Books by Austin Coates published by Oxford University Press

A Macao Narrative

China Races

City of Broken Promises

Macao and the British: Prelude to Hongkong

Myself a Mandarin

The Road

Other Oxford titles

Historic Macao
C.A. Montalto de Jesus

Images of Asia: Macau
César Guillén Nuñez

Macao: Mysterious Decay and Romance
Donald Pittis and Susan J. Henders

Macao Remembers
Jill McGivering

Macao Streets
César Guillén Nuñez

CITY OF BROKEN PROMISES

Austin Coates

OXFORD
UNIVERSITY PRESS

OXFORD

UNIVERSITY PRESS

Oxford University Press is a department of the University of Oxford.
It furthers the University's objective of excellence in research, scholarship,
and education by publishing worldwide in

Oxford New York

Athens Auckland Bangkok Bogotá Buenos Aires Calcutta
Cape Town Chennai Dar es Salaam Delhi Florence Hong Kong Istanbul
Karachi Kuala Lumpur Madrid Melbourne Mexico City Mumbai
Nairobi Paris São Paulo Singapore Taipei Tokyo Toronto Warsaw

with associated companies in Berlin Ibadan

Oxford is a registered trade mark of Oxford University Press

Published in the United States
by Oxford University Press Inc. New York

First published by Frederick Muller Ltd 1967
First issued, with permission, in Oxford Paperbacks 1987

This impression (lowest digit)
5 7 9 10 8 6 4

ISBN 0-19-584200-6

Printed in Hong Kong
Published by Oxford University Press (China) Ltd
18th Floor, Warwick House East, Taikoo Place, 979 King's Road, Quarry Bay
Hong Kong

Contents

To MARIE ATIENZA

Prologue

'AT DAWN WE sighted the coast of China. Numerous islands, small and hilly, little but rock covered with rough grass and scrub. On this grey, humid spring day an inhospitable shore, though doubtless under fine weather it would have a certain rugged, if not even noble, beauty. A sailor observed to me how clumps of trees in such sheltered places as the islands afford indicate the presence of unseen China villages, concealment being needed due in part to this being a region of lawlessness, and in part to violent summer winds called typhoons.

'It is eight months exactly since we left London, and almost with surprise we learn it is a Sunday. Here, then, is my life's destination. This is the place where I must remain for fifteen years, perhaps even twenty. It could be for all my days, as God in his wisdom knows and as I have myself seen. The graves on St. Helena—there were many names from the China station. Yet if I can prosper in this remote Cathay, and in prospering aid those dearest to me to live as it is fitting they should, this will be life well spent.

'With a favourable wind we were soon in among the islands, and at half past ten o'clock we anchored in Taipa roads amid a great concourse of shipping. Three other Indiamen had preceded us, the four of us together, the greatest ships to ride the seas, creating a fine spectacle. Among the larger vessels I noted the flags of several European nations. Under the British flag, apart from the vessels of the Hon'ble Company, the greatest number of ships are those engaged in what is termed the country trade, plying solely in Eastern waters, in particular between China and India. These are

I

the ships that bring opium to China.

'Taipa is an island differing in nothing from those about it save in affording excellent shelter. Ashore is little but a China customs house, though this is important, for it is here that ships are measured for dues before the Chinese permit them to enter the river and approach the city of Canton which lies some 83 miles inland from this place, or 60 as the crow flies. I shall endeavour to keep this journal of my sojourn in Cathay, not that these pages will contain anything notable concerning myself, but that it is in man's nature to leave in some permanent form a record of his passage through distant and curious places.

'I was met by my immediate senior in the Hon'ble Company's hierarchy—this is the only word for it—which is strictly an order of seniority based on the date of first arrival. The encounter was not without amusement. It chanced that I was dressing in the inner room of my cabin—I had the great cabin in the stern of the *Grenada*. Hearing a movement outside, I took it to be John, who had been acting as my servant throughout the voyage, and called his name. When no one answered I went out to find this milord—a coin of doubtful alloy—a regular Cathay buck, a kind of rough dandy. "My name does not happen to be John," he remarked superciliously. I inquired what it might then be. "George Cuming," he answered, proffering his ungloved hand, which was cool and damp. Aware of my mistake I hastened to make amends by means of a jest and by clapping him on the shoulder, but when he observed this latter intention he drew away as if fearing I might break his bones. He is a narrow-faced, thin man, more or less my age, excessively pale, and with eyes as blue as my own, though I would hope mine were never so cold in their stare as his. This Cuming is a man who does not readily reveal his motives, and these are perhaps devious. I would have been plainer with him had I not reflected that it may be my lot to have him at my side for many years to come.'

Thus wrote a twenty-four-year-old Englishman of Anglo-

Dutch parentage named Thomas Kuyck van Mierop, and there is something almost prophetic in the words he uses to describe this first encounter with the colleague whom he was indeed to have at his side throughout the whole of his time on the China coast. Moreover, in the excitement of his first day ashore he omitted to date the entry in his journal. Here the archives of the East India Company supply the missing information. The Honourable East India Company's ship *Grenada*, on this particular voyage, reached China on the 12th of March 1780.

The China they came to was an empire powerful and impenetrable, with no knowledge of, or interest in, anything lying beyond its frontiers. The handful of Europeans who conducted trade with China were kept in complete ignorance of the mysterious land whose luxurious products the Western world so eagerly sought. Under severe Chinese rules no foreigner was allowed to learn the Chinese language or set foot beyond the narrow enclave reserved for foreign residence along the Canton riverfront. In addition it was a society of men only, no European women being permitted by the Chinese to come to China.

From this exceedingly restricted life there was no such thing as leave. Once in a China lifetime an officer might have the good fortune to be sent on duty to Calcutta. This apart, a term of service on the China station was, as Thomas' journal rightly infers, a sentence of fifteen to twenty years' exile in a land so alien and remote as to defy imagination. Many never returned from this exile, or if they did so it was to die along the homeward route at some such lonely spot as St. Helena, which was used as a watering place for ships sailing on the immense voyage from China to Europe round the Cape of Good Hope. Though the foreigners lived in China surrounded by teeming thousands of Chinese humanity, their lives were in some respects as lonely and strange as had they been sequestered in a small group on the furthest uninhabited island of the Antipodes.

Foremost among the nations trading with China, their

3

trade outweighing that of all other foreign nations put together, were the British. The East India Company, operating under Royal Charter, with the monopoly of all British trade in Eastern seas, was the largest commercial organization on earth. In India its activities extended far beyond those of a commercial company. It had assumed full powers of government over entire provinces of India, a fact recognized in the previous year, in 1779, by the appointment of Mr. Warren Hastings as Governor-General of these Indian possessions, with his headquarters at Fort William, Calcutta. At the head of the East India Company sat the Court of Directors in London, and the attention of the Directors, as well as public interest in England, was mainly concentrated on the Company's affairs in India. In fact, however, the Company's very much smaller China station, about which the English public seldom heard anything, was in one way equally if not more important, in that it handled the Company's main source of profit, the tea trade, of which the commercial centre was Canton, the only city in China open for foreign trade, and even then only partially open—for six months each year, after which all non-Chinese had to leave. It was as a supercargo, or commercial officer, in the tea trade that Thomas van Mierop had been appointed.

His father, Martin Kuyck van Mierop, after a stern Dutch upbringing in his native Utrecht, had come to London in his early twenties, and by integrity and strength of character built himself a reputation as the most highly respected underwriter in the City of London in the days when the business of underwriting ships and their cargoes was conducted at Lloyd's Coffee House. After the long war with France, and in part as a result of the sudden ending of high profits on war insurance, standards fell at Lloyd's till the place was little better than a haunt of gamblers, and it was at this time, in 1769, that the more serious-minded and reliable underwriters gathered under the leadership of Martin van Mierop and moved away in protest, eventually leaving coffee houses behind for ever, and founding Lloyd's of London. Martin Kuyck van Mierop was the first Chairman of Lloyd's, and remained so till his death in January 1778.

A devout Protestant and a stern disciplinarian, Martin was a somewhat intimidating father, raising his children in a God-fearing atmosphere in which application to their moral duties, to God and to society, held the foremost place. But he was just and benevolent, and Thomas, his only son, had never seriously disputed the rightness of anything his father did or said.

Thomas' mother, Elizabeth Jane Bentham, was English, attractive and intelligent, with a strain of the intellectual in her. Coming from a family whose moral tendencies made them concerned about social injustices in a complaisant age —one of her nephews, Thomas' first cousin, was Jeremy Bentham, who had recently made his appearance in the London firmament with his demands for a reform of the laws of England—Mrs. van Mierop was an accomplished hostess, attracting to the riverside family home at Twickenham men and women of liberal ideas, whose conversation was more often than not concerned with poor law administration, prison reform, the emancipation of slaves, conditions in the American colonies, and even—though this only rarely —the illegal traffic in opium to China, a subject to which young Thomas listened without realizing he would one day be directly confronted by it and obliged to reach his own personal decision.

The combination of a somewhat puritanical father and a progressive, reform-minded mother had provided Thomas with a background unusual for a young man sailing to make his fortune in the East, and though he had no advance knowledge of this, he was to prove something of a phenomenon on the China coast, being the first representative China had seen of that significant group of people who came to be known as the humanitarians.

As his journal shows, he came to China not from any particular wish to go there—few would have entertained such a wish—but because of family duty. Though Martin van Mierop's leadership had inaugurated a new era for the London underwriters, his years as Chairman of Lloyd's were marked by a number of serious financial reverses in his own affairs, and at his death his family found themselves in straitened circumstances. Thomas was at this time working as a writer for the East India Company in London. Realizing that on his meagre salary he would never be able to support his widowed mother and his two sisters, he made application for a post in India.

The fortunes, the larger part of them illicit, made by Company officers in India were of such spectacular dimensions that vacancies in the Company's Indian service had become a preserve of the highly influential, for whom to have in gift a commission in the Bengal Army, for example, provided a satisfactory method of rewarding hangers-on whose services were becoming inconvenient, or of disposing of unruly members of cadet branches of the family. For a young man with the patronage of a marquess or a Member of Parliament, the more unscrupulous the better, the riches of India were as good as in his pocket before he left the shores of England, provided he too was sufficiently unscrupulous. The van Mierop family, belonging to the world of commerce, could not enjoy such patronage, and Thomas' application was refused; but by using such influence as the family had, they finally obtained for him a post in the Company's less lucrative China service, in which nonetheless, with opium to be reckoned with, men did not do too badly.

The journal continues:

'Accompanied by Mr. Cuming I was rowed by barge the mile or so that lies between Taipa roads and the city of Macao. This is, I am sure, a city like no other in the world, for though situate in China, and though infested—by day, at least—by Chinamen of every quality, it is of itself a part of Europe, a down-at-heel part it may be said, subdued by Roman Catholic superstitions, yet all the same it is Europe, and I rejoiced at this.

6

'Macao stands on a narrow peninsula at the mouth of the river leading to Canton. The outflow of mud from the river causes its waters to be shallow, but for craft of moderate size it has two well-sheltered harbours. One of these, which I observed only from a distance, lies on a stretch of water which by riverine channels reaches Canton, but is used only by the Portuguese and by small vessels. We approached by the more spacious harbour facing the Pearl River, which is the main channel to Canton. This harbour is a majestic bay, as regular in form as a crescent moon, its shore lined with houses of great dignity, all of them painted in bright colours (by order of the Portuguese), behind which rises a gentle slope covered with gracious buildings, including numerous churches and walled gardens planted with many trees. Each hilltop, of which there are three, is crowned by a fort, the use of which would appear to be ceremonial.

'Macao is a Portuguese possession—or so claim the Portuguese. Their claim would seem to be belied by the fact that, according to Mr. Cuming, they pay the Chinese an annual ground rent for the use of the place. They do, however, exercise a certain jurisdiction, having some soldiers and a watch force. But then, it is said, the Chinese too have a watch force, the two forces taking care about their courses in the streets of the city at night, lest they collide.

'One would have thought that the Chinese, at least, would have *wished* for a collision. But this is apparently not the case. "Unique conditions prevail here," said C. obliquely— he is tediously oblique—rendering it inadvisable for me to ask more.

'The Hon'ble Company's house (it is in fact three or four houses joined into one) dominates the waterfront, being the most splendid building in what is unquestionably a crescent of great elegance. Next to it is the so-called palace of the Portuguese governor, a more modest edifice guarded by two African soldiers wearing uniforms which I could swear are thirty years old. In general, all that concerns the Portuguese is old and decrepit. It is remarkable that they have

7

remained here so long. The place is priest-ridden. I have never seen so many churches for so small a population.'

In fact, this is an accurate observation. The Portuguese population of Macao at this time was about 3,000, nearly all of them of mixed race, born and bred in Macao. Only the Governor and a few senior officials were Portuguese from Portugal. To minister to the spiritual needs of this small community were some 90 priests.

'It was said in London that the Canton trade is seasonal. Now that I am here I begin to understand this. The China Government insists that no foreigner may become permanently resident. It is for this reason we are not allowed to bring women to China. The trading season at Canton is during the winter months. After this we are expected to go home to see our families—the China Government is benevolent. Having no conception of geography, however, they believe it quite possible to go to England and return to China in six months! The outcome of this misconception is that at the end of the season we merely descend to Macao, which by some inexplicable logic is not part of China for these purposes, despite the ground rent. This is no place for a lawyer.

'C. explains that the Hon'ble Company has just come down from Canton for the summer. "I need not advise you of conditions in Canton," says he, "since it will be some months before you have cause to go there." Which, being interpreted, means that we move there in September.

'It astonishes me to discover that the tea trade, immense in proportions, is handled by only fifteen supercargoes. Of these the three most senior form the Select Committee, the chief being styled the President, responsible to Fort William. I had expected to be brought to this eminent personage, but this, Mr. C. said, could wait a day or so—no one seems to be in any haste here. Instead I was advised to put my time to use by examining the possibilities of obtaining a Macao residence, it being no longer in vogue to dwell in the Hon'ble Company's house alongside ancient folk whose stock

8

of anecdotes ran dry ten years ago.

'There being some evident wisdom in this, I resorted to an intermediary in this matter, an intermediary being required to deal with the Portuguese, who alone are permitted to own property in this place. My motives here were partly to be in vogue (and to there being nothing more profitable to do on a Sunday), and partly to humour this Cuming, the ambivalence of whose attitude requires study, he being a person who must be fed sometimes with sour, at other times with sweet.

'I must confess my self-composure was somewhat exercised when I actually beheld the intermediary he recommended . . .'

PART ONE

The Decorated Side of the Screen

ABRAHAM BIDDLE'S HANDS smelt of money, and the lines about his heavy, churlish mouth expressed an intimate and practical acquaintance of sin. Thomas noted the smell of money when, a few moments after shaking hands with Biddle, he put his right hand reflectively to his chin, while listening to the man's grandiose yet Cockney flow of language, and the smell thus indirectly reached his nostrils.

Biddle's shop, if this was the correct word for it, was situated on a cobbled hillside street with stone-paved steps every ten yards or so down its descent, looking for all the world as if it were part of a small coastal town in Portugal. Only the pig-tailed Chinese in their dark brown jackets, toiling up and trotting down the street shouting in lively fashion with loads balanced on poles over their shoulders, indicated that this was not Portugal, but a land ten thousand miles away.

A sign outside the shop declared in Portuguese that the business being conducted within was that of the sons of the late João Gonçalves Sequeira; but this was as far as the shop's outward connexion with the Portuguese extended. The interior was Chinese. There were orange tiled floors, half-length swing doors of dark polished wood cunningly carved, with decorated porcelain plaques inset; and there were partitions, also of carved wood, giving reasonable privacy in what was in fact one large room stretching far back from the street. In every section of it indoor plants were growing in quaintly shaped pots and jars.

China fashion—for years had toned him into the landscape—Biddle took time to approach the point of discus-

II

sion, though well aware that the visit concerned the acquisition of a house. Meanwhile he studied the new gentleman of the coast.

Thomas van Mierop had wavy copper-coloured hair and blue eyes deep-set in a rugged, handsome face. He wore a buff surcoat and breeches, a plain white kerchief, and cuffs that extended no more than an inch beyond his sleeves, with only a hint of embroidery—the latest London fashion. There was a quietness, a sense of purpose, about this young man, Biddle noted. He was not like some of the other supercargoes he had seen in his time, who, albeit they were gentlemen, took time to imbibe the extremes of reserve and caution required in the tight European society of the China coast. There was honesty in him. It could be observed in the clear, almost Nordic, look of the eyes, in the firm chin, and in the strong, broad-knuckled hands. Honesty was a quality Biddle mistrusted. On the coast it was invariably a nuisance, and could be dangerous. There was strength of character too, undoubtedly; the young man's entire person expressed this; and about the mouth, the lips casually compressed, was a streak of cynicism, and much patience, an unusual capacity for patience. Taken altogether, something of a problem, Biddle concluded; something of a problem, needing careful handling.

"We'd long been expectin' yer comin', Mr. van Mierop," Biddle said, rubbing his smelly hands slowly together, "and assumin' yer were a person of certain taste—in short, a gentleman of refinement—I'd taken the liberty of makin' certain provisional arrangements which me worthy client Mr. Cumin' may 'ave mentioned to yer."

"No, he did not," Thomas replied firmly. Indeed, the existence of a premeditated plan caused him to reflect with some curiosity how Cuming should even know such a person as Biddle.

The older man was undisturbed.

" 'E was possibly affected by emotion, Mr. van Mierop, since the matter concerns our lately departed and dear friend Mr. William Urquhart, a Company gentleman of a quality such as I've known few."

About fifty years old, Biddle had allowed his hair to grow long—it was white and unkempt, with patches of what had once probably been red—though on a skull-shaped stand beside his Chinese chair of blackwood and marble he still kept a wig, a poor thing, Thomas noted, curled without artifice. From the wig he calculated that Biddle must have been out of England at least fifteen years, while as to his origin, his accent spoke for itself. In China, however, there was the difference that, as a member of the small English community, men like Biddle rose in stature. Constant dealing with educated Englishmen had polished the Billingsgate boy, till as a middle-aged man the only obvious indication of his background was his Cockney accent, which resounded imperturbably on a flow of prose sometimes worthy of Mr. Gibbon himself.

"Moral rectitude, Mr. van Mierop," Biddle was saying with a slight, rather fond, lingering of the tongue, "and habsolute respect for the wishes of others. Without these two qualities no man can confidently remain in China in independent commerce, least of all one engaged, like meself, in business demandin' the exercise of the greatest confidence."

Concerning the nature of Biddle's business Thomas was left in uncertainty of all save that its basis was illegal. For as conversation proceeded it appeared that none but Portuguese citizens were allowed to trade in a Portuguese possession. Biddle explained equanimously that he evaded this restriction by hiring the name of the sons of the late João Gonçalves Sequeira and conducting his trade through them, as if he were an employee.

"And I take care never to ignore me employers," he added unctuously. "The gentleman yer may 'ave observed beside the front door, sir, stretched out insensible on a bed, is one of 'em. 'Is only demand is for a liberal supply of first-quality Chinese liquor—an easy demand to meet, praised be the Lord! But as a gesture of goodwill 'is nephew's allowed to carry messages to the European 'ouses.''

With a sigh Biddle then proceeded to enumerate some of the many other restrictions, Chinese, Portuguese and English, aimed at preventing the country traders from becoming permanently resident in Canton or Macao. Biddle's long survival on the coast would have assumed almost the nature of a miracle had he not, a little later on, explained that by taking appropriate measures and keeping quiet, most laws could be ignored.

Then his voice fell and became more oily, his heavy-lidded eyes lighted up.

"Our lately departed friend Mr. Urquhart was among me many Company clients, Mr. van Mierop. 'E rented from the second generation of Goncalves Sequeira a property of some distinction, situated on 'Ospital Street. It'd occurred to me, sir, that yer might not consider it an 'abitation unworthy of yerself, and 'oldin', as I do, power of attorney for Mr. Urquhart, I could arrange for yer immediate occupation of the premises, at a modest rent and fee, should yer so desire.''

"When will Mr. Urquhart be returning to China?''

Biddle shook his head sadly.

"Alas! never, Mr. van Mierop. 'E departed this life at St. Helena on 'is 'omeward journey, greatly debilitated by the rigours of the climate and, it must be added, by an excessive partiality for port wine. Of the furnishin's in the 'ouse, when the will's been proved, I shall be in a position to sell such as yer may deem sufficiently elegant to keep. The 'ouse is staffed adequately, I'd say, with its own compradore, four 'ouseboys and body servants, a cook, two laundry women, two gardeners, a bell boy, and two chair bearers.'' Two bearers, he explained with care, was the usual number for members of the supercargoes' mess, at least for the first few years. More than two could be considered ostentatious.

The compradore, it appeared, was a Chinese merchant who provisioned and in effect managed the house.

"Should yer wish to make domestic changes,'' Biddle continued, "such matters should be dealt with through the compradore, who is security for everyone in the 'ouse. This is China fashion. That doesn't, of course, apply to the late Mr. Urquhart's pensioner, for 'om yer'd become responsible if yer decide to occupy the premises. It's a point of honour in these parts, Mr. van Mierop, that when a newly arrived officer replaces one deceased or finally departed 'e continues to support that other officer's pensioner."

"It would appear to be a most charitable and proper arrangement."

A smile that was almost a sneer altered Biddle's face.

"I 'ardly think in this particular case yer'll find the pensioner in any way what one might call a burden. Shall we make an inspection of the premises?"

With this he rose, obsequiously inviting Thomas to precede him into the outer passage connecting one delicately partitioned section with another.

In the depths of the building they entered a gloomy room with only one small interior window. There was a scent of sandalwood and Chinese incense. The walls were lined with what at first looked like panelling, but which more careful observation showed to be several hundred sliding drawers built into the walls, each drawer marked with a name and secured by a small lock.

"On this side, Mr. van Mierop, the officers of the Company—the quality, as one might say. On that side, the gentlemen of the country trade. 'Ere," he said, swinging round and pointing into the darkest corner, "the deceased."

With his hand well above his head he unlocked one of the deep, narrow drawers, which he pulled smoothly out and laid on a table. The drawer contained documents chiefly—legal documents, bills of credit on Calcutta and London—and a large key, which he extracted, thereafter replacing the drawer.

"Company or country, livin' or dead, each Englishman comin' to China makes work for someone; but it's morals, Mr. van Mierop, and knowin' 'ow to keep yer mouth shut,

15

that brings the work in 'ere. Now let's proceed by way of the smaller streets."

Though it was past the siesta, the shutters of the high, narrow Portuguese windows of the Rua do Hospital remained shut; but as Abraham Biddle, key in hand, mounted two paved steps to a tall double front door, Thomas observed by the slight movement of an upper-floor shutter that though Macao houses sometimes wore an air of somnolence it should not be inferred from this that the people inside them were asleep. Just as small as the world of the foreign traders in China—though more settled, in that its inhabitants came and went only by birth and death—was Macao itself, a world in which it was prudent to keep shutters closed.

Before they were fully inside the hall two Chinese servants in white tunics hurried down from the upper floor, noiseless in neat black cloth slippers, the shape of which stood out markedly in the dim light against the white stockings and puttees in which their baggy black silk trousers were gathered. Without waiting for orders they began flinging open the shutters in the ground-floor rooms, although in fact there was little to see in them—being level with the street, they were conspicuously empty of possessions.

Upstairs other servants were opening shutters on all sides, filling the house with light, bringing its quiet old dignity to life.

"I needn't labour the fact, Mr. van Mierop, that these are premises fittin' for a gentleman."

They were standing in what William Urquhart had used as his living room. It was in complete contrast with the arid lower rooms, the life of a Macao house being conducted (with the exception of cooking) entirely on the upper floor. Persian carpets of appropriate sizes covered nearly every foot of floor space, out across the landings and into other rooms beyond. There were some good pieces of English furniture, but the larger cabinets and almeiras were Portuguese, ornately carved with pilaster and acanthus, with which were blended peonies and other Chinese motifs, masterpieces of the cabinet-maker's art. The room was large, stretching from the front of the house to the back, divided centrally by an arch decorated with some Chinese craftsman's painstaking imitation of Portuguese manueline. The arch, giving the room two distinct parts, enhanced it with a subtle intimacy. Urquhart, it appeared, when not tippling, occupied himself sketching local scenes. A sketch of the broad sweep of the Praia Grande, 'the more spacious harbour', hung between two of the tall, fanlighted windows, the little panes of which were made of transparent seashells permitting a soft grey-green light to penetrate. There were pipes on a small round Spanish piperack table, and a finely carved cheroot box which, as Biddle casually opened it, Thomas saw was still half full of Manila cigars.

But it was someone else's house—not Abraham Biddle's to rent or to sell, nor yet the property of the second generation of Gonçalves Sequeira. It was William Urquhart's house. His character rested on it with quiet endurance, even from so distant a place as the cemetery on St. Helena, and from the life beyond.

"It's not every gentleman, even from the Honourable Company, that I'd bring to this 'ouse, Mr. van Mierop."

"I appreciate your sentiments," Thomas replied. "But I would not be able to occupy it as it is."

Biddle assumed an expression of innocent astonishment.

"Is there somethin' yer object to, Mr. van Mierop?"

"Object? No. But these are the late Mr. Urquhart's effects. They will be wanted by his relatives. I—"

"Set yer mind at ease on that score, Mr. van Mierop," Biddle interrupted in a sterner tone. "When I say that once the will is proved yer may purchase from me whatever furniture yer wish, I mean *just that*." He mollified his voice. "May I be permitted to explain, Mr. van Mierop, that this too is China fashion. It's the custom for a new officer in China to in'erit—if I may use the word in a not very correct sense—the possessions of the officer 'e's replacin'."

But Thomas had made up his mind. The house was pre-eminently a home, and with fifteen years or so to consider, this was what mattered.

"At the same rental?" he inquired.

"With somethin' additional for the 'ire o' the furniture," said Biddle softly.

"Agreed."

"Yer've made a wise choice, Mr. van Mierop. May I congratulate yer. I think I may prophesy yer'll find this 'ouse satisfactory in *every* way," he said with the strange implication of sin that entered his voice whenever he was being polite; and as he smiled, with the rumour of a chuckle in it, he closed the shutters of one of the windows facing the street, thus depriving of a view two sallow-faced Macao Portuguese women whom Thomas had not noticed, but whom Biddle, even without apparently looking in their direction, had detected as they gazed, with their fixed Asian expressions, through a partly open shutter on the other side of the street.

Thereupon Biddle, obsequiously looking his client straight in the eye, handed him the key and took his leave. A moment later a deferential intake of breath at the doors to the front staircase indicated the compradore's arrival.

The compradore was a small wizened man with greying hair beginning to go thin. He had cadaverous cheeks, a few teeth missing, and wore a dark brown Chinese longcoat, with the same cloth slippers as the servants. He looked more like an ancient sage than a purveyor of fruit and vegetables. He bowed and grinned.

"Morning, Master," he began, despite the fact that it was afternoon. "My velly solly, Master, you good flen Uk Hak Master him die. Velly bad joss pidgin."

It was Thomas' first encounter with business English, as it was uncritically called, and spoken at speed it was somewhat breathtaking. He furthermore found that unless he too spoke in the same way the compradore had difficulty in understanding him. He made a somewhat uncertain *début* in this new art, after which the compradore snapped his fingers and the servants, waiting just out of sight, came in to be presented.

"Number One, Number Two, Number T'ree, Number Four," announced the compradore, who did not trouble himself with names.

A series of pale, ivory-skinned faces, with foreheads shaven, giving their heads an unrealistically dome-like appearance, came in and bowed. Last to be presented was a short, dark-skinned lad with grey eyes.

"Him velly fool boy," explained the compradore benevolently.

"What does he do?" asked Thomas, appreciating that the house was monstrously overstaffed.

"Him open door when Master come back nightee time. But him velly fool. No talk talk."

The compradore smiled significantly. The fool boy grinned. At another snap of the compradore's fingers all withdrew.

In solitude Thomas took in the strangeness of it. It was as if, in taking the house, he was taking on the life of another person where that other life left off. He felt he was prying into the secrets of that other man, as if within these walls he himself were little more than an eavesdropper.

The light was failing, and a wind was rising from the sea. A servant quietly set down a silver tray on which were a decanter of port, a glass, and a covered silver dish which on inspection Thomas found contained shortcake. The intrusion drew his thoughts back to practical matters. There was still one more person he had to interview. He asked to see the compradore again.

"I understand Mr. Urquhart had a pensioner, whom I'm responsible for. I should also see him."

The compradore looked blank.

"No savvy."

"Pensioner," Thomas repeated. "Mr. Urquhart's pensioner."

At the corners of the compradore's eyes intelligence awakened. His mouth, half open in perplexity, opened a little more.

"My savvy. Master like him come?"

"If it's convenient."

The compradore waddled away.

Thomas glanced casually at the view from the rear french windows. Immediately behind the house a granite rock rose exactly to the level of the upper floor. On the rock's flattened top was the garden, consisting solely of potted plants. A wrought-iron bridge connected it with the rear balcony, and beyond the rock, on rising land, were the grey, double-tiled roofs of a number of low Chinese houses—no walls or windows were visible—beyond which grass and rocks rose, filling the view, to the central hilltop fort, the Monte, which he had earlier seen from the sea. Observed at closer range the fort was less imposing. Despite its cannons nosed seaward over the roofs, an air of dereliction invested it, as though, not having been used for a century or so, the cannons might emit only birds' nests.

Drawn by the lonely sadness of the view, he moved nearer the windows, and as he did so became aware that in the fading daylight a figure was standing in one of the inner doorways. That it was a girl—one of the servants, evidently —he saw at once, and equally dismissed further thought about it. He had already seen below the french windows that the servants had their wives and children staying in the compound, their quarters occupying the lower parts of the hill like a small village.

From the front staircase a servant entered bearing a globe lamp with a candle in it, which he placed near the polished but empty fireplace. In the new brightness as the lamp was brought in—the candle was placed before a polished reflector—Thomas took a second look at the girl. She was younger than he had imagined. She stood to one side of the doorway, her body held in an attitude neither bold nor timid. She seemed to have come up neither to transmit a message nor to make a request. Having neither of these motives, her presence assumed the nature of a statement of fact—a statement, he judged from the way she avoided the centre of the door, of unwilling fact.

Her eyes, up-tilted and almond-shaped, and her pale, exceptionally smooth skin suggested that she was Chinese; yet the way she wore her fine black hair, and her black dress, short and shapeless, was more European than Chinese. Still no more than a child, could she have been one of the servants' daughters, influenced in some way by the Portuguese?

"Yes?" he said, expecting to give her the confidence to speak, and moved a pace towards her.

Something in the ivory stillness of her face altered. Across her temples he noticed the pulsating of two slender veins close to the surface of her limpid, youthful skin. He went no nearer. Despite his inability to read the meaning of an oriental expression he sensed, more than saw, that her look was of fear.

Aware of something moving on his left, he glanced towards the street where, in a window of the house opposite, a lamp was passing. In the concealment of darkness those sombre Asian eyes were still watching him over there. They were excited about something.

He turned back to the girl, and as he did so, feeling suddenly hot under the collar, understood the China fashion meaning of the word pensioner.

He closed the shutters. Only when he had done so did the significance of the action occur to him. Embarrassed to a degree which even he himself was surprised by, he moved with a kind of aggressiveness over to the fireplace, leaned with hands outstretched against the marble mantelpiece, kicked the grate, and stared uneasily at a little clock which he found before him, ornate with golden flowers and birds. Just at that moment small mechanisms whirred inside it, and in silvery tones it played 'For he's a jolly good fellow' and struck seven.

He swung away from it. The girl still stood in the far doorway. There was an instant of silence, then she said:

"You like?"

It was so simple as to be almost an affront, the voice of the streets brought into the house, and presumably it demanded politeness—and caution.

"Of course I like," he replied, "but—the circumstances are somewhat strange."

"No savvy," she said. She had a pleasing voice, he noted, and she was now staring at him—longingly, he thought, though he could not understand why this should be. It could hardly be love at first sight.

He tried some business English.

"I like. All man like. But no savvy China fashion."

"My no China girl," she answered swiftly.

"Then what are you? Portuguese?"

"My—" and she stopped. Nor was she looking at him any more, but staring into her own distance, as if struggling with some problem of her own.

It was beyond him.

"China girl, no China girl, I'm new here, no savvy anything," he replied, and in an endeavour to dismiss her returned his attention to the little clock. Its inner whirrings having ceased, it was ticking away obediently.

But she did not go.

"*O senhor fala português?*" she asked.

He switched about in surprise.

"No. I regret."

"*Que pena!*" she said with a little sigh.

He returned some way towards her. She did not flinch as she had earlier. She was no longer afraid of him.

"You're still only a child," he murmured softly.

"No savvy."

She was very pale, in the manner of the southern Chinese, and had a round little face which he now began to observe was full of determination, and she had dimples.

22

"You how old? Years—how many?" he asked.

The little face, turned up to his in mute trustfulness, made no sign of understanding. Placing his hand at different heights, he tried again:

"Baby—little girl—young girl—one two three four—how many?"

She caught it.

"Fourteen," she answered eagerly.

"Fourteen?" he echoed in a shocked tone. Admittedly, he noted, with a sharp eye for such matters, she was a good deal more mature than most European girls of such an age. All the same . . .

At this juncture a line of servants entered bearing some of the luggage from the ship. Methodical in his affairs, Thomas saw at once from which part of the great cabin this particular consignment had been taken, and that his continental portefeuille, a farewell gift from one of his Utrecht cousins, was missing.

"Have they brought my portefeuille?" he asked.

Number One clearly had no idea what this meant, but as Thomas asked the question the girl, who he noticed had made to leave as soon as the servants came in, turned in the doorway, her expression one of timid surprise.

"*Le Seigneur sait parler français?*" she asked.

"*Mais, Dieu!*" Thomas exclaimed. "*Combien de langues savez-vous parler, petite?*"

It was like opening a floodgate. A torrent of words poured forth in lucid French, spoken with a slight Portuguese accent.

"I am not sure I speak any very well, but I know a little, and if I had only known the Seigneur spoke French as well as he does I would have—"

"Gently!" Thomas interrupted. "I said 'How many?' Enumerate."

Joining her hands, with a little dimpled smile she subdued her enthusiasm. It was a gesture that made her seem suddenly very European.

"Well, of course, Macanese, the *patois*," she began. "Everyone speaks that. And a little Portuguese, but it is not very good. And then some Cantonese, but that is not very good either. And French."

"Astonishing! Where were you educated?"

"Educated?" she asked in surprise. "I am not educated. I just learned."

"But you read and write?"

"Oh no, Seigneur! Only men read and write."

"Anyway you know what a portefeuille is?"

"Yes, of course."

"Then will you please explain it to Number One."

A quick exchange in Cantonese elicited the fact that the portefeuille was downstairs. But as the exchange took place Thomas observed how the intrusion of French, which the Number One could not understand, had produced a change in his manner towards the girl. Hitherto the Number One had been master of the situation. He proceeded now with more caution. It was Thomas' first glimpse of the inner complications of the household.

"Where did you learn French?" he pursued, his voice betraying a certain suspicion. He had once had a costly experience in London, a girl used as a decoy, and he was on his guard.

But she answered with complete candour.

"My protector was a Frenchman. I lived in his house till he died. I am an orphan."

"I see. Do many people here speak French?"

"The Seigneur means Macao people?"

"Yes."

"I think very few. I may be the only one. It has never really been of any use to me till now, and then—"

His expression darkened, and her words died away in apprehension. He returned to the fireplace.

"Yes," he murmured to himself in English, "it certainly is uncommonly useful." His own name, known in advance on the coast, would suggest ability to speak continental languages. The planning was exceptionally thorough.

But she was not to be put off.

"I did not know any Englishmen spoke French as well as the Seigneur does," she said flatteringly.

"It is no great accomplishment, I assure you, for the English. France is our neighbour."

"A neighbour?" she queried in puzzlement.

"Yes."

She made a little frown.

"But France," she said with awe, "is one of those places from which people never come back. How can there be neighbours in those places?" She spoke of them exactly as if they were places beyond death, and he perceived that this was indeed how she thought of them.

"Of course there are," he answered with a laugh. "France is very near England."

She remained unconvinced.

"Brazil is near France," she said. It was a statement of fact.

"Brazil?" he exclaimed. "Good heavens, no! Brazil is the other side of the world from France."

"Near Macao," she commented firmly.

"No. Even further from Macao than it is from France."

"But Macao is on the other side of the world from France."

"Yes. But Brazil is on yet another side."

She eyed him doubtfully.

"But the world is round," she said.

His blue eyes dwelt upon her with delectation.

"Miraculous! Who told you that?"

"My protector. Why? Is it not right?"

"Oh yes! Do not let me for a moment attempt to convince you otherwise. The world, as your protector so wisely said, is indisputably round. But Brazil is nowhere near France."

"It is not true what you are telling me, Seigneur. In those places, do you have only one 'neighbour'?"

He gazed down at the little face, placidly Chinese yet imparting the naughty whimsicality of an Italian cherub, orientally composed yet occidentally impudent.

"And why, pray, this interest in Brazil?"

"Because I may have to go there," she replied calmly.

"Indeed? You have the money for such a voyage."

"No. I shall find the means."

"And why should you have to go to Brazil?"

"Because the Seigneur does not wish me to stay in this house."

Their eyes met in sudden, swift intensity. As another consignment of luggage was borne in, he switched away from her.

"I made no mention of your leaving," he said. But when he turned for an answer, she had gone. "Come back!" he ordered. The heavy trunks had arrived. "I did not give you leave to go," he said as she diffidently re-appeared. "What is the matter?"

She hesitated.

"It is not the custom for me to be seen in this room when the servants are present," she replied.

It was another domestic insight. Exactly what, he wondered, was this life of a pensioner, with its strange limits and exactitudes?

Even the fool boy had been roped in to carry things up. At this moment he emerged at the tail end of the servants' procession triumphantly holding above his head an ornate Spanish guitar, its wood inlaid with mother-of-pearl. Laughing with delight he was plinking its loosened strings.

Thomas was not without talent as a musician, and this guitar was one of his most precious possessions.

"Hey! Don't you damage that!" he cried, whereupon the Number One, alert to a crisis, rushed at the fool boy with a Chinese oath and tried to wrench the instrument from his grasp.

The fool boy's face grew sullen and dangerous. Holding the guitar to himself as if it were his baby, he closed his strong rough hands over it. Bidding the Number One desist, Thomas approached the fool boy, who watched him calculatingly. The other servants had come out from the inner rooms. At first they chuckled at the sight of the fool boy with the guitar. Then they were silent, the attention of each of them riveted as Thomas plinked an untuned string, lifted the fool boy's finger off it, tuned it quickly, and struck a musical note.

The fool boy's expression altered to a vacant smile.

"More," he muttered excitedly after the third string had been tuned. In a moment all the strings were tuned and free from his grasp.

"Now you play," said Thomas with a gesture.

"No can. You," answered the fool boy.

"Come then. I play." And gently he lifted the guitar from the fool boy's hold.

From the men in the room there was a murmur of approval. In some strange way the incident had made Thomas more master of the house, less of an intruder. He struck a series of chords, the fool boy, mouth wide open, laughing silently with pleasure.

"More," he repeated. "Fool boy happy."

In the darkness of the doorway beyond the fool boy Thomas observed someone else watching him, a taller figure than the rest, wearing European black with a high white collar. He silenced the strings.

"A scene of perfect domestic bliss," said George Cuming, strolling with affected nonchalance into the light.

In what seemed less than a second the room was empty of all save the two Europeans.

What next took place is recorded in Thomas' journal, but before proceeding to quote from this it should perhaps be pointed out in fairness to George Cuming that he was not quite the rough buck from the backwoods that Thomas casually described. In his well-tailored black evening attire —*de rigueur* at the Company house in the evenings—and embroidered white linen kerchief, Cuming, with his slim

27

figure and narrow, pallid face, the lips a little heavy and unduly red, the pale eyes with a certain harshness about them, was a stylish young man whose smooth manners to some extent glossed the underlying coolness of his character.

'Mr. C. called on me at a somewhat inconvenient hour,' the journal reads, 'to invite me to attend supper with him at the Hon'ble Company's house. I appreciated this condescension on his part, yet so mixed is his goodwill with obscure sarcasms and *double entendre* that frankly I do not know what to make of him. While expressing the hope that I found my house satisfactory he seemed to take it amiss that I had settled in with so little discomfiture. He next complained about the difficulty of finding suitable talent for the theatricals, or charades, with which evenings at Canton are enlivened during the season, saying he hoped he could call on me to impersonate female rôles, this being where talent was most lacking. Meanwhile he drank port—Urquhart's port—and consumed excessive quantities of shortcake (he is very thin, of course). I felt constrained to tip him over in his chair at one point (the theatricals), then reflected that this might damage a good piece of cut glass, and refrained. He sat there very dandified in a high-backed chair, exquisitely dusting shortcake crumbs off his fingers into a silver tray.

'Our conversation later took a more serious turn. I shall endeavour to set down these passages as fully as I recall them, since they are, if true, of a disturbing significance.

'He asked numerous questions about the house, leaving no doubt that he is not unfamiliar with it, despite, he says, never having visited Urquhart here. Indeed I perceive that this is a society in which one's every action, even the most private, is attended by a certain covert publicity. Lest he take too much for granted I saw fit to say that there were aspects of life on the China coast, inasmuch as I had any experience of it, which it was difficult to equate with the standards normal to our race.

' "This is no place for scruples, Mr. Mierop," he replied, taking more shortcake. "China is a law unto itself, and so are we who are forced to live in China. Matters of this kind cannot be explained to people in England. If we were to tell there how we lived here, most of them would never speak to us again. English people have scruples. You, fresh from England, have brought yours with you. Forget them, I assure you. Accept what is set before you. You will find it not disagreeable. We come to China to make money, after all."

'He next recommended that I see this Biddle concerning opium. Biddle's connexions in Calcutta are excellent, it seems, and for trade in opium he is considered, C. said, an expert second to none. With a degree of innocence which I am almost ashamed to record I said that I was under the impression the Hon'ble Company did not trade in opium.

' "The Company is neither here nor there," he answered. "I was referring to the private trade."

'It now falls out that the notices posted in every vessel of the Hon'ble Company saying that no opium may be carried to China are so much nonsense. According to Mr. C., opium is carried in every Company ship in those parts of the hold reserved for the private trade of the Company's officers. This holdspace is not examined. It explains certain remarks made to me by the master of our good ship *Grenada* and which I did not fully grasp. I have indeed been an innocent, but then so too are the Court of Directors who I am certain from my experience with them have no knowledge of all this, and would be horrified if they knew.

'Well, they would profess themselves horrified at any rate. Righteous indignation is one of the attitudes of which they are most fond.

'I said I understood opium to be a drug poisonous to mind and body, and that the importation of it into China was absolutely forbidden by that country's laws. Laws could be ignored, C. said (it accorded with Biddle's view).

' "You make it sound simple," I said.

' "It is simple, provided you put scruples away," was his answer.

' "Forgive me if I presume to contradict you," I replied. It was an uncommon experience having to come to the defence of principles so universally recognized that one is seldom required to examine the reasons for them. A man without scruples, I said as best I could, was a person plunging forward with nothing but his own whims as his guide, and would surely be the first to break his neck.

' "Not in an unscrupulous society," he answered undeterred, "such as this. In such a society it is exactly the opposite. Here it is the man *with* scruples who will be the first to break his neck."

'The tone in which it was said was one of reasoned argument, but the undertone, and the cold stare of the man's eyes, seemed like a warning, almost an ultimatum.

'Finally he informed me that this house is mortgaged against a consignment of opium due from Calcutta later in the year. In mortgages of this kind, it appears, there is no cash transaction at all, opium consignment notes being treated in China as if they were actual currency!

' "So you see yourself already associated with the nefarious trade," he said in a faintly mocking tone. "Have no scruples. Everyone is in it."

'On the point of departure, his manner becoming more friendly, he came forth with another choice piece of advice. "Your guitar," he said with a kind of sniff. "In our Canton theatricals, as a diversion—yes. Apart from that I think the less said about it the better. Sketching, or writing Latin verses, are appropriate intellectual exercises here—not music."

'From which it will be observed that we do have *some* morals here, though they are somewhat strangely based.'

The Company's house, where Thomas dined that night, was of a sombre magnificence. It was also much larger than he had estimated when observing it from the harbour. The four houses of which it was formed—there was internal communication between them—stretched far back from the Praia Grande on a mounting hillside, the buildings rising sectionally to culminate in an alternative frontage on the Ridge, facing the tree-shaded largo in front of an aged Portuguese church. Within the house, as Thomas complained in his journal, one was thus 'everlastingly mounting or descending stairs'. They were, however, very magnificent stairs, sumptuously carpeted, as was every reception room and office, creating a hushed atmosphere throughout.

Nothing about the house, either inside or out, suggested its commercial character. No building facing the Praia Grande was permitted to display a commercial sign. This was one of the very few Portuguese laws with which the Honourable Company agreed, few things being so displeasing to its 'aristocrats' as to be reminded that they were in commerce. Thus from the outside the building wore the appearance of four adjacent family mansions, while within it resembled nothing so much as what it was, a superlatively luxurious men's club in typical London style.

It reeked of wealth. In the principal reception room, designed in classical style by a London architect, enormous Indian landscapes replete with Mughal palaces, minarets, domestic laundry, white cows and turbaned chaprassis hung in gold frames of such monstrous ornateness that it was a wonder the wall held them, while from the centre of the gently domed ceiling hung a chandelier of such ostentatious virtuosity as in circles of discernment in Europe would have been described as verging on the vulgar. Over an immense marble fireplace, seldom used, for in the winter everyone was away in Canton, was a portrait of King George III by Ramsay, and at the opposite end of the room, extravagantly pointed in gold, red, blue and silver, the Arms of the Honourable Company.

Supper, served exactly at ten o'clock, was a ritual formidable in its formality. The gentlemen of the Company, that is to say, the President and Members of the Select Committee, the two Trade Superintendents, the ten other supercargoes, the masters and officers of visiting Company ships, the Master Attendant and other marine officers of the shore-based staff, and others of officer status, such as the surgeons, assembled in the great reception room, uniformly dressed in black and wearing hats. One glass of sherry was served—there was no choice in the matter—after which, at the sound of a ship's bell, not a gong, the concourse proceeded in order of precedence up a majestic staircase to the supper room, entering which each officer removed his hat.

The repast was served at a single long table glittering with cut glass and the Company's gold plate, and adorned with bowls of gardenias, the scent of which was everywhere. At the head of the table, beneath a portrait of Queen Charlotte, also by Ramsay, sat the President of the Select Committee. Thomas, as the most junior supercargo, with George Cuming beside him, sat at the furthermost end facing the President. For every diner there was a servant clad in a long white Chinese robe. On taking his place, each diner handed his hat to the servant, who laid it beneath his chair.

Thomas had been introduced briefly to the President beforehand, but his arrival occasioned no more emotion than if he had just come down to Tunbridge Wells from London. Only at the end of the meal, which was an extravaganza of semi-oriental dishes served with every culinary art and which, Thomas reflected, would have put a royal banquet to shame, did he leap with alarming suddenness into prominence, as the President distantly fixed his eye on him, and said:

"Mr. Junior, the King."

Thomas rose hastily.

"Gentlemen, the King!"

All rose.

"The King."

Thomas was about to sit down when Cuming prompted him in a sharp whisper: "The Directors!"

"The Directors of the Honourable Company!" Thomas

proclaimed.

"The Directors," everyone murmured in a bored way.

Flushing slightly, Thomas noted he had said more than was necessary. To those around the table, no other directors existed.

When they had sat down the President drank exactly one glass of madeira—even this was part of the ritual—after which he and the members of the Select Committee, inviting the four masters of Company ships to accompany them, withdrew to a private room, and the atmosphere at the long table relaxed somewhat.

As an experience, however, the supper certainly proved to Thomas the wisdom of Cuming's advice to him to rent a private residence. Only men of a certain temperament, and of these there were quite a number, could support life in the Company house, and these did so by making themselves petty lords of this or that corner of the various public rooms, round which they constructed invisible frontiers lacking nothing of national dignity save the imposition of customs dues.

The result was that Thomas' attitude towards George Cuming softened, and Cuming too was as affable as his natural coolness would allow. With amazement Thomas observed that some of the older Company men wore the elaborate ruffles fashionable in England fifteen years before. "They send them to be laundered in Calcutta, I might say," Cuming murmured in an undertone. "No Chinaman has ever known what to do with them."

"Time moves more slowly here than it does in England," Thomas' companion on the other side remarked, "and we tend to be left behind."

"But will this not change?" said Thomas.

"Not, I think, while there are no women here," the other replied.

Thomas surveyed again the two lines of faces at the table. No women. An enclave of supposed celibates. For in addition to being unable to bring European women to China,

33

Company officers were absolutely forbidden by the Company to marry local women. Thinking of the conveniently organized domestic regime he had inherited, as Biddle put it, from Urquhart, Thomas mused as he studied the well-fed features of his colleagues with their powdered hair sprucely waved and lacquer-set. Of those officers with rooms in the Company house, he thought, it might indeed be true that they were celibates; there seemed to be precious little privacy. For the others with residences in the town, how many, he wondered, had these mistresses, these half-wives, these women of the shadows behind them, to be left to others, as Urquhart had left his? Probably all of them. And with fifteen years or so to be reckoned with, was there not wisdom in this too? Had not Cuming, in his veiled allusions to the subject, again advised him rightly? He had entered the frame of an extraordinary way of life, with conventions entirely its own, a state of affairs demanding special adaptations, special recourses. Have no scruples, as Cuming had said.

As the madeira circulated—port was only taken in the mornings—Thomas recalled a small incident that had taken place earlier. On the point of leaving the house he was detained by the Number One—he was a man of about fifty and should have known better, Thomas considered—who in his most confidential, faithful and discreet tone of voice, asked, "Master come back nightee time like girlie come topside?" The blatancy of it had disgusted Thomas, and with a brusque "No, certainly not" he had walked out of the house.

Beginning now to understand more of China coast life, he was left with the uneasy sensation of having done the girl an injury. Like the servants, she had her duties, and should be allowed to carry these out. Lulled by the multiplicity of wines served at supper, he wished he had responded otherwise to the Number One's suggestion. It would have been pleasant to have her waiting for him on his return, waiting beside that ridiculous little clock . . . A puritanical upbringing could be a confounded nuisance—specially, it seemed, in China.

It was past midnight, Macao lampless and silent, every shutter of every house closed, as Thomas was borne home by chair. As he mounted the steps to the house the door opened silently before him, as by magic. The lower parts of the hall were dark and still, the higher parts dimly illuminated by two nightlights fixed against the staircase wall. Vaguely silhouetted beside the door was the fool boy, already able to recognize his master's footfall without even seeing him. Thomas put down his hat and surcoat.

"Master and fool boy make ding-dong," the fool boy whispered excitedly, his grey eyes glinting in the dim light.

"Not night time," said Thomas benevolently. "Night time fool boy sleep."

"Fool boy no sleep." He swung his body away in the manner of a saucy girl, and attempted a wink. "Master not likee girl?" he said archly. "More better Master one-man with fool boy. Nightee time make ding-dong."

To create a diversion Thomas pointed at the unlocked bolts across the door. It was a measure that succeeded. In a silent leap the fool boy bounded to the door, his attention absorbed in locking the bolts. Thomas mounted the stairs uneasily, certain now that he had not only done the girl an injury but had probably made her suffer. Having taken the house, he was expected to call her to his bed. This was China fashion, it seemed; and China fashion was in its own way as ritualistic as the East India Company sitting down to supper. Should anyone fail to follow the ritual there would be definite and predictable consequences, and in this particular case the fool boy's behaviour suggested that the outcome could well be complete domestic disorder.

He entered the living room at the same moment as, from the rear door, the Number One entered with globe lamps, followed by the Number Two with what turned out to be a hot rum toddy in a chased silver cup. It was his first real introduction to the services provided by the mysterious Orient, and he appreciated instantly that he would never know how it was done. He wanted to hold the Number One in conversation, discreetly ask about the girl, even command her presence. But this time there were no confidential looks or other indications. The staff had had their orders in the matter. A decision had been taken, and everyone knew where they stood. The two men bowed and withdrew for the night, leaving their young master in a state of aggressive but silent frustration with himself and his scruples.

He glowered moodily about him at the opulent room, innocently displaying its occidental arts in a land so utterly remote. Only the ticking of the infuriating little clock broke the absolute silence of the house and the city.

But still, damn it, he tried sternly to tell himself, someone else's mistress—and only fourteen at that . . .

The sounds of a new day started long before it was light. By equally strict Chinese and Portuguese rules Chinese were not permitted to remain in Macao at night. The daytime population of the city was thus seven or eight times larger than the nocturnal population. Each day ended with a Chinese exodus, began with a Chinese invasion, and needless to say, the restrictions were run fine at both ends. Habitually an early riser, Thomas awoke in the stillness of pre-dawn to the sounds of quiet stirrings in neighbouring compounds, the squeals of pigs being slaughtered somewhere not far off, and to rising tumult in the market places as the first crates of vegetables, live chickens and ducks were borne in from the fields and farms of Heungshan.

Flinging on a shirt and a pair of breeches, he agitated the silk-embroidered bell-pull. There was an answering clang from within the house, but no further response. He stepped on to the balcony of his bedroom at the rear of the house. The hilltop fort was re-outlining itself against the sky; the servants' cottages were dark and silent, every door shut.

There was a movement below. The girl had come out

into the dim grey light of the compound.

"Can you make me a cup of chocolate?" he called down. But she did not stir.

"No, Seigneur. I regret."

A frown of impatience crossed his brow. It was the fact that she was in the house for one sole purpose, and for nothing else, he now realized, that offended his sense of propriety.

"Very well, then. Ask someone else to prepare it."

She crossed the compound, knocked timidly on one of the doors, and said something in Cantonese. More by instinct than by actual sound the knock was heard in every cottage. Within the little tiled buildings the servants, like the crew of a ship in an emergency, hastily tumbled to. Wooden slippers clanked on tile floors, male spitting reverberated through the rooms, sleepy women complained, and one by one the doors opened to emit the men. Unaware of being watched from above, they eyed the girl irritably as they set about the activities of morning, lighting the first fire, lowering the first wooden bucket into the well, cursing softly as the sky changed from night to day.

But Thomas had seen what he wanted. He had suspected it from one or two indications the day before. Now he was certain. The girl's position in the household was worse than that of a slave. Passing quickly through the darkened upper rooms, he descended the rear staircase and came out into the grey compound.

"Where is your room?" he asked the girl.

In silence she led him to it. From the back door a covered way led across the compound to the servants' cottages. Just to the left of the back door, and similarly facing the compound, was the room. Evidently originally intended as a store, it had no ventilation of any kind apart from the door. With the door shut there was darkness. The blank walls had not been painted for years. It was dank and airless, with only a string bed and a chair.

As Thomas appreciated at a glance, no place could have

been more cruelly selected to perpetuate what he now saw was the girl's dual isolation, from the master of the house and from the servants. Part of the house yet without inner access to it, facing the servants' compound without being part of the servants' quarters, the room was an embodiment of her status, classing her with the servants while with subtle finality excluding her from their company.

"Come upstairs," he ordered her. There, before the fireplace, he took a plunge at domestic reorganization. "You understand that I am responsible for you," he began, distantly aware that men are not very good at this kind of thing. "You must be given some proper duties."

"Duties?" she said in wide-eyed surprise.

"Yes. Now"—it came forth weightily—"what can you do?"

"What had the Seigneur in mind?" she asked in astonishment.

"Well, I am not sure I know. Can you sew?"

"Yes, Seigneur."

"Then at least one thing you can do is repair my clothes when that is needed."

"The wife of the Number One does that, Seigneur."

"Well?" he queried.

"Not very, Seigneur."

"So you repair my clothes in future."

She did not reply for a moment, then:

"She receives a tip."

"I see. Could she not be given equal remuneration for doing something else?"

"What, Seigneur?" she said fair and square.

"Yes, precisely. What?—Are you good at arranging flowers?"

"I know a little, Seigneur, but that is Number Two's duty and he is very clever at it, better than me."

"How about waiting at table?"

"Men, Seigneur. Number One and Number Three."

"Laundry?"

"The wives, Seigneur."

"Tips, I suppose."

"No. Face."

"Face?"

"Yes, Seigneur. They would lose face if any of their work were given to me."

He swung round impatiently and leaned with his elbows high along the mantelpiece.

"Can you do embroidery?"

"Yes, Seigneur."

"Well, could you not embroider tablecloths and—er—other things?"

Her dimples showed as she smiled at him.

"We would soon have more tablecloths than the Seigneur could use," she replied. She reflected. "We could sell them, I suppose."

"You could sell them," he corrected with dignity. "Still, that is not quite the answer, is it? We are not a shop. Could you not help with the marketing?"

"I do not leave the house, Seigneur."

He looked up sharply.

"You do not leave the house?" he repeated, at a loss for words.

"No, Seigneur. Never. Nor may I go near any door or window that is open. I may not be seen."

"But this is monstrous!" he expostulated. "On whose orders is all this?"

"On no one's orders, Seigneur. This is the custom. People know we are in the English houses. But it is supposed to be secret."

"Ridiculous!" he muttered. "So far as I am concerned, you may go out whenever you please."

She bowed her head.

"How can I," she asked in a low voice, "since coming to this house? Do you not see what I am?"

With remorse he observed he had made her cry. Her skin turning to an exquisitely soft pink about the eyes, she cried in silence, tears streaming down her drab black dress as if nothing would stop them.

"Come now," he said softly, as if speaking to a child, but before he could say more, with a sudden moan of anguish which surprised him by its intensity, she ran from the room.

He did not follow her. But she had taught him something, and it had ruffled his straitlaced composure. You could not reform or alter China fashion. You had to apply it.

Late that same afternoon a visibly irate Thomas van Mierop confronted Abraham Biddle across the latter's desk.

"I trust yer've no complaints about the luxurious premises yer've ser wisely taken, Mr. van Mierop," said that personage with more than ordinary unctuousness.

"As a matter of fact I have," Thomas answered, "and I wish a satisfactory explanation."

"The 'ighest standards of honour, Mr. van Mierop, are the criterion of the second generation of Gonçalves Sequeira. I trust there's no doubt in yer mind about that."

"I was not suggesting anything to the contrary. What was the compradore doing this morning sending his man to make an inventory of the furniture?"

Across Biddle's face ran a flicker of surprise, but he replied imperturbably.

"Yer've been misinformed, Mr. van Mierop. I already 'old the inventory. The compradore's nothin' to do with it."

"As I would have thought. There is no question of a misapprehension, however. This man came with a note from the compradore. The Number One showed it to me. The visit seems to have occasioned some considerable commotion."

Abraham Biddle's eyes narrowed.

"That Number One's makin' trouble, is 'e? We'll 'ave 'im removed forthwith."

"You will do nothing of the kind, Mr. Biddle," Thomas answered sternly. "I, after discussion with the compradore, will decide who will or will not be removed."

In fact, Thomas, who was unable to throw off the suspicion that Biddle's aim in leasing the house was to use this as a means of controlling his tenant's affairs, was not entirely dissatisfied to have returned that afternoon to find his staff in a state of agitation. It afforded him an unexpected opportunity to put Biddle in his place.

"Very right and proper, sir, I'm sure," said the latter with deference.

"Furthermore," Thomas pursued, "I understood you to say yesterday that I was responsible for the late Mr. Urquhart's pensioner."

Biddle's eyes, momentarily lowered to the papers on his desk, darted up.

"Pray proceed, Mr. van Mierop."

"Where is she?" Thomas inquired coldly.

"You mean she's out?" Biddle exclaimed, glowering and rapping the last word out like a knife.

"I understand so."

"Was this intruder a Chinaman?"

"No. A Portuguese, I'm told."

"A Portuguese?" Biddle lisped with a hiss like a snake, the blood running to his head with rage. Taking up a pen he scratched some words on a piece of paper, rang for a clerk, and handed him the paper without a word. The clerk hurried out. Biddle leaned back slightly. His body relaxed from its tense attitude, but his hand trembled as he withdrew it from the desk. His voice tight and cold as ice, his eyes half closed, he said quietly, "Give the matter no more thought, Mr. van Mierop. The pensioner will be found, and there will be no further intrusions, of this or any other kind. And now, if I may take this opportunity of yer very welcome visit to mention another matter," he went on, all affability, "there's a cargo bein' shipped this season from Madras in which I think yer might be interested and concernin' which I've a small suggestion to make. I'm expectin' it to yield a not inconsiderable profit—in the region, should we say, of three times the purchase price. I 'ad in mind to inquire whether I might inscribe yer name, Mr. van Mierop, against a thousand-dollar share in the said cargo."

"It is certainly an interesting rate of profit," Thomas replied equivocally, his difficulty being that he did not possess a thousand dollars.

"But would yer be interested?" Biddle asked.

"Well, I—"

"Newcomers to the coast," he continued, restraining Thomas with a gesture, "need 'elp an' guidance, I'm sure yer'll agree, and to give it, that's our policy 'ere. Mis'aps, too, can occur, which must be properly guarded against. This brings me to the detail of me suggestion. In the un-'appy event of the cargo not fetchin' the anticipated profit, me company would not expect yer to be a loser, Mr. van Mierop. Any loss we'll carry ourselves. But if success favours our enterprise yer profit is yours. Cash transactions can wait till the cargo's sold and we see 'ow we stand."

"It is an uncommonly handsome arrangement," Thomas said, endeavouring to conceal his amazement.

Biddle reached for a ledger.

"May I then inscribe yer name, sir? The expectation is unusual."

"Certainly."

Biddle began to write.

"Yer initials, Mr. van Mierop?"

"T.K."

"Mr. T. K. van Mierop," Biddle enunciated quietly, writing it down. "One thousand dollars. There it is. Let's 'ope we may later on congratulate ourselves."

Though he had taken care not to let Biddle see this, Thomas was quite seriously worried about the girl, fearing that she had run away. Due to being unable to understand business English he had only grasped fragments of what the Number One had reported to him. Where the Portuguese came in he could not fathom, but from what the Number One said, the intrusion seemed to have no connexion with the girl's disappearance. Thomas was convinced she had run away because of himself.

Not till midnight was he able to return to Hospital Street. This time the door did not open before him. Letting himself in with a key, he entered the gloomy hall and stopped.

In front of him, lying on his back in the middle of the floor, his legs curled up in the air, lay the fool boy, grinning from ear to ear and triumphantly clutching the Spanish guitar which Thomas had earlier ordered the Number One to hide where the fool boy would not be able to find it. Chuckling gleefully, he was rolling from side to side on the orange tiles, plinking the guitar's loosened strings, producing shadowy flat notes at random.

"Master now one-man with fool boy!" he gurgled amid his chuckles. "Master make ding-dong. Fool boy happy."

The house was still. The customary lamps were lit. Yet in the orderly stillness was this personification of chaos—the fool boy with the forbidden instrument.

"Number One!"

There was no answer. Thomas strode into the deeper gloom near the rear door.

"Number One!"

"Yes, Master! Coming!" exclaimed an alarmed voice issuing from the discreet lower room in the house where the Number One sometimes awaited the master's return at night. "Velly solly, Master. My sleeping," he explained as he emerged uncertainly. A smell of double-distilled Chinese liquor indicated that this explanation was incomplete.

"Is the girl here?" Thomas asked.

"Girl?" said the Number One, swinging round unsteadily. He frowned. "My no savvy," he said, lowering his eyes and looking about as for something lost on the floor. "She no sleeping?" he asked tentatively.

"I don't know."

"My look see."

Re-entering his room he came forth with a lighted candle. In the clearer light there was an inverted splendour about him. Still immaculately coiffed and clothed, his entire face was puffed and rosy, and he swayed slightly as he walked, adding to his ever-discreet and dignified manner a hint of abandon, a lurking jauntiness which, had he ever been to sea, would have been plainly identified as nautical. He advanced round to the storeroom beyond the back door and shook his head.

"She no sleeping," he sighed.

"Well, where is she?" Thomas demanded impatiently.

"My no savvy. My more look see."

With padding steps on a somewhat uncertain course he walked into the hall. Seeing the fool boy lying on the floor he shook his head sadly—"Him velly fool boy. No can make ding-dong like Master"—and proceeded upstairs.

Thomas mounted after him in a silence of steadily mounting anger. In the upper doorway the servant looked cautiously into the living room. He turned round with a smile of inexpressible relief.

"Ah! My savvy now. Girl say she likee die. My say no can. Must be asking Master first." He nodded benevolently. "She good girl. She waiting."

Thomas strode past him into the room. Her fine black hair falling freely about her white shoulders, the girl was standing beside a chair of red velvet in which she had evidently been asleep.

"Die?" Thomas muttered. "What is this?"

"Many many way can die," the Number One explained cheerfully. "Can eat bad thing, can *quh*"—he made a gesture of slitting his throat—"can jump in water off Plaia. Many many kind, but all same die."

With concern Thomas went over to her.

"You really wish to go away?" he asked gently in French.

She lowered her eyes to the carpet and did not answer.

"You loved William Urquhart very much. Is that it?" he pursued.

She still did not answer.

But at this juncture the Number One, who had caught the word Urquhart—or, as he pronounced it, Uk Hak—

weaved his way across the room till he stood beside them.

"Uk Hak Master him no-use man," he interrupted firmly. "Master no savvy all thing here. My savvy. Beforetime girl no happy. Girl happy with Master."

"How can?" Thomas asked. "You say she wants to die."

The Number One spread out his hands like an Italian waiter.

"Master no happy," he explained. "This why." And pressing his lips together he gave a nod of age and experience. "Master telling all time this Uk Hak Master him girl. This not! Uk Hak Master number one drinking man. Him no can. Him like, but no can. Him look see, finish."

It was a second before Thomas disentangled it.

"You mean—?"

The Number One expanded his chest in self-satisfaction.

"My savvy all thing, Master. Now Master savvy all thing. All thing velly good."

"Go to bed, Number One. You're drunk."

The old servant smirked, but with dignity.

"My velly solly, Master. Little bit drinking. My also no-use man." And noiselessly he withdrew.

Only to the top of the landing, however, for he had not forgotten his duties entirely. There he awaited the recall which force of habit had trained him to expect.

No recall came, however. Only silence. When he thought this had gone on long enough he coughed slightly and addressed the empty upper spaces of the hall and stairway.

"Master like drinking?"

The silence endured another instant.

"Not just at the moment, Number One."

The Number One smiled to himself and descended. The house was in order at last, all things China fashion.

The President of the Select Committee of Super-cargoes of the Honourable The East India Company Trading to China sends his compliments to Mr. Thomas

Kuyck van Mierop and requests his attendance at the President's Office at Ten of the Clock.

Splendidly written in copperplate script on the heaviest and most expensive paper, it looked at first sight more like an invitation to a levée than a summons to an interview, but this was part of the air of grandeur and sanctity with which the East India Company—and in particular the Select Committee—invested all their doings, and it arrived with the morning chocolate a couple of days later.

Thomas was received in a large upper room facing the Praia Grande, not by the President himself, but by Mr. Pigou, the third and junior member of the Select Committee. Mr. Pigou, greying and in his late forties, had the appearance more of a man of letters than a grandee of East India Company commerce. Bidding Thomas be seated, he ran his fingers through his hair, a vexed expression on his overwined features, as if international commerce was everlastingly beyond him.

"In a general way we try to obey the laws of the China Government, Mr. Mierop. We truly do try. With annual uniformity we report to our masters in Calcutta and London that we never fail to obey. From time to time, however, as in the present unfortunate instance, the laws of China prove too much for us, and we are forced into the position where we have to choose between obedience and depriving thousands of our countrymen of the pleasure of drinking tea. The demand for tea being what it is—inordinate, almost amounting to a vice—the balance swings invariably in favour of tea and disobedience. This too, provided we never report the disobedience, satisfies our masters better.

"The present deplorable case is an illustration of what I mean. A large consignment of tea, delayed for months in delivery by the bankruptcy of one of the thirteen China merchants, is now, out of season and at a moment of fundamental inconvenience, being sent from the tea districts to Canton, where it is expected within the next two weeks.

There is not a single Company officer in Canton to super-intend the consignment's arrival, and if we are not to be subjected to all kinds of subsequent botherations it is essential for someone responsible to be sent to Canton forthwith. It has been borne upon me that you, Mr. Mierop, newly arrived on the China station, fresh and healthy (as I see you to be) and without the need of such old-timers as myself to recuperate in this salubrious climate and gather strength for the ordeals of another season's trading, might advantageously be sent with a commission to ensure the tea's safe arrival and storage."

He coughed into an embroidered handkerchief, and continued.

"The Committee has accepted this timely and sensible suggestion. You will travel by fastboat to Canton by the inner channels of the river. You will appreciate that travel by fastboat is not permitted to us out of season. It is theoretically possible to obtain permission to go up by chop-boat by the main channel of the river, but the chops are obtained after such great delays, and sometimes not obtained at all, that in the present juncture we cannot afford to rely on this system. The Committee wishes you, therefore, Mr. Mierop, to be discreet about your departure, which will be made this day, in the late afternoon. The China officials at the three customs posts you will pass on the river will require cash bribes, and these, at the standard rate and appropriately marked, you will find in your cabin in the fastboat. A linguist will accompany you."

He leaned back reflectively and said with a sigh:

"We labour here under monstrous difficulties. But at this point in our history, with the American colonies at stake and things going from bad to worse in India, one is obliged to assess matters in their true perspective. The British nation, in these grave times, cannot be deprived of tea."

Thomas' first thought was of acute disappointment at being deprived of the girl who for two nights had delighted him.

Her name was Martha, and like many orphans—it was to this he attributed it—she was mysterious, unwilling to say very much about herself, her self being all she had. There was even a mystery about her name. When he first asked her she said she had no name, and only when chided with the unlikelihood of this did she finally relent and tell him her name, though even then in a strangely indirect way—*"On peut m'appeler Marthe"*—as if it was not quite true. When it came to her surname she would give none. She had no surname, she said, and from this she would not budge. Nor would she admit to being either Chinese or Portuguese. She was neither, she said, beyond which he ascertained nothing.

It only made him possessively more sure of her. He would understand her as others had not. To him she would yield her reticences, and to him alone—for he sensed she had already told him more than she would ever willingly have told anyone else—and thus would she be his completely. This was his desire, and he was sure of his ascendancy, sure of his ability to penetrate every one of her mysteries.

When he told her he had to leave for Canton and she almost fainted he was secretly flattered. He caught her in his arms. But as he felt the anxious beating of her heart and observed she was not weeping, he realized he had missed the point. She was frightened of something.

There was no time to wonder why, however. Diverting her attention as one does with a child that cries, he proceeded with the plan he had already decided on. Martha should have an upstairs room in the main body of the house, separating her from the servants.

This, as he had foreseen, cheered her up at once, but produced unusually violent objections about being contrary to custom. He listened to none of it, all but carrying her protesting through to two unused rooms on the far side of the house. One faced the street, the other faced the Chinese houses at the foot of the Monte; both had shutters. He asked

48

her to choose.

"In this place you can always be seen by somebody," she said, showing her dimples—she was excited—"so I would prefer this room." She indicated the one away from the street.

He asked why.

"That side, Portuguese eyes. This side, Chinese. Chinese eyes are small, Portuguese large."

He gave the necessary order, but her words had somehow taken the pleasure out of it for him. There was still so much he did not know about her.

"You think, do you not, Seigneur, that giving me this room is an assurance," she went on.

"Against what?" he inquired.

"The Seigneur does not understand Macao," she replied, and her voice trembled. "We are so easily brought, so easily taken away."

He smiled.

"Now tell me, just who is going to take you away?"

"The Seigneur trusts Senhor Biddle."

"Do I?"

"Yes. And against Senhor Biddle there is only one assurance."

"What is that?"

She looked him straight in the eyes.

"You could buy this house."

"I understood that was impossible in Macao," he replied.

"No. In the name of a Portuguese—someone safe—it could be arranged."

Pressed to explain more, she would not. She had a way of cutting off a conversation, completely preventing further inquiry. It was to be another of her mysteries.

But he hoped he had not made a mistake in giving her the room.

What with pensioners, country traders, security, business English, chops and linguists, Thomas was not slow to grasp that the China coast was a world of euphemism. On arrival in Macao's inner harbour, however, even he was startled by the sheer literary daring underlying the choice of the word fastboat.

To begin with it was very hard to see that it was in fact a boat. It looked like a house, and appeared to be as solidly attached to the wharf as were the other wooden constructions, sheds and stores, on either side of it. It was also clear that if it did indeed prove capable of aquatic movement, the least likely epithet to describe such movement would be fast.

Its superstructure, if this word was applicable to it, was architectural in character. It had rusticated walls of stone which on closer approach one providentially realized were imitation, a colonnade complete with pediment and architraves, and well-proportioned windows and doors, both real and imitation. The only items missing from the complete presentment of a modest country house were a carriage drive and a garden, but there were potted plants on both sides of the front door, and other flowers painted round the imitation windows. It was apparently to be poled or rowed, depending on the depth of the river, by ten half naked Chinese; and if the clamour these were already making gave any indication of what was to come, it was hard to foresee any alternative to five or six days and nights of sleeplessness.

George Cuming, bearing a message of good wishes from the President, had come to see his colleague off. He conducted Thomas round the interior of the fastboat, which was appointed with an eye to the highest standards of comfort, explained more about the Canton bribes, and was generally as helpful as he could be, till it was time to go.

Cuming on the wharf, Thomas amid the potted plants at the front door, last words were exchanged as the inconceivable craft revealed that its lower regions bore certain relationships to a boat, and the footage of watery space between the two men gradually increased.

"Oh, and there was one other point I omitted to mention," said Cuming with the slight trace of affected weariness which preceded his more barbed observations. "About Macao, not Canton. You may wish to pass a word to your household staff. They do not seem to appreciate that in certain matters"—he lingered over it—"discretion is expected of us. Certain people should not be seen outside the house." He made a gesture of resignation. "You know how it is. Most of them have their Portuguese relatives, and some have friends as well, flashy youths with swords and the counterfeit manners of the fidalgos of former times. The Portuguese never quite recovered from their golden age. I thought I should just mention it. God be with you!" he concluded with a lazy wave of his white-gloved hand.

Thomas clutched the rail, his face suffused with anger. The girl's words rushed back at him. He could buy the house—in the name of a Portuguese—someone safe. And her secrecy, her disinclination to answer questions. He wanted to grab Cuming by the kerchief and demand to know more. But Cuming had chosen his moment with strategic care. No arm could grasp over that distance of water, and no order to the sailors, unless delivered in Cantonese, would have the effect of interrupting the slow motion of the fastboat.

Cuming merely smiled with a slight inclination of the head, waited till the boat was in the stream, when with another gentle wave he turned on his heel and coolly strolled to his chair, leaving Thomas Kuyck van Mierop, Esquire, heading in gathering dusk into the empire of China, to chew that one over for six months in solitude.

PART TWO

The Reverse Side of the Screen

FOURTEEN YEARS EARLIER—the records of Macao's ancient charitable institution, the Santa Casa da Misericordia, suggest it must have been on or about the 12th of January 1766—the Reverend Mother Clemencia, Abbess of the Convent of Santa Clara, was returning home at dusk, accompanied by a servant, when, passing the locked doors of the church of São Domingos, she noticed a bundle of rags lying on the church steps. As she drew near it the bundle stirred slightly.

The Abbess bent to examine it.

"A babe!" she exclaimed. "A pretty babe!"

Though the Convent looked after a certain number of orphans, Mother Clemencia's main concern in Macao was prostitution, a matter in which, to her great mortification, a succession of Governors and Bishops, despite her haranguings and entreaties, had failed to take any interest, due, she suspected, to their belief that the large number of entertainers, as they were politely called, was one of the factors attracting foreigners—and with them money—to what a few years earlier had been an impoverished colony.

The sight of the child, however, so touched her heart—a lonely Portuguese heart ever a little aloof from Macao and its people—that she yielded to her own deepest disposition and, seeing that it was nearly dark and too late to summon help from the orphanage, ordered her servant to pick up the bundle and bring it into the Convent. The servant, more wary than her august mistress, took care to separate the rags and examine the sex before obeying this order. Mother Clemencia, with a precise knowledge of life, had

53

not considered such an inspection necessary. Nobody threw boys away.

Next morning, when the priest came to say Mass in the Convent chapel, the child was baptized Martha, "because," said the Abbess, "poor child, she will have to work as soon as she is able, and be trained to work. Even this one additional mouth is more than we can afford to feed."

Which accounts for the entry in the records of the Santa Casa da Misericordia, to which Mother Clemencia applied for a subsidy to maintain the child. The Santa Casa, with two hundred years' experience of administering charity in Macao, granted the Convent, for Martha's upkeep, a monthly sum sufficient to provide two bowls of rice per day, and a small once-for-all payment for clothing. One of the Convent servants, who had recently borne a child, nourished Martha in addition to her own baby—and described Mother Clemencia as an unreasonable woman who should have had babies of her own.

Nine years later Mother Clemencia faced frankly—before God and her own conscience, that is to say, not before her subordinates—the possibility that she had committed an error.

"The Devil is in the child," Sister Grace said as a statement of fact. "I can do no more, Mother." Sister Grace, in charge of the domestic requirements of the Convent, was directly responsible for Martha, who worked in the laundry and the kitchen.

Mother Clemencia sighed, reflecting on the mysterious ways of God. There was no reasonable explanation of the child's temper. Sister Grace was right, it was infernal. There were long sullen silences, the refusal to obey orders, the helpless bouts of weeping. Worst of all was the tendency, of which the latest and gravest example had just taken place, to pick up the kitchen knives and throw them at whomever was the object of her anger. The Mother Abbess was wise in the ways of human beings. She might have been described as, among many other qualities, accustomed to women who threw things about. She was not, however, accustomed to little girls who threw knives with such dreadful accuracy as this Martha. She was dangerous. It so happened that Sister Grace, a nervous person, had reacted in time. Had she not, the knife would have inflicted a serious wound. For all of this Mother Clemencia blamed herself, recognizing in Martha's behaviour, not the Devil, but a great gift of God—intelligence—which, because the child had not been taught to read and write, manifested itself in such physical aspects as accuracy of throw.

Once more she sighed, as a servant brought her morning cup of chocolate. Dismissing Sister Grace's remark about the Devil with a plea for never-ending patience, she called for the child and questioned her. What was the reason for her unhappiness? Did she not realize that everyone in the Convent wanted to love and help her, but that she herself must try always to love others, even those who sometimes made her angry?

"I know it, Mother," the child replied, staring at the ground.

"Kneel then, and make your penitence to me," said Mother Clemencia gravely.

Martha knelt and kissed Mother Clemencia's hand.

"I repent my wicked thoughts," she repeated word for word after the Abbess, "that led me to wicked action. I humbly ask to be forgiven before the Holy Mother of God and before all those who have care of me."

Mother Clemencia smiled, for she loved the virtue of obedience.

"Now kneel and repeat the same before Sister Grace."

The child did not move. Mother Clemencia cajoled her. She stayed kneeling, eyes downcast, fists clenched. She loved Mother Clemencia, who in her imagination was nearly the same person as the Holy Mother of God. Mother Clemencia *was* her mother. Her loyalty was uniquely given to her. It was because she knew Sister Grace was disloyal that she hated obeying her orders and had thrown the knife at her. With the wit of those born with nothing she knew that Sister Grace was secretly putting money aside from what the Abbess gave her to spend on food for the Convent inmates, in order to provide a dowry for a niece who urgently wished to get married and who had come to beg Sister Grace's help. She knew other things too about other sisters. Most of them she hated because, taking advantage of Mother Clemencia's trust in them, they were in one way or another disloyal to her. Martha would thus not make her penitence before Sister Grace, even though Mother Clemencia, her mother, asked her to. Martha knew what her mother-in-God did not know.

Sister Grace pursed her lips and walked from the room, leaving the Abbess to her chocolate and the decision to send the rebel child out into the world.

But to what family, Mother Clemencia asked herself? If a Macao Portuguese family could be persuaded to take her it would only be as a servant, and with the financial difficulties chronic in so many such families it was an arrangement unlikely to last. Once dismissed, where would there be for her other than the Street of Happiness? With her firm, fair skin and shapely body she might experience the even worse fate of being sold as a *mui tsai*, a slave girl, and shipped to Manila, with which there was constant traffic in young girls for Chinese in the Philippines. No, if a place of security was to be found, it could only be in one of the foreign homes. No Protestant could be approached, of course. This ruled out the English, the Dutch, the Danes, the Swedes. Of the Catholics, Macao's few Spanish and Italian residents tended to be birds of passage. There remained the French, for whom Mother Clemencia, educated partly in Paris, had a particular sympathy.

Among the French permanent residents the middle-aged Monsieur Auvray pleased her most. He was a private trader who, as often happened, when the time for his retirement had come, rather than return to Europe had chosen to live out the rest of his days in Macao. Admittedly his was an establishment, not a home. Since his arrival many years earlier, when private French traders were not allowed in China, even by the French, he had lived with a Macao woman whose daughter, said to be the offspring of someone else, he had brought up. There being no known local impediment to marriage, Mother Clemencia had concluded with regret that Monsieur Auvray, on leaving France, must already have been married. In such circumstances the question of adoption could not be raised. Nevertheless, with Monsieur Auvray there would be hope for the child.

"She will work hard for you," she said to Teresa da Silva, the woman who lived with Monsieur Auvray, "and perhaps in time you will come to love her as a younger daughter."

She told Martha that if she was obedient God would provide all things for her, after which the little girl fetched her bundle and, without a tear of farewell, accompanied Teresa da Silva out of the Convent gates.

Teresa was not pleased, but the pressure of the Church was strong in Macao, too strong to be resisted. Her man, old Monsieur Auvray, was kind to Martha and was soon calling her his little daughter. Mother Clemencia was sad because of the tearless parting from the soul whose life she had preserved and whose salvation she had caused to be insured through baptism. True, Martha had asked ever to be allowed to return to visit her. But Mother Clemencia had expected tears. When they did not come, she knew she loved the child, despite her difficult temperament, with a possessive love, contrary to what was permitted under the Rule. Stricken with an unhappiness no one else in Macao would have understood, not even she perceived that the child's dry-eyed departure was due to devotion to doing completely and without complaint the will of her mother-in-God.

"What's your name?" asked Dominie, Teresa's daughter, a year Martha's senior.

"Martha."

"Martha what?"

"Just Martha."

"That can't be," said Dominie. "You must have more than one name."

"Why?"

"You must. You're not a real person if you haven't."

Frightened by an extra-convent existence of which she knew nothing, Martha clasped the rosary Mother Clemencia had given her and prayed to the Holy Mother of God for safety. She did not of course know that Dominie's interest arose from the contradiction in her own life that to some she was Dominica da Silva Auvray, while being to others plain Dominica da Silva. The discovery that Martha did not know her own surname gave Dominie a sense of power over the newcomer. Adding to this the knowledge that her mother did not like Martha, Dominie gained, by Martha's coming to the house, an unforeseen ascendancy in regard to her mother, from whom henceforth she was able to ask more or less whatever she liked, as well as acting just as she pleased.

"Martha doesn't even know her own name," she crowed at old Monsieur Auvray in his rocking chair.

"Why have I only one name?" asked Martha, standing solemn and pale in Mother Clemencia's room two days later.

"Child, you have hardly slept," the nun replied, her heart beating faster with the tender realization that there had at last been tears.

"Why have I only one name?" the child repeated.

Monsieur Auvray had brought her to the Convent. He had consented to this after Teresa da Silva had several times refused. He was now sent for by the Abbess.

"It is true the child should have a surname," Mother Clemencia said in French. "She knows her own story, Monsieur Auvray. We were never able to find out who her parents were." How inconvenient it was, she thought, that adoption could not be mentioned! "Should you wish to keep her in your house," she continued, skirting the subject with care, "there might be certain advantages in her taking the surname of one of the members of the household."

"I would be glad to give her my name," said the fat, tender-hearted Monsieur Auvray. "Would you like to be called Martha Auvray, my little daughter?"

Martha looked inquiringly at him. Her eyes penetrating the meaning in his, she took confidence and gave a small smile.

"A pleasant child," the Frenchman commented, patting Martha's head. "All the same, Mother Abbess, there are other thoughts on my mind. Supposing I were to make the voyage to France—you know I have long projected one—and, for reasons known at present only to God, never return. I speak entirely in the conditional, Mother; such an eventuality may never occur. But I do not think it should be overlooked that, while I myself am in a position to return to France, this little girl is destined in all probability to spend her whole life in Macao. You may consider in such circumstances, Mother Abbess, that my name—though a name not to be despised—might not be entirely suitable for her."

Whether the reason for his refusal was sincere did not seem important to Mother Clemencia. Listening with enjoyment to Monsieur Auvray's polished French, she was borne momentarily away to the days of her youth. Apart from this link between them, there had to be added the implicit understanding that nearly always lay in Macao between one continental European and another. Because there was something managerial in this—something aroused by mutual incomprehension of the apathy and ignorance of the Macao Portuguese—it is probably to it that should be attributed the decision with which the Abbess' interview with Monsieur Auvray ended.

After a domestic upset which Monsieur Auvray recognized as unavoidable and handled with the nice sagacity of experienced middle age, the child was allowed to call herself Martha da Silva.

Martha's relations with her (as it was commonly said) foster-sister Dominie became personal to the point of sisterhood in blood. Dominie was lonely in the old house of high ceilings on the Rua da Penha, amid the silent, sensuous mystery of her mother's life with the ageing Frenchman. Because the old man did not really love her, Dominie never learned to speak French, an accomplishment which Martha rapidly gained due to the trust that came to subsist between herself and her *soi-disant* foster-father. Despite this defect, however, Dominie considered herself superior to Martha. She was older. The house they lived in was her mother's (though Monsieur Auvray had bought the house the title deeds were of course in Teresa's name). Above all, Martha was Chinese. Dominie was not old or subtle enough to appreciate that Monsieur Auvray's love for Martha was an enduring rebuke to his concubine for having foisted on him Dominie, whom he had not fathered. Dominie and Martha, needing each other's companionship, came to share their secrets, and thus to hate each other with the cordiality of real sisters.

Distinctive of the household was the fact that Monsieur Auvray, despite his long years in Portuguese surroundings, remained unalterably French, which meant that the most unalterable part of his physical make-up was his palate. Though he found it undeniably convenient that Teresa cooked for him, equally undeniable was the fact that he found her meals extremely dull. Perhaps Martha's Chinese ancestry here exercised its silent influence in endowing her with a similar finesse in regard to food. Whatever it was, though she had never known in the Convent anything but the plainest of plain cooking, from the moment her Little Papa began demonstrating the niceties of the French cuisine she found herself completely in agreement, with the result that when Teresa and Dominie went out together Monsieur Auvray would take Martha by the hand and lead her down to the kitchen for a secret meal which they would cook themselves, using specially fragrant spices, wines and other ingredients the use of which Teresa did not appreciate. With every spice or herb he used Monsieur Auvray would teach Martha two names, the name of the ingredient itself, and the name of the place from which the best quality could be obtained. When the meal was over —and the outcome of these adventures was invariably delicious—he would make her recite the names she had learned.

"And be sure you never forget them," he would conclude, "because as long as you remember, someone in Macao will know, whereas once you forget a single one, nobody will know."

Martha had not the slightest idea what the names of the places were, in that having no knowledge of geography (never having even seen a field) she made no distinctions between countries, provinces, islands, towns, rivers, mountains or what you will. She did not know if you went to them in a ship or whether you walked. She simply obeyed her Little Papa and memorized them.

That Martha had become Monsieur Auvray's favourite did not disturb Teresa, who calculated that her man would die well before her. M. Auvray had also thought of this.

"When people die and go to Heaven, my little daughter," he told Martha one day, "they give away their money and everything they own, because in Heaven they have no need of money. When I go to Heaven, I shall give you some of my money, to use for yourself, to keep you safe and sound. It is all written down on a piece of paper which is kept in that bureau over there, locked up."

But when, Martha being then thirteen years old, Monsieur Auvray sickened and died without making his projected voyage to France, matters were otherwise.

"I will tell you a secret," whispered Dominie. "Inez says we should all feel sad because Little Papa has died, but my mother is not sad. She is not sad because now she is rich. Little Papa has left her all his money."

Dominie was growing beautiful. She had soft curly black hair and skin paler than that of any other Macao girl, most of whom were dark—darker than the Chinese. Believing that it was her destiny to be beautiful, Dominie dreamed of wealth, of being accounted a true European and marrying an officer from Portugal.

Late that same afternoon Martha opened the bureau, trying as many of its drawers as were unlocked. There were many pieces of paper inside, but she could not tell if any one of them had her name written on it.

Neither could Teresa, for she too, like every Macao woman, could not read and write.

"What are you doing?" she asked with intuitive suspicion as she saw Martha coming away from the bureau.

"Is it true that we are rich?"

"We?" Teresa asked cautiously—she had not washed her hair since her man died, and looked old and dirty. "Of course we are rich. Your foster-father's money naturally now is mine. Provided you are obedient I will look after you, though you need not expect the idle life you led while he was alive. You will work for what I give you."

"There is money for me also."

"You? Why should there be?"

"I don't know. But Little Papa promised it. He said there was a paper in there, in the bureau."

Teresa looked malevolent and frightened. She walked rapidly to the bureau, opened it, picked up every piece of paper she saw.

"Dominie!" she called quietly and urgently, remembering not to shout, for the shutters were closed and the house was supposed to be quiet with mourning. "Bring an ember from the kitchen."

She bundled the bureau papers into the empty grate. It was summer, and the fireplace was not being used. When Dominie returned with an ember her mother applied it. The papers began to burn smokily, damp in the humid weather.

Martha stood a short distance away, beside her foster-father's writing table.

"How does this open?" Teresa asked irritably, banging the top of the bureau's secret drawer.

Dominie rose from in front of the grate.

"Like this," she said, pressing the lever movement.

"Clever child."

Digging her arms deep into it, Teresa brought forth some heavy papers, grey-blue in colour.

"Don't burn them!" Martha whispered, but loudly. These fine documents, she was sure, must be the ones her foster-father intended for her.

"Put them in the fire," Teresa ordered.

"They're mine!" said Martha. "If you burn them, Dominie, I shall hate you all my life."

" 'Mine!' " Teresa imitated her with contempt. "What is yours in this house, you Chinese waif? Burn them."

Dominie bent again to the grate, feeding the heavy blue paper into the fire.

Beside Martha, on her foster-father's writing table, was a silver inkpot which it had always been her duty to keep filled with ink. With a swift movement she opened the silver top, took out the small glass inkwell, and flung it at Teresa's face. In the instant before throwing it she thought to herself, I must not hit her eyes because that would be a sin. So she threw the inkwell at Teresa's cheek.

Made of fine glass it smashed with a wet, flat sound as it hit her. The ink blackened one side of her face, spurted up into her left eye, dripped down her neck. The glass pieces scattered, some of them sticking to her black dress. Teresa bent down, putting a hand to her face. As she raised herself again, blood mixed with ink oozed over her fingers.

It happened so quietly and swiftly that Dominie noticed nothing till she leaned back from the fireplace to pick up the last remaining papers and saw her mother's face. The papers fell from her grasp. A practical girl, she went at once to fetch water and a cloth.

The instant she moved, Martha drew near to pick up the papers.

"Stop her!" whispered Teresa stridently. She herself did not move. Her head tilted up, her bloodstained fingers outstretched, she was as if paralysed.

Martha snatched up the papers and darted back, watching as a wild animal does for the first move in a fight.

"Make her give them back, Mother! I shall have no dowry!" Dominie screamed, bursting into tears.

Teresa shook her off. She glared at Martha hideously. Teresa had been meeting in secret a gentleman from one of the Spanish ships calling regularly from Manila. She had counted on him being her next man, after old Auvray. With hatred and fear she saw this gentle dream shattered. There would be a scar. She had been made a kind of widow. She would never love or be loved again. She spoke quietly, icily.

"I curse the day you entered my house. I was forced to take you in. For five years I have fed you. I nursed a viper. Go, and never enter this house again."

"I will take my bundle with me," said Martha calmly.

"You will go now, with what you have and no more."

Teresa stood between Martha and the room where she kept her few belongings. She modified her demand.

"I will take my rosary with me."

"You black-souled Chinese devil!" Teresa ejected with fury. "What need have you for a rosary?"

Martha's face went puffy with anger, the whites of her eyes reddening.

"I am not Chi..." she began to say through gritted teeth. Yet as she reached the word Chinese her voice died away. Anger ebbed as rapidly as it had flowed in, to be replaced by a look of incomprehension. What she was trying to say was not true. She was Chinese. She had been told so, even by her mother-in-God. But she had also been told that she was not a real Chinese, not like other Chinese who worshipped devils and would go to hell when they died. She belonged to the Christian family, and would be cared for by the Holy Mother of God. When Sister Grace had called her a daughter of hell who would go to hell Martha had not believed it. Yet here was the same assertion from the lips of the woman to whom her mother-in-God had entrusted her. All Martha knew of the world and her place in it slid away beneath her feet. It was true, then. She was not, and never had been, accepted truly into the Christian family. They had all told lies to her.

In lonely, adult dignity she drew the papers from behind her back. She was conscious of the room, its foreign furnishings, its homely smell of tobacco and sandalwood, and of all it had meant to her when Little Papa was there. Without a gesture she let the papers fall at Teresa's feet.

"Now go," Teresa muttered. "Go before I kill you." She tottered forward a step. Her eyeballs rolled up. She sank senseless to the floor, falling where the will lay, her blood-stained cheek pressed against it.

In fear and horror Martha sped from the room and down the stairs. As she reached the front door, Dominie from above—the only time she had ever been brave without her mother to support her—shouted:

"Good riddance! May you be the last stinking heathen we ever have in this house!"

It was the last half-hour of daylight, and before dark Martha had to find the only other place in Macao she knew: the Convent. She had never been out alone before. The Ridge was a maze of narrow cobbled streets, with mounting and descending calçadas twisting among high walls and shuttered houses. Darkness was almost complete when with a prayer on her lips she found the stucco façade of the Convent. The bell-pull had been removed for the night. She hammered on the great door with her fists.

The slats of a shutter on an upper floor opened slightly. "Who is it?"

Martha recognized the voice. Her mouth set hard as lamplight glinted down.

"It is I, Martha," she answered in a low voice from which she could not drive out hate.

"Martha?" queried Sister Grace. "There are many Marthas."

"I am Martha da—" she began. But the name dried on her lips. Her whole being refused to let her pronounce it. "I want to speak to the Mother Abbess."

"Are you by chance Martha da Silva?"

Martha bowed her head.

"No," she said. She was a stinking heathen. She was not Martha da Silva. She never had been and she never would be.

A few spots of rain fell. Banging against the door with all her might, Martha cried out for the Mother Abbess.

"Mother Abbess?" the voice above asked coldly. "Which Mother Abbess do you wish to speak to?"

Martha gasped. Unable to believe her ears, she turned despairingly to face the street, and with a cry of fright shrank back against the door. Immediately before her in the gloom a man was standing motionless and silent.

He was fairly tall, and in his tricorn and cloak, just discernible in the dark, he appeared to be a European. Yet when the tricorn moved, and out of the complete blackness beneath it the man spoke, it was in the Macao *patois*, in which he was fluent, his accent authentic.

"It was you I saw crossing the largo as I came out of church, was it not?" he said in a mocking, dangerous tone of affected casualness.

"I have no idea."

"I thought it was," he said, as though she had replied in the affirmative. The manner of it was familiar.

"Who are you?" she demanded.

The man chuckled.

"Don't you intend going home to my little cousin's house tonight?" he asked lightly.

With a shock she knew who he was. His name was Pedro

66

Gonçalves Sequeira, and he was a young second cousin of Dominie's. Unlike other Macao young men he wore proper European clothes, carried a cane, and affected the manners of the fashionable English. Last winter he had tried to kiss Martha downstairs outside the kitchen while he was calling on his aunt (as, China fashion, the relationship between him and Teresa was described), and had said something that had disturbed Martha and made her hate him, though he intended it to be pleasing. After he had gone the servant Inez had warned her about him.

"You be careful of that one," she had said gravely. "He likes very young girls—like you, dear—and he likes them Chinese."

It was not so much of this that Martha was afraid as of the danger that he might try to deliver her to the Rua da Penha.

"I am not going to that house again," she said.

"Really? Where are you going then?"

"To my mother-in-God."

"Tut-tut, there's a nice child! To Mother Clemencia?"

"Yes."

"Doesn't my aunt ever tell you anything in that house? I thought the whole world knew."

Martha's voice fell.

"Knew . . . ?"

"Your famous mother-in-God left yesterday for Brazil. She is to be Abbess of the Convent at São Paulo."

And Sister Grace, Martha thought, was the new Abbess in Macao.

"Is that far?" Martha asked timorously.

"Brazil? Quite far."

"She went in a ship."

"Yes."

"On the great sea."

"On the great sea."

She fell back loose against the wood of the Convent door.

"Brazil," she said starkly. "It is a place from which people never come back." And her mother-in-God had gone without calling for her. They had told her the truth. She was a heathen. She belonged to none.

As if confirming it, a shutter in the wall above clicked to.

She walked forth into the dark street, and Pedro, who had made his plans, did not impede her. He followed a few feet behind.

Macao, with its elaborate and varied traffic in women and girls, provided young men such as Pedro with opportunities which, even by oriental standards, were remarkable; and Pedro, whose life was otherwise humdrum, liked nothing more than novelty and change. Though one day he would probably have to marry someone like his second cousin Dominie, he intended to delay that day as long as possible, enjoying meanwhile the other attractions the city offered. He had an understanding at one of the houses in the Street of Happiness where he was permitted to hire a room when he required it. It was thither he intended to steer his quarry.

The Convent sank into anonymous night behind them. Above the roofs of the old Portuguese houses and out over the sea thunder growled amid flashes of distant lightning. Ahead lay the lanterns, the smoke, the babel of the Chinese market glowing orange-gold. It was a world no respectable European ever entered at night, and which no woman ever saw unless she was from the Street of Happiness. As Martha came into the mellow lustre of the flares and lanterns, on all sides the pale, half naked stall-boys broke into ribald, foul-mouthed jests. From the house of a Chinese guild a group of rough, gnarled men, talking loudly and laughing, came out, their faces suffused red with liquor. One of them uttered a revolting word, the rest guffawed as she passed.

The congestion of brightly lit stalls on either side made the street exceptionally narrow. There was no concealment, no escape from the obscenity. She struggled on a little further, then stopped.

"Where am I to go?" she asked.

"As a matter of fact I was beginning to wonder where you thought you were going," Pedro replied with urbanity. "Allow me to conduct you by a more sensible route."

Pedro was standing with his black cloak thrown over his right shoulder, twiddling his cane between his fingers, a smile on his handsome face. He was perspiring slightly beneath the inordinate weight of his clothes.

She was about to return the way she had come when, jogging uncertainly through the smoky, clamorous street, a closed sedan chair hove into view and, upon a gruff order from the man being borne in it, swung abruptly sideways, blocking any further advance.

"Master Pedro!" someone called from inside in a displeased tone, a voice thick after eating too much rice. "Do I see yer up to yer tricks again? Let's 'ave a little more hintegrity, shall we? Allow the little lady to come forward, will yer be ser kind, and let yer Uncle Biddle take a look at 'er." Pedro uttered a soft oath of disgust. "That's better," Biddle said with satisfaction, bending forward at the window. "That's the perfect gentleman. Opportunities, Master Pedro, should never be missed. Business before gallivantin'. In other words, 'ands off!"

"Not this time, Mr. Biddle!" he muttered pleadingly.

Pedro Gonçalves Sequeira was a fine-looking young man, fair-skinned for a Macao-born, with large leisured eyes set wide apart, a Grecian nose, sensitive and straight, and a firm chin indicating an over-insistent obstinacy which was his only outward mark of weakness. By Macao matrons with unmarried daughters he was considered a most admirable catch, and by the daughters themselves as the city's most handsome bachelor. Yet when Abraham Biddle spoke his self-confidence vanished; his lower lip twitched; his manly face became that of a thwarted child. It was as though between Biddle and himself existed a relationship of hypnotist and hypnotized.

"No?" queried Biddle. "'Tis a word I don't appreciate 'earin' on the lips o' the very young. Now, take two chairs—

yer walk the streets like a pauper and give no credit to yer uncles—and bring the little lady with yer. 'Ave no fear, me dear. Uncle Biddle'll look after yer as one of 'is very own."

So saying, he signalled his chair to proceed.

Martha had understood little, for Pedro and Biddle were speaking in English. All her life she had had to struggle for the most rudimentary necessities of life, for food when greedy novices deprived her of her share of the Convent's meagre meals, for pieces of cloth to patch her worn-out clothes, for sacks to cover herself with to keep warm in winter, for a needle someone had carelessly mislaid, for pieces of thread no one wanted. Perhaps as a result, more than anything else in the world she wanted to stand on her own, independent. What she most despised in Dominie was the girl's insipid wish to submit to others, to be led, her terror lest her mother, who ordered all her ways, should die before a man be found to replace that leadership. Turning her back on the Convent, Martha had for a few moments stood alone; and her passage through the Chinese market had taught her a lesson. Occurring at that moment, when the Christians had thrown her out and only the Chinese world lay before her, its impact on her was immediate and ineffaceable. In a world dominated by men, for a woman to act prematurely, to attempt to stand alone before the time is ripe, is infinitely worse than being a slave. Stepping into the litter to follow Biddle she resigned herself to such slavery as he might choose to design for her. Slavery she knew it would be.

Late that night she was delivered to the house of William Urquhart. She had wept at Biddle's office, and they had given her green tea containing a drug that so dulled her consciousness it was almost like being asleep. She remembered nothing of the journey in the locked sedan chair. When awareness dimly returned to her she was lying on a bed. Staring down at her was Urquhart murmuring something appreciative.

"What's your name?" he asked in Macanese, in a flat

English accent.

The question penetrated through the fog of dreams enveloping her. Somehow, for a reason she could no longer remember, at some time—a time she could not recall—she had finished with her name. She still had her Christian name, but for some reason she had ceased to be a Christian.

"I have no name," she answered, and with a roar the rain which had been threatening all evening fell like a curtain between the house and the rest of existence.

The Number One's description of the limitations of William Urquhart's amorous proclivities was exact. To meet these strangely austere demands Martha was engaged on a permanent basis, Abraham Biddle obtaining a sizeable sum on the deal. This paid, Martha found herself in the *corps d'élite* of the entertainers, and became an East India Company pensioner—this term, incidentally, being used solely in accountancy, to cover the contingency of wives at home in England examining their husbands' disbursements in China. Genteel names might be given to it and definitions of relativity expressed, but the fact was that she had become a prostitute at the age of thirteen.

Being an orphan she had known loneliness at all times and among all people. Countless nights at the Convent she had cried herself to sleep in despair at her loneliness. She had prayed and prayed that one day a mother and a father would appear wonderfully from nowhere and take care of her.

Scorn she had known just as closely, from Sister Grace and others at the Convent, and endlessly from Teresa and Dominie when Monsieur Auvray's back was turned. Not till Martha entered the house in Hospital Street, however, did she learn what it was to endure both loneliness and scorn without any form of protection whatever.

Thomas van Mierop had evaluated with precision the status to which the allocation of the storeroom as her living quarters condemned her. There day after day she sat waiting for her nocturnal call, obliged to have her door open (because when it was shut there was no light) and thus to be seen by the servants, as well as to hear every sarcasm aimed at her. The experience would have been less bitter had some of the servants been bachelors. Men on their own would have accepted her presence with easy-going camaraderie. But all the servants except the fool boy were married with their wives living in the compound, and the wives were coarse, grasping women for whom marriage was a unique security, and who were nervous of having their husbands see every day that security set at naught with a prostitute living in the house. Of low origins themselves, the wives treated Martha as a creature unspeakably lower.

One of the outcomes of old Monsieur Auvray's death was that Inez the maid was dismissed as redundant. Shortly after her dismissal she called on Martha to inquire if the house in Hospital Street held any prospects for her, which of course it did not. But the visit afforded Martha an opportunity to find out what had been happening on the Rua da Penha.

Teresa, who had suffered severely from shock, had been left with a scar below her left eye. The scar was white with small dots of black in it, as if the ink had made indelible marks in her skin, and it gave her left eye a drooping appearance which made small children frightened of her.

When at last it had been considered safe to allow her to see her face in a mirror she had flown into a terrible rage in which she had sworn to bring Martha to justice. She had already sent for a lawyer when the matter came to the attention of one of her cousins who was a city elder, a member of the Senate of Macao, who in a state of considerable alarm hastened round to her house and begged her to desist.

He explained that should a case be brought involving Martha the danger existed to a high degree that the dreaded Mandarin of the Casa Branca, in whose juridical area Macao lay, and who resided at Chinshan some miles north of the city, would intervene, stating that Martha was Chinese, and that a case concerning her could only be heard in a Chinese court. Martha being a baptized Christian, the Portuguese, as a matter of national honour, would certainly refuse to send the case to Chinshan, and this would precipitate one of those confrontations of which Macao had had all too many previous experiences.

The method used by the Casa Branca to bring Macao to its knees was invariably the same. Chinese notices would appear ordering all Chinese to leave the city, which they promptly would. The barrier gate north of Macao would then be closed, leaving the city's inhabitants to starve, which with equal promptness they would begin to. Since the city's foundation the Portuguese had seldom engaged in manual labour and never in agriculture or animal husbandry. Within the walls of Macao not a pig was reared, not a cabbage grew, and no hen ever laid an egg. A Macao which no Chinese could enter was a Macao with nothing to live on but well-water.

The Senator foretold in lurid detail the sufferings of the people. With metaphor and hyperbole he begged Teresa to show Christian forbearance, and for the good of all the people to suffer to go unavenged the terrible injury she had been done.

Teresa consented, but a mood of brooding silence came over her thereafter, and it was clear she harboured thoughts of revenge by other means. Here the principal obstacle was that Martha resided in an East India Company house, which was one of the places no Portuguese authority would dare to interfere with. It was the knowledge that only by remaining in the house would she be safe from Teresa's vengeance that gave Martha's first meetings with Thomas van Mierop so crucial an importance.

Thomas himself had sensed that on his first evening his brusque "Certainly not!" had caused repercussions below stairs. Could he have seen and heard what actually happened he would have been even more repentant then he was. Even Ah Sum, the Number One, who among all the servants was the most daring in flouting his wife by pausing occasionally to chat with Martha, read the new master's decision as the writing on the wall. For the rest of the servants, every one of whom had been anxious about his own future employment throughout the months during which the house was without an occupant, it was the completing touch bringing jubilant self-satisfaction at the end of a day of frayed tempers and nervousness. All of them were re-employed and the girl would go. Husbands were happy because their wives would be less nasty to them. Wives were delighted, only waiting for the triumphal moment when they would be able to stand there crowing while the little harlot was taken away where she properly belonged. When word came through that the new master had left for supper, taunts and cackle rose to a crescendo. The cook having sent Martha a bowl of hot water and bones, the rest of them celebrated at two round tables set in the open air. They had decided there was no further need to feed her.

That night, after the servants' feast had been cleared away, there was a soft knocking on the door.

"It's your friend," a girl's voice whispered outside in Cantonese. "Come up to the garden."

It was Fong, Ah Sum's daughter, roughly Martha's age and who, when Martha first came to Hospital Street, was of all in the household the one she most dreaded to confront. From the start she had seen her, a squat, solid girl, well-developed for her years, her breasts already high-pointed beneath the revealing tightness of her drab brown samfoo, scrubbing floors and polishing to oblige the Number Four, who was one of Ah Sum's clansmen. From Fong's expression Martha feared that none would be more condemnatory of her. In fact, Fong's searching stare symptomatized a passionate interest in Martha's experience, and in Martha herself.

One day Fong, discharging her duties to excess, had polished the tiles along the covered way in front of Martha's room, and without raising her eyes from the half of a coconut husk, the flattened side of which she was pushing back and forth over the floor with her bare foot, said:

"My father and mother don't want me. They'd sell me if they could. Will you be my friend, Sister? I'll do anything for you if you will."

From that day forth began a friendship in the loneliness and secrecy of which Fong unburdened her heart. In the apparently convivial surroundings of the servants' cottages she was as lonely and desperate as was Martha herself.

In order to escape detection the two girls would meet after dark in a lonely spot above the cottages, where boulders lodged in the foot of the hill created a small plateau on which the gardeners cultivated row upon row of potted plants. There was a little shed on the plateau. When it was raining the girls crept inside it. It was thither that Fong now bid Martha come.

There, beneath a moon dusted in rivulets of cloud, Fong, from the depths of an abnormal passion, made a proposition. Martha had already told her that she could never return among the semi-devils (the Portuguese), and Fong had accepted this without asking for reasons. If the only alternative now was to be sold into the Street of Happiness, why did not Martha escape into the world of the Chinese?

As the idea sank in, Martha appreciated how tempting it was. If she did not belong to the Holy Mother of God, if it was true that she was a Chinese as other Chinese were and would go to hell, was there not wisdom in entering the world of the Devil?

"But where could I go, with no family?" she asked.

"You could become someone's adopted daughter," Fong replied ardently.

Martha shook her head.

"I've been adopted before, Younger Sister. Think of something real for me."

"You were only adopted by semi-devils. We Chinese are not like them. Adoption by us is good. You know the head gardener's wife? She has a sister, a religious woman. She spends her time in temples. She wants an adopted daughter to help her when she is old. Last New Year she sent the gardener's wife to ask if she could adopt me." Fong trembled with excitement. "Why should that old woman not adopt you instead of me? I am supposed to go to see her tomorrow. I will tell my mother I don't want to go. I want you to go instead."

In all Martha's life no one had ever offered to make a sacrifice for her, not even to the extent of ten grains of rice. Altruism was a frame of mind unknown to her. In a rough movement Fong clasped her to her soft, excited breasts.

"Let me, Sister!" she whispered, her voice choking. Tears were streaming down her cheeks.

But Martha was too frightened to consent.

"I shall never forget you," she said softly, responding to Fong's embrace. "I swear it."

Mid-morning next day Pedro Gonçalves Sequeira gained access to the house. He was still prepared, of course, to enjoy himself with the liberated African slaves in the Street of Happiness, or with the wide range of mestiças available, ranging from the ebonies of Moçambique to the bronzes of Timor. But from the day he first saw Martha and forced her into a kiss below stairs at his cousin's house his whole life had in fact changed. The floating world no longer delighted him as it had; it became a mere substitute for a love he desired above all else, but which it seemed he could never attain, even the last resort of marriage being ruled out, since if he married anyone in that house it would have to be Dominie. When, against all expectations, he had Martha in his power only to have her snatched from him for some Englishman, the effect on Pedro was far deeper than he would ever have dared to reveal. While Urquhart remained at the house there was nothing Pedro could do except gnaw at his soul. But as the time for Urquhart's departure drew near, the thought of Martha alone in the house so consumed him he could think of nothing else. He day-dreamed his way through the commissions he was charged with. He could not eat.

The listlessness, of poetic proportions, into which this flung him did not go unremarked.

" 'Eaven forbid that yer uncle should ever give yer an unnecessary warnin',", said Abraham Biddle on the day Urquhart left, "but I trust, Master Pedro, yer'll be ser good as to stay away from 'Ospital Street; and let it not be reported to me that yer've been practisin' any of yer well-known deceptions." The childish, hypnotized look came over Pedro's face. "The 'ouse o' Gonçalves Sequeira subsists," Biddle continued, flavouring his own words, "on its bein' the indispensable purveyor of all a Company gentleman requires. Let no one 'ave any misunderstandin's on that."

The indispensable purveyor thereupon addressed himself to his next opium deal, while Pedro slouched out into the front of the shop where he vent his fury by telling his uncles they were a collection of good-for-nothings. This shocked them very much, causing them to make lugubrious prognostications in family circles to the effect that the boy was going to the dogs due to pernicious English influences.

The morning after Thomas van Mierop's arrival Pedro rose early, button-holed Ah Sum at the market, and asked him how he found his new master. When the servant gave an evasive reply, Pedro, calculating that his hour had come, went at once to Chin Fui, the compradore, and asked for a chit to admit him to the house to make an inventory, a request which Chin Fui granted because, like Biddle, he used the Gonçalves Sequeira name for some of his business transactions, and thus usually saw fit to accede to such petty requests as the family made from time to time.

When Pedro found Martha in the storeroom he assumed, knowing nothing of the internal workings of the house, that she had been sent down there because the new Englishman did not want her. He was all the more surprised by the fierceness of her refusal to come away with him, for although Martha's interview with Thomas that morning had ended in tears she had not given up hope of winning his favour, and not for one moment would she go with Pedro, whom she regarded with contempt.

He promised to rent a room for her in the city, a place Teresa da Silva would never find out about. For Pedro had correctly interpreted his aunt's silences, and well knew the danger Martha was in from that quarter once she left the English house. Martha dismissed the idea scornfully.

"Very well," Pedro said, "—and I give you this on my word of honour. If you will come with me I will marry you." It was a desperate throw, but if it was the only way to convince her, he thought, so be it.

She looked at him witheringly.

"You?" she taunted him. "Would you dare be seen with me in the Cathedral, in front of the Bishop, with all your family looking on? What kind of a simpleton do you think I am?"

At this moment Ah Sum returned from the market, and for Pedro the game was up.

"I give you five days in which to think this over," he said to Martha as he prepared to withdraw. "If then you still refuse to come with me, I will see you are removed from here to another house, where perhaps you will be more responsive."

Martha had no illusions about Pedro's ability to make good his words. She had thought of the Englishman as being the deciding factor in the house, his will superior to that of others. Pedro's threat showed her the reality, which was that Europeans were powerful only in the sphere in which they moved, to which she herself did not belong. Hers was the Macao world, in which the English were mere visitors, exerting no influence whatever. The pressures to which she was subject were those of Macao. It was with these she had to reckon first, at a lower level to which no European descended. On this level the English could be seen to be no more than elaborately dressed puppets, seeming to act of their own volition, actually manipulated in such matters as concerned Macao by crafty operators unseen and unremarked, of whom Pedro.

It was thus that she agreed to take Fong's place, and go to see the gardener's wife's sister.

Ah Sum's wife was the hardest and most intractable of all the women in the compound, and she was a skinflint. She made little secret of the fact that she despised her husband for his soft nature in being unwilling to sell their unwanted girl, nor did she care for the compromise he had suggested, that Fong be disposed of by adoption. True, a cash transaction would be involved, but the sum was small by comparison with what Fong would fetch in the open market.

Ah Sum's wife had wanted to refuse the gardener's wife's sister's request, but had been troubled about how to do it without causing the gardener to lose face, an experience he would not forgive. To provide an acceptable substitute not only settled this problem but, seeing that Martha belonged to nobody, would mean that such cash as the old woman could afford would be paid to Ah Sum's wife, who would thus into the bargain get something for nothing. Meanwhile, the possible avenue of adoption being temporarily closed, she could continue her efforts to persuade her husband to sell Fong.

She refused pointblank to take Martha to the temple wearing her shapeless black Macao dress, saying that this was the clothing of a prostitute, which in Chinese eyes all foreign women's clothing was. Shortly after noon, in a grumpy and irritable mood, she took the unprecedented step of crossing the compound to Martha's room, where she made her put on Fong's best samfoo of black Shuntak silk, dressing her hair in Chinese style, and plaiting her a pigtail.

The change of appearance was so complete that it could not be called a disguise. For the first time Martha had put on the clothes of her race. When she saw herself in the hall mirror she thought at first it was Fong, who was beside her. Only the movement of her lips when she herself spoke revealed the unfaceable truth that she, who had been brought up to fear the Chinese, was a Chinese girl like any other.

She repudiated, feared what she saw. She had lost her identity. This was not she, Martha.

Yet she had said she had no name.

She had never been inside a Chinese temple, and when Ah Sum's wife, with tiny mincing steps—she had bound feet —led the way in under the three huge characters carved in granite declaring the name of the god, Martha was filled with mistrust. The black, smoky atmosphere within, the faded silk pendants and altarcloths adorned with flowers and mysterious beasts, the smoke-blackened tablets hanging from the roof, the huge bronze bell held in its sturdy frame of wood, the bronze censers stuck with dozens of joss sticks sending upwards their acrid, heavy-scented fumes, everything combined to utter a greeting to her which was inimical. Peering in gloom at the small curtained recess behind the altar she looked in disgust at the small fat black image of the god, clothed in what looked like a dirty doll's dress, in its arms a cluster of paper pennants bearing Chinese characters. Remembering the churches old Monsieur Auvray used to take her to, with their soft-smelling European incense and their statues of the saints with gentle, smiling faces, their rich purple or green dresses glinting with golden stars, she knew with fearful conviction how Christian she was and how grave was the step Fong had prevailed on her to take.

They found the gardener's wife's sister. In an even darker corner of the temple she was squatting on a two-inch-high wooden block in front of a shallow box of sand used for divination, a thin, frail old woman, her brown skin lined by veins which seemed to be almost on the surface they were so prominent. Negotiations were taken as far as Ah Sum's wife considered appropriate for the first day. Arranging to return the following afternoon to continue and, it was hoped, conclude the discussions, Ah Sum's wife and Martha took their leave, emerging into the grey glare of the temple forecourt to walk almost literally into the arms of Pedro, who had discovered that the gardener had a relative at the temple, and had come with the aim of repeating his threat to Martha through her. For a moment Martha was rooted to the spot with fear, and for a moment the disguise held. Pedro stared hard at her, unable to penetrate it. Then he uttered the single word "Incredible!" and she panicked.

The temple was situated on the inner harbour, which at this point was fronted by a wide stone quay across which merchandise of all kinds was being borne to and from a row of large junks lined up all along the waterfront. In a flash Martha was out of her clogs and away barefoot across the quay, twisting in and out among the junk coolies, bumping into some of them, rousing curses as she ran. Pedro followed her fast. Ah Sum's wife screamed. People turned from what they were doing. Martha was pelting along over the cobbles in front of the junks when she tripped on an iron ring fixed in between the stones and used for securing ropes. Seizing her by the wrist, Pedro wrenched her round to face him.

"Have you gone crazy?" he demanded.

He had no time to say any more, for the reaction of the dozens of Chinese men on the quay was as fast as cannon-shot. These people knew nothing of Martha or Pedro. All they saw was a girl of their own kind being molested by a foreigner. With astonishing speed, leaving whatever they were doing, a group of about fifteen men surrounded the two of them, and were rapidly joined by others. Within seconds, from all parts of the quay and from the buildings facing it, a crowd of a hundred or more collected, men and boys, a weird expanse of stern, expressionless faces, some pale, some bronzed, each with that identical black hair drawn back into a pigtail. Some carried the poles they had been using to bear their loads. One or two had sticks, and one from an eating house carried a kitchen chopper. In the sudden murmuring stillness that came over the quay women and children poked their heads out of the windows of houses, while others came up from the lower chasms of the junks which were their permanent home, as from the unwonted quiet they knew that above them something unusual was afoot.

Pedro kept his head, explaining in Cantonese that the girl

was not Chinese, but from a Portuguese family. But at the rear were some men shouting at those in front to strike him. Quick to sense that he would be unable to control them with words, with a flick of his cane Pedro drew the sword concealed within it and flashed it round, the men closest to him bounding backwards on their fellows.

A few moments later George Cuming, who had been designated to inspect a house the East India Company were proposing to rent, and for this purpose had been provided with the magnificent white and gold palanquin of the President of the Select Committee, resplendent with the Arms of the Honourable Company and borne by four liveried bearers, was descending in this conveyance down a narrow travessa leading to the inner harbour when he found his way blocked by a large crowd of Chinese. Peering through a window, he saw over their heads a strange procession advancing. Along the quay, midway between the houses and the lined-up junks, came a barefoot Chinese girl followed by a Portuguese, elegantly attired, brandishing a drawn sword, and after him a wave of several hundred Chinese men, clothed and half clothed, their murmuring mingled with the hissing mutter of their naked feet treading stone. A hush of surprise and wonder stilled the waterfront's normal turbulence. Boys in the rigging of junks ceased their shouts and swung where they were, staring silently down. Coolies uncertainly lowered their burdens to the ground. At every window, and even on rooftops, the heads of more humanity appeared.

At a word from the Portuguese the girl turned and began walking towards the mouth of the travessa. The palanquin was now hopelessly surrounded. Ordering that it be lowered, Cuming stepped out, pale and disdainful in a pearl grey suit, a brilliant sparkling in his embroidered neckerchief.

"What on earth is this preposterous inconvenience?" he demanded with an air of such absolute authority that even the Chinese, comprehending not a word, drew back from him, leaving a way between him and Pedro. "Can this be, sir, your customary manner of dealing with the ladies?"

82

Cuming demanded disapprovingly. "And must you wield that offensive instrument?"

As Pedro sullenly sheathed his sword—for the English in Macao were to be obeyed—a low, warm rumble of approval went up from the crowd. Bidding Pedro make himself scarce before he was set upon, Cuming turned his attention to Martha, discovered with a distinctly raised eyebrow which house she came from. He made a calculation. By choosing a careful route to Hospital Street to avoid observation by anyone from the Company, he could put the President's palanquin to good use.

"Explain to these people," he said to his principal bearer. "This girl lives in the house of my friend, an Englishman. We will conduct her home."

The next thing Martha knew she was lying beside Cuming amid the sumptuous gold-crested cushions of the palanquin, being driven off with what appeared to be the guarded acceptance of the crowd.

Nor did Cuming waste any time. He spoke Macanese, but she was more concerned by his hands than by what he was saying. The palanquin being designed to carry one person, she found herself inescapably pressed against him, as if they were two in a single bed, and with bold indecency he took the opportunities this offered. Her Chinese clothes protected her more than her Macao dress would have done, but he quickly discovered how these could be loosened. She struggled, but this only enabled him to improve his position.

"Lie still," he murmured. "D'you want the whole world to see what we're doing?"—for the palanquin was swaying revealingly.

With which, prelude to having his will of her completely, he kissed her full on the mouth, and she bit his tongue for all she was worth. He drew back, concealing his pain. But a man of his inclinations needed more than this to deter him.

"You have spirit," he said, holding her down; his eyes were bloodshot. "A pity you are never alone in that house. When you are, I will come and see you."

83

Wary of attracting attention he tipped her out at the end of Hospital Street. It was raining slightly, the soft rain of the Chinese spring. Hot, ashamed and angry, grasping the trousers which she did not know how to resecure, she entered the servants' compound to a scene of crisis. Ah Sum's wife, terrified by her experience on the waterfront, had returned in hysterics, screaming that she had narrowly escaped death at the hands of a mob, cursing Martha as a whore, and venting her fury on Fong, whom she disliked anyway, and whom she now blamed as the source of all her misfortunes.

Seeing at once that they were united against her, Martha went straight to her room. Fong joined her.

"Why is my mother so angry?" she asked in consternation.

"Your trick of making me into a Chinese doesn't succeed, that's all," Martha answered angrily, tugging at the small, unaccustomed fastenings of the Chinese jacket and flinging the clothes on the floor.

The sight of her silk—her one and only best—lying there crumpled and wet, and a momentary glimpse of Martha's firm white breasts, more beautiful than her own, maddened Fong, converting her passion for her friend to even more passionate anger.

"You have not told me the truth, have you?" she said, her voice trembling with aggression. "You are afraid of the semi-devils, aren't you, because you did something wrong."

"Why do you worry yourself about it, Sister? You will never understand my life. It is different from yours."

"So you did do something," Fong said incriminatingly. "We are harbouring a criminal."

"Is that what your mother told you?" Martha asked, sensing it from Fong's adult choice of words, and realizing with alarm that something from the Portuguese world had penetrated the compound.

Fong, for an instant deflated, reverted to friendship.

"If you did, you can tell me," she said passionately. "I

84

won't tell anyone."

"If I'd murdered someone I wouldn't tell you!" Martha replied.

Fong's stolid look returned.

"So what my mother said was right," she said. "You are bad, and I should not speak to you."

The rain had increased in volume and the gutters were overflowing, a sheet of water descending outside the door.

"Anyway I didn't murder anyone, Sister," Martha said.

"Don't you dare call me that any more!" Fong answered savagely, snatching up her clothes and clasping them wet to her breast. "I will never speak to you again!"

She plunged out through the sheet of rain and was instantly lost to view.

Closing the door and locking herself in darkness, it was then that Martha resolved to do away with herself. For unwittingly she had committed the worst error of all. She had delivered herself into the hands of the servants.

The rain did not dampen the rumpus outside, but it did at least cause it to retreat inside the cottages, where it was, as it were, segmented. Ah Sum had the worst segment. What with his daughter howling and saying horrible things about Martha, whom he really rather liked, and his wife mincing round on her lily feet, puckering her face and making scoffing noises, he ended by becoming so angry that he slammed the door on them and went to take refuge with his clansman Number Four, in whose room he drank nearly a catty of Chinese wine and said a great many things he should not have said.

Meanwhile Martha waited till she heard the servants had retired. She then slipped into the hall. The fool boy, unnoticed amid all the disturbance, had found the forbidden guitar and was in a happy mood. With Martha on such occasions he was like a puppy, and she was teasing him with the aim of tricking him into unlocking the front door for her when Ah Sum, who had no intention of going back to his

85

wife that night, entered the house to sleep in his downstairs room. Apprehending at once that something was wrong, he broke a small earthenware pot of wine over the fool boy's head—it had no effect—and having elicited the reason for Martha's presence in the hall, delivered his dictum that she was not to commit suicide without first asking the master's permission.

With this he escorted her firmly upstairs, scolded the fool boy roundly, and retired to sleep it off. As already observed, he had not slept off very much by the time Thomas van Mierop returned.

A postscript to the day's proceedings took place at the premises of the second generation of Gonçalves Sequeira.

In Thomas van Mierop's presence Abraham Biddle had sent a peon to find and bring Pedro to him. Pedro, ashamed and discountenanced after his collision with Cuming, had been skulking about in obscure back streets, and it was some hours before he was found.

On his presenting himself in the inner sanctum, his face drenched of its colour with the oncome of that rare kind of fear which Biddle could reduce him to, his benefactor rose in silence from his desk, his eyes hooded, his thick lips curled in an expression of contempt and fury. Slowly he came towards him, and menacingly raising his thick, dirty hand, gripped Pedro's neckcloth.

"What is my name?" Biddle rasped out, shaking him.

"You are Mr. Biddle, sir!" Pedro gasped.

"Just so," the other answered. "My name is Abraham Biddle, and if I'm not too much thwarted and interfered with by idiots like you I'm goin' to be rich. D'yer understand that, yer young fool? I'm goin' to be rich!" he whispered in Pedro's face. "I'm goin' to live in one of the grand 'ouses of Calcutta, like a king! Why, ask yerself, do I concern meself—I, Abraham Biddle—with the whims and fancies of these young society jackanapes? The Honourable East India Company—what is it to me?" He shook the neckcloth. "It's the *means*, my boy!—the means by which we shall attain gigantic riches!—I say we. I'd always thought that you and I, Master Pedro, were in this together. I could be rich in me old age in Calcutta, you 'ere in Macao, indivisible partners. From the time yer were fourteen I set me twinklin' eye on you, Master Pedro. I'd 'igh 'opes of yer. I still 'ave. Understand, yer young fool— if yer foller me we'll 'umble 'em all! We'll make these gentry be'olden to us for petty favours which we may or may not condescend to confer."

He smiled, twisting the neckcloth till the blood rushed to Pedro's head.

"This is yer final warnin' about 'Ospital Street or any of yer other monkey business. Yer little adventure today 'as cost yer uncle a minimum—d'you 'ear? a minimum—of two thousand dollars. If yer want yer uncle to love yer any more, see it don't 'appen again!"

With which, giving the cloth a last savage twist, he flung the youth out backwards through the swing doors, where he collapsed on the corridor tiles.

PART THREE

The Summers of His Presence

SOLE OCCUPANT OF the East India Company's majestic buildings—known as the Factory—at Canton, during the ensuing six months Thomas had time in which to exercise that capacity for patience which Biddle had observed in him. He had been pretty shaken by the discovery of how little he knew of Macao or of what went on in his own house. Yet as the weeks passed and he came to view matters more calmly, two factors influenced him uppermost. The first was that George Cuming had done what he had as an act of meaningless spite, so patent and deliberate as to provoke suspicion that the content of what he had said was exaggerated. The second was the sheer physical desire he experienced for Martha, desire so compelling, and which he believed she also experienced for him, that it obliged reason to shape itself in conformity with the overriding demand for the act of love. There were girls to be had in Canton; at the Factory services of every kind could be discreetly provided. But the bronzed, buxom boat-girls and pale, painted courtesans who could be produced on the flicker of a request held no interest for him. He wanted Martha desperately. He recognized his luck in having found her. He did not believe there could be any other like her in Macao, so attractive to him, at the same time so lively a companion, and—as it seemed to him on reflection—so devoted to his interests. He faced the fact that before coming to the house she had had a life of her own, a life not entirely sealed off, as he would wish it to be, from her present existence. He felt no sympathy about that life of hers; he suspected it to have been, like the little he had seen of Portuguese Macao itself, mean and seedy, and of course full of Roman Catholic superstition. The less she had to do with that life the better. He was her protector. With him she would enjoy a life altogether better. As for the youth with the manners of a fidalgo—but it took a good number of weeks before he reached a state of calm appraisal on this particular subject— he had seen such youths in the streets of Macao. With their swords and elaborate manners they would bow politely and beg for a copper. What had such a youth to offer her? Thomas furthermore felt certain she would still be there when he returned. George Cuming might needle him with suggestions to the contrary; Thomas knew something on this score which was hidden from George Cuming. Which was that Thomas had made a conquest with Martha. She adored him. To sleep with someone is to know things about them that can be known in no other way, to know with certainty; and Thomas knew and was certain.

He reached Canton in March. In September, with the coming of slightly cooler weather, the East India Company and the foreign community in general moved to Canton, the Factory burst into life, and the trading season began.

Two days after the Company completed its migration there is a revealing entry in Thomas' journal.

'Mr. C. is haunting me,' he notes. 'He can seldom be persuaded to leave me for a moment, and while there for me to bump my elbow into every time I turn round I am conscious that his affable exterior conceals a quivering desire to ask questions or have me ask them of him. He cannot understand what has happened to me. Why do I not gnash my teeth, and why have I not pulled my hair out? This is indeed most diverting, not only providing me with a private source of infinite comedy, but strengthening my cautious belief that I have no need to fear anything untoward.'

As a recompense for having spent a whole year in Canton he was permitted to leave a week or so ahead of the others at the end of the trading season the following spring. Returned to Macao, he was given a jubilant welcome by the grinning and chattering servants. Everything seemed in excellent order. He was impressed by a superb display of flowers in the rocktop garden, and by the evident warmth of the regard in which he was held by everyone, not least by Martha, who, he observed, had grown up considerably in the year that had passed. She was more seductive than he remembered her to have been, less of a little girl. The slight tremor of disquiet this gave him was quickly dissipated, however, by her seemingly transparent happiness at beholding him returned.

The house was eminently as luxurious and pleasant as he had remembered it; but somehow the living room seemed smaller. Not till the servants were out of the way did it occur to him that the reason for this seeming diminution in size was due to the room being full of flowers. There were flowers everywhere, not just in the living room and in the garden but, as he now observed, in the hall and in other parts of the house as well, even in his bedroom. They changed the entire atmosphere of the house, giving it a more lived-in appearance.

Flowers. But nobody knew he was coming in advance of the rest. Martha, the Number One, everybody had been taken by surprise. Who then were the flowers for?

Then he noticed something else. Little mounds of sycee were lying about. Sycee was the currency of the China trade. It consisted of many nations' silver coins chopped up by the Chinese to suit their own weights and measures, together with 'shoes' of Chinese silver, officially stamped, so called because they were shaped like tiny slippers. There was a small pile of sycee on the mantelpiece, another on top of the bureau, chips and pellets of gleaming silver. He was alone with Martha.

"Is this mine?" he asked, touching the pile on the mantelpiece.

She looked startled.

"Yes," she said hastily. "We found it after the Seigneur

left."

It was possible, he thought, though he did not think he had left the pockets of his unwanted suits quite so substantially lined with silver.

"Oh? I had forgotten I had so much," he said, feigning to be satisfied. "Why yes, and here's some more." Digging into his pocket he drew out another handful and added it to the already existing mound.

As he did so he saw her stare at the sycee in an inexplicable way.

"Is that also mine?" he inquired, indicating the pile on the bureau.

"No. That is money for the house," she replied quickly.

"But I thought the compradore handled the housekeeping."

"Yes, Seigneur. It is the compradore's money."

"It's a large sum to leave lying about."

"Yes."

It was one of those full stops of hers which cut off further inquiry. He had the uneasy sensation that someone else had been living in the house during his absence. Yet the Number One, who had been so quick before to report an intruder, had given no indication of anything being amiss. Very much the contrary, he was behaving as though things were delightfully in order. As indeed they seemed to be.

He was detained with work at the Company house till quite late, and dined there. When he returned, Martha was waiting for him. It needed no words to tell him that she was longing for him as he was for her. Everything about her pleased him more than it had a year ago.

"So you have taken away the sycee," he observed. All but the pile he had added to had gone.

"Ah Sum took it," she explained.

"To the compradore?"

She looked up into his eyes with a little smile.

"I have waited a whole year, Seigneur. Have you only come back to ask questions about money?"

In the same instant she was in his arms, and the passion of her private greeting to him allayed his doubts. His need of her was so deep, moreover, that did it not make questions seem futile? Provided she was his, and his alone—as he felt her to be—while he was present, was it not wisdom, he thought, to inquire no further? Would not inquiry lead but to half-truths or to things he would not fully understand, and in the end serve only to madden him? The gods never give with both hands.

That summer he gave her English lessons, and such was her aptitude that in a few weeks they were speaking English nearly all the time.

"Why will you not allow me to teach you to read and write?" he asked her one day. "You could then write me a letter when I am in Canton, and I could write a letter to you."

"What about?" she asked in astonishment.

It was high summer, and the white punka fringed with red was gently swaying across the ceiling, creating beneath it a little existence of delectable coolness which laughed at the heat-saturated, sun-drenched street without. She was sitting demurely before him, hands folded, in a high-backed chair of green patterned velvet, adoration for him perceptibly streaming out of her in the indefinable way adoration has, something to do with posture, the positioning of thumbs in folded hands, the holding-in of breath, the height at which the chin is held, the little swept-back feet.

Her point-blank questions, however, sometimes baffled him.

"Well," he answered lamely, "you could write to tell me you were well, and I could write to tell you—er—I was well."

"It is good," she said, taking it in. "But how would the letter come to me?"

"By the Company's letter service."

"The Company!" she exclaimed, awed. "How will they

93

know it is my letter?"

"It will have your name written on the outside."

"How can?" she said with a little pout. "You know I have no name for writing down."

"I can write down Martha."

"Can you?" she asked in surprise.

"Of course!"

She frowned.

"But I think there is something wrong with that."

"Wrong?"

"Yes. It is not safe. What is writing down must be safe."

"What is *written* down."

"Written," she repeated obediently. "I have no real name for writing down."

"Oh!" he exclaimed, grasping it at last. "You mean you have no legal name."

"A legal name?"

"Yes. A name for writing down on important papers."

"Yes. That is it," she said slowly.

"Well, you do not need a legal name in order just to receive a letter."

"No, I suppose not," she replied uncertainly. Then her expression brightened. "Do you have a legal name, Seigneur?" she asked excitedly.

"Naturally."

"May I know what it is?"

He told her.

"And do I have to say all that?" she asked in wonder.

"No. You may call me Thomas if you wish, or simply Tom." There were too many occasions when to be addressed as Seigneur was scarcely appropriate.

"Tom!" she uttered, vibrating the name with wonder. "But that is a very wonderful name, like a church bell. TOM!" she repeated, wide-eyed and in a ringing tone.

It was a house one could move about in quietly, and later that evening he re-entered the empty living room unheard. He was about to ring for wine when from another room he heard a voice say "TOM!" in a tone of wonder, as if the word itself were a very grand statement, and again "TOM!" —still like a bell, but more reflectively this time. There was silence for a second, after which came a little laugh of pride and happiness.

There was probably much that he would never understand; but taken all in all, things seemed to be all right, he thought.

The unorthodox commercial arrangements Thomas had come to with Abraham Biddle had achieved results little short of spectacular. In June of the previous year, while he was still on his own in Canton, he had received a letter from Biddle informing him that his credit, as Biddle put it, now stood at over three thousand dollars, half of which (Biddle uncannily interpreted his exact wishes) he had taken the liberty of reinvesting in a promising cargo expected in August. By the following summer Thomas had still larger sums out on investment and was good for nearly ten thousand, even after sending to London credit bills for substantial amounts to clear the family debts.

But the sense that, by looking at it in a different way, he was in fact heavily indebted to Biddle had become irksome. He saw now what he had not seen earlier, that he had become dependent on Biddle in just the way Biddle had intended he should, Biddle's aim being to control and, if need arose, utilize the supercargoes to serve his own ends. Furthermore, when Thomas had written to Biddle inquiring specifically about certain cargoes, the latter had ignored his query, leaving Thomas with the uneasy sensation that he owed his improved financial position to opium. One of his first actions on returning to Macao was to visit Biddle.

He found that extraordinary person in capital good humour.

"Wise investment, a steady run o' luck, an excellent beginnin'," was his comment as, rubbing his smelly hands together, he surveyed the account on his desk. "I trust yer satisfied, Mr. van Mierop."

"Yes, indeed. I am beholden to you."

"Express no gratitude to me, Mr. van Mierop. Old Biddle only does 'is 'umble duty," he said with a leer.

"To be sure," Thomas answered, coming to the point. "And the returns have been remarkable enough to whet my curiosity. I would be interested to know more of the nature of the various cargoes."

"General cargoes, Mr. van Mierop," Biddle answered with a light flourish. "A little 'ere, a little there. The common run, as one might say, of the country trade. But conducted with sagacity," he said resoundingly, "an' on the solid foundation of 'igh morals."

It proved impossible to penetrate further. Yet what was 'the common run of the country trade', Thomas asked himself, if it was not Bengal opium? No other commodity could produce such startling profits. Unwittingly, he now saw, he had himself become an opium trader—and again, exactly as Biddle intended he should.

His opinions about opium had hardened since coming to China. He was determined that whatever the Company or private individuals might be doing, he himself would have no dealings with the drug. It was quite clear what Biddle was up to. British private traders were not allowed to become permanently resident on the China coast, and the East India Company, if it had been doing its duty properly, should have sent Biddle back to Calcutta years ago. This danger Biddle staved off by making himself beholden to Company officers, and, taking thought for the morrow, a salient item in his technique was to cultivate promising young juniors who in due course he could expect to become his patrons, though in another sense also his servitors. Exceptionally well-informed and acute, Biddle somehow either knew or sensed that Thomas did not approve of the opium trade. Thus Biddle's caution on the subject. As Thomas saw it, unless he extricated himself from the coils of the opium trade in which Biddle was quietly and smoothly encompassing him, he would end by becoming Biddle's creature, at the same time forfeiting any claim the future might offer him to restrict or reform the opium trade—and he was born with reform in his blood.

Over the next three years—and cautiously, without drawing any attention to the matter—he inaugurated a gradual withdrawal of his affairs from Abraham Biddle, dealing with other country traders who were specific regarding the nature of their cargoes. The financial results were less remarkable, but Thomas was of an easier mind. To complete his withdrawal from Biddle would of course mean buying the house, the provision of houses being clearly the foundation of Biddle's power *vis-à-vis* the Company. But Thomas hesitated to do anything about this. He trusted Martha. The same three years saw his confidence in her grow and deepen into a love which, in the nocturnal solitude of their annual separations, he knew too well was the mainstay of his life in China. It was the knowledge that he possessed her which alone made life endurable.

Yet he still knew curiously little about her. He knew of Mother Clemencia and Monsieur Auvray, and how a Portuguese woman had burned the latter's private papers. But he knew scarcely anything else—certainly nothing about knives or inkwells. And though he trusted her, the censorship she imposed on anything connected with herself made it difficult to trust her completely. If the chance should come to buy the house it would have to be purchased in the name of a Portuguese, someone safe, she had said. He could not entirely rid himself of the suspicion that her aim in saying it was that he should pay for the house, while the buyer would be the youth with the manners of a fidalgo —of whose existence, parenthetically, there was never the slightest indication.

During the same period Thomas' understanding of George Cuming deepened profoundly.

'Have been cheek by jowl these past days with Mr. C.,' he noted during the next Canton season, 'rehearsing a diverting piece by Mr. Sheridan. Due to height, it is established that I am suited only to male impersonation. Mr. C. caught the lady! He has undoubted talent. Would he but confine himself to it! For I perceive him now more plainly. He is a great gatherer of information, and this he hoards against a ripe time, when he uses a piece of it to strike whomever he dislikes. I could swear he knows to the last cent the investment of every one of us. Removing his female wig he extols to me the high quality of our opium, the acumen of Biddle. "Have I not always given you good advice?" he asks. It is another *double entendre*, wearisome, but were I to have hit him in the face it would have damaged his powder and ruined the comedy. He harps on the theme, however. I note about him a kind of desperation, and fear I am marked to be his next victim. His methods are exquisite. I have observed him promote, out of nothing, a rumour of a fall in price of a commodity in which *such and such* a person has an investment. The horrified investor dashes to his agent, who assures him the price is steady and is for his pains promptly branded a liar. Casually, and by the merest chance, our gatherer comes to learn of the predicament of this panic-stricken investor. "I will sell it for you. Why not invest in this instead?" he says, and earns undying friendship. Meanwhile the price of the original commodity rises, but some months later, when everyone has forgotten the incident. In fact, our Mr. C., who so skilfully directs the players in the comedy, seeks so to direct each one of us, in his passion to order and control, meanwhile enriching himself. It is a form of covetousness. He covets our lives. What he can least abide is to be ignored. To ignore him gives me, I am ashamed to say, subtle pleasure.'

Actually, as a slightly earlier reference in the journal shows, he had already begun to form a pretty low opinion of George Cuming, and the extract which reveals this is of particular interest, in that it concerns one of the most extraordinary aspects of European life on the China coast in those times. The previous summer a group of the super-cargoes had taken a walk to the southern tip of Macao, passing the fishermen's temple of A-Ma, from which Macao takes its name. Thomas wrote of this occasion:

'Concerning the local mistresses whom some men have, the code of "honour" in these parts enjoins silence and that children be bastards. Such as break this code will be hunted down ruthlessly. No quarter is given. Three years ago an Englishman, a country trader, defied the convention and married his Macao mistress in a Roman Catholic ceremony. He was forthwith repudiated by his business partner, who appropriated his goods and denied him access to his office. He was refused any form of passage abroad, and ostracized from European society. At first he lived with his wife's family, but after a time he dared not leave the house, being unable to endure the shame of being passed in silence in the streets by his former acquaintances. His savings dwindling and himself unemployable, he took his wife and child to a hut on an island south of Macao, where he now lives by growing vegetables and fishing. We saw the man. He had come to Macao to buy provisions at the cheap market provided for Chinese fishermen, who are the outcasts of their society, even as this man is the outcast of his. He was barefoot, wearing ragged Chinese clothes, but recognizable from his beard and colouring, and from having no queue. Detecting that he was observed, he shrank into the shadows within a Chinese temple. Mr. C. pointed him out to me and laughed the most heartily when the wretched man fled from us. Others too appeared to take enjoyment from the scene.' In fact, this man was not the only one. Others subjected to the same terrible social ostracism quite simply disappeared, while still others committed suicide.

Meanwhile, as Thomas gradually withdrew his affairs from Biddle, his domestic life with Martha proceeded in tranquillity and contentment, the pivot of his existence.

His fourth year on the coast registered an unexpectedly

high demand from Europe for sandalwood fans, and quite early in the year he received a tip from a Chinese source to the effect that long before orders could be met there would be an acute shortage of sandalwood in Canton, where the fans where made. During the off-season therefore he instructed Biddle to buy shares in a cargo of sandalwood from Macassar in the Indies, being obliged to do this, Biddle being the shippers' Macao agent.

"If I may say so as 'as yer interests at 'eart, Mr. van Mierop, a second-class investment unworthy of yer," was Biddle's comment.

Considerably irritated, Thomas made several visits to Biddle to insure that his instructions were complied with, but his difficulty here was that Biddle conducted his affairs very much as the Chinese did, with few if any documents or signatures, solely a matter of word and memory.

During the subsequent Canton season an entry in the journal reads:

'Mr. C. has been buzzing like a bluebottle. The subject, sandalwood, the dangers inherent in handling East Indies products, the shipping of qualities unacceptable on the Canton market, the certainty of a loss, etc., etc. The extent of his information, the virtual impossibility of placing a single dollar without his knowing of it, I find increasingly tedious. For some reason he seems particularly excited on this occasion.'

At the end of the season he returned by fastboat ahead of the others, reaching Macao after nightfall. Entering his house unexpected, he perceived at once, from the demeanour of the servants, that all was not as it should be. Martha was not there.

Significant of how immeasurably their relationship had deepened, his reaction was perceptibly that of a husband. He did not dare ask the servants where she was, for fear of losing face.

He did not have to wait long. In the stillness of the Macao night the latch of the rear gate to the servants' compound clicked, light footsteps mounted the stairs, and she walked swiftly into the room. Seeing him, she halted aghast. Guilt sped out from her.

Her surprise, however, was evenly matched, if not surpassed, by his. The figure he saw before him was a changed being, at whom he stared in disbelief and wonder. He had left her six months ago, a simple, modest Macao girl. He returned to find her a young woman of strange sophistication and style. She had coiffed her hair in European style, drawn up from the temples, giving her a more mature appearance, and was wearing a superb, long-skirted European dress of black taffeta, low at the neck, very high at the sleeve, but with her arms and all that part of her breast and neck which in Europe would have been revealed, modestly and entirely covered with tight-fitting black embroidered Spanish lace, through which her white skin glowed. She carried lace gloves and a fan, and from her sleeve hung an embroidered purse. Over her head and falling to her feet on either side she wore the black *do*, or mantle, of the women of Macao, of taffeta that rustled against her dress.

"Well, well!" he exclaimed gently, gathering half-an-inch of the lace between his thumb and forefinger. " 'Tis so elegant I feel I hardly dare ask for a kiss of welcome."

"Oh, Tom!" she whispered anxiously. "I had it made to please you!" And she flung herself in his arms.

It was a movement, he concluded, as much to conceal her face from him as to express her welcome, however. He was conscious of her heart beating furiously.

"It pleases me greatly," he said absently. "Pray wear it often." Then the warmth, the closeness of her awakened him. "You look beautiful," he said in a deeper, more familiar tone. "You have taken me unawares. Forgive me."

She wept, suddenly and copiously.

"I will never wear it again!" she sobbed, and wrenching herself from him, sped rustlingly away to her own room.

But, aroused by this time, he was having none of this kind of nonsense. Striding aggressively after her through the darkened rooms, he came to her closed door and tried it. It was, of course, not locked.

He was present, and she was his.

But it was a good deal longer that off-season before he came to the same guarded conclusion of former years, that all was well.

"You told me you never went out," he said to her two days later. He had learned to phase his inquiries.

"It was the first time," she answered.

He asked her where she had been.

She did not reply at once. Then she came and kissed the palm of his hand.

"You have to trust me, Tom," she said simply. "There is no other way."

And with this, though not liking it, he desisted, because he was a man of reason, and was this not the truth that she had uttered? What marriage, for example, he asked himself, could endure on this impossible basis of six months' absence every year, with no means of communication whatever (because all in the house were illiterate), unless founded on absolute trust? But as he discovered, trust cannot be striven for, and even where it exists it uses only one eye and one ear. The rest is mistrust, and there were times that summer when he wanted to threaten her with an injury unless she obediently told him all—all—all the things about Macao which he did not wish to hear.

Questioned about the sandalwood, Biddle was evasive. In August, long after the cargo was due, the list of commodity prices posted daily on the Company notice boards recorded a sharp drop in the price of opium, and three days later Thomas received from Biddle's office formal notification of a loss in the spring cargoes. It was plain that, contrary to his expressed wishes, and to his intense annoyance, his money had been placed, not in sandalwood, but in opium.

Waiting for him in his office that day Thomas found an unknown visitor. He was a Spaniard, by name Hernandez, a small, nervous man with a waxed moustache and overt symptoms of dishonesty. Surmounting difficulties of language, he managed to convey, beneath a good deal of hispanic flourish, that he was in difficulties. The Mandarin of the Casa Branca was after him, it appeared, for some misdemeanour committed, and he was anxious to embark in a ship sailing later in the day for Manila. Despite a fine flow of words he was plainly frightened for his life. He had sold what opium he had, he said, acquiring thereby the mortgagee rights in a Macao house. Discovering at the last moment that in Macao it was illegal for anyone other than Portuguese to own house property, and having no prospect of returning to China, he had come, he explained, to seek the advice of his tenant.

Thomas found himself confronting the present, if transitory, owner of the house in Hospital Street.

He made an immediate decision. He would make the final severance from Abraham Biddle.

His mind switched back to his first extraordinary conversation with George Cuming on the subject of opium.

"You hold consignment notes," he said to the Spaniard with unerring prescience.

Tremblingly the notes and other documents were submitted. Thomas read them briefly and made a calculation in winds and distances. It was a short-term mortgage, the date of redemption January. It was now August. It was most unlikely that orders placed on Calcutta could be confirmed in Macao before the mortgage expired.

Hernandez' nervousness to be gone operating to advantage, Thomas concluded terms, assembled the sum required, and at an agreed time met Hernandez at the office of Senhor Barros, the Portuguese lawyer whom the Company retained for services connected with their transactions and property in Macao. A purportedly legal document having been signed and witnessed, and Hernandez, with many protestations of esteem, having departed with his money, Thomas said to Barros:

"I have a stipulation to make. No deviation of any kind must be made in redeeming this mortgage. As you know, it is common practice here to extend the dates of mortgages of this kind. If it is only a matter of weeks people face the fact that they are more interested in opium than houses. I happen to be more interested in the house. And I will not accept cash in lieu, Mr. Barros. This house is mortgaged for first-quality Bengal opium of this year's Calcutta auctions. If precisely this cargo is not delivered by precisely this date, I wish you without fail to take the proper action, and trust that, for the usual fee, you will arrange to transfer the property to your own name on my behalf."

The season that followed was a grim one, dominated by the gravest crisis there had ever been involving Europeans on the China coast. A country ship, the *Lady Hughes*, firing the customary salute on arrival at Whampoa, the down-river port of Canton, accidentally hit and sank a small boat, seriously wounding three Chinese, two of whom subsequently died of their injuries. The incident, report of which spread like wildfire, caused the greatest public excitement in Canton, where foreigners were for several weeks unable to leave the Factories for fear of being stoned by hostile Chinese crowds.

In accordance with normal Chinese procedure, the Viceroy of Kwangtung and Kwangsi demanded that the gunner who fired the shot be surrendered to him for 'investigation', which in such a case would mean death by strangulation. The gunner, with some knowledge of China, disappeared—in itself a remarkable achievement in crowded Whampoa, where a foreigner was exceedingly conspicuous.

When this was reported to the Viceroy, order was given that another Englishman—any other—must be surrendered. On behalf of the British community, Mr. Pigou, who was now President of the Select Committee, refused to obey. There was a week of ugly suspense, during which the Viceroy repeated his order. Then, in the space of a single hour, the country trader who had chartered the *Lady Hughes* was seized and thrown into prison, the Factories were totally surrounded, by war junks on the river and by a thousand armed Chinese troops on land, every Chinese servant in every Factory walked out, and all communication with foreigners was forbidden, the entire foreign community being imprisoned in the Factories without food or water. Again the Viceroy called for a man.

With the unseen assistance of the Thirteen, the great Chinese merchant financiers who held the monopoly of all foreign trade with China, small supplies of food and water were poled over the rooftops by night from adjacent buildings into the Factory area, but after a week this misdemeanour was observed and stopped. Pigou took every recourse possible, explaining in missives to the Viceroy that the deaths were accidental, and pleading for recognition of the distinction between murder and manslaughter. The difficulty here was that no foreigner, however senior, was ever allowed to appear before even the most junior mandarin to plead a cause personally. Communications between foreign traders and Chinese officials invariably had to be conducted through the Thirteen, who in a case such as this, involving Chinese law, were powerless. The Viceroy did not yield.

For some days the community hung on, living on the only commodities the Factories stocked—rice, salt and wine. The rice supply ran out. Meanwhile it became clear beyond doubt to Pigou that the Viceroy intended to starve them into submission. Acting on his sole responsibility, consulting no one, Pigou sent down to the master of the *Lady Hughes* an order to send up a man. The majority in the Factories —national differences were scarcely perceptible during the crisis—were for holding on, even if it meant starvation; and Pigou's order produced a response of horror and indignation. Feelings ran so high that for several days the President was obliged to remain behind the locked doors of his private suite, for fear of being assaulted by his own supercargoes and captains.

But the master of the *Lady Hughes*, with a starving crew to contend with, complied. The actual gunner still not having been found, he sent up a sick old man, the oldest sailor he had aboard. The doomed man reached the Factories bearing a pitiable letter from the shipmaster to the Viceroy begging for clemency. A violent demonstration within the Factories marked the old sailor's passage from the river to the square on the landward side where the Chinese soldiery awaited him. Those loyal to the President surrounded the sailor and forced their way through a crowd of their own countrymen howling abuse and roughly manhandling them as they passed. In the square on the other side of the vast buildings continental Europeans joined in the booing and insults, and it was solely this that prevented an outright *mêlée* among the British. At the sound of foreign insults there was an observable closing of ranks among the British, who regarded this *au fond* as their own affair. In silence the old sailor was handed over to a contingent of Chinese troops, bound with thongs, and escorted away to prison.

Again, within the space of a single hour, the charterer of the *Lady Hughes* was released, servants returned to the Factories, the war junks and soldiers departed, food was borne in as copiously as ever, and conditions returned to normal.

Since the case involved the death sentence, the matter had to be submitted to the Emperor in Peking. A further two months of grim suspense ensued. In February, shortly after the Chinese New Year, the Emperor's will was known. It came in the guise of an act of clemency. Although two Chinese had lost their lives, only one Englishman need die for it, the Emperor decreed. Before any form of protest could be made, that same afternoon the sailor was publicly executed by strangulation within the Chinese city.

Conditions returned to normal, but only in a limited sense. Socially the Company had been vitiated by the crisis. Unsuspected personal enmities, hitherto concealed by the cloak of reserve, flared up in the bitter virulence of controversy between the factions for and against the President. For once, the masks were off, with the outcome that a great many relationships were never to be the same again.

That year there were no charades or other entertainments. In keeping with the sombre mood that had fallen over the Company, the only evening diversion, organized after the crisis was over, was a chess competition, held over a period of two weeks, in which the finalists were George Cuming and Thomas van Mierop. Throughout the season an uneasy peace had prevailed between these two. Both had supported the President, once the latter had taken his decision; and both had been prominent targets for the contempt and criticism of the majority. But Thomas had sensed, as seldom before, that the co-operation he received from his colleague bore upon official matters only, and was devoid of personal goodwill.

It was past midnight when they resumed their game after the supper recess. At supper Cuming had been drinking heavily. He was flushed, his speech slightly blurred, and this condition had not improved his play. He was losing, and his occasional remarks to the bystanders were becoming increasingly acerb. Already playing a defensive game, he inadvertently allowed one of Thomas' pawns to reach the far side of the board, thereby enabling Thomas to restore his lost queen and, barring a flagrant error, win the game. The murmur of applause which greeted this move was cut short by Cuming's voice, thick and harsh.

"When playing with an Achilles," he said waspishly, "you need to know how to wound his heel. How, I wonder, do I succeed in wounding your heel, Achilles van Mierop?"

There was a ripple of amusement among the bystanders, but the cold intensity with which the words were spoken caused Thomas to look up at his opponent. The flush had all but left Cuming's face. He was white with anger. As their eyes met, he rose away from the table, his chair falling behind him on the carpet.

"I will play no more," he rasped. "There sits the champion."

Voices begged him to desist. The Company had seen too much of this kind of thing over the past weeks. But Cuming threw off those who laid restraining hands on him.

"No!" he said loudly. "Mr. Mierop attaches so much importance to being master in his own house. Let him be master of this one! I concede a win." And turning on Thomas he added, his voice vibrating hatred, "But for the moment only, sir."

Thomas had half risen from his chair in sheer astonishment. As Cuming stalked out of the room amid the embarrassed undertones of those present, he sank back at the table, mentally absorbed in piecing together what the outburst had disclosed. It was February. The mortgage on the house at Hospital Street had expired, and the opium had not been received. The house was his. But the venom with which Cuming imparted the information revealed something more insidious and far-reaching, at the mere suggestion of which five years of ambiguity resolved themselves into a single, undivided conclusion. George Cuming was in secret the business partner of the disreputable Abraham Biddle.

A call on Senhor Barros, upon return to Macao, confirmed the news about the house. Five more weeks passed before the documents of transfer were completed and signed. Only then did Thomas impart to Martha what he had done. It was a morning of heavy summer rain and the living room was rather dark. The off-season had begun with her usual jubilant welcome, followed by his own usual cautiously-arrived-at conclusion that all was well. But for some days now she had been moody and dispirited, and when he told her about the house her only reaction was to clasp a hand to her mouth as if she were about to be sick, and to run away to her own room.

Always careful not to intrude on her when she was in one of her moods, he waited ten minutes or so, then sent a servant to inquire about her. The man returned grinning.

"She little sick, but Master lucky," he announced.

Thomas leaned back deeply in his high-backed Spanish armchair, uttered a long, low whistle of surprise, and waited.

When she returned she was composed and looked better. Unable to restrain his impatience, he rose at once and went to her, took her hands in his.

" 'Tis not a child?" he asked with gentle excitement.

But to his surprise the little Chinese face was averted from him.

"No," she answered. She was trembling beneath his touch.

"Then what is it? What is wrong?"

She turned a little towards him, her eyes lowered. She was on the verge of tears.

"Yes," she admitted in a broken voice.

"But this is wonderful!" he exclaimed softly. "Why do you look so worried?"

"If it is daughter I look after that matter. That is the custom," she said rapidly, but in a voice as commonplace as if she were buying a fish in the market. It was a tone, he knew, which covered the expression of her deepest emotions.

He drew her to him.

"I don't understand."

"That is Chinese custom," she said.

"What has Chinese custom to do with it? This is not a Chinese chil—"

But he did not quite complete the word. It was, was it not, almost a Chinese child? "You've never worried about Chinese custom before," he pursued in an attempt to conceal what she must have noticed.

She bit her lip.

"When there is a child, what does it matter whose customs we speak of? We are all one."

"Granted. But why do you say it?"

"What if it is a son?" she asked in a choking voice.

"By whatever custom, he will be yours and mine," he answered firmly.

But he had once seen Pigou's children, frightened little brown things who played in the back yard when no one was looking.

"We could perhaps do without one of the servants," she said more calmly. "I could then have one of the cottages in the compound."

The implications flooding in, he moved away in concern.

"In God's name, not that," he muttered.

"How else? You cannot have a child in the house. It is a disgrace."

"No, it is not a disgrace," he answered. "And you must not grieve. You must be proud and happy. As I am." He had halted at the fireplace, staring at his own reflection in the mirror. "Let me think about this. There must be a way. And you must not grieve," he repeated with force, returning to her and laying one finger under her chin. "No worries, d'you hear? What kind of a child will that be, born in grief and sadness?"

"It is what I wish to know myself!" she cried in sudden despair, burying her face in his shirt and sobbing.

In effect, he thought as he held her to him, what did become of children born in Macao when their fathers returned home? It was a subject he had never considered. Macao being what it was, girls might be sold. But boys, what would happen to them? What, for example, would be the future of Pigou's sons, or of any other such child? Neither Portuguese nor Chinese, and certainly not English, born between two worlds, trusted by neither, brought up by illiterate women and thus themselves unlettered, what future could there possibly be for such boys but to become petty criminals of some kind, or one of the elegantly tailored, English-speaking beggars sometimes encountered, hawking their sisters?

It was with a moody frown that he left later in the morning for the Company office.

When, towards evening, he returned, he had come to a

decision. The sky was still black with rainclouds, and the streets were still wet, but the rain had ceased, and in the west, beneath a shelf of cloud, a glorious golden sunset was streaming over the hill and fort of Monte.

He found her in the living room. The previous summer she had asked him if he would consent to her departing from customary Portuguese black and having what she said was her heart's desire—a dress with white lace and a ribbon of blue. She was wearing it when he came in. The material was of the palest lemon yellow, but in the glow of red light through the french windows the yellow, the blue and the white sank responsively, as did the colours of the magnificent flowers in the rocktop garden, into shades of a single colour obedient to the fiery sky.

"There is something I have to ask you," he said (the punka was swaying, deliciously cooling the room), "which is very important. You may not wish to answer immediately. But I want you to think about it very carefully."

"Tom, of course I will!" she said with awe and excitement. "What is it?"

"It cannot be at once," he said, "but as soon as it is possible to us, will you marry me and be my proper wife?"

Her look of hopeful wonder altered by unanalysable degrees into a stare—a stare of bafflement.

"Whatever would you want to do that for?" she asked.

"Because we should," he replied gently. "We should have been married these five years. I am at fault for not having considered this before. The child has made me realize."

She considered it a moment.

"You love me, Tom?"

"More than I can say."

"That is very good," she said, folding her hands in satisfaction. "And I love you too, more than I can say. But I don't think I could agree to our being married."

"Why ever not?"

She gestured.

"If we marry we should become like—well, like the servants. They are married, and what happens? They are always fighting each other. Not married, we love each other and don't fight."

"And when the child is born?"

She looked down at her hands.

"Marrying will not make the child English."

"No, in a sense that is indisputable," he said uncomfortably. "But as soon as marriage does become possible to us, in one way or another, do you not see that it would be better—for the child, Martha—if we were married?"

"When you have gone it will make no difference."

Her words cut him, yet he hesitated to speak of taking her to England, hesitated before the suffering he might bring her in words that seemed so fair.

"Would you not prefer to be married than to live like this, neither of us able to show our faces together?"

She brightened.

"That's fine talk, Thomas van Mierop!" she said in a mock deep voice. "Are you telling me you would dare be seen with me in public?"

"If we were married I would—if you'd dare be seen with me."

She clapped her hands in jubilation.

"Oh, how exciting that would be! And then—" Her expression changed as an astounding possibility dawned on her. "Tom—!"

"Yes?"

"If I were married"—her voice sank to a whisper—"would I have a name?"

He laughed.

"Of course you would!"

"I mean, Tom, a writing-down name, a—what was that word you said?"

"A legal name. Yes, if you married me you would have a real legal name."

"A real legal name!" she echoed with solemnity. "Whose

name would it be?"

"Mine, naturally."

"Yours, Tom!" she exclaimed glowingly. "Oh, but I would be too proud," she said, flouncing out her dress and parading about like a little bird. "I would put on such airs and graces. I would be—I can hardly imagine it—Senhora van Mierop."

"Mrs. van Mierop," he corrected her.

"Missis? What is Missis?"

"A man in England is Mister; his wife is Missis."

"What a funny word! Missis van Mierop!" she announced, laughing with delight. "In Macao that would be very astonishing. I would be the only Missis in the place, and how grand that would be!"

"Not for ever, I think. The day may come when there will be others from England."

She checked herself at once.

"If that happened they would say I was not a real Missis. 'Tis better I shall be Senhora van Mierop," she decided with finality. "Would it be correct to have Mr. van Mierop and Senhora van Mierop?"

He chuckled.

"It's a tidy explanation of the situation."

Making no reaction, she went on thoughtfully:

"Then when people wrote things on paper they would be able to write Senhora van Mierop?"

"Certainly."

"Would they be able to write them on—I don't know what the word is in English, but in Portuguese they say *compromisso*. Would they write Senhora van Mierop on that?"

He frowned. He knew the word. It was used in Macao to express commercial agreements, the formation of companies and partnerships.

"Where did you learn such a word?" he asked.

She ran her hand down the curtain.

"I—just heard it."

"It is a word of commerce."

"Yes. You have not answered my question."

"I would wish to know first why you want to know the answer to such a question."

She hesitated, then said with diffidence:

"Silver is stored below in the godown—your silver, Tom."

"Yes?"

"Might I also use the godown—to store my silver? There is not very much."

There was a stillness such as falls just before a storm breaks.

"Where is it?" he asked in clipped tones of restraint.

Without a word she led him through to the inner, central room of the house. With a door in each wall, it was window-less, its gloom partially relieved by being totally surrounded by Chinese-ornamented mirrors. It was a room he never entered. Stacked beside a wall were two chests of the kind used for storing sycee.

"Full," she said, tapping them. "But 'tis better they should not be lying here."

"How did you come by so much silver?" he uttered gruffly.

"I earned it."

"How?" he demanded.

"Nothing very remarkable," she answered, all equable-ness. "But in a modest way I'm in commerce."

In the Company halls it was said to be impossible to make him lose his temper. At this precise moment he had seldom been closer to doing so.

"What kind of commerce does a woman engage in, pray?" he demanded hotly.

She was still equable, but very cautious.

"Do you like the wine we serve at dinner?" she asked.

" 'Tis the best table wine served in any English house here," he replied at once, for he was proud of the fact that guests always praised it.

"I import it," she said simply.

He glared in disbelief at the composed, placid little round face. She was nineteen.

"Anything else?" he demanded, waiting for the next extravagant falsehood.

But the irony was lost on her.

"Oh"—she gestured vaguely—"sundries."

"That covers pretty well anything, doesn't it!" he rapped out.

"It is honest money, Tom," she said slowly, with a tone of warning in it. "And it is not what you think."

She was challenging him to dispute it. His voice altered, softened.

"Do you mean you are telling me the truth?" he asked, for he had never been so taken aback in his life.

"Why should I tell lies? You could so easily find out if I did."

"But why did you not tell me all this before?"

"It was not necessary," she said, tapping the sycee chests.

He glowered at her and walked away.

"*Compromisso!*" he murmured under his breath. "Anyone would say that while I was away you did not have enough to eat!"

In fact, he said it in genuine perplexity. Just as in the morning when he had learned she was with child, so in the evening with this new discovery, he had difficulty in spearing into his emotions the fact that they were not husband and wife. It was all of a husband's resentment which he felt at the sight of her standing there patiently, one hand resting on her boxes of money.

"It began by accident," she explained. "And it is only very little trade. But, as you see, it makes money."

"I do not understand you!" he exclaimed in exasperation.

"I'm lonely when you're away, Tom. I cannot have an ordinary life like other people. My trade gives me something to do."

"I appreciate that. But making money—! Why, of all

things, must you do this? Do I not give you everything you need?"

"You are the most wonderful man I have ever known," she replied simply.

"Well, then," he demanded, "—why?"

"Men who come in ships also go in ships," she said.

"Yes. You've thought of that."

"Often."

"Then will you now also think about what would happen if at that time you were married to me?"

She was silent, and he faltered. He could not say the rest. An oppressive sense of doom overcame him, a stifling English summer evening, the garden at Twickenham, his sisters, loneliness and hate, an imprisonment more absolute than any either of them had known or could even have imagined in China. He saw her eager, pretty face as if it was the last time it would ever be so, as if from this critical and inescapable second the rest would be decline into pain and bitterness.

"You must not be angry with me, Tom."

"I'm not angry."

"No? Not just a little angry?"

"Not at all angry."

She came close to him.

"Just a very, very little you are. That is one thing about not reading things that are written on paper. You read faces instead. And you know really it has all been very strange and wonderful, and I have found out about myself many things I did not know at all, and I do very much wish you could be happy about it. Do you know what they say, Tom?"—her eyes glinted with excitement—"They say I have fingers of gold. I did not know what it meant at first, but they say that gold is a kind of dust, and if you have it on your fingers whatever you touch becomes a little golden. Of course, I laughed when I knew. But, Chinamen specially, they are superstitious. They believe people really do have gold fingers; and it is very strange, but that is how they look at me. They believe I am lucky, and when I say that they should do something with their money they believe it and do it. And they say it always succeeds. Is it not just a little wonderful?"

"Doubtless highly remarkable. Fairy tales are very comforting." He took her chin between his thumb and forefinger and gently waggled it from side to side. "But don't expect me to be too interested, d'you see?"

"I wish you to be interested. I'm doing it for you."

"For me?" he expostulated. "Where in heaven's name do I come into it?"

"So that you will not have to worry about me when you go."

He drew away with one of those expressions that contains an unuttered sigh at not knowing what to say.

"Have the servants bring the chests downstairs," he ordered. "I will open the godown."

He returned to the living room. The sunset was much less strong. By the rear stairs the servants were carrying up the lamps.

"And I would be obliged," she said, following him, "if inside each box you would put some writing to say this is my money."

"Yes, yes," he said with another of those unuttered sighs, selecting a pipe and opening the tobacco jar.

"You must make the writing, Tom. No one else. If you write it, everyone will know it belongs to me, and no one will be able to take it."

"You're a careful one, aren't you?"

"I learned before," she said quietly. "I told you about it."

"Very well. I will write something for you to put in both chests. Better still, you also will write something."

"How can?" she laughed.

"Make your mark with a pen. I will show you."

Going to the bureau, he took out two sheets of the stiff blue-grey paper used by the Portuguese when drawing up legal documents. He had been using it for some time, it being readily available. When she saw the paper she uttered a little "Oh!" of awe.

"What is it?" he asked.

"That was the kind of paper I told you about, the paper that Portuguese woman burnt."

"This is the paper you will write on."

She nodded slowly and solemnly.

"It is very good," she said, coming to the bureau holding out both hands, uncertain which one would hold the pen. "If you show me, I will write. On this kind of paper it will be sure."

That night after supper Thomas sat alone beneath the swaying punka, staring into the darkness beyond the open french windows, while from the other room came the sound of sycee being shovelled on to the scales, weighed, and dropped into small sacks. The sound, normally so comforting when it was his own sycee, deepened his unease. He would have nothing to do with it.

Only when she said all was in readiness did he rise and go silently downstairs with her, unlock one by one the massive double doors of the strongroom, and descend after her, candle in hand, into the gloomy vault of damp stone where his own chests lay in ranks along the walls. The two chests were brought down empty by the servants, followed two by two by the sacks of silver which were secreted in the chests. In the suffocating, airless cool of the godown the flame of the candle shrank till it was no more than a small point of light, the only sounds the strained respiration of the bearers and her voice counting softly as each sack went in. Towards the end the light was so dim they could scarcely see each other.

But without light he knew she was absorbed and had forgotten him; and there came over him that which he had most desired to avoid and had hoped that with her beside him he would never experience—a deep, unbearable loneliness.

PART FOUR

The Winters of His Absence

"THAT WOMAN," Ah Sum's wife said angrily, referring to the gardener's wife's sister, "wants to know when you're coming to see her again."

It was five years earlier, March 1780, the day after Thomas' first departure for Canton, when he had been in China only a few days. Martha, aged fourteen, had just been given her upstairs room, her adoption by the gardener's wife's sister was still to be finally negotiated, Fong had sworn she would never speak to her again, and George Cuming had threatened to call on her as soon as Thomas was out of the way.

"Not for the present, Aunt, and perhaps never," Martha answered.

Ah Sum's wife gave a huffy snort and minced out. It was presage to further trouble.

The trouble below stairs was such that, although it had started in Ah Sum's cottage, it could not be prevented from spreading. Ah Sum's wife, in a fit of bad temper and frustration at being thwarted in her design to sell Martha to the gardener's wife's sister, refused to go again to the temple. Instead she misdirected her temper to the gardener's wife, telling her in a truculent tone that she would have nothing more to do with the matter. The gardener's wife, deducing that aspersions were being cast on her sister, was furious, and communicated this to her husband in no uncertain terms, the trouble thus spreading to their house. Her husband, the head gardener, was a gentle person, but even he was aggrieved and upset, blaming Martha for the trouble and saying things had gone to such lengths with his sister-in-law that there should be no turning back. Fong, in a mood of complete non-co-operation, refused to help the Number Four any more by cleaning floors for him, the trouble thus reaching out to him as well.

On top of it all—and it was this which exercised Martha's mind more than anything else—was the danger that Fong, in her hatred of Martha, would start making wild accusations against her, that she was a criminal and should be in prison, which if sufficiently repeated outside might arouse the Portuguese authorities to investigate.

Three days after Thomas' departure George Cuming paid his threatened call. Having already made up her mind about George Cuming, and not being the kind of person to change her mind about anyone once it was made up, Martha welcomed him with a display of the utmost pleasantness and complaisance. The first thing she lighted on was the port decanter. The Senhor must have a glass of port. She found the biggest glass there was, and filled it to the brim. Port with Urquhart was better than a drug to induce sleep.

In a moment of abandon she said so.

"And so, Senhor, you must be sure not to drink too much. Is that not a very large quantity I have given you?"

"Not too much for me, I assure you," he answered. He was already a little flushed after a heavy Sunday breakfast, and smelt of brandy. Observing him more carefully, she concluded she had done better than she thought.

"Can you drink *all* that?" she asked in wonder. "You are truly a remarkable man, Senhor, if you can drink it all in one."

"Do you doubt me for a moment?" asked Cuming, delighted at the progress he was making. "Watch!"

Down it went, and in, thanks to a complaisant Ah Sum, went another glassful.

"I think Urquhart must have been a fool," said Cuming rather weightily for his narrow frame.

"He certainly did not know how to drink like you do, Senhor," she replied. "One glass like that and he went out like a candle. I believe you could drink two and feel no effect whatever."

"Two?" queried the Englishman, almost insulted. "I could take half-a-dozen without the least effect. Watch this!"

But when yet another glass went down she perceived that Cuming was a better drinker than she had thought. Other methods were needed. Rising to go in search of something fictitious, as she passed Ah Sum she said in Cantonese the single word "Powder", not being sure what to call it but hoping he would see what she meant. His aged face jerked into activity. He hurried away.

It was the moment Cuming had been waiting for. He rose and came to her. With agility she skimmed out of his way.

"Oh, and there!" she exclaimed prettily. "Your glass is empty. What a hostess I am!" They were phrases remembered from Dominie's fancies of life as it would be married to an officer from Portugal.

This meant a little more time fetching the decanter and refilling his glass.

He hardly touched it, however. His lustful stare followed her every movement. It was imperative not to be alone with him a minute longer.

"There are one or two things I would like to consult you about, Senhor," she said, thinking quickly. "May I beg you to come and let me show you. And pray bring your glass with you," she added—one free hand was less dangerous than two.

She led him downstairs and out into the servants' compound. It was a risky move. If the servants intended to have her out of the house, this was their opportunity. Any of them who spoke business English had only to repeat to the Englishman the allegations which Fong and her mother were making against her, and in the interest of his duty to the Company he would be obliged to act.

She thus kept up a running flow of amiable conversation

about domestic problems, pointing out the servants' cottages, the difficulty of the rocks being so close to the house, the danger of the well drying up, etc.; and all the time she was leading him the furthest possible distance, towards the ascending path to her special meeting place with Fong.

Contrary to Martha's expectation, the response of the servants to the sight of an Englishman, rather flushed and holding a glass of wine, being taken on a conducted tour of the demesne, and this too in a self-possessed chatter of Macanese which they could not follow, was one of astounded silence. The men watched. The wives, put out of countenance, withdrew into the cottages. Even Fong's angry voice from inside was subdued upon a rasping whisper from her mother.

Mounting to the shed and the hillside nursery Martha pointed out the extravagant beauty of the flowers the head gardener produced, the gardener himself standing by respectfully. Cuming, all Company gentleman again, was quite prepared to go through this comedy in the interests of better things to come. He was also genuinely impressed, as indeed it was difficult not to be, by the gardener's handiwork. Albeit the time of year was best for a varied display of flowers, the daytime appearance of the nursery was magnificent. Among the rows of pots sheltered by an ageing boundary wall grew not only all the usual spring flowers but numerous rarer blooms exquisitely flowering entirely out of season. Chrysanthemums and poinsettias of mid-winter still flourished happily beside the more seasonal narcissi, foxgloves, begonias, asters, African violets and daisies, tearoses and carnations of the Chinese spring, while already the firecracker honeysuckle sprayed over the wall in a cascade of orange, and the summer's first gardenias were heavy in bud. Under glass rare orchids from the South Seas dangled from hanging pots and carefully preserved coconut shells. Dwarf trees, each with a high market value, were being twisted into weird shapes, and highly unusual plants seldom seen in South China were flourishing as if in their natural habitat.

"Flowers of this kind," Martha was saying in the manner of an impresario, "are only fit for the great houses in Macao —the Company house, for example, and your house, Senhor."

Cuming nodded. He glanced at his timepiece. He had not all day to spare.

His movement alarmed Martha, determined as she was to keep him outside as long as possible. In her desperation to find a means of keeping the conversation going she recalled her talk with her own Englishman about having a shop and selling things.

"We could supply the Company house," she hurried on brightly. "There would be something to pay, naturally, but we could guarantee a figure well below the market price."

"Could you contract to provide regular supplies?" Cuming inquired, visibly bored and impatient to move into the house.

"Certainly," she answered, not having the faintest idea whether she could or not, or even being quite certain what these commercial words meant.

"I could tell the Number One at the Company house to call and make some arrangements if you like," said he casually.

"I should be your servant for ever," she exclaimed enthusiastically. It was another of Dominie's phrases, usually accompanied by a tremendous curtsey.

"Very well. I will do so," said Cuming.

But it was no good. He had begun descending the hill. There was no other course but to follow.

In the compound she at last saw Ah Sum. From behind Cuming she cast him a despairing look of inquiry. He merely lowered his eyes as she passed and uttered in Cantonese the single word "Dissolved".

She looked in amazement from Ah Sum's face to Cuming's glass. She had noticed nothing. She glanced at Cuming's face. It had turned white.

123

Whatever Ah Sum had succeeded in doing, the effect of fresh air had brought about a quick reaction. For several minutes Cuming had been feeling queasy. As he re-entered the tiled hall he apprehended with concern that in very few minutes he would vomit everything he had eaten. He made excuses and said he must leave at once.

"Must you really, Senhor?" Martha asked, heartbroken. "I was hoping you would stay and taste some of my Macao cakes."

It was the *coup de fusil*. No Englishman in Macao had ever been known to like Macao's extremely sweet and sticky cakes, made of glutinous rice, coconut, molasses, and other less identifiable ingredients in which the confectionery arts of Europe, India, China and Africa were weightily combined. The mere thought of them at this moment nearly made Cuming sick on the spot.

"Thank you—most kind," he muttered, his lofty walk reduced to a lurch as he made for the front door. With a handkerchief over his mouth he stepped into his waiting chair and signed to the bearers to move off.

By custom Martha could not approach near the front door when it was open, but from the depth of the hall she called out gaily:

"And you will not forget about the flowers, will you, Senhor?"

As the chair moved out of view the Englishman nodded with a groan.

"Close the door and lock it," she said to Ah Sum quietly, "and may we never have to unlock it again to that devil. You did well," she added, and was about to ask him what he had used when everything went green, her knees gave way, and she fainted on the tiles.

It was a turning point.

Martha had long observed the head gardener's cleverness with potted plants. Not only was he skilled, he had green fingers. Anything he tended would grow. She had also long observed that the number of potted plants in the nursery far exceeded the number ever brought into the house or to the little rocktop garden; and she suspected that somewhere above the hillside nursery was a track which circled the lower slopes of the Monte and ended up in the Chinese market.

"You have skill," she told the head gardener next day, "but no business sense. In a week I can find more customers for your plants than you could in a year. I suggest that from now on, if Chin Fui agrees, you should have a one-third increase in pay and one-tenth of the profits of anything we sell, on condition that you no longer take a single pot out of this compound into the market."

The gardener looked scandalized.

"How could you say I ever did such a thing?" he declared.

"With a better return for your work I hope you will no longer find it necessary," she said.

The gardener, who, like many of his kind, was more craftsman than man of commerce and detested haggling with the market dealers, did some quick arithmetic, and after protesting his honesty was pleased to accept the new terms. As Martha was sure he would, George Cuming kept his word, and that same afternoon she received a call from the Number One at the Company house.

He was smooth and soft-spoken, with a pigtail glossier than a woman's and a puffy but well-tended face the colour of uncooked pastry. A very considerable personage, the Number One of all Number Ones by virtue of his position as senior domestic employee to the East India Company, when Ah Wing saw that he had been ordered to interview a chit of a Chinese girl who might have been suitable as an additional concubine but was certainly good for nothing else he was not at all pleased. He conducted himself with lordly disdain, addressing himself entirely to Ah Sum, who was present throughout.

Ah Wing was impressed by the flowers, however, and as

Martha saw him mentally revolving the financial possibilities she quickly summed him up. From his well-manicured hands alone it was clear that he was far richer than he should be, was really more business man than servant, and, like every business man, on the look-out for opportunities. He must, she concluded, be known to more or less every Englishman in Macao, and could be useful. Gradually, dwelling gently on Ah Wing's exalted position and substantial connexions, Martha took over the conversation, and gradually Ah Wing perceived that the person he was dealing with had perhaps other uses than as a concubine.

Flowers were peculiarly difficult to obtain in Macao. People with gardens produced for themselves alone, and supplies from Heungshan (they came in by junk) were irregular and uncertain, the market not being quite large enough for sound commerce when transport costs were added. Agreement was thus reached without much trouble about regular supplies to the Company house. By dusk that day, and entirely by accident, Martha found herself in trade.

During the next few weeks Ah Wing, who saw he had stumbled on a good thing, became positively friendly, and money began to flow in. In modest quantities at first. But with Ah Wing's assistance these quantities increased till by midsummer the distribution of the gardener's products had been so extended that it embraced nearly all the Company officers' private houses. Inquiries then started to be received from other foreign homes, to the satisfaction of Martha and the gardener, and to the wide-eyed surprise of the servants, whose behaviour perceptibly improved as profits rose.

Not quite as much as Martha would have wished, though. Due to its anomalous nature a pensioner's position in regard to servants was always fraught with difficulty. Martha knew that unless she could settle the servant problem she could have no more than a fictitious semblance of security. As the weeks passed and September neared, when the Europeans would leave for Canton, it became evident that Thomas would not return till the following spring. In the house Martha was to be alone at the helm for a year. It was a long time.

The development of the flower industry had healed the breach between Ah Sum's family and that of the gardener, but there was still an air of discontent below. It was evident that this was being fomented by someone, and it did not take much reasoning for Martha to realize by whom.

At her mother's firm insistence Fong had resumed her tasks for Number Four. He was only partially pacified, however, and the reason for this, Martha deduced, must be that what Fong had formerly done with good grace she was now doing under protest. Since the day of Martha's visit to the temple the two girls had not exchanged another word. If they ever encountered one another while Fong was working, Fong would look the other way. Where possible she avoided Martha completely.

Fong had come perilously near to the truth about Martha's background. In the days of their friendship Martha had spoken perhaps more than she should about the Portuguese, and with friendship succeeded by enmity the presence of Fong, aggrieved and angry, assumed an aspect of danger.

Ah Sum having proved unwavering in his insistence that Fong must not be sold, Martha concluded that the most effective course would be to persuade Ah Sum and his wife to find Fong a husband. Knowing she could not mention this openly to any of them, she waited till Chin Fui, the compradore, paid one of his visits, when she cautiously raised the subject with him.

Because of Macao's residence restrictions Chinese business men desiring to reside in the city did so by means of various innocent subterfuges. Ah Wing, for example, obtained residence rights by being technically a menial. Apart from menials the only Chinese entitled to reside in the city were the Christians and the boatbuilders. Chin Fui in his younger days had been strongly advised to become a Christian, but being a man of principle he had decided against this and become a boatbuilder instead. That is to say, he acquired from the Goncalves Sequeira family the lease of a piece of land on which stood an old shipyard producing junks and sampans, thus making himself technically one of the privileged, and enabling him, under the registered occupation of boatbuilder, to carry out an extensive and diverse trade which had nothing whatever to do with boatbuilding. Though Thomas, on making his acquaintance, had not perceived it, Chin Fui was a highly versatile and enterprising merchant, probably the richest Chinese in Macao. He derived little as compradore, merely using it as a classic Chinese form of insurance, keeping a foot in everywhere, in this case with the wealthy and prosperous English.

Such was the strange importance of the part which pensioners played in the maintenance of domestic equilibrium (and thus, for Chin Fui and his kind, steady profits) that when Martha raised with him the subject of Fong's marriage Chin Fui judged it wise to listen to her and act. In the following weeks a marriage was arranged between Fong and one of Chin Fui's distant clansmen, who travelled from his village far out in Kwangtung to be married in Macao.

When he came to the house (Fong having by decent custom been hidden away) Martha chanced to see him. He was a dour, dark-skinned country lad with a head as round as a cannon ball. As usual with peasants, his hair was shaven completely from his forehead to the middle of the dome of his head. Seeing herself for a moment in Fong's position, Martha was shocked by what she had done. Looking down from the french windows she was on the point of calling for Chin Fui, who was with his clansman, and commenting on the boy's unsuitableness as a match for Fong when the fool boy, rushing out into the yard, flung himself into the boy's arms, beating him on his hard shoulders, shouting with delight, and dragged him round and round. Sending for a servant, Martha learned that the bridegroom was the fool boy's elder brother.

Her objections diminished. She had for some time wished to have the fool boy out of the house. She was afraid of him.

In his disordered mind he saw her as coming between himself and the new master, for whom he had formed a dog-like attachment. Sometimes when Martha was downstairs he would follow her about, muttering softly, and occasionally giving a little clipped laugh. He was the only other person who slept in the house. Alone as she was in an upper room, she was completely at his mercy. On the eve of the wedding she persuaded Chin Fui that it would be wise to allow the boy to return to his village, together with the bride and bridegroom. A day or two later she watched the three of them depart from the side entrance with appropriate cracker-firing and ceremony. And her conclusion about Fong proved right. From that day forth the attitude of the servants changed rapidly for the better.

When September came and the Europeans departed, the demand for pot-plants abruptly dropped. Realizing that if the gardener was disappointed the situation below stairs could easily slip back to where it had been, that basically it was the success of her little business venture which was keeping things in order, she concluded that some means must be found of establishing her enterprise on a firm all-the-year-round footing. This meant stimulating a further extension of trade in the direction of the only Europeans who remained in Macao all the time, the Portuguese officials.

This presented a new problem. Since she herself was unable to leave the house, and neither Ah Wing nor the gardener had any dealings with the Portuguese, an entrepreneur was needed. How to find one with the requisite contacts?

It was the custom in Macao for hawkers of fruit and vegetables to cry their wares through the quieter streets of the city. The slight movement caused by an alteration in the angle of the lattices of a shuttered window was sufficient to make any hawker stop. Unseen from the street the lady of the house would call down through the lattices for what she wanted, and lower a basket tied to a cord. After the required fruit and vegetables had been hauled up, the basket would be lowered again with sycee in it.

Despite being absolutely forbidden to go anywhere near Hospital Street, and having too much respect for Abraham Biddle's means of knowing what went on in Macao to venture to disobey this order, Pedro Goncalves Sequeira had not by any means given up hope of making Martha his mistress. He had taken the trouble to find out which hawkers frequented Hospital Street. Sometimes, should Martha purchase anything by this method, the hawker would include with the goods a folded slip of rice paper on which was sketched a Portuguese youth in European attire kneeling at the feet of a woman wearing Macao dress. On other occasions the picture would be of a girl wearing Chinese clothes with a pigtail, and the Portuguese youth would be shaking his finger at her warningly.

Martha was well aware of the message all of this was intended to convey. 'Your Englishman is a bird of passage. What will become of you when he is gone? I, Pedro, will still be here, and you will still be young.' It was convincing and disturbing, for Pedro, if not given his way, could prove dangerous, being related to Teresa and knowing of that woman's desire for revenge. But who, Martha thought, strictly in commercial terms, could be a more ideal intermediary with the Portuguese than Pedro, who through his uncles' firm must have connexions with all the Portuguese officials? And in view of the risks in thwarting him too long, what better means of holding him at bay than by using him, thereby filling him with false hope and making him doubly wary of committing mischief against her?

If she received Pedro he would have to come in by the front door. She was sure he would never agree to enter by the side door. He would thus be observed from across the street by people who, for all Martha knew, might be connected with the English. The master might thus come to know. Apart from this, having Pedro in the house at all, by whatever door, was a risk. Ah Sum and the other servants had been impressed by the way she had handled and disposed of George Cuming. All the less easy would they find it to accept visits by Pedro.

Wisely foreseeing that messages delivered by Ah Sum might be considered by Pedro as an affront, she used Chin Fui as her channel of communication, and without ever meeting Pedro, came to a financial understanding with him by means of which the potted plant enterprise resumed its growth, the gardener smiled again, and tranquillity reigned.

Not another word was heard of George Cuming, who had come to suffer from vague suspicions of having been made a fool of by the gentle harlot of Hospital Street, and of perhaps having made a fool of himself. Occupied with various other intrigues—he was a very various person—he allowed the summer to slip by without making a second attempt. So far as Martha was concerned this was satisfactory. She had got the best out of him.

The significance of George Cuming's involvement in the matter—the fact that she knew him and that he had been to the house—did not occur to her till the day Thomas returned from Canton and found sycee lying about. In Macao houses sycee lay about everywhere. There was a great deal of it, and nowhere else to put it. Theft was unknown. When Thomas commented on it Martha grasped with sudden alarm that such was evidently not the custom in other places, and at almost the same instant perceived that on no account must Thomas be told anything about the flowers, the money, the connexions with Ah Wing and Pedro, springing as it all did from the visit of George Cuming. Jealousy, she knew by instinct, runs most swiftly along channels of race. There were many things Thomas might one day be told, and understand. Cuming's visit, she knew, was something he would never understand. He would never entirely believe that it befell as it did. Thus it was better he should know nothing of it. Thomas had become the recipient of that same unswerving loyalty she had once given to Mother Clemencia, to Monsieur Auvray. That given, she considered she had the right to deceive him in moderation. It was for his own good, after all.

When Thomas then took some sycee from his own pocket and added it to hers, it brought further revelation. At sight of the two portions of silver inextricably mingled, an entirely new principle occurred to her—separate ownership. In Monsieur Auvray's house sycee had more or less belonged to everyone—with the old man's permission, *bien entendu*—because they were like a family. Here it was not like a family. Anything that lay about was his. By adding his sycee to hers the whole pile became his and she made a loss—visibly. It must not happen again. Leaving him, she went quickly round the house, picked up all her sycee lying scattered about, and secreted it in a Chinese chest in the windowless central room with mirrors.

That summer, the first Thomas actually spent in Macao, was a tremendous season for potted plants. Everyone seemed to want them, even the Bishop, who would doubtless have been startled had he known that in purchasing them he was lining the purse of a pensioner. The comings and goings in the nursery and compound were so extensive that it was quite difficult to confine them to times when the master was out while at the same time meeting all orders.

This was achieved successfully, however. Ironically enough, Thomas had been appointed house secretary for that particular off-season, and thus had to authorize all the Company's domestic expenditure. On several occasions the entry 'Florals and Fanciful Greeneries: To Sequeira's, such-and-such dollars' had passed beneath his eyes and received his approving and unsuspecting initials.

One evening late in the September of the following year, at the very end of the off-season, Martha was summoned below to receive from one of the clerks in the Gonçalves Sequeira office an urgent message from Pedro.

The firm of Gonçalves Sequeira—that is to say, the part of it which the family actually controlled and which was not merely a borrowed name for the activities of Abraham Biddle and Chin Fui—had in the past dealt in imported sundries. These had included Portuguese wines, Indian condiments and spices, carpets, muslin, European ornaments and clocks, Spanish wines, cigars, snuff, scented and hard woods, incense and lace. Before the British became so powerful in Macao the firm had been one of the city's best.

Their commerce had been too insignificant, however, to interest Abraham Biddle, who, apart from paying in cash and kind (liquor) his annual fee for the use of the family name, helped the Gonçalves Sequeiras not a tittle. Despite the vast transactions conducted through their premises—Biddle was the largest opium merchant in China—the family was chronically short of money.

The clerk explained to Martha that a Spanish firm in Manila, with which the Gonçalves Sequeiras had had a long association but to which they were in default on certain payments, was refusing to land a valuable cargo of wine unless the Gonçalves Sequeiras forthwith settled their account with them. The firm had put together everything they had, but it was still insufficient. They were holding some silver due to Martha, and Pedro now urgently begged that he might be allowed to use this and beg a loan of seventy taels of silver in addition, which would enable him to weather the day.

"I certainly have no intention of lending Senhor Gonçalves any money," Martha remarked with asperity when she heard this.

The clerk looked understandably disapproving.

"I might invest some money, though, might I not?" she said on second thoughts. "Have you a sample of the wine?"

The clerk expanded his empty hands.

"Do you take me for a nitwit?" Martha asked imperiously—it was the manner she had always longed to be able to use with Sister Grace, and the poor clerk now received it in good measure. "Go at once and fetch me two bottles. And don't shake them about," she warned, remembering old Monsieur Auvray and the rituals he employed with wine.

She had no idea why wine should not be shaken about.

133

She just knew it should not be, and in the clerk, who was only a few years older than she, and who had shown signs of being insulted by being asked to make a financial bargain with what he considered to be a sixteen-year-old prostitute, it inspired a suitable degree of respect, in that he did not understand the reason for the injunction either.

At dinner that evening a new wine was served. Martha, sitting as was now customary at the end of the table (she had her meals alone), said nothing, watched and waited.

Sure enough, towards the end of the meal Thomas commented on it most favourably. Waiting till from the scent wafting from the living room she knew he was enjoying an after-dinner cigar, she went quietly to the central room. Weighing sycee on the scales could not be done without making a noise, and as a precaution she had prepared for just such an eventuality as this by buying a number of purses, filling them in advance with definite amounts. Neither she nor Ah Sum could read the markings on the scale weights, but he could identify each simply by sight and by lifting it, and had taught her to do the same. The requisite amount was quickly and noiselessly taken out of the house, and that night Thomas van Mierop, though he did not know it, embraced and bore to his bed a young lady in the wine trade.

Pedro was not the fool Biddle sometimes made him look. Since coming to man's estate—and more pertinent perhaps, since becoming enamoured and being deprived of Martha, an experience which had very much brought him to his senses—he had seen clearly that unless he found something to do, independent of Abraham Biddle, he would still be a messenger-boy at the age of fifty. Furthermore, the means lay at hand. If he could resuscitate the family business from the sterile chaos to which his uncles had reduced it, there might be a chance for him to stand on his own. It was on this endeavour that he was engaged when he appealed to Martha for a little financial aid. How little was required showed the sorry depths to which the old firm had sunk.

His way was by no means easy. The daily ridicule which Biddle extended to the activities being conducted in the front office Pedro suffered in silence because of his deep respect for Biddle. A far worse problem was presented by his own uncles.

The uncles were actually the third generation after Founder João. It was typical of the hazy knowledge one community had of another in multiracial Macao that not even Biddle had this right. Pedro was thus the fourth generation of a family accustomed to money and position, a family afflicted with two peculiarly Portuguese tendencies—an inability to give a negative answer to anyone's face, and a belief that the word miser was about the worst in the dictionary.

To each generation the distribution of largesse was a cherished ideal. It was thus that the men of the family saw themselves. Pedro had been brought up with it. He had not considered it unusual, nor even recognized its consequences, until he became the disciple of Abraham Biddle, when to his surprise he observed that Biddle was not always giving money away to people. In fact it was very hard to extract even a tael of silver from him. He counted what he had (or rather, weighed it), guarded it, and used it. To Pedro this was a revelation; and as he saw, it was productive of results.

When he tried to apply these most un-Portuguese principles to the resuscitation of the family business he quickly appreciated what he was up against. On the very first occasion when he made some money he returned after lunch to find that one of his uncles had given half of it away to an indigent relative. All three of the uncles were shocked when Pedro remonstrated with them about this. Where had his Christian manners gone, they asked? Had he forgotten who he was? There was no answer to this, no means of convincing them that in days of success such actions were perhaps permissible, but that with the firm on its beam ends they were not.

Thus not only had Pedro to conduct business, he had to watch like a hawk his uncles' every activity, not let them out of his sight if possible, and never leave them in the shop alone.

Despite the fact that the Europeans were within days of departing for Canton, he managed to sell the whole of his wine cargo. Rapid sales of this kind were possible due to there being no general provision stores in Macao, no counters across which small daily sales could be made. Every shop was an importer, and when a ship arrived it behoved householders to purchase quickly and in quantity, since no more such goods might be available again for many months.

Martha, of course, only had a share in this cargo, but she made a profit which surprised her and set her thinking. When the Europeans had gone, and people had more time on their hands, she questioned Ah Wing and certain others employed in the best houses concerning the drinking tastes of Europeans. As a result of these inquiries she suggested to Pedro, still without meeting him, the names of a number of brands which the firm had never handled, and asked that he make inquiry whether any of these could be obtained from Manila. The names were conveyed correctly to him through old jars and bottles rescued by the various servants who were her advisors.

Word from Manila was favourable. At this point, though, the Gonçalves Sequeira uncles stepped in, insisting that to invest in unknown brands was sheer foolishness, and that their nephew was trying to ruin them. When this was conveyed to her, Martha went to her silver chest, made some calculations with the aid of Ah Sum, and decided she could just manage it. She sent word to Pedro that if he would place firm orders forthwith she would underwrite the cargo. The uncles, when they heard this, shrugged their shoulders, and with misgivings gave in. The wines were ordered.

A few days after this, Inez unexpectedly reappeared at Hospital Street. Though Inez had little European blood in her veins she was very much like a plain-spoken, good-natured Portuguese countrywoman. Pious, downright, and with no illusions about anyone, she had worked like a buffalo (to use her own phrase) for the past twelve years to maintain herself and her two boys, the paternity of whom, if she knew it, she had never been known to reveal to anyone; and though she would not have taken kindly to anyone who called her a gossip, she liked to have someone to impart her thoughts to. In Monsieur Auvray's house this selected person had been Martha.

After a long period without work she came with the good news that she had been engaged as a cleaner (really a caretaker) at the Santa Casa da Misericordia. She had obtained the job through the good offices of the powerful and terrible Father Montepardo, senior secular priest and Canon of the Cathedral, of whom people were so scared that until the desperate and hungry Inez came along the priest had never been able to persuade anyone to clean his room on a regular basis. This function Inez had now been performing for some time every other Wednesday afternoon.

To Martha, with her increasing interests in trade, outside information of all kinds was becoming important, and it was difficult to think of anyone better placed than Inez for knowing the latest news. The Santa Casa, with the aid of whose funds Martha had herself been raised, was an institution of great importance. To be a member of the Board of the Santa Casa was Macao's highest local distinction. Meetings of many kinds were held in the Santa Casa's offices. In the course of a year nearly every Portuguese of any standing came there. As caretaker, moving about the building more or less as she pleased, Inez was no longer just a friend. She was an opportunity too good to be missed.

But to insure that Inez would come to Hospital Street regularly, friendship was not enough, Martha considered. In addition to friendship there must be interest. It must somehow be made financially advantageous to Inez to come.

A small scene on the Rua da Penha came back to Martha,

one of Teresa's guests expressing surprise to see Inez working as a servant when she was known to be so good at dressmaking, Teresa not believing it, saying it must be someone else, so unlikely did it seem to her that the old warhorse of the scullery could have nimble fingers.

Having at last a little money of her own, there was nothing Martha wanted so much in the world as to spend it on beautiful clothes. From her meagre childhood, from the austerity and hardness of life with the Franciscan Sisters, from never being allowed by Teresa to look pretty lest she spoil Dominie's chances, Martha longed to wear dresses finer and more wonderful than any Dominie ever dreamed of. She was sick of her little black Macao dresses. They were symbolic of hopelessness and sorrow.

"Inez, do you still use your needle sometimes?" she asked.

A nucleus of hidden friends, linked by the strong bond of kindred financial interests, began to grow up around her. There was Chin Fui, reputed the richest Chinese in Macao. There was Ah Wing and a number of others like him who, though outwardly servants, were actually business men. There was the invaluable Inez. And there were to be others. It was a circle Martha cultivated with appropriate small gifts when babies were a month old or daughters were being married. Through it she came to develop an intelligence system which, though not dealing with quite the same matters, came to rank in efficiency with that of Abraham Biddle.

By means of this system she came to know about Pedro's difficulties with his uncles, a matter which gave her grave concern. It was one thing to have a small share in a Goncalves cargo. If one of the uncles gave some of the profits away it was up to Pedro to see that Martha herself lost nothing. It was a very different matter to be financing an entire consignment through the firm. If the uncles gave away any of those profits it was her money they were giving. She saw that as things stood she was entirely dependent on

Pedro being able to control his uncles, which was a point in doubt. If only she had a name for writing down on those magic sheets of paper called accounts she would be able to trade through Pedro under an account of her own. This, she now knew, was what Biddle did, and Biddle, though a scoundrel, was wise.

For trade had become part of her life, and none knew better than she how vital it was to her. The house in Hospital Street would not be hers to live in for ever, nor would she be young for ever. Englishmen came and went, and their women, like flowers whose bloom is over, were cast away. The very best they could expect was dingy penury, outside the pale of society, with their half-caste children bearing their mother's name and, in their eyes and faces, something of the English father they would never see again. It was the age-old story of the women of Macao, known to every woman, feared by many. Those in penury were the fortunate. Others, when the end came, went to the Street of Happiness and were lost, even to their own children.

But if she herself was to survive when the time of departure came, she would need that most precious of all things, a name of her own.

One evening the following April, shortly after sundown, Pedro was sitting alone in the first of the inner offices. His uncles had gone home, and on the wooden floor above him Abraham Biddle, who lived there, was, judging by various weighty movements, changing his clothes.

For the third time in four weeks Pedro had had a bitter exchange with his uncles. It had arisen over a consignment of spices in which his uncles refused to take any interest and Biddle had laughed at. In desperation Pedro had once more turned to Martha for help, but the sole response had been the return of the clerk saying, "She wants to know where the spices come from."

Pedro blew up with impatience.

"Mother of God! Where does she think they come from?

Go back and tell her, the East Indies of course! Where else? And what on earth does it matter to her anyway?" he expostulated. "She doesn't know Brazil from my backside."

Comparatively restrained comments of this kind, when he was in a bad temper, were apt to throw his relatives into a state of tight-lipped shock. They considered him very coarse.

He had waited about forty minutes when the unaccustomed sound of the rustle of a woman's dress drew him hastily to the outer office. Before him, in her superb creation of black taffeta and lace—the first product of Inez' needle—stood Martha.

Later that same evening Thomas, returning unexpected from Canton, was to be surprised by her appearance. Pedro was utterly dumbfounded, gazing at her in awe and admiration. For the Martha he saw belonged to a higher order of things, no longer a little girl to be cajoled or fooled with—or threatened either, for that matter, he thought with a displeasing recollection. It was an exciting but uncomfortable miracle.

"I have come, Cousin," Martha said, cousining him for the first time and rather pleased with the effect she had produced, "to tell you personally what I could not have told you through a messenger. Which is"—she dismissed the clerk with a gesture—"that if we are to do business together, when I ask a question, Cousin, I want a proper answer!"

"I sent you a proper answer," Pedro said, collecting himself.

"Yes. The East Indies. What does that mean to me? Where is the cinnamon coming from?"

"From Timor, of course."

"No," she said firmly. "Ternate."

He was so taken aback that again he was momentarily speechless. What could have been going on in that house, he thought, that she should know the names of such places? He did not know she was trying out on him what she had learned from old Monsieur Auvray, and which this evening had suddenly begun to make sense and be useful.

"Well, it probably is Ternate cinnamon," he said in hasty justification of himself, "but we buy it through Timor."

"And the nutmeg?"

"Again, Timor."

"Banda," she answered, not daring to say more than this lest she reveal she did not know quite where, what or who Banda was. "Better value for money."

He stared at her in astonishment.

"It may or may not be Banda nutmeg, but it comes through Timor."

"You will always be cheated if you buy Timor. Trouble with the Dutch. You should open a new channel." They were Monsieur Auvray's very words.

"How can we? Where?"

"Through Chinese in Siam. Have two channels. We are then in a position to bargain."

This was indisputable. Timor was one of the last Portuguese possessions in an area now almost entirely Dutch, and there were constant supply difficulties.

"Where would you wish the mace to come from?" he inquired, wondering if there were any more marvels to come.

She raised her eyebrows.

"Naturally from the same place as the nutmeg, Cousin."

"Really? Why?"

"Pedro Gonçalves, have you never opened a nutmeg?"

"No, I can't say I have," said he, recoiling slightly before so close a suggestion to manual labour.

"Well, if you do, the first thing you will find is the mace, wrapped round the nut."

He felt rather foolish.

"And now about that wine," she went on. "I think I should have a separate account."

"Yes, yes, certainly," he agreed, dismissing it.

"How do you propose to make it separate?" she asked sternly.

"It's very simple. A separate account under your name."

"You may discount that name. It is not a real one."

"Of course it's a real one," he said, feeling that a member of his family was being insulted.

"No. Think of something else."

The name Martha da Silva might be real or it might not. She had no means of knowing. But she perceived that to use it on magic slips of paper was an admission of relationship to Teresa, and could be dangerous.

He too, remembering this point, conceded her objection.

"We could open a new account and call it Number Two."

"Number Two? Can that be written down?"

"Yes, of course it can."

"On pieces of paper? On purses and chests containing my money?"

"Yes"—he was careful not to smile.

"Very good," she said, guardedly satisfied. "Let my account be Number Two, and be sure you always put it. Now I must return." She glanced up at the ceiling. "What is all that noise?"

"It is Senhor Biddle. He stays up there."

"Does he?" she said with interest.

She looked round the empty office, noting the disposition of the rooms. Between his uncles on one side and Biddle on the other, Pedro was caught between two fires, Biddle's attitude to his disciple's attempted independence fanning the flames of the uncles' opposition.

"Why do you not tell him to go?" she asked.

"Go? Where?"

"Take a house of his own. He knows so much about houses, he should have no difficulty."

Pedro frowned. It was an inconceivable idea. How could he ask Biddle, his benefactor, to go?

"Try it, Cousin," Martha said quietly. "Have courage."

Silence fell between them, implicit in it a new and stronger togetherness. He nodded.

"It's good to see you."

Each was thinking the same—how ideal a marriage would

be if only it could be! She was impressed by the change the years had made in him. He had always been handsome. Today he was not merely that. He was altogether improved, more stable—and more in need of her. It would be an extraordinarily practical solution ... And then she remembered Teresa, deprived of a European man in her house and thus cut off from European society, with no prospect of ever entertaining an officer from Portugal whom Dominie might marry. Teresa had been using every wile, Martha knew, to bring about a marriage between Dominie and Pedro, and it was better so. And better too were the four walls of an East India Company house, with a man she loved but who in the end would go, than a marriage in which a single disagreement would be enough to deliver her into the hands of Teresa.

"Marry Dominie," she said hastily, trying to conceal her awareness of the emotional bond between them.

His eyes ran over the lace at her breast.

"The one piece of advice you've given me this evening which I don't think I shall take," he answered.

He was very near her.

"Don't touch me, Pedro Gonçalves," she said in a low voice, "and remember, if you ever dare come to that house without my permission, it is the end between us," she added with a flick of her black lace fan.

She left him staring incredulously after her, with a rent feeling of sadness such as no woman had ever roused in him before.

"Mr. Biddle," Pedro said a few days later, "my affairs have expanded to a state where I require the use of the upper rooms of this building. My uncles and I would be pleased if—"

After the first upward glance of surprise, Biddle, his ugly mouth contorted with anger, rose slowly from his chair, and Pedro's words died away. A shadow of the old hypnotized look flickered across his expression, but he held his ground, and as he did so he watched Biddle's face soften as he mentally reckoned up the balance on which his existence in Macao depended: the Company's tolerance (unauthorized by the Governor-General in Calcutta), the goodwill of the Macao authorities (which a word from the Gonçalves Sequeiras could alter), the need to be the indispensable purveyor of Company requirements (again dependent on Pedro's family). Anger ebbed, and caution, the all-important, the sole remaining moral basis of things, took its place.

"Yer pushin' yer uncle, me boy, in the direction 'e's been thinkin' for a long time o' takin'. What d'yer say? A fanciful 'ouse on the Ridge?"

Tears came into Pedro's eyes. It was the first sign he had ever had of the influence he might possess over the man.

"We hope you will always remain associated with us, Mr. Biddle."

"With you, me boy, always. Yer like me own son." He frowned, fearing to reveal himself further. "This, Master Pedro, in a manner o' speakin', was comin' to yer, and to me 'umble self. Yer'll be what I've made yer."

For of course, as Biddle and soon everyone else in Macao saw, to rise to the Ridge was an enhancement, not a defeat. It was to be business as usual, but with a chair and coolies.

Martha's advice proved wise, moreover. Biddle retained an office at the shop, but seldom used it, transacting most of his business in the pleasant house on the Ridge to which he moved shortly after, with a walled garden in which he installed the aviary of tropical birds which he had originally started in the rear court of the Gonçalves Sequeiras. With Biddle out of the way, Pedro's control over the firm increased, and new lines of commerce were opened.

But Martha was still not satisfied. She was Gonçalves Sequeira Number Two, a name shouted out between the junks and the houses of the inner harbour, while coolies trotted to and fro with their loads, quills made marks on paper, and wooden tallies were handed in and counted. But when it came to it, the whole of her trade was in Pedro's name, and while she trusted Pedro, as the volume of the trade and its profits rose she became less sure. While he could be counted on in the good times they were passing through, would it be the same should there be reverses? She would never be at ease, she knew, till she had found some way of placing her connexion with the Gonçalves Sequeiras on a firmer footing, on a legal basis.

Meanwhile it became progressively more difficult to conceal from Thomas the increasing amount of sycee in the central room. The weight of it was too heavy for even the sturdiest cabinets, and in May, when the usual slight lull in investment occurred with the coming of summer rains and high seas, and coincided with the height of the pot-plant season, with cash coming in all the time, she was finally obliged to purchase two sycee chests and ask Thomas for the use of the godown.

Thomas never returned to Macao with more disturbed and mixed feelings than he did at the end of the next season, his sixth in China. Impatient to arrive, he yet dreaded his arrival. Hopeful of glad tidings, he yet knew with a sense of hopelessness that the tidings he expected to hear could in no circumstances truly be glad. Hastening his pace as he threaded the narrow streets, it was not out of eagerness that he did so, but in order more speedily to end uncertainty, and come to grips with the most difficult domestic situation he had ever had to face.

It was a sunny spring afternoon. He scarcely noticed the excited welcoming chatter of the Number Three as he entered the hall. His hearing was attuned to the upper floor rooms of the silent house. Striding swiftly upstairs, he went to her room. There were signs that she was still occupying it, but she was not there. In a corner of the landing outside stood a wicker basket cradle. It was empty.

The Number Three, padding after him more slowly, came upon him staring at the cradle. He grinned.

"Beforetime baby, Master. Him nice baby. But him die."

And with the Chinese protective reaction against the impact of displeasing news, he laughed.

In the agonized rush of sympathy for her which swept over him, Thomas ignored it.

The child, he learned, had been an exceedingly beautiful boy. The servants had been in raptures over it. He would have been very tall, they said. But the child did not cry, and seldom opened its eyes. It just slept. Neither Martha nor the wet nurse who was hastily called in could feed it. It lived for a little less than two days. In consternation Thomas knew what Martha herself must have thought. It was an unwanted child, and it had returned whence it came.

They met in silence. She had changed. The childlike impudence which so often and enchantingly haunted her expression had gone. Her dimples were no longer mischievous; they had somehow become thoughtful. Even her features seemed to have been refined, giving her a dignity beyond her years.

But their eyes did not meet. From her left arm dangled a purse heavy with sycee. She had been out, and had entered in haste, her black *dó* thrown back from her head but still lying over her shoulders. The purse and the *dó*, symbols of her right to do as she would, symbols of his own impuissance.

On her side she wondered why the purse made her feel guilty. He stared at the purse and wondered why it was to him an accusation. Each was distraught, but not with grief. Each hesitated conscience-stricken before expressing in terms of sorrow what was not a sorrow. Each faced with paralysed hearts the transformation which had brought a liaison simply and innocently entered upon to a spiritual and emotional entanglement so unfathomable that neither of them knew any longer how to speak to the other, what would please, what would wound, and why each was filled with such appalled sorrow which had nothing whatever to do with the lost child.

Towards evening he at last found voice to speak of it.

"I wish you to know," he said gravely, "that what has

befallen in no way alters my desire that we should be married."

"You are very kind," she replied in a matter-of-fact way, for the moment of embarrassed meeting past, she was restored to her normal self. The child had died two months ago. Since then, domestic matters and trade had re-absorbed her life, and his gravity and emotion belonged to a moment in time which for her was already over.

"It was not for the sake of the child I asked you to marry me," he pursued. "It was for our own sakes, for your sake and mine."

"What you say is very good, Tom," she answered. "But it will not be necessary for us to marry." And as she said it she spied a purse of sycee which she had inadvertently left where he would see it. She took it up by its rolled silk strings, the sycee inside it making a sound like water sprinkled on loose sand.

"It *is* necessary!" he insisted, angered by the sight of her again with a purse.

"Why, Tom?" she asked in innocent inquiry. "I tried to explain to you before. No one will ever be better prepared than I. You will be able to go away with less worry than any other—"

"Listen to me!"

"But many Englishmen go away very worried, Tom," she said insistently. "We all know that. We do not blame them. We know they—"

"Have you considered what it means when I say I am asking you to marry me?"

"Well, yes, but—"

"Then what does it mean, if we are married, when the time comes for me to return to England? Is it usual, do you imagine, for married men shifting from one country to another to leave their wives behind and never see them again?"

"It would make no difference in Macao, Tom. England is one of those places—"

"But imagine yourself married to me at that time."

She shook her head.

"That is not the way of it. Englishmen never marry."

"I am asking you to marry me!" he said loudly. "And when my time comes to leave, I wish you to come with me to England. If we cannot be married before we leave, we will be married in England, but whichever way it is, you will marry me and come with me when I go. And," he concluded with a flick of his fingers against the purse, "you will give up this ridiculous nonsense forthwith."

Seldom was proposal of marriage made with stranger countenance, and seldom can proposal have been received with less sign of flurry or emotion. His reference to her purse reminded her of something.

"Ah Shek!" she called down from the french windows. "Don't forget the candles need changing."

"Come inside!" Thomas ordered.

"Yes, Tom," she answered obediently.

"And pray pay attention to what I am saying. It is important."

"I know it is."

"You are going to give up this trading business because it is entirely unnecessary. There is no need for you to worry about money, now or for the rest of your life."

She was in black, a full-length dress of great elegance and simplicity. She gave a little laugh.

"In Dominie's dreams—the Portuguese girl I told you about—that was how it always was," she said, her eyes bright with humour at the remembrance of it. "All her young men—they were always very, very handsome, and had cloaks and swords, even in summer, and green cock feathers in their hats—bowed deeply to the ground and offered her their slavish obedience. And the one thing above all which they promised was that if she would accept their hand she would never have to do another day's work in her life. She always thought that was splendid. I always thought it would be terrible, but never dared say so for fear of being told to scrub the kitchen floor. But those were dreams, Tom. Life is not like that. You can observe it anywhere in Macao. Men are often lazy, and women have to do all the thinking and planning. Ask any grandmother."

"I am not speaking of Macao," he answered vehemently. "I am speaking of you and me, and of England. Can you not comprehend that every Englishman is not the same? I promise you, Martha, that if you will agree, when I go you shall come with me. Now will you not agree and trust me, as you have never truly trusted me yet?"

"It has never happened before—going to—those places, I mean," she said.

"In this case it will."

"No," she answered slowly. "I do not say it will not. I would ask you only to remember that you are not the only one, and neither am I. Many, many have promised to others what you are promising now to me. None, Tom, none has ever kept his word. This is a city of broken promises. I know it. I was born here. It may be that you will try to keep your promise. If it still pleases you to keep me here, I am sure you will. But this you must know. Though I might dearly love to, I would be a fool if I believed you. In Macao we know this, that when the time comes it is always otherwise. Whatever words may have been said, whatever promises made, when an Englishman goes, it is alone."

She was trembling and could say no more.

"That is your answer, then?" he said quietly.

"Yes. That is my answer." And flying in a rustle of black silk across the room, she flung herself at his feet, tears streaming down her cheeks. "Pray God you will forgive it!"

PART FIVE

Through the Hinges of the Screen

THOMAS' UNEXPECTED APPREHENSION of the secret commercial activities of George Cuming was succeeded in the ensuing months by detailed observation, all of it tending to confirm a discovery. Partnership, of course, was one of those legally finite words of limited application to the commercial ambiguities of the China coast, and whether George Cuming and Abraham Biddle actually operated in partnership business might still be doubted. Unquestionable was the fact that there was a close commercial tie between them.

The discovery—for George Cuming recognized instantly that he had in the heat of the moment revealed himself to Thomas—significantly altered relations between the two supercargoes. Thomas had become the possessor of a secret the revelation of which would bring about Cuming's disgrace. The secret known, Cuming would also face dismissal, but this compared with his social downfall would be mere formality. He would be hounded out of the place by his peers.

Aware of the danger he stood in, Cuming from that date simulated a warmth of friendship for his adversary which deceived everyone except Thomas himself, who never in his seemingly pleasant dealings with him overlooked the fact that his courtesy masked what had become an implacable enmity.

As for Biddle, the worst that could happen to him as a result of the secret's revelation would be expulsion from China, and though this might not harm him financially it would none the less be a bitter blow, for Biddle was now said to be the richest man on the coast, and had begun to look towards a dignified retirement in Calcutta.

In short, Thomas held the strongest card, and could play it at any moment he wished. Characteristically he considered its greatest value dwelt in lying unused in his hand. Knowledge of its presence there insured at least nominal compliance with his wishes when opinions were divided, while its security value augmented in measure with a movement of events rendering his relations with Cuming progressively more critical.

The Company personnel had greatly increased, and among those junior to Thomas were several more humanitarians. These were instinctively drawn to Thomas as to a leader. When Thomas first came to China opium was an institution, not a subject for argument. With more humanitarians present new voices were heard. Opium was not yet a specific issue, and Thomas' circle of friends, which was a large one, included those who traded in opium and those who did not. It was observable, however, that on Cuming's social occasions the company nearly always consisted exclusively of opium men. The possibility had come to exist of a division occurring in the Company's ranks, creating a pro-opium party led by Cuming, and an anti-opium party led by van Mierop, each of whom was rising in seniority. In Thomas' twelfth year on the coast Cuming was appointed Superintendent of Imports, while Thomas became Superintendent of Exports, these two posts being the threshold of elevation to the Select Committee.

Other developments were no less significant. Three years before this, in 1788, a particularly fair and handsome young man was a cabin passenger in an East Indiaman sailing from Calcutta for China. Five days out to sea the young man astonished the ship's officers by appearing in woman's attire. The wife of a Company surgeon, she had broken the iron regulation, and was coming to spend the summer with her husband in Macao. There was uproar in the Select Committee when she arrived, but nothing like the uproar among the Company personnel in general in Macao. Never was a woman so feted. She slept all day and danced all night. And never did a husband have such a difficult time of it, the China station beaux contriving to insure that the poor man was seldom alone with his wife for a minute. Socially it was a hilarious summer.

But it forewarned the death-knell of an epoch. The sanctity of the regulation once sullied, other wives would come in future years, as come they did, two or three each off-season; and as they did so another rift appeared within the Company, a rift between those who maintained pensioners, and those who did not. It manifested itself from the very first. Men with pensioners in the unseen mystery of their homes were not entirely acceptable socially in the new conditions. Though they were invited, it seemed to others as if they stood apart, estranged from the gaiety of the proceedings; and as time passed they were invited less. Privately the ladies referred to such men as 'Asiatics'. George Cuming called them the conservatives. He himself, prudence personified, had no pensioner, and on the one occasion, so it was said, when he kept a woman in his house for several months he threw her out the moment he discovered she was with child. Thanks to this piece of prudence he was able to shine as a respectable member of the new society, in fact as the leader of that society, in that he was the most senior person on the China station to be unencumbered by a Macao woman or by illegitimate children. In strict conformity with the illogicality of things China fashion it was George Cuming, the opium dealer, and not Thomas van Mierop, the humanitarian, who had become the upholder of morals on the China station. And all the more important was the card in Thomas' hand as the cleavage deepened, as two separate and highly complex groups aligned themselves between two leaders mutually antagonistic, and as men of the old dispensation shrank from the new social glare of the Macao summer into the shadows of their world of shutters and screens, a world that was passing away.

At Hospital Street nothing more was said about marriage.

Outwardly it was treated as a matter closed. But in fact, as the new society came in, and as Thomas felt himself being steadily forced in upon the more restricted society of men with domestic lives similar to his own, so did his determination increase to marry Martha and put an end to what he came increasingly to regard as the shamefulness of their existence together. He was determined too to bring her with him to Europe when he retired. She would suffer, he knew, but it would not be for long. Women in England might smirk at her behind the concealment of their fans; even his own sisters would find her very strange. He knew her capable of holding her own with them all when it came to it.

They would probably have to wait till reaching England before they married, and she would thus be unable to travel in a Company ship. No British country ship would carry her either, but in a continental ship, Spanish or Dutch, there would be fewer objections, and he knew the masters of many such ships, men who had often been his guests at Hospital Street.

Then war came—the War of the French Revolution—and the number of continental ships coming to China fell sharply, the few that came being classed as hostile. Thomas was undeterred. War would not last for ever. In due course he would be able to arrange matters. Martha would come to England, live in the beautiful riverside house at Twickenham, enjoy beneath the willows of England the wealth of a career in China.

But of all this he said nothing, intending to leave things as they were until she should be faced with the imminence of his departure, and see with her own eyes that he meant what he said. To leave her in Macao would be unendurable.

In April 1793, two vacanies having occurred simultaneously, George Cuming and Thomas van Mierop were promoted to membership of the Select Committee, Cuming as second member, Thomas as the third.

'I accept what has come to me this day,' Thomas wrote in his journal, 'with pride but without joy. Casting my thoughts back, it seems as if these years have been only as a dressing of the scene. Now is the piece itself. We are in our places, and the curtains will part, and I gaze at that self-appointed adversary who, he also, is in his place. Already we feel the heat of the candles. It will begin.'

Hitherto their respective duties had kept the two men reasonably far apart. At Canton entire weeks could go by without their being required to do more than greet each other before supper, while at Macao they often saw each other no more than once or twice in six months. Membership of the Select Committee demanded an entirely different pattern, daily discussions, frequent confrontations, and—a new ritual—supper at the President's house, just the three of them.

The President's house was an official residence acquired by the East India Company after nine years of negotiation with the Portuguese. Situated on high ground just within the old city wall, it was an attractive mansion of classical design standing in a garden large enough to be lost in, and which gave the place its name among the English—the Casa Garden. Ramsay's portrait of the King had been moved from the Company house to the Casa Garden dining room, and beneath its pallid smile and silver wig the Select Committee, seated at one end of a long and otherwise empty table, took supper in an atmosphere suggestive of the reluctance with which one begins a meal to which the invited guests have failed to come.

The President was Henry Browne, a heavily built man of military appearance, with a bushy black moustache and ferocious eyes, a bold exterior behind which crouched rather a timid soul, slow at evaluating situations and dreadful of facing serious issues. The cross-currents between the three men typified the complexities which the changing times had introduced. Browne and Cuming were united against Thomas in being opium men, while Thomas and Henry Browne were united against Cuming in being men of the old dispensation. Somewhere in the Casa Garden there was a pensioner and children.

In August 1793 Thomas refers to one of these dinners in his journal, in the same entry giving an unconscious revelation of how his daily confrontations with Cuming were beginning to wear him down.

'We are tight in this place, but not snug,' he wrote. 'We fire at each other with quips each containing a little gall, until our repartee is exhausted. After this our combined pipesmoke darkens the saloon. We puff because then we need not speak. We suffocate. How willingly would I forego the dignities of this office in exchange for those former days that now seem so free! Stayed away from supper for ten days last month, though it is not wise to do so. Mr. C. will be up to his machinations if he is not kept under surveillance. But a strange weariness has come over me this summer. It is probably the weather, which has been unusually heavy. In truth I should expose the man and have done with him; is this not what is needed to restore my humour? Why die a little every day when there is a remedy at hand?'

At about midnight after one such supper towards the end of the off-season Thomas returned to his house to find that apart from the two little nightlights on the staircase wall the place was in darkness. On the rare occasions when Martha retired before him a light was left burning in the living room. Such was the meticulousness with which his every requirement was attended to, the absence of a light assumed significance.

Mounting the stairs, he found in the darkened living room that the heavy red brocade curtains had been drawn across the windows. It was the first week in October, and still very warm, far too warm to have curtains drawn. The atmosphere in the room was airless and heavy. Groping into the gloom he found a lamp. The globe was still warm. From the inner rooms there was neither light nor sound.

Finding a taper, he lit it from one of the nightlights, and had just re-lit the lamp when a sound behind him made him turn. Wearing a billowing white night-dress, her fine black hair falling about her shoulders, Martha was standing before one of the windows, everything about her expressing in silence an extreme agitation. A slight movement of the curtain behind her showed that she had been concealed in the window recess between the curtains and the shutters.

She had been behaving strangely ever since he came down from Canton. At first he had attributed it to difficulties with her trade. Due to the war and to an unusual number of typhoons, it had been a bad year, and more or less everyone was affected. He seldom questioned her about her trade. In that her continued interest in it was an expression of her unwillingness to believe in his intention to marry her and bring her to England, it was a subject he did not care to discuss. But one way and another he knew a certain amount about it, mainly from the occasions when the godown had to be opened for her, when from her movements of silver—outward in years of good investment, inward in bad years to lie unused beneath the house—he could assess how she was doing. Occasionally she would offer an explanation of some unusual increase or disbursement, and would sometimes ask his advice, particularly about wines. Apart from this, her trade was a subject which she too avoided with him, knowing as she did that in his heart he regarded it with resentment. In fact, from the day he first came to know of it, her trade had lain between them, an irremovable obstacle to a complete understanding, yet equally a perpetual reminder of the reality, that in the end he would go, and she would have to fend for herself.

In any case, so far as he was concerned her trade was small fry when compared with his own private trade (as the serried ranks of sycee chests in the godown demonstrated), and he knew about it all he felt he needed to know, namely, that it was, as she had said, legitimate and honest trade, and —equally important from his point of view—that she was not engaged in the opium business. This he knew without even having to inquire of her. Being prohibited by the Chinese authorities, opium was subject to more severe price fluctuations than any other commodity on the market. Martha's movements of silver to and from the godown bore no relation to the ups and downs of the opium price (posted up daily in all commercial premises), and thus Thomas could be certain—and to his satisfaction—that she was not in it. She was also well aware of his own views on the subject, and so far as he knew, she agreed with him.

But as the weeks of summer passed he had decided that the strangeness of her behaviour could not be attributed to the year's trade reverses. There was no sign of her being in financial difficulties, and he gradually concluded that her moods—she seemed constantly nervous and was easily irritable—were being caused by something else, something stemming from that Macao life of hers in which he had no part, from which he would willingly have separated her if he could, and which was another thing about her which he had come to resent.

In fact, as the journal shows, Thomas himself was by no means in his usual easy-going frame of mind. He was on edge—almost certainly due to his daily confrontations with George Cuming—and there are several journal entries which are critical and sometimes frankly unjust.

'It is true I detest all that part of Macao which is Portuguese,' he writes around this time, 'with its feasts and processions, its pride, superstition and ignorance, its priests, prostitutes and borrowing idlers, its climate of sanctity and decadence. All that pleases me here is this house.'

This year that world—her world—had inexplicably begun to impinge on the life of the house, eating into his closely guarded privacy. As he saw her pale and distraught before the dark red curtain he felt as if his domain had been invaded—as perhaps indeed it had been. Was there someone else, he wondered, concealed behind that curtain?

"You were in another room," he said.

"Yes," she lied.

"We have received a despatch at last. The ships will soon

be here." Because of the war, ships were obliged to sail in convoy, with consequent delays. It was the main reason for the Company being still in Macao so late in the year.

She had come away somewhat from the curtain. Continuing to speak of everyday matters, he moved by slow steps towards it, seeing which she came swiftly to a space between a table and an armchair, obstructing his further approach.

"In any case," he went on, ignoring her move and turning away, "it means that in a day or so we should be leaving for Canton."

"Oh, no!" she gasped in distress. "I hoped this year you would remain."

Her distress was genuine. All through the summer she had been alluding with dread to his departure. She had never done so before. His eyes were fixed on the curtain. It was completely still. What lay behind it was evidently an object, not a person.

"Does it so trouble you that I should go? This year's season will be short."

She came slowly to the fireplace.

"Once, long ago," she said, "you told me you wanted to marry me. Do you remember?"

It was the breaking of seven years of silence.

"Yes, of course I do."

In fact, the question had been much on his mind that very evening. At supper George Cuming, having his own way of it, had been subtly needling him and the President in an endeavour to find out if either of them had any matrimonial intentions. It was done with extreme indirectness, but it indicated, as Thomas perceived with some anxiety, that Cuming had got wind of something—by instinct perhaps, since it was a subject that could be mentioned to no one—and it had served as a warning to Thomas of the depth into which it behoved him to conceal his personal intentions. Cuming was playing for President, and for the victory of the new society.

"I gave a foolish answer," she said. "I did not understand about marriage. You were angry with me."

"Was I? I've forgotten."

At the fireplace he saw two of her, her face as it was, and its reversal in the mirror.

"Could we be married now?" she asked in a low voice.

"Now?" He frowned.

"Now," she repeated urgently. "As soon as possible."

"I would be dismissed."

"Does it matter?" she asked with a gesture of anxiety. "You said last year you had enough to retire with."

"True, but I would not wish to return home a dismissed officer. I would no longer qualify for a cabin. I might not even find a ship prepared to take me."

"Why should the Company ever know we were married?" she asked, coming to him ardently. "We could be married in secret."

"How would that be possible?"

She uttered a little sigh of impatience.

"You don't know, Tom! Macao is full of stories of secret marriages."

"You misunderstand me, beloved. Who would marry us?"

"I know someone who would, and no one would ever know," she said, her eyes sparkling. "Moreover he is powerful. He would protect our secret."

He took her in his arms.

"Do you remember my telling you once that in Europe there were different kinds of Christians who went to different kinds of churches? If you and I were in Europe we would worship in different churches."

She drew back from him incomprehendingly.

"But what difference can there be in that? We are neither of us pagans, like the Chinese."

"No, but a minister—a priest—of my kind of church is the only one who can perform my marriage, and there is no such minister here, nor is there ever likely to be. Even if there were, the priests of your church would say that a marriage performed by a minister of my church was not a true marriage."

Her alert eagerness was replaced by a blank stare. Freeing herself, she moved away.

"So you have changed your mind. I said you would."

"I have not changed in the least, Martha," said he firmly. "As soon as it is possible it must be as you say. But it cannot be in these present circumstances. First we must have the Company change its marriage rule."

"Then why do you not have them change it? You are powerful. You could do it."

"Not powerful enough. We are pitted against a hundred years of convention."

She looked at him steadily.

"So you will not marry me, will you? You could be honest and say so."

Knowing the value of outward unconcern, he sat down, reached for the tobacco jar, and filled a pipe.

"Last year," he said quietly, "Mr. Browne was third member of the Committee. This year he is President. Has it not occurred to you that the same thing could happen again? Mr. Cuming is a year my senior, and might well be retired before me. With good fortune I might then have a year or two as President. If that day came we could have the marriage rule changed."

But by this time she was in tears, and when he observed this she stamped her foot and turned her back on him, her shoulders shaking with sobs.

"If you loved me you would change it now! Why must it always be wait and wait?"

But it had never been a question of wait and wait. Her words were completely unreasonable, and it showed him the depth of her unexplained mental disarray. Cloaking his own anxiety about her, he replied:

"Because if I were to say a word about it now, the only result would be an adverse one. I assure you that on this particular subject, only if I am President can I speak and be listened to. Will you not be patient and trust me?"

But it was useless. She burst out tempestuously:

"With you English it is always promises and telling people to be patient! I've had enough of it! I can't endure it any more!"

In the depth of the house a bell rang. With an exclamation of terror she fled into his bedroom, her night-dress billowing out behind her. Surprised, he rose and followed her as far as the door to the inner rooms. She had flung herself on the bed and was sobbing uncontrolledly into the pillows. On the stairs he heard the padded footsteps of a servant. Reluctantly he returned to the living room.

A foreigner below wished to see him, the servant said. It was a decidedly unusual hour for social calls. Thomas went to the head of the stairs.

In the gloom of the hall stood a young man attired in the customary evening black. The Company had so enlarged that it was no longer possible to know each officer personally, and this was one whom Thomas knew only vaguely. A junior surgeon named Duncan, of two years' standing on the coast, he was a rough-hewn, red-headed Scot reputed more adroit in commerce than in surgery, and he was one of Cuming's men. With evident marks of anxiety, and begging forgiveness for the lateness of the hour, he asked in a gentle Scottish brogue if he might have a word on a matter of some urgency.

With misgivings Thomas invited him up, and was relieved to note, on re-entering the living room with the surgeon, that from the bedroom the sound of sobbing had ceased.

Declining port but accepting a glass of water which he drank with avidity, Surgeon Duncan unfolded a tale of woe. With shame, he said, he had to confide in Mr. Mierop that he had heavy gambling debts owing to a group who had now rounded on him, threatening that unless he paid up by noon next day they would bring the matter to the attention of the Select Committee. Knowing that such a step might well lead to his dismissal, the surgeon had come to Mr. Mierop to plead in advance a little more time in which to discharge his obligations.

Yet why, Thomas thought, should Duncan choose the middle of the night?

The case was unusual, however, and in the course of its narration Thomas uttered a syllable or two of sympathy. The surgeon's rustic features, Thomas concluded a moment later, should have warned him that the man had a peasant's capacity for insinuating himself. Having sturdily established that Mr. Mierop and he were two honest men in a world of duplicity, Duncan admitted that in fact there was a means by which he could pay his debts immediately, if Mr. Mierop would be good enough to help him. He had a valuable cargo aboard a country ship, the *Clarissa*, already on her way from India, but which by no conceivable chance could arrive by noon next day. If Mr. Mierop would consider underwriting this cargo, Duncan's problems would be at an end.

"The *Clarissa*?" Thomas asked. "Who are the agents?"

"Dadabhoy, Rustomjee and Watts, sir, of Bombay."

Thomas nodded. The Macao agent for this firm was Abraham Biddle.

"Then I take it your cargo consists mainly of opium."

"There may be some small quantity of opium in it, sir."

"Opium is a light commodity, Mr. Duncan. Quantity is less significant than value. Why did you not ask Mr. Cuming to help you?"

"In truth, sir, it was Mr. Cuming who advised me to consult you, knowing as he does your great generosity."

It was too blatant to be a lie. Cuming was up to one of his tricks again, it seemed, using the young surgeon as a tool; and as he detected this Thomas recalled how at the end of supper that evening Cuming had asked for a private word with the President, and the two had withdrawn to Henry Browne's study. What could be more likely, Thomas asked himself, than that the subject of their discussion was opium? Why else should they exclude him? Vaguely he sensed the beginning of a chain of circumstances.

He decided he must give the surgeon short shrift. The young Scot was so persistent, however, that in order to be rid of him Thomas was obliged to reveal himself more than was his wont, telling him plainly that he did not deal in opium and would in no circumstances underwrite a cargo that contained any. The surgeon, embarrassed and crest-fallen, having departed, Thomas went at once to the inner rooms.

These, to his increased disquiet, appeared to be empty. Only when he had fully entered his bedroom did he realize that she was behind him, hidden by the door. She had been listening to his conversation. Without a word to her he passed through to his dressing room, took off his coat, and loosened his neckcloth.

She came to the dressing room doorway. Her mood, he observed, had changed. Her little face composed and set, her fists clenched, she was passionately angry.

"Who is the woman you were talking about?" she asked darkly.

Unbuttoning his cuffs, he paused.

"What woman?"

"You know," she said accusingly. "You think you can cheat me, you and your English friends. You think I do not understand what you talk among yourselves. Who is she?"

"I don't know what you mean."

"Clarissa. That's a woman's name, isn't it? It's because of her you don't want to marry me."

Despite himself, he burst out laughing.

"Clarissa! My dearest child, that isn't a woman. That's a ship."

"It's a woman's name," she said firmly.

"True, but in this particular case it's the name of a ship. Many ships have women's names."

"Why?"

"I hardly know. It's a tradition, I suppose. Ships are somehow considered feminine, so people give them women's names."

"I didn't know," she said, with the implication that he was still deceiving her. "There are many things I do not know." (And indeed she did not know, for Pedro handled the shipping side of her business. The largest ships she had ever seen were the Chinese junks in the inner harbour, and these did not have names.)

She returned to the bedroom. Waiting till he knew she was in bed, he passed swiftly into the living room, ostensibly to blow out the last globe lamp. Instead, however, he traversed the full length of the room to the window in which she had been hiding, and drew back the curtain.

There was nothing behind it, just the closed white-painted wooden shutters and an empty recess. The shutter latch was unfastened. Methodically he adjusted it. With the usual preliminary whir of its insides, the gay little clock on the mantelpiece broke into the silvery tones of 'For he's a jolly good fellow', and struck one.

The following morning the bottom fell out of the opium market. The news that caused it to do so came from Canton during the night. Chinese dealers in Macao, due to the fact that Chinese woke up earlier than Europeans, managed to sell a certain amount to unsuspecting persons before the news became widespread, and Chin Fui was seen hastening early up the Ridge to warn Biddle to sell before it was too late. By nine o'clock business in the tea houses had stagnated. An hour later the value of opium was zero.

What had happened was that a Chinese trader, arrested on a charge in no way connected with opium, had lost his head in a Canton court and accused numerous high mandarins, including the Viceroy's principal private secretary (and thus by implication the Viceroy himself), of fattening themselves on the illegal trade. To the consternation of the Canton government, the arrested man turned out to be that all-important person euphemistically referred to in Chinese as the water-bearer, the agent through whom the mandarins received their opium squeeze from the foreigners. The Viceroy's face being involved, the sole recourse was a demonstration of virtue. Two Chinese suspected of opium smuggling had been arrested and sentenced to death in Canton, all foreign ships arriving at Whampoa were being ruthlessly searched, their entire cargoes being seized in the case of any found carrying opium. In the phraseology of the mandarins, a 'great threatening' was in progress.

At eleven o'clock the Select Committee met in emergency session. The chain of circumstances apprehended by Thomas the night before had manifested itself. Cuming had clearly received an advance warning from Canton, though how he had had the effrontery to send Duncan round was difficult to imagine. Possibly Duncan had irritated him in some way. One could never tell precisely what Cuming was up to. One simply had to watch him.

At present he was being astringent and practical, giving no indication of personal anxiety. Cuming had aged more than Thomas, who at thirty-seven, slim, bronzed and fit, had changed little in thirteen years. Observing Cuming's greying hair, and the cold blue eyes beneath which lines of dissipation had appeared, faintly pink in colour, Thomas none the less wondered whether the somewhat sallow face was not a shade more grey than usual.

As for Henry Browne, though battling to maintain the soldierly appearance he presented, he was almost incoherent with nerves, never having been called upon to handle a crisis of such dimensions.

From the viewpoint of the East India Company it was a situation of the utmost gravity. Three country ships had had their cargoes confiscated. Two large convoys of ships, Company and country, were on their way from India, due any day. In every one of them, somewhere in the holds, was opium, from the sale of which by country traders the Company would normally purchase the year's tea. Against these now valueless cargoes the Company had issued to country traders bills of credit, in expectation of being paid in silver gained in their private opium sales. As things stood, not only would there be no silver, and thus no tea, but due to the China fashion practice of treating opium consignment notes as if they were currency the Company was down on credit bills alone to the tune of three hundred thousand silver dollars.* Unless the situation eased, this dual deficit in tea and silver would have to be explained to the Court of Directors, and it was hard to see how this could be done without touching on the deadly question of the consignment notes.

There was furthermore another complication. Before entering the Committee room Thomas had checked up on outstanding bills and discovered that five-sixths of them stood in the name of the sons of the late João Gonçalves Sequeira, in other words Biddle. Had the bills been more evenly distributed among the traders there would have been a likelihood, by bringing pressure to bear on them, of recouping at least something sizeable in silver. As it was, everything depended on Biddle, and rich as he was—there were rumours of his floating a vast new enterprise in Brazil—it was unlikely that he would be able to lay his hands on silver amounting to more than a fraction of that with which he was credited.

Finally there was the question of the degree of Cuming's involvement. As a Company officer, and personalities apart, Thomas had concluded that there was only one possible course of action open to the Committee, and that it must be taken immediately. It might ruin Biddle. Would it also ruin Cuming? As Henry Browne hummed and hawed, and Cuming made a crisp comment now and then, both of them evading mention of the crucial measure, Thomas continued to hold it up his sleeve, wondering uneasily to what extent, if he introduced it, it would wear the guise of a declaration of outright war.

Cuming was for doing nothing. It was the old cry of the opium men. There were frequent petty crises over opium,

* In today's money, about US$8,000,000.

167

and almost anything could spark them off. Cuming, whose attitude to the Chinese was one of tolerant amusement, regarded the great threatening as of no more importance than these earlier crises. Sit tight and let the storm blow over, was his final advice to Henry Browne; opium storms always did blow over.

"Not so easily, I fear, where the Viceroy's face is involved," Thomas put in. Loss of face in China demanded retribution as perhaps nothing else did to quite the same extent.

The President, who had been tugging at his moustaches in the hope that perhaps Cuming was right, gave way to a burst of emotion.

"Sit tight?" he cried in a kind of anguish, covering his face with two hairy hands. "Mr. Cuming, I confess I do not understand your reasoning."

"Mr. Cuming's suggestion," said Thomas, "is that after a week or so the Canton government will consider it has done sufficient, and conditions will return to normal."

"Quite so," added Cuming, deferring to his colleague's assistance.

"By which time every merchant owing us money will be bankrupt!" Browne exclaimed angrily. "Frankly that is no solution at all."

Whenever an issue of any gravity came up, this was how it went. Despite the enmity that separated them, the two junior members were obliged to combine in order to cradle the President along. Thomas had for some time been noticing Cuming's increasing impatience with Henry Browne's indecisiveness. It almost seemed to Thomas as if Cuming was for once in sympathy with him. From the first day he had known him there had always been sympathy there somewhere, a streak in Cuming's nature which yearned for companionship but had not the gift of inspiring it.

Thomas spoke.

"Then I propose that we have no alternative but to take immediately such steps as may be feasible to effect restitution of the moneys we have advanced." Addressing the President, he was intent on Cuming's reactions.

"How can we do it?" the President asked hopelessly.

"Perhaps Mr. Cuming would agree with me," Thomas pursued, not taking his eyes off him, "that a first step might be the summary recall of all outstanding bills of credit, to whomsoever issued, or cash payment in lieu within forty-eight hours."

The President shook his head despairingly.

"Mr. Mierop, I cannot believe my ears," he muttered.

Thomas affected to take no notice.

"Would you agree, Mr. Cuming?" he inquired.

"I see no alternative," Cuming replied. To Thomas' intense interest he had not batted an eyelid.

"Gentlemen," Henry Browne implored, looking mournfully from one to the other, "are you totally insensible of the Company's name?"

Thomas hazarded a glance at Cuming who, meeting his gaze, shrugged his shoulders equanimously.

"Name be damned," Thomas answered quietly, with this encouragement, "if you'll forgive the expression. We trade in China by monopoly, and can afford to be autocratic. Short of taking this action I can see no way in which we can report to the Directors."

Henry Browne leaned forward, his elbows on the table, like a man undone with the burden of his responsibility.

"Mr. Cuming," he said in a broken voice, "do I understand you to say you support this?"

"Yes, sir," Cuming answered curtly. "Entirely."

In his expression Thomas could read nothing. Either Cuming, like himself, had nothing to lose, or, as so often demonstrated at the Canton charades, he was a talented actor.

Abraham Biddle, true opium merchant that he was, was unconcerned by the events of the early morning. When Chin Fui, for years his Chinese intermediary and right-hand man, came to warn him, Biddle chided him for running up the hill so fast at his age. Opium storms blew over. Besides—and with more than twenty years to prove it—nothing could upset the perfected financial arrangements of the indispensable purveyor.

Early in the afternoon, however, he received at his house a demand note from the East India Company accompanied by a notice, the wording of which gave him what he called a nasty twinge. To be more closely in touch with events he put on a surcoat and descended to Sequeira's.

In the city, among the commercial community—country trade Europeans, Armenians, Parsis, Portuguese and Chinese —there was panic. Accosted in the streets by anxious investors, Biddle reached Sequeira's to find more demand notes awaiting him, and more being delivered every few minutes, relating to bills of credit already drawn in Calcutta and Rio de Janeiro. It was unprecedented, inconceivable.

"I don't believe it," he muttered as Pedro, who had nothing to do with opium himself, glanced at the notes on the desk.

"Don't tell me John Company's going bankrupt," Pedro said.

"No," Biddle answered uneasily, "not John Company. Bring me pen and paper."

In haste he addressed a note to George Cuming and despatched it by runner. While he waited, more demand notes were delivered. The reply, when it came, was scribbled on the back of Biddle's message. The old man unfolded it, read it at a glance, folded it again. His face turned ashen grey.

"If any more o' these come, send 'em to the 'ouse," he said, and walked gravely out of the shop.

As evening approached, the aviary was a mass of singing, trilling, piping and chattering, its sweet, strident music filling his garden with sound, eliminating all else.

He did not hear it. Having drawn a wicker chair out among the flowers, he sat in the abasing sunlight and stared sometimes at the blue sky, sometimes at the decaying plaster of the garden wall. In his hand, cold in an evening breeze presaging winter, he still held the message, and from time to time would read it again: MANAGE YOUR OWN AFFAIRS. I WILL MANAGE MINE. And lower down, as if in afterthought: IF YOU TELL YOUR STORY, DO YOU THINK ANYONE WILL BELIEVE YOU?

By the time the shadow of the house reached the top of the garden wall Abraham Biddle owed the Honourable East India Company just over a quarter of a million dollars.* His normally ruddy face strangely lifeless in the waning light, the perpetual sneer about his lips lengthening and narrowing into an expression of dignity, he thought of his early days on the coast. He had met with many reverses. He knew the risks. He had always known the risks lying daily between him and his mansion in Calcutta. Was it possible that he, with his unique knowledge, could be caught—on the threshold of his great Brazilian venture, within an inch of incalculable riches—at the end of his resources? There was no chance of making any gambler's last throw. And from Macao there was no escape.

Above the garden wall the sky, though tinged with faint shreds of evening mist, and though the sun had sunk away, remained as throughout the day—blue, without a cloud, an inexorable blue—and the birds sang as if to burst.

As the Company's demand notes were despatched throughout the city, panic gave way to despair. Even the humblest families were affected, for far more than met the eye depended on opium. That night Macao was a city of financial ruin.

At the same time rumours of the direst kind were circulating. Chinese military forces were said to be gathering prior to investing Macao, seizing every foreign house, and imprisoning anyone found in possession of opium. All trade came to a standstill. A number of people, frightened of more

* In today's money, about US$6,700,000.

noticeable methods of disposal, were burying opium in their gardens.

Late on the second day of the crisis it was reported that Abraham Biddle was no longer at his house. Through the Company halls the news reverberated like cannonshot. Biddle had absconded! He would easily be found, of course, men said, and he must have assets which could be seized. But the fact was, the Committee would be obliged to report to Calcutta and London a serious financial loss, the fat would be in the fire about the opium consignment notes, and so too concerning the depth of involvement of Company officers in the opium trade.

In the conduct of the Company's affairs George Cuming from this moment perceptibly shrank in stature, leaving all decisions to Thomas, while Henry Browne, overcome by events, retired to the Casa Garden, whence he hardly stirred.

"I rely on your judgement, Mr. Mierop," he said distractedly. "Do what you think is right. And if anyone is required to go to Canton to negotiate a settlement, it must be you. You are the only one among us who has clean hands in this matter."

In effect, Thomas van Mierop had assumed charge of the Honourable Company's affairs in China; and every time he entered the great Company house he perceived from the deferential reactions his presence occasioned that this was a reality understood by every Englishman on the China station. What was also understood, and by many with concern, was that once report was sent to Calcutta it was only a matter of wind and sail before Henry Browne and George Cuming were summoned to London to give an account of their stewardship to the Court of Directors, leaving an anti-opium man as President of the Select Committee, a situation which for many might prove to be an uncomfortable new experience.

The immediate difficulty was the disappearance of Biddle. It was manifestly absurd for the China station to have to report that in a place as small as Macao they had allowed their principal debtor to slip through their fingers and vanish. Yet Macao had been scoured from end to end in a search for Biddle, concerning whose whereabouts not even the remotest clue had been obtained.

For years now Thomas had dreamed of becoming President, not for ambition's sake so much as for his own special personal reason. But as the vista cleared before him, and appointment as President became distinct and foreseeable, it brought him no elation. Over the past few days Martha's moods and behaviour had become more and more unaccountable. Every time he left the house she seemed to regard it as a desertion. She plainly resented his being so occupied at the Company house, while on his side he resented what he interpreted as evidence of the increasing encroachment of her Macao life into his home. The house in Hospital Street, in fact, had become a house of resentments.

From experience he knew that to question her directly would only make matters worse. Somehow, by observation and deduction, he had to arrive at the cause of the trouble. Again and again he revolved in his mind each incomprehensible domestic incident. On the fourth day of the trade standstill, alone in his office for a moment, he was rehearsing once more the events of the night of Surgeon Duncan's visit. He reached the instant of drawing back the curtain, staring at the white-painted shutters, the empty recess . . . and suddenly a new facet was illuminated. The shutter latch was not fastened. He had himself closed it. A missing element clicked into place. She had not been concealing anything behind the curtain. She had been looking at something through the half open shutter, something observable from that particular window, something which had perhaps recently altered, something she was certainly afraid of.

Leaving the Company house at the earliest moment, he returned to Hospital Street. It was a warm, sunny October afternoon, and as he approached the house he noticed that the shutters of the upper windows were closed. During the past week one of her inexplicable attitudes was to shut windows and draw curtains when it was completely unnecessary. Irritatedly, on reaching the living room, which was dark and stifling, he swung the shutters open and looked out at the street.

Nothing had changed. For thirteen years nothing had changed except, occasionally, the paint. The gentle spies, to whose insatiable curiosity he had long been accustomed, were as usual at the window opposite. These particular ones he had not noticed before. An elderly mother and spinster daughter probably—there had never to his knowledge been a man in that house—the older woman had white hair. Seeing herself repaid in her own coin, she hastily withdrew from sight. Beneath her left eye was a white scar.

He was alerted by a movement behind him. Martha had entered from the rocktop garden. She had been there without his noticing. She was wearing a full-length, high-waisted dress of maroon-coloured Chinese silk, extravagant for the afternoon, with a jabot of pina elegantly embroidered. As so often during the past week, she simply came in and stood there silent; and not for the first time he found it oppressive.

"Bid them bring hot water," he said, going to the inner rooms.

Moments later, passing through to his bathroom, he observed she had again closed the shutters.

Without comment he entered the bathroom, and with his back to the door removed his undershirt while the hot water bearer filled the various receptacles. There was a definite procedure about this, and when the servant withdrew, Thomas without hesitation swung round and plunged his hands into what was normally a basin of tepid water. He let out a yell. The water was scalding hot. Bounding angrily to the door he flung it open and saw outside a boy whom he took to be about twelve years old staring at him in terror.

Rather dark for a Chinese, he was tall for his age and good-looking in a strangely European way. His soft wavy hair, narrow face, and grey-brown eyes plainly indicated a mixed parentage.

Thomas' expression darkened. He had trusted Martha. It was trust that had never had a more disquieting jolt than at the sight of the boy's features.

"Martha!" he called irritably, trying to steady his voice. "Who is this little fool?"

But in her response there was no guilt. She simply passed a hand across her brow in a gesture of fatigue, in itself an extraordinary reaction for her.

"I'm sorry. I forgot to warn you. I engaged him this afternoon."

"Well, for heaven's sake, train him. What's his name, anyway?"

She faltered.

"I quite forgot to ask. What's your name?" she asked the boy in Cantonese.

The boy looked at her warily.

"You mean my Chinese name?" he asked.

"Yes. Whatever name you use."

"Kwan Po," he said, then changing his language, "But I speak English, you know; and you," he added with a pertinent look ranging between the two of them, "may call me Ignatius, if you wish."

Thomas scowled at him.

"You're a Roman Catholic."

The boy blinked.

"I don't understand you, sir."

"You go to church."

"Yes, sir."

"You're Portuguese."

"No, sir. I'm Chinese."

With a mutter of impatience Thomas returned to the bathroom.

"He's the grandson of Ah Sum, our old Number One," Martha explained hastily.

"I don't care who his grandfather is. If you must keep him, teach him."

And Thomas slammed the door on her.

In fact, in the following minutes he was thankful to be able to sluice water over himself, for he had seldom in his life been so hot with anger and suspicion.

It was suspicion that had communicated itself. There was prolonged rapping on the bathroom door.

"Tom! Listen to me!"

He replied by sluicing more water over himself.

"Tom! I saw this boy for the first time this afternoon. Do you hear what I say?" He was scrubbing himself and made no answer. "If only you took more interest in my life while you are away, you would understand things better." That, he thought, was about the last straw, to blame *him* for thirteen years of forbearance! Had she never thought what her life would have been like if he had given way to the suspicion which six months' absence every year inescapably engendered, if he had interrogated her, spied on her, forced her to explain all her actions when she was apart from him? He rinsed his body in a long and noisy gush of water. "You do not ask questions about me," she went on, "because you do not wish to hear the answers. But about this boy, whether you question me or not I shall tell you the answers, whether you like them or not. Will you please open the door a little."

The agitation in her voice made him pause. He opened the door an inch.

"You remember Ah Sum, our first Number One?"

"Of course."

"He had a daughter, Fong. I don't think you ever saw her. Fong is this boy's mother."

"I suppose you will tell me next his father was Chinese."

"Nobody knows who his father was."

"How singularly convenient! Why do you not despatch him back where he came from?"

"We cannot now that Senhor Biddle is not coming back."

Clad only in a towel, Thomas swung the door full open. "What was that you said?" he demanded.

"Senhor Biddle? Fong was his amah. I obtained the post for her."

The detested Macao world seemed to envelop him.

"How do you know he's not coming back?"

"He said so this morning."

"He said so? Where is he?"

"I have no idea. He sent a message."

"Where from?"

"I don't know. An unknown man brought it. It was in Chinese writing. It said, DO NOT EXPECT ME TO COME BACK. That, and a silver dollar. Fong was in that house with no other money and no food. To help her I took in the boy."

"Very charitable, I'm sure," he said, walking through to his dressing room where fresh clothes were laid out. "So Biddle is somewhere in Macao?"

"I think so."

"Are you seriously telling me that he can just disappear without anyone knowing where he is?"

"If he wants to, yes—from foreigners, I mean. No foreigner would ever find him."

"But you, I suppose, could," he said with sarcasm.

"If I tried," she replied calmly.

"We shall use our own methods to find him, thank you." She was at the dressing room door.

"And about the boy—you believe me . . . Tom!" There was a note of alarm in her voice. "Tom!" she cried out. "Look at me!"

He looked.

"Yes, I believe you," he said in a dry way.

But for the life of him he was not sure whether he did.

For two more weeks the great threatening continued. Each day anxious people mounted the hills of Monte and Guia, scanning the approaches by land and water for signs of the reported Chinese besieging force. By the first week of November, when not a single soldier or war junk had been sighted, it became apparent that the Viceroy did not propose a military seizure of Macao.

It remained to be decided what should be done about the debts owing to the Company, in particular the staggering debt of Abraham Biddle, of whom even after three weeks and exhaustive inquiries, not a whisper of information had been received.

For Martha had told Thomas the truth about Macao. With its different linguistic and racial communities, each almost watertight from its neighbours, despite daily commingling in the market, along the wharves, and in the houses of international commerce, Macao was peculiarly suited to acts and movements of secrecy. A man need only have connexions with two of the watertight compartments to enable him to pass from one to the other, leaving the first in total ignorance of his whereabouts. A man like Abraham Biddle, whose contacts overlapped many of the compartments, could if he put his mind to it live or die in secrecy, as he pleased.

Finally accepting this extraordinary fact, Thomas prevailed upon Henry Browne and George Cuming to attend a meeting, with the Superintendents of Exports and Imports and three other senior supercargoes, with the aim of deciding what action was to be taken.

It was a disbalanced gathering. His downfall already as good as sealed, Henry Browne was at his most indecisive, while Cuming, whose behaviour continued to leave Thomas mystified, remained silent, though still showing no actual sign of discomfiture. From the outset attention thus focused on Thomas.

After explaining the financial position he turned to the legal aspect of the affair. It was to be assumed, he said, that Biddle was bankrupt. Had this been London or Calcutta everyone at the table would know well enough what to do about that. In Macao the situation was more complicated.

"The Court of Directors will, I think," he said, "expect us to take the action normal in the case of bankruptcies. The question is, under whose laws relating to bankruptcy are we to proceed? Manifestly, I suggest, we cannot turn to the Chinese. In the first place, so far as we know, they have no bankruptcy laws. In the second place, the precise extent of their legal powers in Macao is not known. We cannot turn to the Portuguese, because to do so would oblige the Governor of Macao to recognize the fact that we are established here as a company, contrary to the laws of Portugal.

"I thus put it to you, Mr. President, that we have no alternative but to proceed without too much regard for legal niceties. I suggest we post some of our men as bailiffs in Biddle's various properties, proceeding, in other words, somewhat under our own laws. Biddle must have interests in Calcutta, where our laws apply, and after a few months we should be able to lay hands on some of what is owing to us. Meanwhile we shall have to take the usual proceedings against Biddle, *in absentia*, as we would if this were Calcutta."

As he spoke he noticed George Cuming twisting in his chair with suppressed impatience, wearing that warning look of affected weariness. Manneredly Cuming addressed himself to Henry Browne.

"This is not, Mr. President, a matter of legal niceties, as Mr. Mierop would seem to suggest, but one of inescapable facts concerning property and rights. It is indefensible to suggest that we have any right summarily to invest the home and premises of Mr. Biddle, for the single and, I think you will agree, the overriding reason that Mr. Biddle's business transactions are conducted in the name of a Portuguese company. The least attempt to interfere with this company will be interpreted by the Portuguese as an infringement of their rights in Macao, and the greatest possible unpleasantness will ensue, which is the one thing we must avoid. I would have thought, too," he continued with a lilt of sarcasm, "that in respect of this particular company Mr. Mierop would have been one of the first to wish to avoid any such hasty and ill-conceived action as he now proposes."

Thomas was suddenly aware that everyone in the room was looking at him, as though waiting for him to answer something.

"I do not follow you, Mr. Cuming," he said.

"Come now," Cuming pursued mockingly, "this is surely no time for such elementary subterfuges."

"I confess I do not follow your meaning, sir," Thomas answered, his temper rising.

The President intervened uncertainly.

"If what you are saying is in the nature of an insinuation of some kind, Mr. Cuming, I should like to suggest that this is not the time for that either. Now, looking again at the legal aspects—"

Hot with shock and embarrassment, Thomas scarcely noticed what happened after this. Satisfied that Martha was not in opium, he had never troubled to inquire through which firm she traded. When the meeting terminated, without Henry Browne reaching a decision, he was the first away. At the door of the Company house he swung himself into his waiting chair.

"Drive me to Sequeira's," he ordered.

The place had not altered much since his first days on the coast. In the outer office the same down-at-heel Portuguese clerks—different ones doubtless, but looking the same —pondered in a depressed way over documents they did not seem to understand, laid on desks so placed that no light fell about them. Familiar now with the magnificence of Chinese residences in Canton, Thomas was no longer impressed by the ornate Chinese seats and carved 'horsebox' doors, nor even by the indoor flowering plants, all of which had formerly pleased his eye, but which now seemed plebeian. This time what he noted was the Portuguese atmosphere, the typical orange tiles of Macao, the partly European construction of the building, the dark stained wood, the air of gentle propriety and cleanliness, designating a house of activities not over-ambitious, but with long years behind them and many more ahead, a place unruffled by time.

He asked for the head of the firm.

Did he mean the Senator?

The appellation puzzled him. Was it a Senator who was head of the firm? He wished to see whomever handled—he hesitated—the interests of a woman called Martha.

There was a noticeable tremor throughout the office. Oh! Senhora Marta da Silva! Yes, that would be the Senator.

Disconcerted, incensed even, to learn that in fact Martha had a surname and had never told him, he gave his name, and a moment later was ushered into the first of the inner offices where he had once sat uncomfortably with Biddle.

The young man who rose to shake hands with him was shorter than himself, attired in English clothes of dandyish cut. Despite certain Asiatic characteristics—an even complexion, an almost beardless chin—he was undeniably handsome in the European sense. His wavy black hair was in some disorder, making him look more like a romantic poet than a trader, and there was in the placid, widely spaced eyes evidence of a certain wildness of mood, the cause of which Thomas did not at once detect.

"I have come to make some inquiries," he began, "about the trade of Miss Martha—da Silva, is it?"

"Ah, you mean my remarkable cousin!" the Senator sighed.

"Your cousin?" Thomas muttered in surprise.

"Not in the English sense, perhaps. Our relations stretch further than yours, Mr. Mierop. Will you take a glass of wine?"

He reached out for the carafe of vinho tinto which Thomas had not observed on the desk, but which now explained a good deal.

"Alberto! Another glass!" Pedro called over the partition.

Thomas declined the wine, but the Senator paid no attention, shakily filling another glass.

"I was given to understand Martha da Silva was an orphan," Thomas said coldly.

"True," replied the Senator with equanimity. "Cousin by adoption would be nearer it legally. But it makes no difference in our Portuguese families. From the day my aunt adopted her she was a member of our family, related to every one of us."

" 'Tis doubtless a large family."

"Like every Portuguese family—endless! You didn't know about us, it seems?"

"No, I did not."

"Well, sir, your visit is timely. If only, I have been saying to myself, someone could reason with my cousin! If only someone could persuade her to compromise! I take it you're familiar with her business affairs?"

"Slightly."

Pedro's face darkened. He cocked an eyebrow and leaned suspiciously forward.

"It wouldn't be you who advised her, would it?" he asked.

"I doubt it. What precisely are you referring to?"

"This affair between Mr. Biddle and the East India Company."

"Oh, I follow you," Thomas answered, having no idea what the Senator was driving at, but deciding to bluff his way on. "This does happen to be a matter on which I hold strong views."

"I suppose I have no right to ask you to change them."

"I doubt if you could, Mr. Sequeira."

The Senator drank half a glass of tinto in one gulp.

"You behold a ruined man, Mr. Mierop," he said, his eyes watering. "She has taken the action you advised. So be it! I am ruined." He replenished his glass. "In Christian consideration I cannot hold it against you. I only wish she would pay heed to the compromise I have suggested, and save us from what we are now faced with—closure!"

He wiped his eyes with the back of his hand and

attempted an apologetic smile for his display of emotion. A large, black, heavily armoured beetle whizzed past his face, causing him to duck out of its way, crashed into a partition and fell to the floor, its noisy buzz temporarily silenced by concussion.

"To what action on her part are you referring, Mr. Sequeira?"

Pedro gestured.

"Of course, to her withdrawal from trade."

Thomas stirred in his chair.

"When was this?" he asked, trying to conceal his amazement.

"It's beyond me. I can't remember. A week or so ago. I've lost count of the days. She called me to Hospital Street. It was the first time I'd seen her there in thirteen years."

"You mean—?"

"No, I never go to Hospital Street. She won't allow it. You knew that, I suppose."

Thomas studied the handsome face. He knew now who he was talking to. The youth with the manners of a fidalgo. It must have been for him, he thought, that Martha had unaccountably worn that elaborate costume the other afternoon.

"She talked about her reputation," Pedro went on. "I told her time and again, 'You're not trading with Mr. Biddle; you're trading with me!' She wouldn't listen."

"But how could her decision so affect your company?" Thomas inquired. "As I understand it, this is a house of agency. Miss Martha da Silva is merely one for whom you have been acting as agent."

"Strictly speaking, that is so. At least, it was so once."

"Mr. Sequeira, either it is so or it isn't. I would be grateful if you would explain the precise position."

"It isn't very precise, I fear. Nothing is. Oh dear!" he sighed, "where was I?"

"Miss da Silva's is agency business."

"To be sure! I'm with you. Well, yes, it started as agency

business. Then as time passed and the Senhora's trade expanded, more and more time was taken up by it. We all had to work very hard. It had to receive far more attention than anything else, until there was no part of the commerce conducted under our name, except that of Mr. Biddle, which could not be described as part of the commercial transactions of the Senhora." He blew his nose and wiped away a few more wine tears. "What can one say? She has a gift for commerce. She knows—even without stirring out of the house she knows—what will sell and what will not sell. I'm sure my great-grandfather's bones would rattle in their coffin if he could hear me, but it might as well be said. The Senhora *is* the house of Gonçalves Sequeira. She has been for years. Withdraw from trade! I told her, 'D'you want to starve us to death?'" He lowered his voice. "I mean nothing to you, Mr. Mierop, and I know I cannot ask for your help. But if only someone could reason with her! It's beyond me, I'm afraid," he added, tipping some more wine into his glass. "Very much beyond me."

On the tiles the fallen beetle started buzzing, while in Thomas' mind the full and frightful situation sank in. The woman in his own house, his mistress, almost his wife, *was*, and had been for years, the house of Gonçalves Sequeira, which because it lent its name to Biddle's transactions was known throughout the entire European community as the largest opium firm in China. Who among his colleagues would know, as he knew, that in fact Martha did not deal in opium? No one. Meanwhile his own actions as an anti-opium man had been clothed by Cuming's well-timed innuendo in the basest hypocrisy. Thomas van Mierop, they would say, could afford to take an anti-opium stand; his opium deals were handled by his pensioner.

"What was the compromise you had in mind?" he asked.

The Senator waved his arms in the air.

"Of course, a new company! Formed under another name and in another building, if need be. I told her, 'I'm willing to forego my father's name—can I say more than that?—

if only you'll listen to me and save us all!' She wouldn't. A long rigmarole about her baptism. She has no name, she says. I said we'd search the registers, have affidavits sworn. She's as much da Silva as I am Gonçalves. Still she wouldn't agree. 'I cannot be the head of a company if I have no name,' she said, and talked about *compromissos*. That's one of the legal words she knows. Forgive me, Mr. Mierop, but she leaves me aghast at the extraordinary muddle of what she knows and what she doesn't know. Saints in Heaven, what am I talking about?"

Thomas had risen, his manner tight and withdrawn.

"Thank you, Mr. Sequeira."

"I do most sincerely hope, sir—" the Senator mumbled, rising in confusion. "Alberto!" he called, unable to guide himself to the door. "Mr. Mierop, please accept my profound apologies!" He fell back into his chair. "Alberto!"

In a noisy rush the beetle rose into flight. Flinging open the swing doors Thomas stalked out, as with a groan of despair the Senator covered his face with a handkerchief.

Striding to the street doors, Thomas recalled from years before George Cuming's exasperated remark about the heel of Achilles. Cuming had certainly aimed his shaft perilously near it.

At the door of the premises Thomas was met by a Company runner bearing a note from the President requesting his presence for yet another meeting. He returned immediately to the Praia Grande.

In the committee room Henry Browne announced that clearance papers had been received from Canton enabling the first of the convoys waiting at Taipa to proceed up-river without restriction to Whampoa. Since it was evident from this that receipt of chops for the autumn migration was but a matter of days, arrangements were put in hand for the immediate departure of key personnel by fastboat. Despatching a runner to Hospital Street requesting Martha to put all in readiness for him to leave early the following morning, Thomas spent the rest of the evening at the Company house attending to preparations for the move. It was nearing midnight when he reached home.

There the disorder customary on such occasions prevailed. In the dressing room, where in dimly golden light the shadows of men heaved and ebbed across the ceiling, Thomas superintended the packing and closing of the final trunks. Amid comings and goings the gay little clock struck twelve in the other room, and soon afterwards a cortege of closed trunks borne by everyone available, including the chair bearers and the gardeners, swung its way out, resembling the simultaneous funeral of five or six soldiers killed in the same affray.

Bringing up the rear in the position of chief mourner, Thomas entered the living room just as Martha, holding back the curtain, flicked a lattice open and shut, enabling her to look for a second into the darkness outside.

Striding forward, setting the cortège in disorder, Thomas made for the window, flicked the latch, and flung the shutters open to the night. Again there was nothing to see, but at the sight of her silently and obstinately unchanged, the pent-up emotion of three weeks unloosed itself.

"Now," he said firmly. "Show me. What is it?"

The procession of coffin-like trunks doubled its pace, its orders and grunts replaced by excited silence.

She drew back where she could not be seen from outside. "As you see, there is nothing."

"There is something. What is it?"

"Pray close the shutters."

"Not until you tell me what it is you were looking at."

She closed the double doors behind the last of the servants.

"Very well, I will tell you. But pray close the shutters first."

He drew them in and clicked the latch.

She wandered disconsolately to the fireplace, the taffeta of her long dress rustling in the renewed quiet.

"There is really no need to tell you. It is only a small matter," she said.

Flicking the latch, with his fist he sent the shutters swinging open again. On the instant she was beside him, grabbing for the lattices. He took her by the wrists, brought her round to face him.

"Let me!" she pleaded. "Let me shut them!"

"Not before you answer my question."

"I cannot explain! It is something you would not understand."

"I will be the judge of that. Tell me what it is."

"I cannot," she said, her voice dropping as she tried to drag herself away.

She struggled with him in silence at the open window.

"I gather," he said without loosening his hold, "you are still worried about having no legal name. Would that be the reason for your sudden interest in marriage?"

"I beg you, close the shutters!" she whispered tensely. "I will tell you nothing while they are open."

"I enjoy the fresh air."

"You are making it worse for me. When you return from Canton I shall not be here."

"What d'you mean?"

He relaxed his grip. In a trice she freed herself and moved away, nursing her wrists.

"I never asked anything of you before," she said bitterly. "I have given you everything I had to give; and you have taken—always taken. Now I ask you one thing, and you refuse. This is the kind of man you are. I know it now. This is how the others were. This is how it has always been with you Englishmen in Macao."

"Must you raise that again?" he asked, himself as a cautionary measure closing the shutters. "Have I not told you I wished to marry you?"

"When it suits you. That will be too late."

"Too late for what?" he demanded. "What do you mean by saying you'll not be here when I return?"

"I don't know. I'm not sure. I meant I may not be here."

"Where will you have gone?"

"To a place from which people do not come back."

"Do not speak in riddles."

She was not looking at him, but he could see her reflected in the mirror.

"I am being watched," she said. "Everything I do is watched. I dare not go to the door. I dare not see anybody from outside. I dare not speak anything to the servants. I dare not carry on my trade. Those who hate me are watching everything—from that window."

He laughed contemptuously.

"A handful of girls and old women? What is there in that to be afraid of?"

Her face passed from the mirror.

"I said you would not understand."

"So it's true, then: you've gone out of business?" he said casually.

"Certainly not!" she retorted.

"They say you have."

"Who?"

"I heard it in town."

"It's not true! I will not have people speaking of me as if I'd failed!—I have temporarily withdrawn from trade. That is all."

"You intend to resume?"

"I would like to, but at present I cannot."

"You could, however, by forming a new company."

"No."

"A company has been discussed."

"I know nothing about it."

"They say it has, though."

"You heard that too in town?" she asked with sarcasm.

"Yes," he replied. "I met that Portuguese cousin of yours, Sequeira."

Her face changed. There was silence. She gave a little laugh meant to contain gaiety, but which lacked it.

"You must mean that silly fellow Pedro. I could never form a company with him!"

"If you were married you could. You would then have a name. I suppose the next step is that as marriage to me is for the moment out of the question, you will marry your cousin instead, and add the completing touch to your connexion with the famous opium firm."

She drew herself up, glaring at him. Her face stiff and angry, she banged her fist down on the back of a chair.

"I will not answer any more of your questions!" she shouted.

"It was not exactly a question."

"In any case, I have taken my money and my interests out of his hands."

"Naturally. You have to save what you can from the shipwreck of Biddle's bankruptcy."

"My decision has nothing whatever to do with Biddle."

"Why then?"

"The Gonçalves Sequeiras are too closely related to them."

"Them?"

"Those who are watching me."

He uttered an expression of impatience.

"This is absurd! You have nothing to be afraid of," he said, walking as it chanced towards the window.

"Don't open it!" she cried. "I beg you!" (He looked back with a frown of disbelief.) "You come from another world. You descend like a god out of the sky. You reside and move about like a god—remote, aloof, with the other gods, your friends. What do you know of us who were born here and must live here? Who are you to say what is frightening to us? It is not the gods we are afraid of. It is our own people, whom none of you know. Have you heard of a country called Timor?"

"An island, not a country—yes."

"It is a place where they send women who live with men they're not married to."

"Nonsense."

"It's true! You are clever. You have taught me so much. But there are many things—here in this very place—which you do not know. They are waiting and watching for the chance to take me out of this house—to Timor."

He sat in an armchair, clapped his hands on his knees, and laughed.

"I should like to see them try!"

"You will not see it. It will be done when you're away."

"Well," he continued with geniality, "we cannot post soldiers at the door. We don't have any. How about a posse of well-built Company chair bearers? They'll be doing nothing these next few months."

"They will be bribed when the time comes."

"Then, let me see," he said, cupping his chin in his hand. "What other form of protection can I offer?"

"I have already told you!" she cried in a tone deep with despair. "But you have refused!"

Hiding her face, she fled into the inner rooms. Within the suite his bedroom door slammed and was locked.

Three nights later, aboard the fastboat, the journal, not kept for several weeks, is resumed.

'At the Heungshan customs post today chanced to see a Chinaman of some distinction, waiting like myself at the jetty while his craft was inspected. From his eyes and manner—it is curious that such things should be unfailingly observable—I was certain he could speak a foreign language, and endeavoured to engage him in conversation. It turned out he spoke Portuguese, and we conversed through a linguist. He is secretary to the so-called Bishop of Peking, has been visiting Macao on clerical affairs. He spoke without much favour of certain measures of a moral nature, drastic in their purpose, being at present enjoined by the Bishop of Macao. What he told me has explained much that I have overlooked, or not troubled myself to be acquainted with.

'Inability to communicate with the house a grave concern.'

And this, incidentally—and it well reflects the age—is the nearest there is to an overt reference to Martha in the entire journal.

PART SIX

The Screen Folded Aside

THOMAS HAD EVERY reason for grave concern. Eleven months earlier, in January 1793, His Excellency Dom Marcelino José da Silva, Bishop of Macao, after weeks of arguing and persuading, had obtained the signature of the Governor and Captain-General on his special measures to improve the city's reputation and the morals of its inhabitants by stamping out prostitution in all its forms, utterly and for ever.

The Bishop was a thin ascetic, with a sallow skin, heavy beardline, and large, sad eyes which concealed both the fire of his reformer's zeal and the depths of tyranny to which he was prepared to sink. He had assessed his problem accurately. Macao was long accustomed to its entertainers. They were numerous and in general discreet, and the ramifications of their family relationships and *connaissances* could in a crisis be extended to embrace practically everyone in the city. It was thus almost impossible for the Bishop to obtain information about them for any punitive purpose. There were no streetwalkers, and no actual Rua de Felicidade; the Street of Happiness was a reference to a way of life, not to cartography. The world of the entertainers lay behind closed doors, requiring an introduction, an address, or a key. All the more important to the Bishop was information.

Because of the apathy of respectable people, the Bishop had concluded that it was necessary to strike terror throughout the city, and the special measures were framed accordingly. Under them the Bishop—in name, the Governor and Senate, but in fact the Bishop—and his priests were given powers to order the arrest and internment without any form of inquiry, public or private—the word of a priest was enough—of any woman suspected of being an entertainer. The place of internment was a disused stables which the Bishop had walled in, adapted for human occupation, and piously renamed the Asylum of St. Mary Magdalene. Here the unfortunate women were to be reformed and taught sewing. Any considered incapable of reform—and here again the word of a priest was enough—were to be sent without other inquiry into perpetual banishment to the penal settlement on Timor.

For the first few days nothing much happened, until the Bishop became aware that the reason his orders were not being obeyed was that many of the priests, who themselves maintained mistresses politely described as housekeepers—another long-recognized Macao institution—were unwilling to persecute a crime which they were themselves abetting. In March the furious Bishop summoned the formidable Father Montepardo, senior secular priest, whom he rightly regarded as the key figure in obtaining obedience, and threatened to defrock publicly any priest who failed to put away his housekeeper and children. He then demanded from every priest an oath of obedience. To the consternation of the denizens of the Street of Happiness, priests' housekeepers were one and all dismissed, and a reign of terror descended upon the city.

Teresa da Silva had for years waited for some such opportunity as this, and there was now a dual reason for her hatred of Martha. Teresa was sick to death of her daughter Dominie. As a child, Dominie's gaiety and beauty had concealed the fact that she was not very intelligent. When Teresa's dream of having another European in the house was shattered, Dominie failed to realize that this in addition meant that she herself would never marry an officer from Portugal, since without the *cachet* of theirs being a European house no officer would care to call on them—at least, not with marriage in view. Unaware of this, Dominie continued to prattle about her officer, until Teresa, unable to stand it any longer, hit her, telling her she would marry her cousin Pedro or be a spinster for life.

Dominie had hysterics, but in the end, as usual, she obeyed her mother, and gradually her dream changed. The officer from Portugal faded away, to be replaced by her handsome second cousin, heir to the important commercial house of Gonçalves Sequeira.

But in bringing about the match, Teresa soon perceived that behind Pedro's ever-polite hesitation lay a definite reluctance, and by rumour she eventually came to know that, incredible as it might seem, Pedro was biding his time, waiting to marry Martha. Teresa also heard a vague report about Martha being in trade, but Martha's activities being concealed beneath her account name Gonçalves Sequeira Number Two—among Chinese along the waterfront she was known simply as Dai I, Number Two—Teresa was unable to find out any more. As Pedro came less and less to the house on the Rua da Penha, so did Teresa's hatred and suspicion of Martha increase. Having unwisely scared away other possible suitors, Teresa with alarm faced the prospect of being saddled with Dominie for life, unless somehow she could make an end of Martha.

Teresa had all but resigned herself to defeat when the Bishop's special measures came into force. The event filled her with an unprecedented hope. Almost crippled now with acidity, when she heard the news she sat silent in her low chair, tapping the floor softly with her stick, a tear now and then falling from her ageing eyes, the sign that she was excited. From the Bishop's secretary's clerk she learned that Dom Marcelino would not hesitate to engage the powerful East India Company on the issue of their privately maintained prostitutes, the Bishop being of the conviction that it was in fact the Protestant English who were principally responsible for the city's shabby moral state. But since the matter was a delicate one, the clerk considered, involving perhaps even a diplomatic exchange between Lisbon and London (Teresa let fall another tear), absolute proof would be required that an East India Company house was being used for purposes of prostitution, presumably during the absences in Canton, before the Bishop could act.

Teresa did not hesitate. She had heard that many people, most of them Chinamen, came to that house during the absences. That same evening she suggested to some distant cousins of hers who owned the house opposite Thomas van Mierop's that her own larger house on the Rua da Penha might suit them better, while their smaller house on the Rua do Hospital would really be rather a blessing to her.

Teresa had always taken the greatest care to conceal her desire for revenge, knowing that among Macao people such actions did not provoke sympathy. Above all she concealed her motives from Dominie, for the girl, who was feather-brained, was apt to blurt out to all and sundry everything that was said to her. Teresa had thus for thirteen years spoken of Martha with nothing but goodwill and forgiveness. With equal care, when moving to Hospital Street, she spoke of nothing except the convenience of having a smaller house. But her eyes watered often. With an extraordinary elation she saw at last how to repay and yet remain on the side of the saints. Revenge would be disguised as an act of virtue.

Martha was forewarned of the move by Inez. It was the main cause of her disquiet throughout the summer. When, in the first week of October, the move actually took place, and Teresa assumed vigil at the window opposite, Martha recognized that she had no alternative but to suspend her trade, thereby sealing off the house from outside contacts.

To Pedro this was the final blow in a series which cumulatively amounted to disaster. On the strength of conducting Martha's trade he had risen to prominence and restored his company's fortunes. A few years earlier Dai I had launched into a new and larger venture, the import of constructional hardwood for houses, shipbuilding and cabinet-making, which had done extremely well and looked set to providing a steady and substantial income. With this and other existing lines the firm was in touch with Siam, the Philippines, India, Burma and the Indies.

The rise to status and influence which Abraham Biddle had long ago envisaged for Pedro had started to take place. Only one of his uncles survived, and he was all but bed-ridden. Pedro's control of the firm was unimpeded. Through a carefully cherished friendship with Macao's Judge, His Honour Dom Paulo Mascarenhas Pereira, he had been elected to the Senate. Aged thirty-four, he was Macao's youngest Senator. With Judge Pereira behind him, with his own business flourishing, and with Biddle to fall back on, it looked as though nothing could prevent his becoming in the course of time the most important Macao-born Portuguese.

Then, one winter night in 1791, two years before the opium crisis, he had inadvertently sown the seed of disaster. Judge Pereira had made a disclosure to Pedro in confidence concerning certain friends of his—this was how the Judge put it—who were thinking of engaging privately in a venture which, were the necessary resources available, was certain to yield remarkable and continuing profits. Pedro had suggested that the Judge might one evening, in the privacy of his house, meet Abraham Biddle. The suggestion had been accepted, and Pedro requested to deliver an invitation.

"A gesture of the greatest condescension," had been the response of that worthy, who despite his long sojourn in Macao had never been taken notice of by a high-ranking Portuguese official. "I shall 'ave much pleasure in acceptin'."

Born in Brazil, educated in Portugal, and reputed to enjoy wealth derived from both countries, Judge Paulo Pereira was noted in Macao for the magnificence of his house and way of living. Unusually swarthy, with an aquiline nose, thick lips, bulbous eyes, and irrepressibly curly greying hair, he bore the traits of a partly African ancestry. He customarily wore black, with a bejewelled crucifix hanging round his neck from a thick gold chain. At a glance he might have been a somewhat self-indulgent prelate. In fact he was one of those rare men of affairs who combine personal generosity, political sagacity, and corruption.

Biddle was received late one night at the Judge's house, and there began a secret relationship. At the outset the enterprise involved a series of deals in opium and general Chinese products with Brazil, but given Judge Pereira's unique position—equally influential in Macao and in Rio—the possibilities of an extended trade were so great . . .

When they left the Judge's house well after midnight, Abraham Biddle had temporarily put from his mind the idea of retirement. He believed himself on the threshold of the greatest venture of his career.

Two years later the enterprise was still in the investment stage, but the sums Biddle had passed to the Judge far exceeded his East India Company credits, and when Chin Fui came with news of the opium shake-up Biddle regarded it as a small affair. The Company's subsequent demand for the return of credit bills or prompt payment in silver put things in an entirely different light. Biddle had already sent his credit bills to Calcutta, and he had practically no silver. Furthermore it was impossible for him to prove that he was good for the sum the Company was demanding, since the only person who knew this was the Judge, and for the Judge to confirm it would reveal instantly that His Honour, contrary to the laws of Portugal and to the rules of his profession, was engaged in commerce.

The Judge however was a rich man, and Biddle thought that he would not object, as a private individual, to advancing him a loan or guaranteeing him in a sum sufficient to keep the Company quiet for the moment. After dark on the first night of the opium crisis, Biddle and Pedro presented themselves at the Judge's house.

The visit was ill-timed. The Judge was celebrating the engagement of his second daughter. A dance was in progress, and the Governor and all the Portuguese *élite* were present. Biddle and Pedro were received in an ante-chamber, in which sounds of music and animated conversation could be heard from other rooms.

When the double doors were opened by two liveried African servants, and Judge Pereira, clad in black evening breeches and cutaway, entered and saw Biddle—Biddle who had no place in Portuguese society, and whom the Judge could not be seen with—he made his feelings plain by addressing his remarks exclusively to Pedro, and in Portuguese, thereby obliging Pedro to interpret between them. For Pedro it was an interview of acute embarrassment. Trapped between his two benefactors, he interpreted as best he could while observing on the one side beneath the social veneer the Judge's temper rising, and on the other the disintegration of Biddle from the reasoning to the anxious, from the anxious to the pitiful, until finally he cringed before the Judge as he pleaded for assistance.

Though he must have been in dread every minute that the Governor or some other high functionary might enter the room, Paulo Pereira dealt with the matter with smoothness and suavity, declining to give even the meanest help.

"The contribution Senhor Biddle has made is being handled by agents in Rio," the Judge said, "persons of impeccable reliability. The investment of these sums, as Senhor Biddle is aware, is nothing to do with me."

Biddle fell on his knees, imploring the Judge in a torrent of Macanese which the latter understood, while with horror Pedro, a helpless onlooker, realized what had happened. For Biddle to beg for money was useless. There was none. Judge Pereira had spent it, all of it. Pride at being received by a high official of the Portuguese Crown, pleasure at being treated with such affability, vanity at being able to offer him the resources and advice of which he stood in need—all this had dulled the perception of the man from Billingsgate, with his dreamed-of Calcutta mansion, his superiority over the gentry, his belief in the power of wealth. Such vanity had suited Paulo Pereira's purposes admirably.

But to be seen with Biddle grovelling before him was more than the Judge could risk. Curtly bidding Pedro, who was an invited guest, to join the assembled company when he would, Judge Pereira returned to the festivities, leaving his African servants guarding the closed doors.

Painfully Biddle rose to his feet, and declining with dignity the offer of the humiliated Pedro to accompany him, walked with all his habitual slow-moving solemnity to the door, and out into the night.

He did not return to his house that night, or indeed on any subsequent night. The only occupants of his house, in the servants' quarters, were Fong, her illegitimate son Kwan Po (Ignatius), and the fool boy, who from a boy had grown into a demented and dangerous man.

Fong's marriage to the fool boy's elder brother was not a success. Forced into the marriage by his parents, the husband had little or no interest in Fong. After a year living in the country the couple returned to Macao, bringing the fool boy with them. Chin Fui gave the husband a small job in his boatyard, and there they lived with Chin Fui and his family in the dark, ramshackle wooden loft above the yard which no amount of affluence could persuade Chin Fui to exchange for a better home.

One night, while everyone was asleep, the husband packed his small bundle of possessions and slipped out. At first it was thought he must have returned to his village, but when after several weeks no word of him was heard from there it was presumed he must have gone to sea, and he was given up for lost. For Fong, childless, it was the final depth of shame. Had her parents still been in Macao she would probably have returned to them, mortified as she would have been. But the year previously Ah Sum had retired, and with a small pension from Thomas had returned to his ancestral village. There was nothing for Fong but to remain with the Chin clan, to whom she no longer belonged, her husband having repudiated her.

She no more had a place at the family table, taking her meals in her dark cubicle, her only companion the fool boy, into whose disordered mind had come the idea that it was his duty to protect Fong against the day of his brother's return. Happily laughing, he would slide his back down the wall till he squatted on the floor, saying, "Don't worry, Sister. He will come back." To which, in more lucid moments, he would add, "I have my responsibility, you know." And every night he slept like a dog across her door.

Chin Fui was prepared to put up with this situation, but his wife soon started complaining about extra mouths to feed. It was just at this time that Abraham Biddle was moving to his house on the Ridge, and Martha, informed about Fong and concerned for her welfare, recommended to Pedro that Biddle employ Fong as his amah.

Biddle did so, and when less than a year later Fong bore a son Martha at first concluded that the child must be Biddle's. But there was a curious feature to it. From the day the child was born the fool boy's madness deepened. He no longer rolled on the floor and laughed. Hour after hour he would stand as still as a post, eyes downcast as if in shame, and he would allow no one to cut his hair. Dedicated to the protection of Fong, it seemed he had failed in his duty. Yet he bore no resentment to Abraham Biddle, whom Macao gossips considered to be the father of the boy Ignatius. It did not seem that the fool boy could himself be the father, Ignatius bearing such distinct signs of being of mixed race. Thus, when questioned by Thomas, Martha stated that the paternity of the boy was unknown, believing this to be the truth. There was something about the story as the gossips had it which did not make sense.

Throughout the winter after the opium crisis Martha remained behind permanently closed shutters, in total isolation from the world around her, while the Bishop's reign of terror entered a more ghastly phase. In the selection of their victims the priests showed less and less regard for whether the women were in fact engaged in prostitution. As Inez put it, no woman with a little story behind her was safe. Father Montepardo warned Inez on no account to give up her job with the Santa Casa, since while working there she might pass as a beneficiary. Father Montepardo knew about Inez' sons.

Certain prominent members of the Macao public had originally applauded the Bishop's intentions, but when the injustice of the special measures came to be seen, public opinion, Portuguese to the core, swung its sympathy entirely over to the cause of the persecuted. The single-minded Bishop was not deterred. When watch force officers declined to make further arrests, on the technical ground that the special measures had not yet received Lisbon's approval, the priests, operating in twos and threes by night, themselves shadowed their suspects and made arrests. Time and again they were heard passing stealthily along Hospital Street, while Martha, the lights extinguished, watched through the lattices, wondering in dread at which door they would halt. All that winter there was not one night when she lay down to sleep without fear. She did not have to be told that she, the most prosperous woman of the floating world, who had dared flout convention by engaging in honest commerce, would be a cherished prize in a ship bound for Timor.

A few days after Thomas' departure for Canton she discovered with alarm that Fong had been engaged as an amah by Teresa who, encouraging her to let her boy Ignatius visit her frequently, was using the boy as a source of information concerning what was going on in Thomas van Mierop's house.

How Fong came to be working for Teresa may be briefly told.

On the day Fong received Biddle's message and the silver dollar, her sole thought was her own survival. She had never been much of a mother to Ignatius, who was the permanent mark of her shame, while the fool boy, standing in ghostly and frightening stillness about the place, was a burden she resented. Desperate, with no one to turn to in her own Chinese world, she took Ignatius and the fool boy with her, and went to seek help from Pedro.

A week earlier, Pedro had received a call from Dominie. Teresa was rapidly ageing, and the excitement of moving house had worsened her cramp. She was now unable to leave her bed unaided, and Dominie, herself worn out and near to hysteria, had come to ask Pedro if he could recommend an amah. When Fong came, Pedro sent her round accompanied by Ignatius. Since Teresa would obviously never consent to house the fool boy he was left at Pedro's office, Fong promising to come back and arrange for him to be returned to the Chin clan, where he properly belonged.

Teresa, however, refused to take in even Ignatius, and Fong, finding herself opposite the van Mierop house, decided to risk loss of face, and went to Martha, not telling her where she had been engaged to work. Having disposed of Ignatius, she then went straight back to Teresa's and began her duties, thus by what almost amounted to a sleight-of-hand trick devolving herself of responsibility both for her son and for the fool boy, who was left haunting the rear parts of the Gonçalves Sequeira premises, clinging bat-like among the upper wall drawers of what had once been Biddle's inner sanctum, descending only when no one could see him, and eating the rice which was left for him on a plate on the floor.

When Fong brought her boy to the house Martha was shocked to see her, so much older, rougher, hardened by suffering. It was like looking at herself as she might have been, had it not been for her Englishman. But there was a slyness about the way Fong had conducted her manoeuvre, and Martha, who could never forget that passionate friendship which had suddenly turned to hate, knew that in that house Fong was an added danger. Either, therefore, Ignatius must be dismissed, or he must be separated from his mother. Of these alternatives the second, Martha considered, was the safer.

Martha had quickly become attached to Ignatius, and he to her. With the wisdom of the young, Ignatius had known from his earliest days that he was not wanted at Biddle's house, that the old man resented his presence, that even his mother resented him, fearing lest she lose her employment because of him. Like a prisoner he had dwelt there, his only happy moments being when he could escape from behind those high garden walls. When therefore Martha asked him not to see his mother again without permission, the boy readily consented. He had never been happy before, he said, and would do anything Martha asked of him. Throughout that anxious winter, in fact, he was her sole consolation. It was as if, without any of the grievous social problems, a son had entered the house.

But when winter ended, and early in April the Company descended upon Macao, with the new season came a new and graver anxiety. Thomas returned sick. Brought in a litter from the inner harbour, on arrival he collapsed in the hall and had to be borne upstairs by the servants.

He had been ill intermittently during the winter, victim of an unknown distemper which, from a surgeon's report which has by chance survived in the Company archives, appears to have been a recurring form of dysentery. Browne and Cuming, awaiting the inevitable wrath of the Governor-General of India, to whom they had finally referred the problem of what was to be done about Biddle, had been obliged to emerge from their doldrums and assume shadowy sway over the Company's affairs. Thomas, however, was such a cheerful patient that no one had any doubt that, once away from the muddy river water of Canton, to which the surgeon ascribed the complaint, he would quickly make a complete recovery and take his place as President for the next season, as soon as despatches were received from Calcutta. The atmosphere at Hospital Street was positively festive as throughout the summer what seemed to be the entire Company flocked round to inquire after him and pay their respects.

Martha, instantly adapting herself to the situation, became his nurse, and proved herself as one born to such a vocation. No sick man in that age was ever tended with more solicitude and understanding. That Thomas realized now the danger she stood in—his journal shows that this had been weighing on his mind during the winter—gave her the courage to be more open with him; and with the psychological impediment of her trade removed, in his sickness they grew closer to each other than they had ever been.

As the surgeon had said it would, Thomas' health improved on reaching Macao. But two recurrences of the disease in Canton had greatly weakened him, and recovery, the surgeon said, would be a gradual process. Martha was the epitome of confidence. There was a clear aim, a time schedule for his recovery. By the time the first vessels arrived with despatches from Calcutta he must be well enough to assume the position that would then await him. He would be President. The schedule was implicit in her every conversation.

The surgeon assigned to Thomas was one of the more promising youngsters named Pieter, a serious, kindly young man who led the general confidence in his patient's recovery. Thomas was advancing well, and Surgeon Pieter was about to assent to his making an excursion by chair, when in August, amid the summer's most oppressive heat, occurred a relapse with all the same symptoms.

In the house the regimen, the activity, the vigilance continued, but the time schedule changed. Tom had to be well enough to make the autumn migration to Canton. Everything in fact depended on this, for if an officer missed a season it was the end of his career. This, then, was the aim. Even should despatches be received tomorrow, and Browne and Cuming leave for England while Tom was yet unready to assume the full duties of President, it would not matter provided he was ready and fit when the time came to go to Canton.

Ships came. Despatches came. But no despatch concerned the opium crisis or the Company's losses. In the remote grandeur of the Casa Garden the President and George Cuming with wondering inquiry allowed themselves for the first time in many months a mood of cautious optimism. Perhaps they and everyone else had misjudged the situation. Perhaps their report had not created such furore in Fort William as they had imagined it would.

The number of callers at Hospital Street began to decrease. As summer drew to its end each call was shorter, more perfunctory. Though striving with the help of a good surgeon, Thomas showed no sign of improvement. In the last week of September, the worst of summer, when only a few days remained before the migration was to take place, Surgeon Pieter with tactful reluctance warned him that his recovery might take longer than expected, and Thomas saw himself confronting the dread process Urquhart had experienced and which he had himself witnessed in the case of others whom sickness had carried off according to an immemorial pattern—in an East Indiaman which, so far as the patient was concerned, never reached home.

The next step in the process followed a few days later when Surgeon Pieter announced that he had been ordered to proceed with the others to Canton. It was the practice to leave sick persons to winter it surgeonless in Macao, when if they survived, the next step followed: permission to leave, the letters to this effect being termed death warrants. Since normal practice could not be followed in the case of a member of the Select Committee, another surgeon had been deputed to remain behind. Thomas requested that his thanks be conveyed to the President for this special consideration. That night Pieter brought his colleague to pay a courtesy call. It was Surgeon Duncan.

In the same week the number of callers fell to nothing. The most assuring friend was elsewhere. The most regular visitor found he had other engagements. The centre of power dwelt once more firmly in the Casa Garden. On the 4th of October, as by now accepted as unavoidable, Surgeon Pieter gave his certificate to the effect that, due to severe debilitation, Mr. Thomas Kuyck van Mierop was unable to go up to Canton for the season.

His signature was no longer required on Committee documents. No more messengers with despatch boxes hurried to and fro. The President paid a ten-minute call, after which none came save the surgeon. The rest of the Company had gone.

Thomas recognized that time and his own helplessness had robbed him of his opportunity. His chance of promotion had gone for ever. However quickly he recovered he would not be able to remain on the China station with others junior to him promoted. He would be retired. But he still had a great deal of life before him. He was not yet forty. In England, with a sizeable fortune behind him, his prospects were good and he intended to enjoy them. He had written to his family, telling them at last about Martha, preparing them for her arrival when he retired.

Haggard and frail as he had become, shivering in the least draught, he daily insisted on being dressed fully and brought into the living room where, erect in his high-backed Spanish armchair upholstered in red velvet, immaculate in black longcoat and breeches and white stockings, he would sit awaiting the daily visit of the surgeon. Before him on a lectern lay a heavy family Bible open at a page which day by day advanced like a rare type of hour-glass in which it was paper, not sand, which ran out. He was reading the Bible from beginning to end.

In the evenings he wrote in his journal, the handwriting as always well-rounded and unhesitant.

'Mr. Duncan suffers more than I do,' he noted mid-November. 'It is written plain in his face. I refuse to die. I even feel better. Every day that passes increases his sensation that he is being ruined, kept so far from the commercial exhilarations of the Canton season. He disguises his suffering, of course. Indeed, while with physic he seeks to restore me, he threatens to assassinate me with bonhomie. In fact he is a prying man, with his eye on every distant door which, strolling about as he speaks, he will glance through in search of I know not what. Each day is a gentle battle of wits, he noting with apprehension every symptom of improvement which may entail his further delay here, I assuring him that if anyone has gloomy expectations of me I intend to cheat him of them.

'The reality is different. He has been assigned to me since, being impatient for his affairs, he is likely to be swift in giving me warrant for departure, while I—God grant me speedy recovery! Help me, O God in whom I trust.'

In fact, Thomas had been gravely affected by the change of surgeons, perceiving too well the hand that had designed it, and his condition had worsened.

'I begin to doubt I can stay in this race,' he wrote a few days later. 'I pray God I may have strength to dispose all matters in accordance with his law. Give me life, O Lord, to accomplish this.'

The entries in the journal become shorter, and through each one of them runs the same note of urgency.

'I will readily depart from China and from this dismal place, but give me health, O Lord, give me health that I may walk to the quay sound of foot.'

This, in fact, was the point. The war still dragged on, and there would be difficulty in obtaining a berth for Martha. It would somehow be arranged, he was confident, but it would require his personal attention. Furthermore it was essential that she leave first—a situation which again demanded that he be well—since were he to sail first, leaving her to follow, the ecclesiastical authorities would certainly choose such a moment to arrest her if they had a mind to it, knowing that he would not be returning, and that she therefore no longer enjoyed the protection of the East India Company.

In the margin of his journal he noted each day the chapter and verse of the Bible which he had reached in his reading. At the end of November he was in the Second

208

Book of Kings. Religion now pervades the journal, religious thoughts appearing in every entry, unmentioned beneath each the impelling determination that his long liaison with Martha, to whom he felt he owed all that he had known of happiness in China, must be solemnized in wedlock. On the night when she had locked him out of his own room he had sworn so to contrive matters that whatever else might befall, never would she marry that Portuguese. But this was an oath taken in the heat of jealousy, and it was now only of secondary importance when set beside his desire to give Martha the status of a married woman and to right themselves before God.

As for Martha, the long ordeal of nursing him was beginning to tell. Sleep descended on her at any hour of the day or night. Living from day to day, too occupied to think of the future, her every thought and action was concentrated on restoring him to health. And she was becoming a Christian again. Unbeknown to him, she started on a table, which she set against the wall on the rear landing, a collection of sacred objects which gradually became a household altar, with candles, vases of flowers, an embroidered altar-cloth, and a statuette of Our Lady holding the infant Jesus.

Before it she placed a silk-covered stool to kneel on, and very early each morning, while Thomas, exhausted by sleeplessness, finally had an hour or so of real slumber, she prayed, racing urgently through every prayer she could remember from her Convent childhood. The prayers were in Latin, and many of them she had not remembered correctly. She did not know what any of them meant. But she knew that this was the language of the Holy Mother of God, and that if she spoke in it she would be heard.

'December,' Thomas wrote in the second week of that month, 'the year's perfection, the air crisp, the sky always blue, the garden warmed by a gentle sun. I am improving with the weather. I feel strength returning to me every day. Thanks be to God, I shall accomplish all things that are necessary.'

The following morning Surgeon Duncan informed him that he must leave Macao for a change of climate, and at the earliest moment.

Surgeon Duncan was cunning but maladroit. He had been very angry when George Cuming had made a fool of him by sending him to Thomas on the eve of the crisis; and when Cuming had suggested that he stay in Macao to attend Thomas the surgeon had accepted with alacrity, believing that in the special circumstance, could he cure him, van Mierop would become President, and he, Duncan, would acquire a new patron. But with his remedies unavailing, and Cuming still firmly at the helm of affairs, he had come to regret the alacrity of his acceptance.

When the surgeon told him, Thomas' gaunt head, momentarily bowed, drew back in proud anger between the curved horns of the chair.

"You speak of the impossible," he said. "Leave I must. But not till I am in a fit state to do so."

"I speak, sir," replied Duncan, grave for once and ill at ease, "of your sole chance of recovery. I am prepared to give the required certificate."

"But this is monstrous. Given another month, I shall be well."

"Not fundamentally, sir. My remedies can allay, but only climate can cure."

Thomas studied the ruddy, rough-hewn face, and marvelled that after so many years of responsibility and influence he should be at the mercy of this young churl with his cunning peasant's eyes and gross hands itching for their share of the season's spoil.

"What are you advising?" he asked at last.

"Return to England."

"And were that inconvenient . . . ?" he demanded, determined to fight it all the way.

Surgeon Duncan was perplexed by so strange a question. "Should we say a long sea voyage?" he replied uncertainly.

"Mr. Duncan, do you sanguinely suppose I can accept your prescription?"

Duncan steadied himself.

"With the greatest reluctance, sir, this is my final advice. You may recall that surgeons, when giving such advice, are required to report the fact to the President at Canton."

Thomas lowered his eyes. The death warrant. He was conscious of his hands suddenly damp with perspiration. He was definitely improving. He had not perspired for weeks. Then it must be a temporary departure, he thought quickly. Above all, the ecclesiastical authorities must know that he was returning.

"I am your servant," he said quietly. "But if I am permitted to choose I will opine for a long sea voyage, on the understanding that if restored to health by the time I reach St. Helena I may take ship in the contrary direction and return."

Duncan shrugged his shoulders.

"As you wish, sir. Then let us say a long sea voyage."

"My thanks, Mr. Duncan." And then, in a manner which caused the surgeon to glance at him with anxiety, Thomas shivered. He remembered from long ago the China station graves on St. Helena. Those men never returned. None had ever returned. In a lower tone he added, "Now go send the clerk to me, and a notary, if one still resides in Macao. It seems I should make a will."

Martha, as was her wont, had been listening from behind the rear door. The instant the surgeon left she came in. She wore a white dress with a red sash high beneath the breast. One of her insistences throughout his illness was always to wear light colours, making herself appear as fresh and pleasing to him as she could. But her face was drawn with sleeplessness.

"What is a will?" she asked in a low voice.

"It is a writing, witnessed by a notary, in which people

say what they wish to be done with their money and property after their death. There is nothing unusual about it. In England everyone makes a will."

"The writing is on that thick blue paper," she said nervously.

"Not blue necessarily."

"With the Portuguese it is blue. It means—"

" 'Tis a precaution only, but one I should take. I might be shipwrecked, after all," he said with a flicker of a smile.

"Yes, you could be shipwrecked," she echoed. "But it means you will not come back."

"God willing, I shall come back restored and well. I shall go as far as Prince of Wales Island or St. Helena. The voyage will quickly give me back my health. From there I shall take another ship returning to China."

"No!" she exclaimed anxiously. "I know the names of those places. They are places . . . It is better you should not go."

"The surgeon has left me no alternative. Don't be afraid. I—" he faltered, and added again softly, "God willing."

Unconsciously he had shown that his doubt was as great as hers. She caught her breath aghast and flung herself down before him, burying her face between his knees.

"Don't leave me!" she begged. "This is more than I can bear!"

Gently he laid a hand on the nape of her neck. She shuddered as his cold fingers touched her. When he raised his eyes from her, it was in the direction of his thoughts—the shuttered windows flecked with sunlight overlooking the street, the endless vigil in the unseen window opposite, the priests prowling the streets at night. If there was a convoy leaving, he might have no more than a few days left.

"Is there not another means?" he said at last. "Supposing I were to take the surgeon's preferred suggestion and return to England. You would take a country ship to Calcutta. There must be someone here who can arrange it. When I reach London"—he faltered—"when I reach London," he repeated in a low voice, "I will arrange for you from there for the rest of your voyage."

"A voyage?" she asked with incomprehension.

"Yes. There must be someone here who can help." There was no one; they were all in Canton. But he was past reasoning. The image of that future he had set his mind on survived the reality of its accomplishment. "You will be happy in England," he said. "My home will delight you. Twickenham!" he mused. "The gardens, above all—a real garden, with poplars and weeping willows beside the river, not a garden of pots such as we have here. Yes. When Duncan told me to go, I knew it more than I have ever known it. I long for England. There I shall become well again, in that air, in that countryside with its thrushes and larks, birds whose voices you have never heard—and in spring a strangely ugly bird, the cuckoo, but with a voice that wakens even the old to the memory of their youth. Every spring I have passed in China how I have longed to hear that sound from the woods! For colour and melody there is no country like it. By comparison Macao, for all its greenery, is a parched, dry place." Her trusting brown eyes were fixed on his. "Will you let me arrange it? I will ask the clerk who is here. There must be someone. There must . . ."

But her expression had become more practical. She smoothed her dress.

"Women are like flowers that are hard to transplant," she said.

"True, but you would be among friends who would love you."

"For your sake only, Tom. They would not really love me."

"They would."

"No. Specially those—how d'you call them?—missis." She rose to her feet. "Macao may seem grey to you, but it is my place, the only place I know. I could not go with you, Tom."

"After staying some time in England we could return,"

he insisted. "I would be in health by then."

"No," she said. "You can go, and you can come back. But I must stay here."

"Then I am to ignore what will be the requirement of the Company. I am not to make the voyage."

"I did not say that!" she replied swiftly. "You have to make a voyage."

"And you?" his voice hardened. "What else have you in your mind?"

She knew what he meant. She was trembling.

"I have always told you the truth, Tom, always—though you may not have believed it. I cannot say what I shall do, because I do not know what others may try to do to me. But I cannot go with you. Wherever you go, near or far, I cannot leave my own place. I will wait for you for ever, if you ask me to. But it is here that I shall wait."

He leaned deep into the chair, the grip of his emaciated hands tightening over the heads of the carved leopards which formed its arms.

"Then, if it can be done in secret," he muttered, "send for one of your priests and let him marry us."

Her breast heaved. Her tired eyes lit up with wonder and excitement.

"Holy Mother of God!" she murmured, falling at his feet. "My prayer is answered!"

"Amen," he whispered exhaustedly. "Be speedy about it. There is no time to lose."

At about noon next day Surgeon Duncan, with an eye to reinstating himself in the favour of his former patron, penned and despatched the following letter.

To George Cuming Esquire,
    At Canton.
Sir,
    It is my duty to inform you that I have found it advisable to recommend to Mr. Mierop that he make a long

sea voyage as the sole likely means left for his recovery.

He has accepted my recommendation, and in due course you may expect to receive his formal application for permission to leave, with my certificate appended thereto.

It would appear that the Roman Catholic Church in Macao is taking some interest in Mr. Mierop, an interest which may bear some relation to matters you had earlier seen fit to discuss with me.

This is not mere hearsay. I was today at his house at the same time as a Romish priest.

I am etc.

ALEXDR. DUNCAN

As it chanced, the surgeon, bringing the ship clerks with him, had come to Hospital Street unusually early that morning. As the front doors opened to admit them, the three men, uniformly raising their eyes, halted in silence, staring at an extraordinary figure descending the stairs. In black cassock and red stockings, wild-eyed and white-haired, a priest of huge, bent frame and almost incredible ugliness, with arms as long as a gorilla's, a lolling lower lip, hooked nose, and deepset piercing eyes each a different shape, reeled and swayed like a drunkard as he came down, one hand clutching the banister, the other holding a tall knotted staff which he crashed on the hollow wood of the staircase. It was the dreaded Father Montepardo, senior secular priest and Canon of the Cathedral, who had come at Martha's invitation, conveyed to him by Inez. At the foot of the stairs Martha and Ignatius knelt and kissed his hand.

As only a few days remained before Christmas, and Father Montepardo was heavily engaged, it had been decided that the secret marriage should take place on St. Stephen's Day, the morning after Christmas, in the presence of two trustworthy witnesses and immediately subsequent to Thomas' reception into the Catholic Church, on which Father Montepardo insisted before he would consent to join them in wedlock. In the matter of Thomas' conversion the Father had asked that an interpreter be present, and himself named the only man in the city who was equally fluent in English and Portuguese—Senator Pedro Gonçalves Sequeira.

When he uttered the name Father Montepardo stared at Martha with his eyes wide open (the left one was the larger of the two), his face puffed round like a balloon as he waited for her reaction. He knew about Martha's trade with Pedro (there was little in Macao he did not know), and when Martha, showing no sign of surprise, asked if Pedro could also be a witness, the Father leered wickedly—he looked like Satan dressed as an old priest—and said he thought this would be most appropriate.

Thus Thomas and Pedro were to meet for the second time, and thus, with life's infinite capacity for irony, Pedro was to be asked by two people—Martha and Father Montepardo—neither of whom he would dare refuse, to seal in his capacity as interpreter and witness the termination of his own long-cherished hope.

It was the last hour of Christmas Eve, and there was a slight chill in the air. Thomas, enveloped in shawls, was reading the Bible in his usual chair, turned now to face a glowing fire from which the soft scent of China fir pervaded the room. Knowing he had no need of her for the moment, Martha resolved on a sudden to enjoy in advance the almost unimaginable freedom which as a married woman would be hers within a matter of hours, and attend Midnight Mass at the Cathedral.

Donning a simple black dress, she threw over her head and shoulders a stiff black taffeta *dó*, and calling a servant to accompany her, made her way down Hospital Street to the largo at the end of it which fronted the Cathedral.

Unnoticed she passed within, into warmth, light, and a multitude of friendly sounds, footfalls on stone, an organ thinly played, the creak of benches, the continuous, harsh rustle of women's mantles. Beneath the high wooden roof, black with age and the smoke of incense and candles, among so many Portuguese and mesticos, men and women, nearly all of them wearing black, memories of childhood enveloped her, in particular of her Little Papa, Monsieur Auvray, beside whom she liked to kneel at Mass, and who, when it was over, would take her round the churches and talk to her about the Saints.

She found a place in the last row of worshippers on the women's side of the nave. The Mass had begun, but though others rose and knelt at the appropriate times, she spent the whole of it on her knees, absorbed in her own prayers and in the golden sense of restoration and fulfilment which had flowed into her, uplifting her from weariness. From the depth of her heart she poured out her thankfulness to the Holy Mother of God, praying for Thomas' recuperation at sea and for his safe return to Macao.

As the Mass proceeded she realized that each worshipper except herself held a candle, and that these, starting from the front, were being lit as, the men on their side, the women on theirs, one worshipper gave light to another. The front of the nave began to glow in the light of hundreds of candles, the light slowly spreading from row to row.

When it came to the turn of the last row everyone was kneeling, and the woman next to her had difficulty with her candle. Its flame remaining very small, she shielded it carefully, turning slowly to offer it to Martha. For an instant she stayed thus, poised, concentrated.

Surprised at the woman's slowness in not seeing her position—that she had no candle—Martha looked into the face. At the same instant the other woman's gaze met hers. It was Dominie, who with a sudden "Oh!" of fright rose to her feet, and the little flame of her candle went out.

"Stay where you are!" Martha whispered. "Don't be foolish!"

Dominie subsided. She tittered nervously, and when she at last passed a flame to the woman on the other side of Martha she tittered again, uneasily swaying her neck about like a swan.

After the Mass the worshippers bore their candles out into the largo where, coolly bathed in moonlight, they stood about in groups, lingering over their adieux for the night, while children urged their parents to make haste for the jolly nocturnal feast they knew awaited them at home.

Dominie and Martha moved past them. The servant materialized in the darkness of a porch. On the cobbles, among buildings dimly alive with lights and movement of festivity, only the women's footsteps cried between the walls. The servant, in cloth slippers, moved noiselessly.

"I must say," remarked Dominie pointedly, "I was surprised to see you in the Cathedral, of all places."

"From now on I hope you'll see me there often," Martha replied. "May I tell you a secret, Dominie?" She could not wait for Teresa to know.

Dominie paused in their walk. The comings and goings at the van Mierop house had naturally aroused the greatest curiosity over the way.

"A secret?" she asked excitedly. "Father Montepardo? The Extreme Unction?"

"No, Dominie. Not the Extreme Unction. Marriage. I am going to be married."

"You? Married?" Dominie gasped. "I don't believe it."

They were alone in the street. In moonlight, and with Dominie's candle burning between them, each could see every detail of the other's face framed in the oval of their black mantles.

"It's true," Martha said.

"To whom?" Dominie asked warily.

"Naturally, the only one."

"Who d'you mean?" Dominie's voice rose towards hysteria. "Is it a Macao man?"

"No."

"Not from Portugal?" she said, unable to believe such a thing possible.

"No."

"Then who?"

"Use your common sense, Dominie."

"You mean," she said, nodding at the servant, "him?"

Martha raised her eyes in a completely European way.

"The servants, my dear Dominie, are married already, and as if I would think of marrying one of them! Goodness gracious, why should it be such a puzzle to you? I am marrying the Englishman."

Dominie tittered.

"But isn't he going to die?" she asked.

"He is not! He will make a long sea voyage and return in perfect health."

"To marry you?"

"No. We shall be married before he goes."

"I've never heard of anything so ridiculous," Dominie sniffed.

"What is ridiculous?" Martha demanded.

"You, of all people, to be so innocent! Surely you know that when they go, they never come back. To marry him when he's just going away—h'm—what kind of a marriage is that?"

Martha turned on Dominie, seized the candle, and flung it lightless to the ground.

"It is my marriage!" she cried passionately.

Dominie shrank into the shadows near her own front door.

"Don't you do anything to me!" she uttered fearfully. "If you do I shall scream and you'll be arrested. My mother and I know all about you! Women like you shouldn't be out in the streets. Don't you come near me!"

To such an extent did it recall scenes of their childhood that to Dominie's surprise Martha simply remained in the moonlight laughing.

"You think you can affront me!" came Dominie's scornful voice out of the shadows. "You think it's so high and mighty to marry an Englishman? I'd have you know I could have married an officer from Portugal—yes, you didn't know

219

8—COBP

about that, did you?—except my mother wouldn't agree to come with us to Lisbon, so I had to stay here with her."

"No, I didn't know," Martha replied, as if this statement were true.

"That's why!" said Dominie, justifying herself. "You think you can deceive me with your fine stories."

But it was Christmas, the time for making amends, and Martha had an idea. If Pedro was to be one of the witnesses, who more suitable as the other than Dominie? Much could come of it.

"I'm not deceiving you, Dominie. Come to my wedding. Come on the morning after Christmas."

Dominie advanced suspiciously out of the shadows.

"You once said you would hate me till you died."

"We were both very young. I no longer think that."

"You do! Just now you showed me you do."

"You mistook me. I want to be friends with you, Dominie. Please come."

The servant opened her door.

"You're telling lies!" shouted Dominie. "You think you can humble me because I'm not married! But any time I choose—any time I choose—I can marry a very important man in Macao. You didn't know that either, did you?"

With a sigh Martha ascended the moonlit steps.

To her surprise there were coats and hats in the hall, more light upstairs, and the sound of men's voices. She mounted cautiously and listened.

In the living room Thomas still sat facing a cheerfully burning fire. Standing on his left was the surgeon. On the other side, in evening black, stood George Cuming.

". . . was seen by Surgeon Duncan and two others. You will not, I presume, attempt to refute the evidence of three witnesses," Cuming was saying.

"What I said was not a refutation," Thomas answered calmly.

"Then you admit that Roman Catholic priests have

visited this house?"

"One priest, yes."

"That is correct, sir," Duncan put in. "One priest was all we saw."

"I am instructed by the President to inquire whether there was a special reason for this visit."

"There is a reason for most visits, Mr. Cuming."

"From indications you have given us in the past, it has been presumed that the visit concerned a marriage."

"I am unmarried, sir."

"Then it was a visit made prefatory to a marriage."

"You are free to speculate, Mr. Cuming, if you will; but do not expect me to reply to questions concerning your speculations."

Martha had heard enough. That Tom, in his exhausted state, should be subjected to this kind of interrogation was more than she could support. Impelled by her new-found freedom, she was no longer the diminutive little pensioner hiding behind the scenes in the world of the mighty English. She was the well-to-do lady trader of the inner harbour waterfront, who would stand no nonsense from anyone; and at this moment, abandoning discretion, and with no clear idea of what she would say or do, she advanced into the open doorway.

As she then discovered, no word or other action was required of her. At her appearance the two men standing on either side of the Spanish armchair faced her with the sensitive speed of conspirators. In the light from the low-placed lamps their faces appeared unnatural, the surgeon's pink and unhealthily puffed up, Cuming's peculiarly white, struck by a flush over the cheeks. In their tight-fitting black attire their faces and hands stood out like sentient islands of agitation.

Cuming quickly recovered himself.

"We are not to be left on our own, I fear," he said without removing his eyes from her.

She made no reaction. It was a battle of wills.

"I shall be brief, then," Cuming said, returning his attention to Thomas. "The President naturally had no means of knowing what your intentions were, but on the assumption that they were"—he hesitated, unwilling to be too precise while she remained in the room—"that they were as I have just mentioned, and that such a development might be likely to take place prior to your leaving China, he considered it advisable to give a ruling in these somewhat unusual circumstances, and he has commissioned me to apprehend you of it verbally, should I deem it necessary."

He paused, still awaiting her departure, and with a slight shrug of the shoulders continued.

"As a result of my conversation with you I do deem it necessary. Forgive me if I am guilty of a misjudgement. It is thus my duty to deliver you the President's warning. The development I was referring to will involve your dismissal from Company service, and the President is not empowered to waive this rule. Dismissal is instantaneous, and the President desired me to remind you that, this being so, with effect from the date of such a development you would cease to qualify for accommodation in Company ships. The President is not prepared to authorize any variation in this rule, and in the event of your dismissal letters would be sent to the national companies of friendly powers advising them of this order and requesting them to refuse any application you might make for a passage in their ships. Short therefore of travelling in a ship of the enemy—a means I would presume you unwilling to employ—you would be reduced, if you wish to leave Macao, to taking a country ship to India. Here again the President wishes to remind you that letters would also be sent to Fort William and Fort St. George advising them that you were ineligible for a berth in any East Indiaman proceeding to London."

Cuming continued to speak, but Martha was no longer listening. Like everyone else in Macao she knew the invariable fate of any Englishman who openly married his pensioner, knew that among the English this was the one step which would neither be countenanced nor forgiven. Like everyone else in Macao she knew of the man who had been driven out to sell vegetables to fishermen outcasts, and who at the sight of another European would slink away with the furtive haste of a rat.

"I shall be returning to Canton tomorrow," Cuming was saying finally. "Surgeon Duncan will remain in Macao with the President's special authority to insure that his orders are carried out should the need for them arise."

Little as Martha knew of the East India Company, she knew enough to appreciate the depth of this last insult, that a surgeon should be given what amounted to authority to dismiss a member of the Select Committee. Trembling with anger, feeling the insult directed as much to herself as to Thomas, she came up beside the armchair and in a movement unconsciously expressive of her wish to be united with him, laid one hand gently on his shoulder. Without seeing her, unaware till then who else was in the room, he raised his hand to clasp hers.

Cuming observed the quiet simplicity of it.

"You still insist you are unmarried?" he queried.

"Yes," Thomas replied.

"Are you prepared to say so on oath?"

"Mr. Cuming," Martha interrupted with deceptive gentleness, "are you asking all these questions because a Father came to the house?"

He studied her without trace of emotion.

"Yes, I heard you spoke English these days," he said coolly, and readdressed himself to Thomas. "Are you prepared to say so on oath?"

"Mr. Cuming, I am asking you a question." Thomas' hand on hers tightened to restrain her. "I must confess," she continued undeterred, "that I see nothing very astonishing about it. It was not Mr. Mierop the Father came to see. I am a Christian, not a pagan. The Father came to see me."

"I want a straight answer," Cuming said to Thomas.

"Surgeon," Martha appealed, "surely you can see that Mr. Mierop is in no state to answer questions. Will you kindly ask Mr. Cuming to desist."

The surgeon flushed to the roots of his red hair and said nothing. Martha uttered a little sigh.

"Then, Mr. Cuming, I will be the surgeon. You may direct your questions to me. Mr. Mierop is not married."

"I wish to hear that from you, Mierop," said Cuming, his temper rising.

"Is there anything else you wish to ask, Mr. Cuming?" Martha riposted.

George Cuming swung away towards the fire, his back to her.

"Will you be so good as to ask this woman to leave us," he ordered sharply.

"To that request you may have an immediate answer," she said. She went swiftly to the rear door, where she halted and turned. "Either you leave the house this instant, Mr. Cuming, or I call the servants."

As the unheard-of command flashed across the room, Surgeon Duncan, aghast at having witnessed such a scene, averted his eyes in dread from his patron and superior. Cuming made no outward reaction, but this concealed nothing. The English were like royalty, never contradicted, far less ordered about, and they had the same mental processes as royalty when their divinity is challenged. The pedestal rocked. There was air beneath the footfall instead of ground.

There was a long and shattering silence till the room steadied itself. Then Cuming began drawing on the white gloves he had carried in his hand throughout.

"I would have wished this otherwise," he said with dignity to Thomas. "Once, many years ago, I gave you some advice—here, in this very room. Do you remember? I reminded you that in an unscrupulous society it is the man with scruples who will be the first to break his neck. It is a warning that still holds. I trust that for your own good, at this late hour, you will see your way not to insist on disregarding it."

There was no response from the sick man. Cuming drew

on his second glove.

"The responsibility is now yours, Mr. Duncan. See to it."

"Yes, sir," muttered Duncan.

Again Cuming waited for his rival to speak, and then, aware perhaps for a fleeting instant of the strange nothingness of enmity, he turned his head away abruptly.

"I wish you well," he said curtly. "Adieu."

Looking neither right nor left he departed, the surgeon following.

In the distance the front door closed. The footsteps in the street died away. The house was silent.

Martha came to the fire.

"If you advise the priest to proceed with extreme caution," Thomas said, "it can still be done."

"No, Tom. They suspect. It is too dangerous."

"I am compelled to take that risk," he said gravely.

"I forbid it, Tom. I forbid it absolutely. You do not know what it would mean."

He shifted his position. His hollow eyes glinted with a reflection of their former vitality.

"Bring me my book."

She swung the lectern round till the great Bible lay before him. With dedicated care he laid his hands on its open pages.

"I have this one great desire," he said. "Before I depart I must set my house in order. For my sake, Martha, my beloved Martha—before God—do as I ask. I cannot board that ship till He has seen me wed."

"It cannot be, Tom!"

"It may be the last thing I shall ever ask of you."

"Do not say that. It is for your sake I refuse. You have not thought what will happen when they find out. If you had to stay here with me in those conditions, it would be worse than to die."

He was silent.

"Then I see only one path before me," he said at last.

"Since the Church is denied us, let this be our church."

"What do you mean?"

"This house, this room—let this be our church."

"But Father Montepardo must not come!"

"The Father need not come."

"No other priest must come, Tom! It is not safe."

"No other priest need come."

"Then—?"

"In this church of ours we will be married by one who is greater than a priest."

"You mean the Bishop?" she queried in alarm.

"Greater than the Bishop."

"There is no one greater than the Bishop."

"There is," he answered steadily, "and he shall marry us."

"No!" she protested. "Tom, I am frightened. I do not understand you."

"Do not be frightened."

"But what are you going to do?"

He withdrew his hands from the Bible.

"Pray bid the servants bring me to bed," he murmured. "And sleep soundly. There is nothing to be afraid of. God willing, in the morning I will explain to you what we must do, you and I."

For surely, he thought, when all else has been tried and has failed, God will look down on this, understand, and sanction it.

Ignatius had not finished his breakfast on the morning after Christmas when the front door bell rang.

It was Senator Gonçalves Sequeira, and by the confidence with which he entered the hall it seemed he had been invited.

"Has Father Montepardo come?" he asked.

"No, Senhor. Were you looking for him?"

"He asked me to meet him here." He took out his timepiece. "In any event I'm somewhat early. Where is the

Senhora?"

"I'm not sure, Senhor. I'll find her."

With feelings of uncertainty Ignatius went upstairs in search of his mistress. Only yesterday he had borne a message to Father Montepardo asking him not to come today. The Father was very angry after Ignatius had recited the message. Ignatius had so shot up in size that people often took him to be older than he was. Father Montepardo made this miscalculation, and Ignatius had not enjoyed it. Dead scared, he had stuck to his guns, but he was glad when he was able to run away. Why, he asked himself as he climbed the stairs, should the Father, after receiving such a message, arrange to meet Senator Gonçalves Sequeira at the house?

Reaching the landing he stopped in surprise. Before him the tall white-painted doors leading to the living room were closed. There was something forbidding about it; these doors were never closed. Passing through the 'horsebox' doors of various inner rooms, he emerged on the rear landing only to find this door also closed, while to his further surprise his mistress' altar, kneeling stool, candles, statue, everything had gone.

Could it be death? he asked himself, suddenly adult. If it was, why had the surgeon not been sent for? Gingerly he padded in his cloth slippers to the door and tried the delicate gilt handle wrought in the shape of an S. It gave. It was dark inside, every window shuttered, and from somewhere within he could hear voices speaking quietly, gravely—his voice, then hers, then his again. He slipped noiselessly in.

"To have and to hold from this day forward."

And her voice:

"To have and to hold from this day forward."

Now that he was inside with the door closed and the light of day shut out, he saw that in the front part of the room beneath the arch two candles were lit.

"For better, for worse."

And her voice:

"For better, for worse."

227

"In sickness and in health."

"In sickness and in health."

The candles were standing on the altar table. The altar with all its decorations had in fact been moved in, and there kneeling before it were his master and mistress, their backs to him, the mistress wearing a white dress edged with ermine, with a white mantle, the master in one of his finest black suits with a shiny surface such as Ignatius had not seen him put on for many months. Even in the semi-darkness he could see it sagged empty about him, too large for his weak and shrunken body. She knelt uprightly in the way of healthy people. He was slumped forward over something which in a little while Ignatius divined as a book.

"To love, cherish and to obey."

"To love, cherish and to obey."

Their voices were low, trembling and solemn, as if each were deeply afraid of something.

"Till death us do part."

"Till death us do part."

Ignatius frowned. He could not understand it.

"According to God's holy ordinance."

"According to God's holy ordinance."

At these words he became frightened. Something was happening which he as a youth was not meant to see, something important, grown-up and secret.

"And thereto I give thee my troth."

"And thereto I give thee my troth."

He wanted to open the door again and go outside, but dared not. That he had succeeded in entering without being observed was little short of miraculous. He could not count on a second such miracle.

The master turned to her, his head almost resting on her shoulder.

"With this ring I thee wed," he said. "With my body I thee worship. And with all my worldly goods I thee endow. In the name of the Father, and of the Son, and of the Holy Ghost. Amen."

228

With an eery tingling through his body, Ignatius began to sense an explanation.

The master bowed his head. He was dreadfully weak. Falteringly he took up the book again.

"Forasmuch as we two have consented together in holy wedlock," he said, but the words became fainter and fainter, "and have witnessed the same before God, and thereto have given and pledged our troth each to other . . ."

He is going to die, Ignatius thought. He did not know how he knew. He just felt sure.

". . . and have declared the same by giving and receiving of a ring . . ."

Should he risk slipping out and fetch help? If the master died, what would happen to them all?

". . . and by joining of hands, let it be pronounced that we two . . ."

Painfully the master wiped his brow. Ignatius saw his hand trembling. The words sank to a whisper.

". . . be man and wife together; in the name of the Father, and of the Son, and of the Holy Ghost. Amen."

The master put the book down, then slowly turned his haggard face to hers, and with astonishment Ignatius saw them kiss. He had never seen a man kiss a woman before.

They began to stir upward. It was time to escape. With silent cunning worthy of a thief Ignatius made for the door, when there was a slight disturbance outside and the door was flung open to admit, peering in satanically, the huge, black, ungainly figure of Father Montepardo, with the Senator behind him.

The two figures at the altar turned to face the sweep of light, she swiftly, he with the gravity of the sick.

Father Montepardo lurched forward.

"Has someone else been here?" he asked.

"Father!" Martha exclaimed in astonishment. "I sent you a message. Pedro, help me!"

Thomas, who was leaning on her heavily, was falling forward, about to collapse. Pedro strode to him, took his weight about his own shoulders, and gently lifted him into a chair.

"Yes, I received your message," Father Montepardo replied with a ghastly chuckle. "But I paid no attention. Requests such as yours do not come every day. What are you doing in this darkness?"

Martha shrank from him, shame and anxiety written all over her face. The unfamiliar words of the marriage service had meant nothing to her. She had never lived with a married couple, never been to a wedding. All she knew of marriage was that it was a form of protection against punitive laws. In desperation she turned to Thomas and said in English:

"Father Montepardo is asking why we are in the dark? What am I to say?"

Hunched low in the chair, Thomas raised his head. Dimly he recalled in his utter exhaustion that he and the priest had conversed in a common language, but he could no longer remember which language it was.

"Tell the Father, with my regret, we are already married," he replied.

Martha heard it, but could not believe it.

"With deep regret," she repeated automatically, "we are already married."

"By whom?"

"He asks, by whom?"

"Tell him, alone before God."

She repeated it simply.

Father Montepardo reeled forward.

"I don't understand. Senator, would you kindly interpret for me. By what authority do they say they are married?"

Pedro translated.

Thomas' eyes searched the room till they at last found Father Montepardo. Extending his hand to take Martha's in his, with head austerely raised, he replied with slow finality:

"By the authority of God alone. We can turn to no other."

Martha understood then, and was terrified. Sinking on her knees before Father Montepardo, she hid her face in his robe and begged forgiveness. With a scowling frown the priest absent-mindedly laid his hand on her shoulder.

At this moment an urgent whisper from a servant outside on the landing summoned Ignatius downstairs. In the hall, with three other servants round her, he found Senhora Dominica from across the way, clad in black with a black mantle over her head. She looked pale and frightened. She had come to the wedding, she said, but the servants said there was no wedding. In fact, she had been forced to come across after an explosive scene with her mother. Her every nerve on edge, she had already assumed that Martha had deceived her.

"Follow me," Ignatius said, and led her through to the rear stairway.

The two of them reached the top of the stairs as the doors of the living room opened. Father Montepardo came out first. Behind him came Martha and Pedro, who was saying something to her quietly, his hand lightly resting beneath her arm.

At the sight of it Dominie's stare widened into terrible, unbelieving dismay, the group as they came out conveying exactly the impression that Father Montepardo had just married Martha and Pedro. Dominie screamed, a ghastly sound of frustration and outrage. With a groan she clutched the banister, groping her way down like someone half blind, uttering convulsive laughter, high-pitched and throaty, and tore out of the house.

By that afternoon the Macao Portuguese world (but no one else) learned with regret that Senhora Dominica da Silva Auvray was no longer of sound mind, having been taken by a fit of madness while attending her sister's secret marriage to an Englishman.

Spies were posted by Surgeon Duncan at either end of Hospital Street, but they were quickly identified by the servants and induced to report nothing. No word of Father Montepardo's second visit reached Duncan, and no more questions were asked. Thomas applied for and duly obtained a berth in an East Indiaman due to sail in a convoy leaving in the second week of January.

He was exceedingly weak, but as the days narrowed to departure he re-gathered strength, buoyed up in expectation of the voyage. If he was not restored by the time they reached St. Helena he would continue on to London. But of this he said nothing, knowing the importance of giving his departure every appearance of being temporary—as it might well prove to be. Apart from furniture for his cabin he took little with him other than clothes, some books, and his journal, leaving all his more treasured possessions behind as gages of his return.

It was decided that he must be accompanied by an English-speaking servant, and inevitably Ignatius had been chosen. This too was in its way a gage. Thomas knew Martha's affection for the boy. To take him away from her was as good as a promise that they must both return quickly, while if in fact they proceeded to London the presence of Ignatius there would be an added inducement to Martha to follow. London would seem less strange to her with Ignatius as her footman, while once Thomas was in London, freed from the East India Company's un-Christian regulation, to arrange for her passage would be simplicity itself. In the end, he knew, she would relent and come; but he also knew that even a hint of such a possibility would at the present juncture be fatal.

There was of course his will, but this, although as with everything he gave great care to it, he considered merely a precaution. He left it to the last moment, completing it only the day before he was due to leave, and when on the last day Surgeon Duncan called he found his patient, beneath the gaunt mask of a wasting disease, in a rare humour. Before him was the President's formal permission to leave—the death warrant.

"You behold me undismayed, Mr. Duncan," he said, and he tapped the letter. "We really must find a new name for these things."

For Martha the fortnight since Christmas had been a harrowing experience, in which she felt herself cast aside while English clerks hastened to and fro, giving orders to the servants and superintending the packing and removal of furnishings for the cabin. She kept to her own room, only coming out when Thomas asked for her, on which occasions she put on as brave a face as she could, though the sight of him and the thought that he was going made her want to die. Her sense of being cast aside had reached its climax in the last three days, the days she had most wanted to be with him, during which he had been closeted with the notary, and she had hardly seen him at all.

He might well say he would only be absent four or six months. This was not how the servants saw it. With foreboding she observed their changed manner towards her. None of the original servants remained, yet though individuals might change, the servants as an entity remained the same. Already the signs were manifesting themselves of a return to the insolence and contempt which it had once before been her lot to endure. The impending departure of the master of the house showed once more what had for so long been concealed—the true nature of her position.

The surgeon was making his final call on the day of departure when to her astonishment she heard Thomas touch his small desk-bell twice—the call for her. It was the first time she had ever been commanded to appear when a visitor was present, and she was utterly at a loss to know why. She had distantly heard that they were in surprising good humour, and she thought she knew the reasons: Thomas encouraged by thoughts of the voyage, the surgeon happy to be returning to his moneybags. But what part had she in this? With misgivings she entered the strangely festive atmosphere, so unlike anything she had anticipated on the

233

last day.

"The surgeon is kind enough to admire this house," Thomas said to her with a faint smile. "He should see the other rooms. Would you care to conduct him?"

Baffled, she remained in silence at the door as the surgeon advanced towards her with a genial grin. He seemed pleased with himself. Too surprised to protest, feeling stiff and awkward, she conducted him as requested.

The inspection proceeded smoothly, Duncan full of praise, till they came to the central, windowless room. It was a grey day outside, and not even the mirrors did much to alleviate the gloom. The room was cold and still, remote from outer sounds.

"And what arrangements, I wonder, is he making about the house?" the young Scot inquired.

"I do not follow you, Surgeon."

"Do I not make myself clear? I was wondering which Company officer he'd invited to take the house over."

In the room's peculiar insulation she felt deprived of air.

"He will only be gone a few months," she replied hastily.

With arms folded across his chest, his legs set wide apart, Surgeon Duncan pushed out his lips slightly.

"I wouldn't wish to see you deceived," he said. "He'll be lucky if he reaches England."

She looked away only to rediscover him in a mirror.

"Be that as it may, I know of no arrangements to transfer the house."

"I suppose he wouldn't have told you. But the Company don't usually leave houses like this empty. There's too much demand for them." In the mirror he came closer. "And when, as in this case, the house has other attractions to offer—"

The mirror converted his smile into a leer. She could only think of the three days just past during which Tom had been closeted with the notary. Between them what had been decided? The East India Company, people said, never changed.

234

"You are very humorous, Surgeon," she said, forcing a smile to her lips.

"But serious too," he rejoined.

She pushed open one of the half-length swing doors. He moved to assist her, resting his hand on the door so close to hers that the fine yellow hairs on the top of his forefinger touched her skin, transmitting something vibrant that made her wish to recoil from him.

"Don't tell me you'd object," he protested jocularly, "if I came to live here. The devil you know is better than the devil you don't. It's a thought worth remembering."

He made to return to the living room.

"In that case, should you not see the other rooms first?" she asked, leading him on with irony.

"Ah, how you run ahead!" he said with a soft laugh. "I only meant if he hasn't promised the house to someone else."

"When would you expect such a change to take place?"

"Just now it'll mean waiting till the end of the season. But don't you worry," he confided. "The time'll come soon enough, and I trust I'll be the lucky one!"

Clinging to the banisters, she stayed where she was till the surgeon had taken his leave in the other room and departed. Then she went to the door and looked in.

Placid and unconcerned, he had resumed his Bible reading. His quiet absorption, the attention to his own life and interests which she saw reflected in him, roused in her a sudden, speechless exasperation. Her face grew sullen with that inexpressible rage which Sister Grace had feared and of which Teresa da Silva had been a victim.

"Who is to have the house while you're away?" she asked, deceptively calm.

He looked up.

"Do you wish someone else to be here?"

"The house will be transferred to someone else."

Setting his finger at the point he had reached, he gave closer attention to her.

"Who told you this?"

"I do not have to be told. How many days will it be before another of you comes?"

"Martha, listen to me. My foremost wish is to safeguard you," he began.

"Yes, and all Macao knows how. This is the way of the English. You are all the same—clever at pretending. You are not going on the great sea, though you pretend you are. You are going to England, and in Macao we know what this means."

In weariness he put a hand over his eyes.

"Martha, listen to me—"

She clenched her fists, her eyes red, her lips trembling.

"I have been thrown in the street," she said with terrible intensity. "I have been given away. I have been sold. And you ask me to listen to you—you or any other man! I listen to no one!"

There was a sound on the front stairs and Ignatius, clad in European travelling clothes, burst in.

"The order's been given to sail, sir," he said excitedly. "They've come to take you to the ship."

At the sound of it Martha rushed to the sick man, her anger gone. Kneeling beside his chair, raising her hands meaninglessly up and down, she implored him:

"I have loved you, Tom. I have loved you. I beg you not to do this to me! I trusted you not to be like the others. I have loved you!"

Her arms outstretched across his knees, she bowed her head and wept.

At the door four burly coolies, conducted by Ignatius, bore in the special litter in which Thomas was to be laid and transported to the ship. Martha raised her head and saw it. With a cry of anguish she rose from her knees and fled from the room.

"Follow her, boy," Thomas ordered Ignatius. "Bring her to me."

The boy went swiftly, but when, Thomas having been

lifted into the litter and borne carefully downstairs, Ignatius presented himself again, he was alone.

"She won't come, sir."

"What use are you to me, boy? Bring her."

"I cannot, sir. She's locked herself in and refuses to open the door."

Thomas' voice fell.

"Where is she?"

"It's an odd place, sir. Just outside the back door there's an old storeroom. We never use it for anything. She's in there."

Thomas closed his eyes. Ignatius was afraid.

"D'you wish me to go to her again, sir?"

"No, boy," Thomas replied gravely. "May God bless her and keep her. I can do no more."

Ignatius gave a sign, and the litter was borne out through the front door.

PART SEVEN

Martha Merop

AFTER HE HAD gone she took all his remaining personal possessions and anything he had ever purchased for the house,
even curtains and carpets, and had them stored in the little-
used lower rooms, ready for despatch when he or his relatives should send for them. She had a window thrown into
the wall of the disused storeroom, and the room was whitewashed. There she transferred as much as she could of her
own belongings, till in her upper bedroom there was little
left save the bed, in which she however continued to sleep.
She still wore her costly dresses, but as she traversed the
upper rooms, themselves now invested with an air of emptiness, it gave the impression that she was a ghost haunting
the house of which she had once been mistress.

Emotionally she was often upset during these operations,
as she handled so many of his things that evoked memories
of him. It was emotion which made her impatient with herself, and which she mentally forced herself to put away from
her. It reminded her of the fool she had been. It was she
who had always known it must end thus, she who had years
ago warned him it would; yet when the time came it was she
who had unconsciously believed it would not be so, that she
and he would be different. She had loved him—the women
of Macao so often did love their Englishmen—and now that
it had ended it behoved her to return as quickly as she could
to the commonsense frame of mind of earlier days when
she had recognized that there could be no other ending—
until perhaps, after some time, she would became calm
enough to think of him, which at present she dared not, and
be grateful for the departed years, as the women of Macao

239

—those who did not let fancies run away with them—were always grateful to their Englishmen, grateful for a security and solace which they knew could never be for life.

She resumed her commerce on a larger scale than before. "I have to make money while I can," she said to Pedro. "Soon it may be too late."

Time and again she tried to formulate a way of escape from being passed on to another man. Ostensibly the most feasible escape would be to marry Pedro. But for more than ten years she had been telling Pedro what to do, and imperceptibly marriage to him had become psychologically impossible. As his wife she would never be able to obey him, nor he to command her. Marriage to him, in fact, would be almost certain hell. The other alternative—to buy a small house of her own, which she could have afforded—posed a risk which she hesitated to take. She was no longer so concerned about having Teresa as a neighbour. No one in Macao was less likely to disbelieve the now widespread rumour of a secret marriage than was Teresa, who had witnessed every one of the external happenings which so strongly suggested that a marriage there had been. Nor would Teresa ever dare report on anyone so evidently enjoying the protection of the dreaded Father Montepardo. But for Martha to buy a house and move into it, signifying as it would that she now considered herself outside the scope of the Bishop's special measures, would wear the appearance of a challenge to the authorities, a challenge they would certainly take up. Reluctantly she concluded there was nothing she could do but await the fate selected for her by the East India Company.

In the house itself the servants, well aware of the significance of the domestic alterations she had made, and knowing too that when an Englishman left China sick he did not return, awaited the day when she would descend to sleep on their level; and on the rare occasions when they were obliged to speak to her, did so in an off-hand way only thinly disguising their contempt. Uncertain for their future, they were waiting for a new master, and to know where they stood.

On the 12th of May, exactly four months after Thomas' departure, the East India Company began to arrive in Macao, and a winter of comparative inactivity came to an abrupt end. The first shocks were felt at the house of Gonçalves Sequeira. The Select Committee had at last received a despatch from Calcutta concerning the opium crisis eighteen months earlier. The Governor-General, with his usual immense rectitude, a characteristic which may have been all very well in India but seldom bore any relevance to China coast situations, had ordered the Select Committee to institute bankruptcy proceedings against Abraham Biddle *in absentia* through the proper machinery of Portuguese law. For the house of Gonçalves Sequeira it was disaster. No sooner was the news known than every reputable trader with whom Pedro was dealing informed him with regret that they were unable to accept orders from him, carry his cargoes, or advance him credit. His explanations went unheeded. His promises were declined. His signature was worthless. That same night, on the verge of starvation, and unaware he was in imminent danger of arrest by the Portuguese, Biddle emerged from hiding, coming late at night to Pedro's office (where a petrified clerk at first mistook him for a spectre) and begging for food and shelter. Pedro thus faced not merely bankruptcy, but the choice between surrendering his benefactor to the Portuguese authorities, or concealing him and perhaps being arrested himself for doing so.

The following night, shortly after dark, a Portuguese captain of the watch force rang the bell at Hospital Street. With him was an African soldier holding a small bundle of Chinese women's clothes. The servant could not understand what the officer wanted, and Martha had to be called to talk to him in Macanese. Fong had been murdered. Her knifed body had been found just outside the city wall, her clothes scattered around in the grass. With the customary speed of intelligence in all that concerned serious crime in Macao, the Mandarin of the Casa Branca had demanded the surrender of the body, which had been sent to the magistracy at Chinshan. It remained to dispose of the clothes, in which the Casa Branca was not interested. The watch force captain had found out where Fong worked, but Teresa's house was in darkness and no one answered his call.

Martha took the clothes. From the nature of the death it was obvious what had happened. Fong's husband had returned after fourteen years at sea, had discovered that during his absence she had borne a son that was not his, and had murdered her in satisfaction of his honour. He had never cared for her; he had deserted her; his clan had thrown her out. None of this mattered when set beside the fact of Ignatius' birth.

And of course no one would ever answer the door opposite. Teresa crippled with cramp, unable to move unaided, and Dominie immersed perpetually in a gentle dream about Lisbon and an officer, without Fong to assist them they were prisoners in their own house, without light and without food. Having asked the officer to notify one of Teresa's relatives who might be able to gain access to the house, Martha withdrew slowly upstairs with the bundle.

The officer's footsteps had scarcely died away when along the street came the soft thudding of cloth-bound feet bearing a sedan chair. They halted outside, a man's voice said something in English, and the bell rang. Awaited in dread for four months, the moment had come, the hour of the successor. It could only be he. She heard a servant padding into the hall, the click of the door, voices, across the tiles the crisp, measured tread of European shoes, falling hollow now as they mounted the stairs. She shrank into the depths of the room, moving behind a low divan in an absurd last movement of search for protection.

In the doorway stood the black-coated, white-kerchiefed, dissipated but still immaculate figure of George Cuming.

He removed his hat.

"Good evening," he said, coming in and seeking a place to

242

lay it. "What immense relief, if I may say so, to be able to speak to a local woman in English!"

She made no response.

"You have no objection to speaking English, I hope?" he pursued.

It was a distinct change from his manner the last time they met. She was conscious of his cold blue eyes and the silvery gleam of his shoe buckles. Drawing a handkerchief from his sleeve he mopped his chin and the back of his neck.

"It's deucedly warm. Do you not use the punka?"

Following summer ritual, the punka had recently been installed across the ceiling, but its lines of white cloth fringed with red hung still. She seldom required it. She touched the embroidered bell-pull.

"It's mounting the stairs that does it," he remarked. "Forgive me if I inconvenience you."

When the Number One appeared she indicated the punka. "And bring wine."

"Two glass?"

"One glass," she replied pointedly.

"And a flask of cold water, I pray," Cuming added, flicking a mosquito off his ear. "What a pestilential season summer is! In England I never imagined I could dislike it so." He regarded her calculatingly. "Tom Mierop was my oldest friend on the China station. It was grievous to see him depart the way he had to."

"He often spoke of your friendship," she replied guardedly.

"Did he? A conscientious colleague. His pious disposition was not appreciated by some, but between him and myself there was a perfect understanding." He tucked his handkerchief away. "You appear anxious about something."

"No."

"If you are, my visit may be timely. It might almost be termed a mission of protection."

"What—form of protection?" she asked slowly.

A servant entered with decanters and glasses. Motivated

243

from somewhere on the floor below, the strips of the punka began to sway, gaining gentle momentum.

"That's better!" he exclaimed. Wine and water were poured. "May I invite myself to a chair?"

He made to sit in the Spanish armchair when a notion made him change his mind. Deferentially he sat in a smaller chair near it. He examined his fingernails.

"Had you heard that Biddle has been found to be alive after all?" he inquired casually.

"I had heard."

"You know that bankruptcy proceedings will be taken against him?"

"I had heard."

He drank the best part of a glass of water before reaching for the port.

"Your affairs are somewhat entangled with those of Biddle."

"No. They are conducted under separate account that has nothing to do with him."

"I wouldn't be too sure of that, if I were you. The transactions dealt with in that building are handled in a surprisingly haphazard manner. Do you see your accounts?"

"Yes."

The port glass close to his lips, he paused.

"Can you read?" he asked penetratingly.

She flushed.

"No."

"Then how d'you know what they show you are your accounts?"

"The items are read out to me."

"By a member of the firm, I'll warrant, who makes such inventions as he chooses."

"That could never be!"—she fumbled. "Sometimes the accounts were read to me by Mr. Mierop."

"Really?" he said with leisurely surprise. "Why, then, did he once tell me he had no knowledge of your trading?"

"That's true," she admitted, flustered. "I remember better

now. When the accounts had been read out I always told them to leave them with me. That frightened them. They thought he would go through them. Actually he never did."

He smiled with a suggestion of admiration, and took a pinch of snuff.

"Allow me, then, to make the position clear. Your money will shortly be scooped up to the last farthing to meet a portion—only a portion—of Abraham Biddle's debts."

"That's impossible!" she expostulated. "I've never even consulted Mr. Biddle. My trade is mine!"

"You conduct it through Sequeira's. So does he. That is all the court will wish to know."

"But inside Sequeira's each account is separate," she protested. "They dare not cheat me."

"Whether you've been cheated or not is immaterial." He snapped his snuffbox shut. "The proceedings will be according to Portuguese law. Under that law Sequeira's itself is the only legally recognizable entity. Biddle's sub-account, if one may so call it, is invalid, because Biddle, not being Portuguese, is not permitted to trade in a Portuguese possession. The same applies to any other foreigner dealing through the firm. As for yourself—pray forgive me, but I cannot envisage a Portuguese court conceding that you had any rights whatever. Any reference therefore to your account, Biddle's, or anyone else's, will be legally inadmissible. Do you see what that means? These accounts, so far as the court will be concerned, do not exist. All are part of Sequeira's, and all will be absorbed in the deluge of Biddle's debts."

She moved away to the black spaces of the french windows. She recalled the day this same man had given her her first order, the promise her trade had always held, the importance she had attached to it, the difficulty there had been with Tom about it, the concealment, the struggle. The Bishop had come with the first reminder that there was no escape from what one was born to; and here now was this. Every ounce of sycee, every cent, every cash, would go; and she would be glad to be a pensioner, even to a man like

Cuming, since only in this was there security.

"So?" she asked. "What is your suggestion?"

He had risen, and was standing arms folded beneath the arch.

"I am given to understand you have Biddle's keys," he said. There was an undertone of threat in both voice and stance.

"And if I do not?"

"I spoke to Sequeira. He was quite specific. A few days after Biddle disappeared you asked Sequeira to lock everything and give them to you."

"Yes," she admitted. "Mr. Mierop once explained to me what a bankruptcy was."

"If this were London or Calcutta you could not have acted more wisely. But this is not British soil. Under Portuguese law what you have done will merely render it more convenient for the authorities to show that Biddle's account, yours—and mine—were an integral part of the Sequeira transactions. We have a few hours—perhaps a day or so—before the law acts. You cannot read. I can. Give me the keys. I will send down someone reliable to bring out the books and every document that can be found. We will go through them here, destroying everything which might suggest that you or I were conducting trade through the firm. I have already destroyed my own papers. I suggest you do the same with yours. So far as Biddle's are concerned, I will make myself responsible for identifying everything that might concern you."

She paced cautiously to and fro.

"I understand another officer will shortly be coming to live here," she said.

"Who?"

"I don't know. I was about to ask if you did."

"Has there been any news of Tom Mierop?"

"I have heard nothing."

"Then what is your information based on?"

"I thought it was certain."

246

"Well, nothing can happen until there's news—by news I mean bad news—and even after that it will be months before there's any question of assigning this house."

"I understand that when an officer went to England, the Company allowed someone else to take his house."

"That is so in the case of Company houses. But this is not a Company house. It belongs to Mierop personally. In the sad event of his demise the Company would probably take it over, but certainly not while he lives."

She did not know what to make of this. It sounded true, but then Englishmen were clever at making untrue things sound true. She decided to parry it.

"Then in that case," she said, "about the bankruptcy, I think I should follow Mr. Mierop's advice."

"What advantage do you expect to gain?"

"No advantage. If I am to lose all I have, there is no more question of advantage. It is simply that I should obey Mr. Mierop until he advises me otherwise."

George Cuming took up the glass of port he had earlier set down.

"When will that be?" he inquired. "How do you know you are not waiting for advice from a man who is already dead?"

"What are you concealing from me?" she asked tensely.

"Nothing. But are you really so innocent as to believe he will return? The voyage he has taken is one from which no man has ever returned. And when the news does come, as it will, what of yourself at that time? I know you. You are an unusual woman. You want a life of your own, do you not? If tonight you do as I ask, I give you my word. When that time comes I will guarantee your independence."

Disturbed, uncertain of herself, she came to her original position behind the divan and laid her hands on the back of it. Feeling her fingers touch something unfamiliar, she looked down. Her hands were on Fong's clothes, resting where she had laid them. The poor, cheap cloth. Fong, like herself, a woman alone. Fong, like herself, a woman with no

247

one to turn to. And before her this grandee of the East India Company offering her protection.

Swiftly unlocking an ornamented Chinese cabinet, she drew out a bunch of keys attached to a chain.

"I agree to your proposal, Mr. Cuming," she said, and handed them to him.

Half an hour after his departure there was the sound of Chinese men's voices in the street, the bell rang vigorously, and Martha, going to the head of the stairs, in amazement beheld both front doors wide open as coolies bore in Thomas' trunks.

A convoy had just arrived at Taipa.

The house sprang instantly to life. Servants whom Martha had scarcely seen for four months embarrassedly hastened to make their presence felt. In the compound the wives fanned charcoal for their irons and hastily pressed their husbands' uniforms, another domestic feature not seen since January. Within minutes everything was functioning smoothly.

The bell rang again. Thomas' correspondence. A package of shirts ordered from Calcutta. His portefeuille and journal. Various odds and ends.

But once recovered from the first excitement, Martha was almost transfixed to the spot by the impact of another thought. What—oh what!—was he going to say when he learned she had given Biddle's keys to, of all people, George Cuming?

"Find out when he's expected to land!" she shouted down to Shek, the Number One.

The foreman in charge of delivery arrangements was uncertain. The convoy had only begun to arrive after dark, there were high winds at Taipa, and it was difficult to tell what was going on; but on the Praia Grande people were saying that passengers were expected to disembark in the morning.

With luck this would give her till about ten or eleven

248

o'clock next day. George Cuming, she estimated, would not risk going to Pedro's office by night; the janitor's suspicions would be aroused, and any attempt to enter would be reported. He would go early in the morning, before most people were about. Despatching a servant to Pedro's house, she asked him to be ready to accompany her to his office at seven in the morning.

After this Thomas' possessions had to be brought up from the lower rooms and re-installed in their proper places. Carpets were laid, curtains and pictures hung, cabinets shifted, and ornaments set out. Her own things too were brought up from the old storeroom, her upper room restored as it had been. Even with every servant working at full pressure it took hours. Not till well after three in the night did the house bear sufficient resemblance to the state in which Thomas left it for her to feel safe to retire for a few hours of sleep. The servants uncomplainingly worked on through the night till all was in order.

Martha had correctly assessed that beneath his calm appearance and relaxed manners George Cuming was a desperate man, his fortune and reputation at stake. Her plan was to forestall him at the office and persuade Pedro to maintain guards in the place, preventing access to the inner offices until the law acted. She was confident that with Thomas' advice—he would have to advise, whether he liked it or not—and the help of a lawyer, the separate identity of the Number Two account could somehow be established.

But when early next morning she reached Pedro's house it was to find he was still sleeping, and when she furiously demanded that he be wakened immediately she was informed that this would be difficult: he had been sleeping since yesterday afternoon. She knew what this meant. As in the opium crisis, so now. Pedro had taken refuge in drink. Resignedly she bid her bearers proceed.

The office, when she reached it, was conspicuously open in the otherwise shuttered and empty street, while some yards downhill, and equally conspicuous, two bearers waited beside an empty chair. Martha alighted at the door. The outer office was empty, but there were voices from one of the inner rooms. Gently drawing open one of the swing doors, she went inside.

"The only help you may expect"—it was Cuming—"is such as will enable you to bury yourself again wherever you've been buried hitherto."

"I'd like to oblige yer, George, but where I've been they're unwillin' to give me food."

"With money, then. A small weekly stipend."

"They're unwillin', George. It's not a question o' money."

"Were you not with Chinamen?"

"Yes."

"Money should put them at their ease."

"Yer don't understand. I can't go back."

Martha was not so much listening as taking in the disturbing fact that Pedro had chosen the alternative of concealing Biddle, and in the office evidently. She had always mistrusted Biddle's influence over Pedro. It was she who had insisted on Pedro being independent of him; and it was from that day that Pedro really began to make money. She knew that Pedro regarded himself as responsible for Biddle's downfall, having introduced him to Judge Pereira. But this, in her eyes, did not justify Pedro's action now. In what was in effect a straight choice between herself and Biddle, he had chosen Biddle. Pedro was no longer to be counted on. There would be no guards placed in the office, no means of preventing Cuming, Biddle, or his tool Pedro, from interfering with the accounts to her own certain ruin. She was in this alone.

"I can save yer, George, whatever laws they stand me up against. I'll go down in the dust, but you'll live as a gentleman. But I need 'elp. Nothin' grandiose, 'ave no fear. Just money enough to keep me alive in a decent condition, and a word from you to allow me to stay in me own 'ouse. And when it's all over, another word to say not prison for an old man like me. Not prison, George. Assure me o' that, and I swear everythin' o' yours'll be safe."

"When everything of your own is finished? Where do you keep your books?"

"Yer've grown defiant, me boy." There was a snarl in it. "I don't look ser good as I did, but I'm not finished. Until I am, yer'll do as yer bid! Gimme them keys."

"Not on your life."

There was a sound of locks being tried.

"If I go down, George, you'll go down with me. That I swear also."

"You're discredited, thank God, at last. What other rooms have we?"

George Cuming strode out through some inner swing doors, and penetrated deeper down the corridor.

"Mr. Cuming!"

He turned sharply in the semi-gloom.

"Mr. Cuming," Martha repeated, "I would prefer we went no further with this."

He returned a pace.

"Are you mad? This has to be undertaken at once."

"I have changed my mind, Mr. Cuming. Pray return me the keys."

He hesitated, assessing the degree of danger he stood in.

"Sink if you wish to," he replied suavely. "I am for survival. Do I undertake this for both of us, or for myself alone?"

"You do not undertake it at all, sir," she replied, drawing back her *dó*. "I withdraw my permission."

He laughed.

"A pensioner speaks! Then, little miss, it will be done without your permission."

With a flick of the keys he resumed his way along the corridor, passing into what had once been Biddle's inner sanctum.

She pursued him as far as the door.

"Mr. Cuming, I beg you!" she pleaded, wondering what

woman's resource she could resort to next. "Mr. Mierop has returned. I must ask his advice first."

"Mierop? Returned?" he demanded in amazement.

His features were momentarily caught in the dimly grey light from the room's solitary little window. There was a dry clicking sound, unidentifiable had it not been followed by a liquid movement high in the gloomiest corner of the room as the fool boy, hideously white, with hair as long as a woman's falling about his body, released himself from his bat-like position, and with legs and arms cunningly outspread like a spider, dropped upon George Cuming and bore him to the ground almost without a sound. As Cuming collapsed beneath him on the tiles, the fool boy's hands closed about his throat.

Despite his white hands and foppish appearance, Cuming was sinewy and strong, heavier in build than the fool boy; but struggle and batter him as he did he could not break the madman's hold. Oblivious to the worst pain Cuming could inflict, he clung on with absorbed concentration; and as, murderously locked together, they rolled wildly over on the tiles, the fool boy's face wore a smile.

And thus, somewhat unexpectedly, Martha came to know the paternity of Ignatius.

At this moment providentially Pedro arrived. The struggle itself caused hardly any noise, but the screeching of chairs on the tiles brought Pedro at once into the depths of the corridor. Instantly he summoned the bearers of Cuming's and Martha's sedans, hard-hewn, expressionless men, their skins darkened by the sun. Knowing without words what was required of them, they chose their time before closing in on the fool boy, when one of them succeeded in hitting him on the back of the neck. For an instant he relaxed his madman's grasp. Dexterously the bearer flung him on his back and hit him with the tips of his fingers at a point high on his chest, not far from the armpit. The fool boy uttered a gasp and lay where he was, momentarily paralysed. With a rope procured by Pedro the four men trussed him up, heels and hands behind his back. Cuming lay limp at the foot of the desk, his face to the wood.

"Get me his keys, Cousin," Martha directed. "Search him."

Uncertainly Pedro went forward. With an effort Cuming lurched up. Pedro sprang back, more from surprise than fear, as Cuming, supporting himself against the desk, stared at them emptily, his glazed eyes bereft of expression. With the palm of his hand he wiped blood off his chin.

"Get his men out," said Martha quietly in Cantonese. There was no turning back now.

But Cuming caught her intent.

"Stay!" he ordered them.

None of the bearers moved.

She sized up the situation, Cuming's bearers on her right, her own on her left, confronting each other sinisterly, only awaiting an order.

There was a sound of sharp footsteps in the front of the shop, and a man called in Portuguese, "Is anyone there?"

Pedro glanced down the corridor.

"My God!" he muttered, re-entering the room hastily. "It's the watch force. They've come for Biddle. I'm done for."

The moment had an unearthly quality. It was as if the whole of the ordered world—Martha's world—had come to an end, Biddle about to be arrested, Pedro reeking of liquor, charged with concealing him, and in the inner room this scene of disorder, blood on the floor, furniture at sixes and sevens, the trussed-up fool boy reviving now and beginning to snarl at Cuming like a dog, Cuming himself with his face swollen and hideous, his clothes ripped to pieces, one of the sleeves of his coat lying on the tiles, while on each side stood the coolies, looking incriminatingly as though they were hired assassins.

Martha thought quickly. Whatever happened, Pedro must be prevented from losing his nerve.

"On the contrary, Cousin," she said. "They could not

253

have come at a more convenient time. They can take Mr. Cuming as well. We are both witness, Cousin," she explained pointedly, "to why he has come here."

Again the officer's voice called out.

"Hold him in conversation," Martha said softly to Pedro, as with harrowed mien the latter went to answer the call. "Also, Mr. Cuming, you and I know why this madman has attacked you, and why he will, if we set him free, kill you. If you do not wish the entire city to know that displeasing story, in addition to your being in Mr. Biddle's office for an illegal purpose, you will give up the keys—immediately. In return I will see you out of this."

Cuming made no movement.

"Do I have to remind you," she went on, "that you are no longer among the English, where your word is all-important and mine means nothing? You have made the mistake the English are always so careful to avoid. You have come down to my level, on which the word of an Englishman means nothing whatever. Do you wish to stay on my level, Mr. Cuming, or shall I send you back to your own?"

Not for nothing had Martha for years listened from the rear landing to those parties of Tom's. She knew too well how the English talked. Through and through she knew their fear of losing caste.

Cuming's eyes fell, and she saw she had won. His blood-stained hand went slowly to his pocket and drew the keys out. He came forward to give them to her. On either side the bearers advanced, hers to protect, his to resist.

"On the floor will do," she said rapidly.

He withdrew. The keys clanked on the tiles. The bearers fell back. She made a sign to one of her men. He took up the keys and gave them to her.

"Now, all of you," she said in Cantonese, "bring him with you, follow me, and be silent."

At the door she paused. Pedro and the officer of the watch force were speaking together quietly in the front room. She could not hear what it was about. Quickly she led the way to the furthest extremity of the building, through the yard and out into a rear alley. In daylight George Cuming looked far worse than he had in the dark study. He could not possibly traverse the city in such a state. Going to the rear door of the adjacent shop, Martha rapped and attracted attention.

The boss was a fat old Chinese who, as Pedro's neighbour, inevitably knew the identity of Gonçalves Sequeira Number Two. A quick exchange in Cantonese, and the boss was grinning agreement. They entered the main building. It was a coffin shop.

At a word from the boss a coffin was brought.

"Get in," Martha said to Cuming. "They will carry you home."

With assistance he was laid in it and the lid was fixed on. A moment later, borne by Cuming's bearers and four men from the coffin shop, the second member of the Select Committee passed innocuously through the men of the watch force mustered in the street.

But on re-entering the Gonçalves Sequeira offices she found it was not Biddle the watch force had come for. The swing doors concealing Biddle were closed, but he was still there. Beneath the doors she saw his broken shoes and torn stockings as she passed. Uneasily she rejoined Pedro. The officer—the same officer of the evening before—saluted her.

Then she saw. In the street, just outside the main doors, the fool boy, still trussed with ropes, lay on the cobbles between two men of the watch. An order had been received from the Casa Branca. Responsibility for the murder of Fong had been fixed upon the Chin clan, and in the normal way of Chinese justice the clan head—the head of the clan for the entire district, not Chin Fui—had been ordered to surrender a man. Unwilling to give up the real culprit, the clan head had selected the fool boy, who for eighteen months had not once left the building and had nothing whatever to do with the murder. The Casa Branca had commanded the Portuguese to deliver him.

In silence Martha walked into the street, where the fool

boy, opening his eyes, saw her, and in a moment of lucidity such as he used to have long ago, said in English:

"Why you angry me, missie? Fool boy have"—he faltered, and muttered it in Cantonese—"responsibility."

Then intelligence receded. His eyes closed. A trickle of blood oozed from his mouth.

The watch force officer was a gaunt, disillusioned man.

"Believe me, Senhora, there are moments when I pray on my knees that we might strike back," he said, his voice trembling, "when this is what they call justice."

Borne suspended from a pole laid on the shoulders of four men, like a pig in a basket the unconscious madman was taken to his fate.

For some moments after they had gone Martha could not speak. But Pedro spoke, at once and urgently, advising her that Biddle had offered to help them, and begging her to let him go through their commercial documents. His insistence restored her to reality. The sun was already well above the rooftops, the day warming up. She had not a minute to lose. On this day of all days Thomas must not return to find her out. Dismissing Pedro's pleas with a gesture, she entered her sedan and was borne swiftly to Hospital Street.

Entering the hall she glanced at the table for hat and cane, saw with relief that he had not yet arrived. She went quickly upstairs. Drawing off her black mantle as she entered the living room, she stepped back in surprise. Standing near the fireplace with his back to her was a European sailor, a youth. At the sound of her dress he turned to face her. His skin darkened by the sun, his features strangely mature after his months at sea, it was Ignatius.

"Yes," he said apologetically, looking down at himself. "The sailors gave me these."

But why had he come first, she thought? And what was he doing just standing there? Tom was still in the roads at Taipa. He had come back, but he was still sick. She stared wordlessly at the boy. She found she wanted to ask the question only if she need not listen to the answer.

"You're as black as an Indian," she said.

"Yes," he answered with a grin. "The sun's terrible in those places."

"Is it? I've been in business again till the last few days. You'll be amazed when you see how many flowers we've sold."

"It's good."

"Yes." There was a pause. "Is St. Helena a big place?"

"I didn't go as far as that."

"But you went on the great sea."

"Oh yes, but only as far as Prince of Wales Island. There they said there was no purpose my going any further. I'd better come back."

She refused to listen.

"Ignatius, I have something terrible to tell you," she interrupted. "When did you land?"

"This morning, Senhora."

"It was yesterday. Your mother is dead. That man returned. He murdered her, horribly, outside the city." She covered her face. "No, I shouldn't be telling you this. She's dead. That was all I meant to say." Her voice fell. "What do you mean—no purpose?"

His Eurasian eyes, with their long dark lashes and pale irises, met hers.

"We buried him at sea. Twenty-nine days out. They fired ten minute-guns."

She stood stockstill, as if frozen. Then like an automaton she continued.

"I was responsible for that marriage, Ignatius. It seemed wrong then. I never believed it could end as it did." But he just stared at her, making no reaction. "You are very calm. You understand, do you not, what has happened?"

"I understand, Senhora. They told me. I'm very sorry," he replied steadily. "It's difficult to explain, though. Somehow this is my home now, and you and—"

He faltered.

257

"Go down and have breakfast," she ordered hastily. "You must be starving."

"Not yet, Senhora. There is something I must tell you first."

"I do not wish to hear it. He is dead. There is nothing more to say."

"There is some more I have to say, Senhora. He told me to."

"Say it later. Go and have breakfast."

But he stayed there doggedly.

"In a minute, Senhora. I'll change these clothes too. Before he died he said there'd be money for me, and it's true there was. But there were no clothes. My own were quite worn out after so much washing in those hot places, and these were all the sailors could spare. They're very ugly, aren't they?"

"Very, and they do not fit."

"I was with him most of that last day—when he told me about the money, I mean. Then later"—he glanced at her warily—"when other people were there, someone said he'd not live much longer, so I thought to myself, 'You've done all you can', and was squatting against the wall of that huge cabin while they stood round his bed.

"Just then I heard him, from out of the middle of them, saying in a terrible, urgent way, like when he wanted to leave for the Company house and his bathwater wasn't ready:

" 'There is something I have left undone!'

"His voice was not very clear. The others didn't understand it. But I knew him so well, I could always follow his words.

"He called my name, twice, in that same terrible way, very loudly. For days—ever since we put to sea—he had not spoken so loudly. None of them knew my name, so when he called I had to go and ask them politely to make way for me, which at first they refused to do, because of course in the ship they treated me properly as a servant, not like it is here. They thought I was being too proud.

"So I had to tell them, 'I am Ignatius. He wants me.' Then they let me come.

"He had raised himself so that he sat up in bed, but as I came to him he began falling back—his face was so white, as white as the shirt he wore—until two of them took pillows and propped him up, because they could see he was still wanting me.

"So I said, 'Yes, Senhor, what is it? I am here.' But though his eyes were open and he appeared to be looking at me, somehow he could not see me, and he went on calling. So I put my hands on his and said, 'I am Ignatius. What are your orders, Senhor?'

"He sighed then, as if he were suddenly happy. He craned forward at me from the pillows—I could remember him then as he used to be before he was sick—and said (I remember every word, Senhora; I shall never forget it):

" 'I am going, Ignatius,' he said. 'I am going.' Like that, very strongly. Then, 'When you return to Macao, tell her this'—he did not have to explain who it was; I knew he meant you—'and promise me now that you *will* return to Macao, no matter what obstacles stand in your way, and that whatever happens you will not forget my words.'

"Everyone around seemed to be holding their breath, they were so silent.

"So I promised.

"And then he said:

" 'Dear lad, tell her this with my dying love—USE MY NAME.'

"His hands moved a little. I think he was trying to grip mine. But his head fell back on the pillows and they told me to go away.

"I went back to my place and squatted down again. It was such a huge cabin, Senhora, almost like a room in a house; and they stayed standing there all about him so I could not see anything; and after a time some of them slowly moved backwards, away from his bed.

"Then they all began walking out of the cabin, and one

of them—he was a friendly man, quite old—picked me up by the arm and took me along with them. I looked back and could see him there on the bed. But they had stretched the sheet over his face.

" 'He's dead,' the old man said to me. 'But don't you worry, son. We'll find a job for you.'

"He was very good to me."

Ignatius paused and looked curiously at Martha.

"I thought it was strange, his last words. No one else understood it either. The old man asked me what it meant. I told him I didn't know. But there could be no mistaking it. He spoke quite clearly. Does it mean something to you, Senhora?"

She nodded swiftly, unable to speak, and turned her back on him. Like Ignatius, she had not the faintest idea what it meant, but it was her Englishman, absolute and real, as if it was he himself who had spoken to her, he who so often said things she did not understand at first.

"You are not angry with me, Senhora?"

She shook her head vigorously.

"I will have breakfast now," he said. He hovered near the door. "It's a strange thing, a burial at sea."

The President's study in the Casa Garden was small and congested with furniture. Between its narrow windows stood heavy cabinets above which, placed too high to be seen properly, hung portraits and English landscapes, gathered there, one would suspect, because there was no room for them anywhere else. It was still the forenoon, and it was hot. One of the cabinets had swung open, and from it bulged a multitude of files and letters in disarray, evidence of the President's forthcoming departure. Across the ceiling a punka swayed, monotonously agitating the papers and rendering it necessary for everything on the desk to be held down by brass weights.

Since Ignatius left her, Martha had been carrying on without thought, in a curious state of drifting confusion. She

260

had no recollection of her actions. Actually, among other things, she had gone to her wardrobe, changed into the same simple black dress she had worn at the Midnight Mass, and it was in this, with a heavy veil of Spanish lace falling over her shoulders and covering her face completely, that she left for the Casa Garden, a palanquin having been sent to fetch her.

As she was ushered into the President's study, Henry Browne was seated in the centre of his large desk, with on one side of him a nervous and cadaverous clerk, Mr. Rogers, and on the other a handsome, pale, tight-lipped gentleman, dressed meticulously in outward image of his mind, whom Martha recognized as the notary. Despite the heat and humidity of summer, all three were fully dressed in European style.

"And where, pray, is Mr. Cuming?" the President was asking Mr. Rogers. "It is he who should be handling this matter."

"He cannot be found, sir," the clerk replied, trembling.

"Most inconsiderate. He knows how intensely I dislike dealing with these matters involving locals."

Henry Browne glanced up at the figure before him, and being of a fiery and lustful disposition where women were concerned, was not deceived by widow's weeds. Beneath the lace veil, and even more beneath the arm-length sleeves of black piña, transparently light, he noticed a glow of skin mysteriously white and seductive. With a pull at his moustaches he lowered his eyes hastily.

"Tell her to sit down," he murmured to the clerk, who did so haltingly in Macanese. "This is a most extraordinary epistle," he continued, perusing with the aid of spectacles the heavy papers in front of him. "I confess I am surprised, Mr. Humphrey," he said, leaning towards the notary, "that you did not see fit to advise him against dictating such a rigmarole."

"I did try to, sir," the notary replied. "But he was extremely insistent, and in view of his condition I considered it my only course to defer to him. In law, of course, the will is practically meaningless."

"Yes. Even I can grasp that," said the President, and feeling he had perhaps been over-critical of the notary, added sympathetically, "No consideration for us, eh, Mr. Humphrey? Leaves us with all the awkward decisions."

"Leaves you, Mr. President," the meticulous notary corrected deferentially, "in your capacity as Probate Officer."

"Let us not stress that overmuch, Mr. Humphrey," said Browne. "I rely on you. Now, where are we to begin?"

"Well, sir, since you ask my advice," the notary replied, his entire appearance tightening into the minutiae of his profession, "there is one aspect of the document which, if disposed of at the outset, might spare us a deal of trouble. He describes this woman as his wife, as you see here." He indicated the line. "I queried this, because the actual words he wished to put were 'my beloved wife Martha Mierop', and I felt obliged to point out warningly to him that in the case of a common law wife this was not correct. His answer —somewhat to my surprise, I might say—was that she was not a common law wife. But when I asked him where he was married he refused to say. I finally managed to persuade him that unless he was willing and able to produce proof of his marriage it would be inadvisable to write the woman's name as Martha Mierop. With considerable reluctance he agreed, which accounts for the name being written Martha da Silva. But he insisted on the words 'my beloved wife' being left in."

The President nodded.

"*De mortuis nil nisi bonum,*" he said gloomily, "but you have my sympathy, Mr. Humphrey. A most obstinate man. I had to deal with him for years."

"Yes, sir. But there's an important point here."

"I'm sure there is. What is it?"

"Simply that if, contrary to the Company regulation, Mr. Mierop was in fact married to this woman, it is arguable that the entire will is invalid and can be ignored."

Henry Browne curled one end of his moustache.

"A point indeed!" he answered. He ruminated. "It would certainly spare us a deal of trouble. I see what you mean."

"Precisely what I had in mind, sir—to save you trouble," said the notary. "Might we take this point first?"

"By all means. What do you wish me to do? Shall we ask her directly if she was married to him?"

"As a matter of form, perhaps a straight question of identity first, sir," said Mr. Humphrey, who was a most tactful prompter.

"Yes," the President agreed. "Rogers, ask her if she's—erm"—he found the place—"Martha da Silva."

Mr. Humphrey, pleased with his prowess, leaned back on two legs of his chair, studying her suavely. There was a slight pause as Rogers blew his nose—the cool air moved by the punka was giving him a cold.

For Martha too the room would have been too cool had it not been for the veil over her face which, perhaps because the punka was shifting small particles of dust about the untidy room, was becoming suffocating and uncomfortable. Unwilling to endure it any longer, and wishing to spare the clerk, who was now sneezing, the trouble of interpreting when he was clearly not feeling well, she raised the veil from her face with a simple movement of both hands, and addressing the dome of the President's head, which was bent over the will, said:

"I have nothing further to add to what Mr. Mierop told this gentleman."

Amid what then took place she was surprised, and rather shocked, to see three Englishmen behave with so little composure. Humphrey swung forwards with a bang which nearly broke the legs of his chair. The President's head shot up as if someone had threatened to shoot him. The clerk, with an awful sound, mid-sneeze, mid-groan, sank shivering into the depths of his chair, his face hidden in his handkerchief.

"Does she speak English?" demanded the President, the first to regain speech in what seemed to Martha a query of unusual stupidity.

"It would appear so," the clerk mumbled in reply, suppressing a sneeze and desperately, needlessly, prolonging operations in respect of his nose.

"Someone might have warned me," said the President in a tone of aggrieved dignity. "If you speak English," he resumed slowly, in the precise way Englishmen use when addressing foreigners, "will you be so good as to tell us whether you were married to Mr. Mierop."

"I understand he describes me as his wife, Mr. President," she answered.

"We are aware of that," Humphrey interposed, repaying her with severity for the shock she had given him. "Were you in fact married?"

"Mr. Mierop has spoken for me," she said.

Henry Browne energetically pushed up his moustaches.

"You speak the most remarkable English, if I may say so. Am I to take it you have understood everything we have so far said?"

"Everything, Mr. President—except when you were speaking Latin."

With a shiver the President took refuge in the documents.

"This is most embarrassing," he murmured. "I think, Mr. Humphrey, the sooner we proceed the better." From mouth and nostrils simultaneously he issued a blast of windy sound, and began. "This document is the last will and testament of Mr. Mierop who, as you know, died at sea three months ago. I will not burden you with those parts of the will that do not relate to you. Mr. Mierop leaves substantial sums of money to his two sisters, to two of his cousins, and to Mr. Rous, who handled his affairs in London. He also leaves a large sum for the maintenance of five destitute families in London, to be selected at Mr. Rous' discretion.

"We now come to the main part of the will. I wish you to listen to this very carefully. I quote: 'To my beloved wife Martha da Silva I leave the sum of ten thousand pounds,*

* In today's money, about US$1,200,000.

264

together with my house in Hospital Street and all the furniture in it. If she will give up her wish to spend all her life in Macao, and will come to Europe, she is to receive a further three thousand pounds.

" 'It is my wish that after my death she should marry, with but this one exception, that if she marries any person of the Portuguese race she is to receive five thousand pounds only, regardless of whether she comes to Europe or not. Anyone else of any other race she may marry, and receive the full ten thousand pounds, and the additional three thousand pounds if she comes to Europe.

" 'My books and furniture, my plate, my watch and ring and wearing apparel, prints, wines, and any musical instruments or other curious articles, together with the house, are to be hers whether or not she conforms to my wishes in regard to marriage.' "

The President paused.

"You appreciate, I am sure," he said, "that the sums involved in this will are considerable. Before probate can be granted—that is to say, before the money and property can legally become yours—we shall need to know something of your personal intentions."

But she just wanted to go home and forget about them.

"This is surely not necessary, Mr. President," she answered politely.

Henry Browne scanned her as he would have a military map on the eve of an invasion.

"Then you have not understood what I read out," he corrected, taking up the will again.

"I understood, sir," she insisted. "And I am deeply grateful to know what Mr. Mierop wished me to receive. But I do understand that this is only a will."

"*Only* a will?" Humphrey queried smartly, on his professional dignity.

"Yes," she replied. "I mean, I don't expect to receive anything. For instance, I know you would never give me the house."

Henry Browne stiffened at what had suddenly become not a dry-as-dust will but a challenge to his personal magnanimity.

"My dear lady," he exclaimed with emotion, "you certainly will be given the house. There is no question about that whatever."

Humphrey stared at him in a stiff, puritanical way. The clerk froze to his papers. Conscious of their reactions, Henry Browne flushed.

Martha watched it.

"Mr. President," she asked tentatively, "what is ten thousand pounds?"

Henry Browne frowned.

"You surely know what a pound is?"

"No, sir. I always weigh silver by the tael."

"You—?" he checked an utterance of surprise.

"I have a small business of my own."

He raised his eyebrows.

"Bring the equivalent of half-a-sovereignsworth in sycee," he ordered the clerk.

Rogers, thankful for something to do, moved awkwardly to one of the cabinets, from which he drew two leather purses. Placing one on a set of weighing scales which was one of the room's many encumbrances, he poured from the other a shower of miscellaneous bits and pieces of silver till the scales balanced. Thereupon he took the purse by its silk strings and laid it heavily on the desk between Martha and the President.

She assessed it.

"About six double handfuls."

"Very possible," the President agreed. He lifted the purse and lowered it. "Two of these makes a pound. Two hundred of these makes a hundred pounds. Twenty thousand of these makes ten thousand pounds—one hundred and twenty thousand double handfuls."

She thought for a moment.

"How much room would that take up?"

266

The problem of storing silver was one with which the Company was all too familiar. Henry Browne made a mental calculation.

"Well, taking the godown of that house in Hospital Street as an example: if you were to move everything else out of it and stack it from floor to ceiling with chests of sycee— every cubic foot, in fact, from top to bottom—" he paused. "No, perhaps that godown would not be large enough."

"Sir!" warned Humphrey. "I think one should not encourage—"

But she felt safe now to interrupt him.

"Thank you, Mr. President. That is what I wished to know. It seems that five thousand pounds is already a great deal of money."

"Five thousand?"

"Yes. With the house, the only sum to which no provisos are attached."

Browne gazed at her in astonishment.

"Remarkable!" he exclaimed under his breath.

"Nevertheless, Mr. President," intervened Humphrey with some haste, "the point I made remains at issue."

Henry Browne leaned ponderously in the notary's direction, considered him balefully over the rims of his spectacles, and said with finality:

"If I may be permitted to use your jargon, Mr. Humphrey, it is arguable that this is a will, and that wills depend upon the laws of England, not on the regulations of the East India Company."

"Yes, sir."

There was silence.

"Limited probate may be granted forthwith in respect of the house, furniture, personal effects, and the first five thousand pounds. There is a key somewhere which she ought to have."

Humphrey scowled. The terrified clerk laid it on the desk. She recognized the master key to the godown.

"With deference, sir," said Humphrey, "the formalities

have not yet been completed. This is incorrect."

"Much in China is incorrect, Mr. Humphrey. The formalities are your concern. Mine is to see the substance of the late Mr. Mierop's wishes carried out. Take the key," he said, pushing it across to her. "All that it unlocks is yours."

As the palanquin—its use by Martha was of course accidental, the Company having no lesser conveyance immediately available—returned her to the house, the earnest conversations of a group of Macao Portuguese women gathered on Teresa's doorstep petered out. One prompting another, the women turned their backs on her, a group of long black mantles facing away in silence.

"The old lady's dead," Ignatius whispered to her as she alighted.

Giving the head bearer a fraction of sycee, she dismissed the palanquin and crossed the street.

"Is Dominica inside?" she asked.

There was no response, every mantled head averted.

She made her way to the door.

"There's no need for anyone else to go in," one of them muttered.

She turned.

"Is anyone with her?"

"Her cousins," answered the woman nearest her without raising her eyes.

"She's hysterical," volunteered another.

"Has a doctor seen her?"

"No."

"Should one not be sent for—an English doctor?"

The mantles stirred. There was a murmur of wonder. None could command such a doctor. For a Macao woman to do so was inconceivable.

Amid whispers of incredulity Martha retraced her steps.

"Ask Surgeon Duncan," she instructed Ignatius, "with my respect, if he can come at once."

Entering her own hall, she was abruptly reminded that it

was not by wills that houses were bequeathed to women. There was still the staff to be dealt with. All four men-servants were standing in the hall, in their faces that expression of neutrality with which Chinese confront personal crises.

"There are two foreigners upstairs," said Shek.

"Then why is one of you not looking after them? Kindly continue your duties, all of you, as you normally do."

She did not like the look of them. They were in no mood to obey, and without loyalty they were a potential danger. Officially this was a foreign house, with servants engaged under security, and the Casa Branca might well ask why a Chinese woman was inhabiting it. Because of this danger she would not be able to dismiss any of them. Somehow she would have to master them.

She went upstairs. In the living room stood Pedro, nervous and on his guard. Beside him stood a much older man, modestly clad in a black coat and breeches which hung about him untidily, sack-like. If they were not the clothes of someone else, then the wearer had shrunk remarkably from his former size. His face was pale, thin and waxy. His white hair, drawn back neatly and tied with a black ribbon, was so sparse that he looked like an old woman.

"You may not remember Mr. Biddle," said Pedro.

She halted.

"The punka—wine—shortcake," she ordered Shek.

"No formalities, I pray," said Biddle oleaginously. "Might I 'ave leave to be seated?"

She motioned him to a chair.

"Me conscience grieves me," he explained humbly, "with the thought of all the troubles I've brought on you and our Pedro 'ere. Before I go to what's facin' me, it's me solemn obligation to try and give yer both all the 'elp an' advice I can."

"My investments are a total loss, Mr. Biddle," she replied nervously. "I appreciate your consideration, but there is nothing more to be said or done."

"That's what I guessed yer were thinkin'," he said, his lined face losing some of its impassivity. "And this is why I've come. There *is* somethin' that could be done. If someone can restore public confidence in Sequeira's, every penny yer talk of today as lost will turn into a profit tomorrer." He leaned back with a flabby shadow of his former evil smile.

"How?"

"What's the source o' public confidence in any firm? The knowledge that it 'as money be'ind it! All yer need do with Sequeira's is find someone"—he lingered over it—"with money, someone willin' to invest it boldly. Quite a deal o' money'll be required, but with it Sequeira's can ride the worst storm, and all yer enterprises'll succeed as yer'd 'oped."

"You are probably right," she said, as frightened of him as she had been fifteen years ago. "But I have faced my loss. I am reconciled to it."

"There's no bein' reconciled to loss such as Sequeira's 'as in front of it!" Biddle warned. "'Ave yer thought about what'll 'appen when I'm in that court? Everythin' Sequeira's possess will go down as a little token to meetin' my debts— the shop, the furnishin's, the land, our Pedro's 'ouse, personal things yer thought were yours for life. Imagine if yer were the owner of this 'ouse. Yer'd lose it!" he said sharply, his eyes wide open. "Yer'd lose it, me dear—and all this fine furniture and any private money yer might 'ave. It'd all go."

Ignatius appeared to announce that the surgeon was below. He had encountered him by chance in the street.

Flurried and anxious, Martha bid them await her return, and descended to the hall. The mere fact that Surgeon Duncan had responded to her call—for to be commanded by a Macao woman, whatever the circumstances, was an insult to a Briton—showed that he too had heard the news about the will.

The crossing of the street—such a simple action—was an event. With fear and respect the women in the street drew aside before the incredible sight of a young woman like themselves, a woman wearing a *dó*, conducting a surgeon of the East India Company into a Portuguese house, a house like their own, explaining to him as she went (in English, which the Macao Portuguese ladies did not understand) the nature of the case he had been called to attend.

Upstairs incense was being burnt. A mass of candles flickered before the family shrine. Women were arranging flowers round Teresa's bed. Some of the women Martha remembered from years before. Others she had seen come and go, but never met. All of them, young and old, knew who she was. Their peculiarly festive preparations came to a sudden stop. In the silence she heard Dominie's voice saying pettishly:

"I'm not a child! Why should I go to bed?"

But Martha did not at once look for Dominie. Herself the focus of every eye, she went slowly to the bedside. Beneath white linen they had laid out Teresa's body, the head revealed. It remained a hard, austere face, yet in death there was humility in it. With wonder Martha perceived what in life Teresa had never shown, that she had a just, sensible face—and the scar had gone, lost in a pallor equal to its own. It was another Teresa, a better woman, of whom it was impossible to believe that afternoon on the Rua da Penha, the papers smoking in the grate.

Recalling it, Martha could not look any longer. She faced the relatives, two of whom, she then appreciated, were holding the distraught Dominie who, with her wonderful black hair falling all about her, was in the midst of a monotonously babyish struggle with them, pulling her hand away, pretending it was bruised, crying, having it taken once more, all the time pleading against being obliged to lie down in the other room. There was something obscene about it. Sometimes she giggled low down.

"I'll get the better of you!" she said. "What makes you think you can tell me what to do?"

Then she saw Martha.

She stood up, her dark eyes livid and wild. She struggled

back, upsetting a chair. She steadied herself, searching to recall who it was.

"Take me away!" she cried suddenly. "She has glass in her hand. What my mother said—never let her pick up glass!"

"I had better not stay with you," said Martha to Surgeon Duncan.

"I'd prefer it if you did," said he. "There'll be language difficulties, I don't doubt."

Martha spoke out.

"Dominie, I've brought a gentleman to see you."

In the act of dragging her cousins back Dominie recovered herself, gazed vaguely through her locks at Martha, and from her to the surgeon.

"Oh!" she exclaimed. Gently drawing her hand away from her cousin, she pushed her hair back from her forehead. "What a terrible welcome! Please come this way."

She attempted to conduct him into another part of the house, but was grabbed by her cousins, who were wise to her vagaries.

"Ask them to set her free," said the surgeon.

Martha did so in Macanese.

Released, Dominie extended her hand.

"Allow me, Senhor," she said graciously.

Playing his part, Duncan took her hand. To everyone's amazement he was led away into Dominie's own room. There, surveying him admiringly, she said in Portuguese, of which she only knew a few words:

"I'm sure you must find this climate terrible. I can't stand it either."

"There's nothing much wrong with her," Duncan said in an undertone to Martha. "We simply need to calm her down."

"You appear to have done that already, Surgeon."

He smiled slightly.

"Ay, so I observe. What a pleasant room you have!" he said kindly in very Scottish Macanese.

"You say such polite things, Senhor."

She bid him to a seat and took one herself, watching intently as from his pocket he took the emblem of his profession as conducted in China, a small ivory of a nude woman recumbent.

"Oh!" she exclaimed, quietly enraptured. "A medical officer!"

Her face had begun to glow, evoking the beauty she had had as a child. The women were crowding at the door.

"She'd better remain here in her own house," Duncan said to Martha, and instructed that the body and anything suggestive of a funeral be taken away as soon as possible. "May I come and see you again tomorrow?" he asked Dominie, as if speaking to a child.

"You are most welcome, Senhor."

"This evening would be better," Martha advised.

"This evening it shall be," Duncan said playfully, "if the Senhora agrees."

"The Senhora will be very happy," Dominie sighed, placidly folding her hands.

Wine was ordered. It was becoming a kind of party. Martha left them. Passing Teresa, she looked once again at the white, humble face, and walked on.

As she reached the street, the President of the Select Committee was just alighting from his gold and white palanquin, and another unprecedented incident took place. In full view of the women assembled in the street Henry Browne walked over and extended his hand to her. There was an audible gasp of astonishment (for the handshake was far more incredible than even Martha knew—Henry Browne momentarily forgot himself) as, in an access of social panic, she lamely put forth her hand into his. She had never shaken hands with a man before.

"It occurred to me," said Henry Browne, his regard containing curiosity and a somewhat brash admiration, "that, as my time here is short, I should use it profitably by discussing with you the more uncertain parts of the will. It also

273

occurred to me that this might best be done at your house. I hope this is not disagreeable."

"You are more than welcome, Mr. President," she replied timidly.

While mounting the stairs she did her utmost to recall Thomas' maxims about introducing people, another thing she had never done before.

"Mr. President, I think you have already met Senator Gonçalves Sequeira—and Mr. Biddle."

It was a hot day, but in a manner of speaking the room froze.

"How do you come to know this man?" the President asked Martha coldly, his geniality gone.

"I have not seen him since I was fourteen."

"What brings him to see you now?"

"He has come to advise me on my business."

"What advice, pray, is he in a position to give?"

"Mr. Biddle and I both trade through Senator Gonçalves Sequeira."

"The Senhora," Pedro explained, "faces a substantial loss due to the refusal of shippers to carry her cargoes."

Henry Browne came to the fireplace, glanced about the luxurious room.

"If your business is as you have described it—small—so will your loss be. I would advise you to forget it. Have nothing whatever to do with this man."

"I am obliged to, Mr. President. From what Mr. Biddle has been explaining to me it appears that—what was discussed at your office this morning—everything—may be treated as part of the assets of the Senator's company, and lost."

Henry Browne considered it.

"That might apply to your commercial assets in the company," he said, "but not, I think, to your private fortune."

"I see you are unfamiliar with Portuguese law," Pedro put in smoothly.

"Is that Portuguese law?" Browne queried in some surprise.

"Mr. President," Martha asked cautiously, "from what took place today, could it be said that I was"—she hesitated before speaking so tremendous a word—"rich?"

Henry Browne eyed Biddle with caution.

"You may speak frankly," she said.

"Without any doubt," Henry Browne replied with gravity, "you are at this moment the richest woman in Macao."

She moved slowly across the carpet away from them. She was lost in thought. She was a woman, after all, and it was a very great decision, a great question. She turned.

"Could I not then trade on my own?" she asked.

"Everyone knows you are connected with us," Pedro said with a forcefulness that betrayed his alarm. "No ship would carry your goods."

Pondering this an instant—for the new idea that had just occurred to her involved an even greater decision—she gently kicked a foot out beneath her skirt.

"In that case, Mr. President," she said, "could I buy a ship of my own?"

"My dear young lady," Henry Browne replied, "with the total sum mentioned in my office you could buy the entire Praia Grande waterfront from here to the Governor's Palace."

"I see," she said thoughtfully. "But could I buy a ship?"

"Buy?" the President queried. "I would not buy, if I were you. There is an excellent shipyard here. Why not build?"

With an audible scoff Pedro interjected:

"It would be called the bankrupt ship before its keel was laid."

Henry Browne ignored him.

"I would not let that disturb you," he said to her. "Build your ship."

"Who would be fool enough even to engage the men to do the work?" asked Pedro with scorn.

Henry Browne continued addressing her.

"Engage them yourself. Pay them by the day."

"And the shipbuilder?" Pedro demanded.

"Pay his fees in advance. You can afford it."

She moved about, absorbed in thought.

"Dare I do it, Mr. President?" she asked. But as the image of a nice little ship such as those she had seen on the inner harbour took shape, she had already made up her mind.

"Of course not!" Pedro protested. "The idea is utterly absurd."

Henry Browne examined him sternly.

"You seem out of sorts, young man. On second thoughts I shall be glad to challenge you on the point of law you mentioned earlier—if indeed it is Portuguese law, as you insist. Instructions will be left with Mr. Humphrey," he continued to Martha, "that in the court your interests are to be represented by our Portuguese lawyer, who will be briefed by us."

It was the point she had wanted to be sure of. Slowly she clasped her hands together.

"Then, God willing, I shall have my ship," she said, grave and deliberate. "Cousin Pedro, ask Chin Fui to see me."

"Who's he?" Henry Browne inquired, raising a bushy eyebrow.

"A shipbuilder I know," she said casually.

"With a name like that I shouldn't think he's built anything larger than a junk. What kind of ship do you want?"

It was a hint. Her image of the nice little ship was evidently faulty. She mentally adjusted the picture.

"I want a big ship, Mr. President," she said, filled with awe at being able to say it, "bigger than a Chinese junk, big enough to go to—big enough to go out on the great sea!"

The President gave a faint smile.

"I know," he said kindly. "There's a Portuguese here who will meet your requirement exactly. I forget his name," he went on, turning to Pedro.

"Ribeiro?"

"Ribeiro, that's the man. First-class designer and builder.

Send for him."

But Martha had once seen a print of one of Ribeiro's ships.

"Senhor Ribeiro!" she exclaimed with respect. "Will he come?" she asked doubtfully.

"Why should he hesitate?"

"No," she answered, reflecting on it. "Why should he? Go to Senhor Ribeiro now, Cousin. Tell him I wish to see him tomorrow before noon—about a—big—ship."

Pedro, running his hand across his brow, turned uncertainly in Biddle's direction. But over Biddle's flaccid, old woman's face a ghastly change had taken place. About his eyes the skin seemed to have fallen, the eyes staring sightlessly ahead without import, the mouth hooked into a sneer from which all meaning had gone.

"Go, my son," he muttered. "Do as yer bid. If yer stick to me now, yer done for."

Pedro withdrew.

"That court'll never see me," Biddle continued. "Some people may say I've nothin' to be proud of, but proud I am just the same. I don't want no one to see me, no one who remembers what I was before."

"Where have you been?" asked Henry Browne.

"I was with a Chinaman an' 'is family," Biddle replied gravely, "good honest souls. In the past I rendered 'em some small favours, and in me hour o' trouble they took me in as one of 'em. But it was not to last. They'd a small son, a bright lad nine years er so. 'E played around me all day long, 'e did, called me Uncle like the rest of 'em. Then 'e caught a fever. They gave 'im Chinese medicine, an' in two days 'e was dead, poor mite. Not that they said anythin' to me, but I knew I was no more welcome. I made an excuse and went to another family where I 'oped to find a refuge. But the story o' the dead child spread before me. I was bad joss. If anyone took me in, they ran the risk of 'avin' their eldest sons die. No one'd give me shelter. For some weeks I lived in a disused 'ut. It was good enough for me. The trouble

277

was findin' food. I begged, and sometimes people gave; but even this they were afraid of. Three days I 'ad nothin'. Then I came back."

"And now?"

Biddle looked assessingly at Martha.

"I need money," he said, not removing his eyes from her. "With it I'll go away again, somewhere else."

"Mr. Biddle's keys are in my possession," Martha explained flurriedly, unable even now to overcome her fear of him, "and I am not prepared to allow anything to be opened."

"Is this absolutely necessary?" the President asked.

"The lady 'as 'er reasons, though I can assure 'er such precautions are unnecessary."

"My entire savings, Mr. President," she answered vehemently, "and perhaps this great inheritance as well, are at stake in Mr. Biddle's bankruptcy. My own small trade was supposed by me to have nothing to do with Mr. Biddle. The documents which come before the court may suggest that it had. I shall have to defend what is mine. In holding the keys I am taking the only step I can to support what I shall say. The court will know I cannot read or write." Henry Browne nodded. "If Mr. Biddle needs help," she pursued, "he should surely look first to his friend Mr. Cuming."

Immersed as she was in Asiatic trade, in which those who were interested knew about the Biddle-Cuming connexion, it had never occurred to Martha that in Company circles it was Cuming's most closely guarded secret.

"Mr. Cuming?" Browne asked in surprise. "An unusual choice. Why should he help Biddle?"

"They are partners. It is only natural."

"Is that so?" Browne asked, looking at Biddle in incomprehending concern.

"We were much together in the common course of understandin', sir," the old man replied with care.

"In China that's as good a description as any of a partnership. Biddle," he pursued, standing over him, "I am leaving shortly for England to give evidence at an investigation into the losses resulting from your failure to meet your obligations. Questions of partnership have considerable bearing on the investigations. I would like to know more."

"Yes, sir?" Biddle replied prudently.

"Were you or were you not partners?"

"No, sir."

Browne relaxed with every sign of relief.

"That is as I would have thought," he said. "Mr. Cuming has this afternoon asked me by letter if he may accompany me to England to assist in the investigation, and in view of the seriousness of the matter I have given him my permission."

Biddle's eyes dilated with sudden anger before this final evidence of Cuming's falsity to him. His lips trembled as he came slowly to his feet—he was taller than Henry Browne —and walked weightily out of the group. Beneath the arch he turned, his churlish mouth distorted, contradicting the old-womanish softness of the rest of his face.

"Yer've 'eard the truth, but not the 'ole truth," he said thunderously. "You asked if we was partners, George Cumin' an' I. No, we weren't partners. But that's only 'alf the truth. 'E's my nephew."

"Your nephew?" Martha exclaimed. "Mr. Biddle, answer me one question. You are different from the other Englishmen. You belong to the same Church as we do. You are a Catholic."

"I was born a Catholic, yes."

"And Mr. Cuming?"

Biddle's lower lip curled up.

"Yes. Let Mr. Browne 'ear it. My nephew George is a Roman Catholic, ineligible for employment with the East India Company. Why did you ask this?"

"His son," she said.

Abraham Biddle nodded. He grew more calm.

"Yes. Me parents died before I was twenty-one. George's father was a sailor, a dangerous man with a temper like

Satan. One night, drunk in a London tavern, 'e killed a man. Before 'e could be arrested 'e slipped aboard 'is ship an' escaped to foreign parts. We never 'eard of 'im again. In those days I worked as an apprentice in Shoe Lane, makin' knick-knacks to send to China. I'd 'ardly enough to feed meself, an' I 'ad to support me sister an' 'er child. The church we worshipped in was in Aldgate, a church for poor folk like us. But next to where I lodged was an English church where the gentry came each Sunday. I joined that congregation. The parson knew me by sight. 'E took it for granted I was one of 'is flock. I became friendly with 'is wife, a kindly soul, told 'er about the boy an' about me sister who was sickly, dyin'. The parson's wife introduced me to a lady and gentleman of the parish. They'd no children o' their own. Fortune favoured me. They took a likin' to the kid an' adopted 'im. They gave 'im an education. 'E became respectable. Then 'is foster-parents moved out o' London, an' I, 'umble apprentice as I was, didn't see 'im again till twenty years later, when we met in China.

"I'd been sent by that same company in Shoe Lane to attend to their Canton accounts, which were in disorder. They paid me a pittance, expectin' me to return to London as soon as I'd tidied up the business. I tidied it up all right, but instead o' goin' 'ome to me pittance I started up on me own account.

"Those were 'ard times for a private trader. At the end o' the season John Company threw yer out o' Canton. When yer came down to Macao they tried to throw yer out of 'ere too. By one device an' another I 'ung on some'ow. I was makin' money, far more than I ever could 'ave in Shoe Lane; an' one thing I knew. I could only win security by makin' meself indispensible to the officers o' John Company.

"I'd set about it well enough when 'o should arrive as a junior supercargo but me grand young nephew George. 'Ere was the opportunity I needed. I knew 'is past, knew 'e was no gentleman, nor no Protestant neither. 'E worked for me like a good boy, 'e did, an' I looked after 'im, made 'im what 'e is today, one o' the richest men on the coast—though 'e likes to conceal it. But even in those days I knew, with 'is gentleman's manners, 'e 'ated me. With wealth, I thought, 'e'll change. I was wrong.

"Tellin' yer this, Mr. President, I'm keepin' a promise. I warned our George that if I went down, 'e'd come down with me. There was no lovin' yer neighbour where I was brought up. That's 'ow I've lived, and that's 'ow I shall die. I 'aven't changed either."

Erect and dignified, Abraham Biddle walked to the door. Before Martha or the President had time to divine his intention, he had gone.

Ignatius had not come face to face with Biddle for eighteen months, and seeing the old man descending the stairs he hoped he would not be recognized. Going to the front door with the same impersonality he would have shown to an unknown caller, Ignatius was about to open it when a hand was laid on his shoulder.

"I trust yer'll say, me boy, in future years that yer uncle gave yer nothin' but affection."

"No, indeed, sir."

"Between you an' me, dear boy, 'as always subsisted a cordial understandin'." He paused, staring at Ignatius with hollow, desperate eyes. "Ain't it?"

Ignatius had originally learned his English from sailors in Macao, and he knew their slang, which Biddle never used except when under stress.

"Yes, sir," Ignatius answered nervously. "You have been always more than good to me."

"That's it. That's what yer uncle likes to 'ear." Lowering his voice, he rubbed his thumb against his index finger. "Give me money, boy."

Ignatius' mouth opened in astonishment.

"I have none," he said.

"Find me a little."

"I must ask the Senhora first."

Biddle was silent.

"Very well, boy," he answered at last resignedly. "Tell 'er there's a small debt I'd like to repay, if she'd kindly 'elp me."

"How much shall I bring? A purse? Two purses?"

"Not ser much as a purse, boy." He spread out his palm. "Just a small 'andful."

Ignatius leapt up the stairs three at a time.

"Give him that purse," Martha instructed. A sense of oppression came over her as she heard the request.

"He asked for a small handful only, Senhora. I think that is all he will take."

With the same oppressive urgency she unstrung the purse, drew forth as much sycee as she could hold, and let it fall into Ignatius' cupped hands. The boy went off with it.

"Don't let Biddle worry you," said Henry Browne. "His powers of survival are infinite. As for the art of telling specious stories, as we have seen today, Mendes Pinto was a mere novice."

"You mean you do not believe what he said about Mr. Cuming?"

The President smiled at her with benevolent tolerance.

"My dear young lady, I have known George Cuming since we were both at school. Not a word of truth in it."

"Yet it agrees exactly with what we in Macao know about Mr. Cuming."

"And what is that?"

"Well, as one example, that boy who has just left the room is Mr. Cuming's son. He was brought up in Mr. Biddle's house and baptized a Catholic."

"H'm. Is there anything unusual in that? All the children born in English houses are Roman Catholics."

"Where the mother is Portuguese, yes; but not, as in this case, where the mother is Chinese."

"H'm," he said again. "Well, Macao has always been beyond me. All I know is that I have known Mr. Cuming a very long time, and a better friend you could not expect to have."

The President thus convinced himself as he wished. It was as Cuming had said. Were Biddle to tell the truth, no one would believe it. The secrets of the leader of the China coast's new and more moral society remained among the many things Macao knew about the East India Company which England never knew.

"And you will never marry a Portuguese," Henry Browne announced with finality. "Though it may not be exactly orthodox, and will doubtless shock Mr. Humphrey profoundly, I propose to use discretion. A note will be sent this evening authorizing the grant of probate in the full ten thousand pounds."

The Number One, at last responding to Martha's repeated bell-pulling, caught this remark as he came in. Though he spoke little or no English, he understood numerals. As Martha asked him in Cantonese why the punka was moving so slowly and where the wine was, his eyes were absorbed in mathematics.

"Nothing for me, I pray you," said the President, divining her meaning. "I must take my leave."

Ashamed that the President should come on a day when the house was in such disorder and gain a poor impression of her, Martha saw it was no use. The last moments of a unique occasion had come. Through the years she had watched the Company officers come and go. No future President of the Select Committee would ever set foot within this house. In a year or two no officer of the East India Company would even know who she was. Today was a day that would never be repeated. It had to be used to the full.

"Mr. President," she said as she hastened to accompany him, "what am I to say tomorrow when Senhor Ribeiro comes? It is a little difficult to order a ship as big as that when I have never seen one."

It was an admission she would have made to no one less than Henry Browne. To her surprise, and not much to her satisfaction, he halted midway on the stairs, his moustaches rose up in the air like birds' wings, and he roared with laughter.

"Tell him what you told me," he cried, "—that you want it to be a big one! He'll catch your meaning." And with a wink he added, "When it comes to the business side of it, it wouldn't surprise me if you weren't a good sight shrewder than he is."

He took his hat and cane. Placing one foot on the bottom stair, his air grew more serious.

"It is not often one comes to know a man only after he is dead. Yet it is only today that I feel I really know Tom Mierop. I too am leaving money to someone here, enough for herself and her children. But she's a very simple woman." He lowered his gaze. "It need not have been like this, I suppose, if I had ever thought about it."

In a swift movement, furtive and precious, he kissed her hand, and walked out into the street.

The door of the palanquin closed on him. His poise recovered, he leaned from the window and added:

"Between ourselves, the most remarkable aspect of this Biddle affair is that I don't believe it will ever come into court. The principal figure in the case, apart from Biddle himself, is Judge Pereira, and the Portuguese lawyers are so terrified of him that we have not been able to persuade a single one of them to touch it. It looks as though old Biddle's going to get off scotfree. There's irony for you!"

His cane fell noisily against the window. At the sound the bearers moved off and he was jerked back against the cushions. The palanquin was borne away.

"Ignatius!" Martha called, re-entering the hall, oppression thundering in her ears. "Have the chair made ready, and come with me yourself!"

"Where to, Senhora? You've had nothing to eat all day."

"That can wait. We must find Senhor Biddle. There is something he should know immediately."

There was delay over the chair—the bearers, like everyone else, were unco-operative. Not till about four in the afternoon, a good hour after Abraham Biddle left Hospital Street, did Martha, with Ignatius striding beside the chair, reach the old man's house. As they mounted the hill they found the door into the garden ajar.

It was hotter than ever, the sun baking the city with all the vigour of early summer. Eagerly pushing open the garden door, Martha and Ignatius passed within—to a scene, an atmosphere, of desolation. Rank grass three feet high rose everywhere wild, choking young trees, hiding the paving stones of the path. In a row of red tubs, brown and yellow stems of plants hung down in death, while from their brick pedestals small wild flowers forced a way.

At the end of the garden, the house looked forlorn and derelict. Some of its plaster had come off in the typhoons of the previous summer. Its black shutters, their paint scarred with the pink they had once been, stood haphazardly, some open, some shut, and one lopsidedly broken at the hinge. A sturdy plant sprouted from the apex of the main gable.

The doors were wide open. Martha stepped inside. The house was silent and almost bereft of furniture. Dust lay on everything. Cobwebs were spun thick from the moulding of the room's central arch down to its capitals. An antique cupboard had had one of its doors ripped off. In the fireplace, amid ash and more cobwebs, emerged the partially burnt leg of a chair. When, she thought, had he really returned from wherever he had been?

"Mr. Biddle!"

Stillness.

"He may be upstairs. Look for him," she directed.

In each of the downstairs rooms was the same dereliction, armchairs stripped of their stuffing, furniture broken for fuel. In the kitchen a curved Chinese pan had been used not so long ago. Coming out at the side of the house, she re-entered the garden at a point where, beneath the shelter of a wall, there was a row of structures made of fine strips of wire, a rarity in Macao, each covered by disintegrating matshed roofs. It was the aviary, which she had so often heard of, but never seen.

Swings and perches bearing remnants of their once gay colours were suspended within the frames, but what had evidently been water and seed receptacles had either fallen to the ground or were dangling loose, broken in a struggle for survival, while on the sand and small stones below, through which the first weeds were penetrating, lay scattered hundreds of tiny bones, exquisitely white and clean.

From a nearby house wafted the heavy perfume of incense. Along the street an itinerant cobbler was passing, beating a piece of toneless metal and uttering a cry.

"He is not there," said Ignatius behind her. "But upstairs I found this."

He held a small blackwood box, its top partly slid open. Inside were a number of pellets of a soft-looking black substance.

"It was like this when I found it," he continued. "Those are his finger marks, not mine. He must have just taken some."

"Is it a medicine?"

He raised the box to her face.

"Smell it."

She drew back repelled.

"What is it?"

"Opium."

Uneasily she looked about her.

"Could opium be harmful?" she asked.

"I don't know, Senhora."

"Somehow we must find him!"

They set off in the direction of Hospital Street at a fast pace. At the foot of the hill they passed the cobbler seated against a wall, drying the sweat off his neck.

"Ask him if he's seen Mr. Biddle."

It proved easy enough. Everyone of every race knew Biddle, the oldest English resident. Once in movement in the city, he was not hard to locate. Yes, he had been home, but had gone out again, walking towards the barracks.

"Follow!" said Martha. "Fast!"

From one information point to another they strode along. Their last informant was a woman vegetable seller. She agreed she had seen Biddle, but when asked which way he had gone she simply pointed up a slight incline in the meandering lane they were on, and said "Out."

Reaching the summit of the incline they drew up uncertainly, the woman's word making sense. Before them the land fell away into open countryside, dotted here and there with small Chinese villages. Away to their left flowed the West River, to their right the grander expanse of the Pearl River, each descending southward from the same panorama of isolated hills and mountains rising from the flat green rice land.

"Not out there, surely?" said the front bearer uncomfortably.

Martha stepped out of the chair. Once away from the streets there was an unexpected sense of isolation. On the slopes that fell gently before them were hundreds of Chinese tombs, low ovals of stone and plaster built into the natural mounds of the land. Among the tombs, and zigzagging crazily to avoid each mound, ran a well-used track, one of the routes by which the vegetable and poultry sellers came and went each day.

"Take the track a little way—see where it goes."

The bearers were nervous and looked disapproving. Ignatius had the air of an adventurer with danger lurking ahead. Martha swung about in the chair as the bearers falteringly made their way down, stumbling occasionally, moving between what seemed on the lower level to be smooth mountains of tombs, a zone significant in its silence, where not even a bird sang.

The pace slackened as courage diminished.

"Hurry!" she urged.

There was a jolt forward, an increased pace maintained for a few yards, then once more a slackening.

"Go back, then, if you're afraid! I'll walk."

There was another jolt forward.

After passing the tombs they reached a zone of vegetable plots, painstakingly laid out wherever the flat land was not interrupted by coarse hillocks or clusters of granite rocks. At a row of grey stone houses they stopped.

The villagers, black-clothed peasants, men and women, were circumspect. Yes, they had seen the foreigner. What about it?

Ignatius, after his months at sea, had learned a thing or two. He spun a yarn. Would the villagers not help him find his old benefactor? He had good news for him which he was anxious to deliver. It took time. Martha, an object of astounded curiosity, a Chinese in European clothes, shifted impatiently inside the chair. At last, armed with somewhat ambiguous directions, they moved off into a wilder, less cultivated landscape. The track, rarely used and sometimes hard to find, neared the beach on the Pearl River side. Windblown sand lay in lines over the coarse grass wherever there was a break in the scrub shielding the earth from the sea winds. When they came on higher ground, they saw water on either side of them, and knew they were near the neck of the slender peninsula.

Once more they asked for directions, this time from a half naked man watering a small vegetable plot sheltered by a bamboo hedge. From him there was less reticence, but only one word.

"There! " he said, inclining his head towards nothing in particular.

They moved slowly forward, past strange cactus-like plants, green-blue and spiky, which grew on the edge of the sand. Then the land dipped, and in a small inlet through which a trickle of fresh water ran between banks of sand, was a hut built of leaves and thatch. Before it lay the expanse of the Pearl River and the blue mountains far away on the other side.

Martha removed her slippers and walked barefoot with

Ignatius down the soft sand. A small fishing boat lay grounded near the hut. Some scrawny chickens dashed away at their coming. A wizened, sun-tanned man in a torn jacket, his pants wound up above his knees, emerged at the entrance of the hut. The door was a piece of sacking from a foreign ship. He looked without emotion at the two of them.

"We're looking for the foreigner," said Ignatius in Cantonese.

The man made no reaction. The bearers meanwhile, their curiosity roused, had followed them down.

"He won't understand that," said the leader. "He's a Hoklo."

"Can you speak his language?" asked Martha.

"A little."

"Then ask him if he's seen the foreigner."

The bearer asked in the outlandish tones of the Hoklo people. The Hoklo wife, tough, dour and golden-skinned, brought out three oblong stools two inches high, and with ingrained dignity bade Martha and Ignatius be seated. Together with the husband, they squatted down on the stools set in the sand.

"He wants to know why you've come," said the bearer, standing beside them.

"Tell him we're the foreigner's good friends," said Martha.

He did so. The fisherman considered them, scratching his leg, which was covered with sores.

"Tell him if he comes to my house in Macao I will give him medicine for his skin," Martha said.

"Foreign medicine?" the fisherman asked. He only wanted foreign medicine.

Martha and Ignatius smiled at the sophistication of this member of an almost outcast race. The conversation wound on among medicines, fish and market prices. Confidence was established.

"My daughter takes the fish to market," the Hoklo volunteered. "But I found her out. She was cheating me on the price."

"How bad of her!" Martha exclaimed.

"Yes," he agreed. "She was giving some of the fish away."

"You stopped her."

"Yes."

"Quite right," she said with conviction.

"I suppose so," he conceded. "But now I feel ashamed." He turned to his wife. "Bring it. Let's show."

"No!" the wife replied, scowling at him.

"These are rich people. It doesn't matter."

Pouting, she entered the hut, coming out a moment later with a tied-up piece of brown cloth which she pushed at him ungraciously.

"Look at this," he said, untying it. "This is what he brought."

He spread it out between his thighs. Piled in the centre of the cloth was a little heap of sycee. Martha nodded. She knew by sight the size of her own handful.

"That's half a year of life to us," the fisherman said. "And to think I stopped her taking the fish!"

"Where is he?" Martha asked urgently.

"He went that way," he answered, indicating the next hill of sand. "I asked him to sleep here, but he wouldn't—said he had someone to see over there."

"Who lives further on?"

"No one. That's what I couldn't understand."

She rose to her feet, but Ignatius did not stir.

"Had he been taking opium?" he asked the fisherman.

The Hoklo shook his head and frowned.

"Never saw him do it before. He asked for hot water, and swallowed I don't know how many taels with it. He frightened me—but maybe it doesn't affect foreign devils like it does us."

Martha did not wait for more. Beckoning the others, she set off up the sand slope. The sun was nearing the horizon

in a blaze of red. As she, Ignatius and the two bearers came
to the top of the slope, each involuntarily stared for an instant westward. Behind them the hut lay in shadow. The
fisherman and his wife were pulling the boat down to the
water.

"Low tide!" shouted Ignatius.

"Low tide!" the bearer repeated in Hoklo.

"Already coming in!" the fisherman shouted back.

"His footsteps!" cried Martha. "Look!"

They shifted their attention to the beach beyond. It was
a bay of sand, shaped as gracefully as a crescent moon. The
sun lit with red the wild grasses growing where sand met
earth. From there the beach sank down into shadow, while
across the Pearl River a single vast cloud mounting
immensely into the sky glowed pink in the reflected glare
from the west.

Where they were standing the sand was fine and yellow.
As it fell within reach of the tide it became firm and
streaked with black. She raced down into the shadow, to a
point where in the firmer sand were footprints of European shoes. The others followed her. In silence they went
forward along the track, which led in the direction of the
sea. Further on the track was less steady. The footprints
veered to the left, then to the right, then in an aimless cir-
cular movement, from which they bent this way and that
away from the sea, towards the western sun. Near the softer
sand there was the sign of a sharp turn. Again the footprints headed to the sea, the heels dug in deep, the steps
more closely spaced. Within a few yards from the water's
edge there was the mark of a heel with loose sand splayed
out from it, and on the other side of the track a soft round
dent.

"He fell down," said Ignatius.

Silently they went on, the footprints leading in unnatural
spaces to where the sand was wet. There they vanished.
They looked along the shore for a sign of their reappearance.
Ignatius walked away to the left, setting quite a distance

between them. Then he called.

Picking up her skirt, Martha ran to him. He was pointing into the sea. Near him she stopped to look, but saw nothing. The water was a vivid mass of pink and midnight blue as the reflected light from the vast cloud vied with the oncoming shadows.

"Can you not see?" he asked with youthful impatience. "There! The buttons on his waistcoat!"

She followed his gaze. She had been looking too far out. Not more than twenty feet away, in what could only have been a foot or so of water, was something floating like a small black dome; and over the roof of it, as Ignatius had correctly observed, were the waistcoat buttons of Abraham Biddle. An air bubble, gathered within his clothing, maintained him thus, at the full extent to which the waistcoat had been made to fit, but which the man no longer filled. His head and legs lay bent beneath the sea.

It was blue and yellow twilight when they reached the graveyard area again and saw ahead of them the dark hills of the city. Not having to ask the way, they came back faster than they went, at a pace inspired by the bearers' fear of what they had seen. Martha had wanted them to drag Biddle's body out of the sea, but they were already shivering with fright, and when she made the suggestion they ran for it back to the chair. As they and Ignatius between them breathlessly explained, should it be reported to the Casa Branca that they had even been seen on the beach, none of their lives would be safe. So overcome were they with panic that it had ended with Martha running after them, entreating not to be left behind.

But being borne home to the hills of Macao, gazing out of the sedan window at the brightening stars, she was no longer thinking of Abraham Biddle. She was re-living one by one the events of the tremendous day; and as she did so Thomas' dying message, brought to her by Ignatius from the great sea, came to make sense. With wonder she saw that what Thomas had left her was not in the nature of some haphazard gifts, great as these were. Placed together, what he had given her assumed the coherence of a complete design.

The sedan was lurching its way along the gloomy path between the mounds of Chinese tombs. Through the window she looked up at the walls of the Monte ahead, dark against the darkening blue. She was the richest woman in Macao. She was the owner of a house traditionally an East India Company residence. But she was still the woman da Silva, the pensioner, the entertainer—call it what one would. People might say she had been secretly married to an Englishman. Did anyone know his name? And until they did, would she not remain the woman da Silva, potential victim of public scorn and of moralists' attacks, she who had given a man more fidelity than many a married woman? The more she thought of it, the more amazed she became that Thomas, in his dying hour, should have had the prescience to recognize this last problem, and to provide an answer for it.

Would the Church denounce her if she used his name? Who would know the truth? None save Father Monte-pardo, perhaps, with absolute certainty, while one unforeseen advantage of wealth was that if the Bishop were to take any unjust action against her it would prompt the accusation that he was interested in her money. Moreover in the past few days a rumour had been circulating in Macao that opinion in Lisbon was adverse to the Bishop's special measures and that the royal authority might be invoked to disallow them. The Asylum was full, but no more arrests were being made, and no women were being embarked in a ship due to sail in a few days' time for Timor.

But if she did use his name, it must be done boldly. To whisper in confidence that she wished to be called Martha Mierop, to hint, to act clandestinely—all these would be indications of fear upon which the Bishop could act. She must beware of pretending she bore Thomas' name. She

293

must assert, openly and to the world, that bear his name she did.

As the perspiring bearers mounted the last rise to the grass-covered remains of the city walls, she decided to make a donation to the Santa Casa da Misericordia, provide a new altarcloth for the Cathedral, which would please Father Montepardo, and pay for Masses to be said for the repose of Thomas' soul.

In accordance with his dying wish, she had become the Widow van Mierop.

It was fully night by the time she reached Hospital Street to be confronted in the dark hall by a stern pan-faced Number One.

"There are complaints," he said significantly as she came in. "They want to talk to you."

"Who?" she asked, imperiously pretending not to know.

"The others."

He followed her upstairs. It was the inescapable and decisive struggle, to be engaged with those whose language contained no decorative names such as pensioner or entertainer, with those to whom, particularly as times hardened, Martha was a whore, to be treated with the contempt a whore receives from one side of the world to the other from respectable people like the servants. The memories of fifteen years, through every one of which the situation had dwelt just below the surface, surged into her thoughts as she mounted to the upper floor. For fifteen years she had endured it, this uneasy acceptance, this silent condemnation, this contempt. Tonight it had to end.

Sand still clinging to her skirt, her feet still bare, carrying her slippers in her hand, she entered the living room to find every globe lit and the servants lined up in silence waiting for her—the four houseboys, the cook, the makee-learn, the gardener and his two assistants. Sounds on the rear landing told that the wives had also come up and were listening outside, it not being dignified for them to appear at what was a man's affair. As Martha entered, the two chair bearers, still shaken and disturbed by what they had seen on the beach, joined the row of stolid, stern faces.

"They want to know if they are still to be employed," Shek began as spokesman.

"Why? Why should they have any doubts?"

Untidy and dishevelled, looking a perfect Chinese edition of a tomboy, she faced them with pale composure, calm and authoritative, her fine black hair, which she had swept back a moment before, lying straight from her temples, but with her bun coming loose.

"They understand you will live here alone."

"Yes?"

"They wish to complain to the compradore. They want a new master. If you are trying to prevent a new master coming, they wish you to go."

Unpleasant words. She could see that with their wives outside, who had goaded them on, the men were in a state in which there could be violence.

"You all hated the master who has just died," she said. "You never obeyed his orders. Deliberately you would come slowly when he called. You always argued with him when he asked you to do things you did not like. You refused to do anything which was difficult or inconvenient."

Along the row from end to end every expression altered in varying degrees of incomprehension and doubt.

"No?" she asked. "Is that not correct?"

Eleven puzzled faces answered her.

"Perhaps the contrary is," she pursued. "You liked the former master better than any you had ever had. You always obeyed him. When he called you never walked, you ran. When he asked you to do things you did not like, you did them without question. However difficult or inconvenient it was meant nothing to any of you. Your only wish was to please him."

The eleven faces softened. They looked like Chinese villagers listening to an itinerant story-teller. What was being said was true.

"If we suddenly found that he was not dead, and he walked in now through that door, every one of you would carry out his orders. You would see to it that his every wish was fulfilled."

Even the wives on the landing were silent, straining to hear.

"He cannot come in through that door," she continued, "because he is dead. But instead of coming himself he has sent a very important piece of writing to the head of the English company. This writing was shown to me this morning, and any of you may see it if you wish. By means of this writing your master has sent his orders to every one of you, and he expects you to obey him as you would if he were coming in now through that door. He has appointed a new master of the house, and he wishes you to obey that new master, all of you, exactly as you would if he himself was here."

Every face brightened. This was easy.

"But they say in the market there is to be no new master," said Shek.

"Those who talk in the market have not seen the important writing," she replied. "They do not know the truth."

"They wish to know who the new master is. When will he be coming?"

"The new master has already come," she said. "Fellow-countrymen, I am the new master. It is I whom the old master, if he came in now through that door, would order you to obey."

Consternation returned all down the line.

"They say that is impossible," said Shek. "Only a man can be master of a foreign house."

"It is the first time it has ever happened," she said, and saying it brought home to her its immensity. Gratitude and pride welled up in her. She could not control her voice. "He has given it to me," she said, but sobs broke her words. "He has given it to me, the house and all his money." She struggled to keep calm, struggled for speech. "Any of you who do not wish to be faithful to him any more, who do not wish to obey the order in the writing, should leave now, pack his things, and go. Those who stay are re-employed in my service."

None said it, but from one end of the row to the other and out into the landing beyond, they were gripped, as if someone had said it, by the rumour ever running along the waterfront, by the words they had heard Chin Fui himself say when, visiting the house, he would glance at the upper floor and give a little wizened chuckle—that she was lucky, that she had fingers of gold, that nothing she touched would ever fail.

The Number Three, a gnarled old man, the oldest of them in years, had been infected by Martha's weeping. Tears pouring down his cheeks, he shuffled forward and with hands stiffly by his side, bowed to her.

"We didn't know," he muttered. "We want to stay."

He looked away to hide his face.

Behind him Martha caught the looks of the others, filled with wonder and shame, some of them also near tears. Not knowing what to do, how to put themselves right, they did as the Number Three had done. One by one they came up, each bowing, each repeating the same words. But after the third she could not face them any more. Groping for a little silver in her purse, she handed it to the Number One.

"Kill chickens. Make a feast. You are all engaged in my service," she cried in a broken voice.

There was a hiatus when the last had come up. They stood about sheepishly.

"Come on, you fools," said the Number Three, taking the lead. "Let's get back to the kitchen."

With relief they followed him. The soft drumming of their feet on the wooden stairs increased in volume as their speed of descent quickened, and with it they found voice again, their chatter growing and diversifying with their enthusiasm, until it culminated out below the french windows

297

in little short of an uproar.

With satisfaction Shek shook the sycee.

"Master number one good man," he pronounced in business English. "All Macao him number one."

His transposition from Cantonese to business English was symbolic and final, the intimate and conclusive sign that the house was at last hers.

"Open the shutters," she said to him. It was the first time for nearly two years.

He opened them fully on the dark street. A faint breeze stirred the air, in its coolness a rumour of the sea.

"Ignatius," she said as Shek bowed his way out, "when I have a ship, it will have to have a name."

"Yes, Senhora."

"Ignatius, how do you give a ship a name?"

"By writing it on it, I suppose," he answered. He was picking his sweat-soaked tunic free from his skin and was not paying much attention.

"By writing? On what?"

"On the ship's side."

"Do all ships have a writing on their side?"

"I think so."

"A writing!" she exclaimed with awe, moving towards the windows in thought. "Ignatius," she said in a low, trembling voice, "dare I give my ship a woman's name?"

But he only scratched the back of his neck.

"Why not, Senhora?"

"Because it will be dangerous," she replied, almost to herself. "The East India Company will not like it. Neither will the Church. They will say it is a defiant name—as in a way it will be. And yet, Ignatius"—and she nodded to herself—"I think I shall do the dangerous thing. I shall give my ship a woman's name!"

Just at this moment Surgeon Duncan, arriving on foot, had come to make his promised evening call on his patient over the way, and was waiting for the door to be opened to him. Martha, coming to the open window, reached it to see Dominie, as she used to be long ago, radiant and smiling in a long white dress, holding a candle and beckoning the surgeon in.

"You've come down yourself?" said Duncan with surprise in which there was an edge of keenness. "Where are the others?"

"I sent them home to have dinner. They'll return presently."

She withdrew invitingly before him. The door closed. In the fanlight above it the candlelight flickered for a moment and went out. Nor, as the seconds passed, did any other light go on.

For with every tale that ends another begins, and the age-old story of the women of Macao had not yet ended. Though not from Portugal, Dominie's officer had come at last; and the maladroit surgeon had proved himself not incapable of curing a patient.

Almost exactly a year later—the 17th of May 1796—at low tide, after work's end at the decline of a mercilessly hot afternoon, Delfino José Ribeiro, Macao's foremost shipbuilder, stood on the foul sand of the inner harbour close to the water's edge, surveying with pride and love the splendid child of his invention, which rode calmly at anchor, her bows facing up-river, her white sails trimly furled, her three masts rising high above those of every other craft, her brasswork gleaming in the reddening sun. Well laden, she rode low, black and firm in the water. Tomorrow shortly after noon, on the highest tide of the month, she would sail on her maiden voyage to Calcutta.

He would have liked to be alone on the beach, but this was not possible. Every day for weeks past hundreds of Chinese from Macao and the neighbouring district had been coming to gape, like those around him now, awestruck at the vessel's size. In fact, she was not as large as an East Indiaman; but the local people who came to stare had never seen an East Indiaman. Such ships anchored at Taipa without ever entering Macao's harbour. For the country people the new ship was a phenomenon.

Listening with half an ear to their chatter, he was reminded of something he still had to do. He walked along the slimy beach to where, without the sun impeding his vision, he could see the bows. In the excitement of completing so large a ship on time, and having her laden and ready to sail on so precisely chosen a tide—due to the river's silt—he had forgotten to order the painting of her name. When he had remembered, there was, as with everything else in shipbuilding, an unexpected hitch. He knew what the Senhora's wishes were, but was uncertain how to spell the name. Useless to ask her—she could not write. It was Chin Fui who had solved the problem, sending a man to the East India Company, from whom the correct spelling was obtained.

Someone hailed him lustily from a sampan. It was the painter, being ferried back from work.

Kwai Suk, Chin Fui's master painter, had been in a philosophical mood that day, and while suspended from the ship's bows in his cradle of bamboo, with a pile of stencils numbered in Chinese beside him, he had wondered about foreign ways. The patterned stencils were said to be the characters of foreign language, but to Kwai Suk they were not characters at all. They were mere lines, devoid of meaning. He contemplated the barbaric simplicity of foreign language.

At some point during this philosophizing he picked up a stencil consisting of a single vertical stroke. He shook his head. There was a single-stroke character in Chinese (meaning one)—more elegant, naturally, than this rude thing looking like a doorpost—but the Chinese character was horizontal, not vertical. He held the stencil horizontally. It did not fit the space allotted to it. Something was wrong. He nonchalantly dropped the doorpost into the sea, and went on with the next character.

Now, with a clothful of tackle over his shoulder, he

waded to the beach, his legs covered with black mud.

"Finished!" he shouted proudly, coming up beside the builder.

Delfino Ribeiro, shielding his eyes from the sun, read in the distance the bold white letters: MARTHA MEROP.

He nodded with satisfaction. Knowing how the name was spelt seemed to bring the Senhora nearer to him.

"Did you paint the other side as well?" he asked.

"Yes, sir."

"Well done."

With a wrench of the heart he turned away up the beach.

One hour before noon the following day, in similar weather, bright and hot, a blue sky peopled by vast mountains of rain-bearing cloud, a strong fresh breeze blowing to keep the rain away, the richest and now the most famous woman in Macao was borne in a new and splendid blue and gold palanquin down to the inner harbour waterfront.

A crowd larger than any that had been seen for years and years had gathered. On the quay, on the short expanse of beach, and everywhere beyond in junks and sampans, there seemed to be no place that was not filled with light-hearted humanity and noise. A matshed shelter had been constructed on the quay for distinguished guests. Some distance from it there ran above the beach and out over the water a long, narrow gangway of bamboo and planks leading to the deck of the vessel which was the object of all eyes. Sampans milled round her, filled with the sailors' relatives and other sightseers. Seven or eight large junks seemed intent on blocking the *Martha Merop*'s way to the sea. The bamboo gangway shook perilously whenever someone passed along it. Hundreds of Chinese bystanders thronged the beach and quay, and mingled with the invited dignitaries sheltering from the sun under the matshed. Somehow amid the confusion the ship had to be blessed, and sail at the full tide.

Martha had known it would be a day of ordeal. But

when the palanquin drew up and she saw the numbers of people who had gathered, her courage failed her. The palanquin was lowered. A bearer opened the door. She was aware of everyone even from the roofs and upper windows of the houses, staring at her. Shivering despite the heat of the day, she was momentarily unable to move. The bearer waited, endlessly it seemed, while she struggled with her fear of walking out to face the possibility that, before so great a concourse of people, the priest might refuse to bless the ship.

A man had come out from among the dignitaries under the matshed. Formally attired in black, it was Pedro, the only other person in the great crowd who knew the danger of the advancing moment.

Things had turned out better than expected for Pedro. As Henry Browne had foretold, the Biddle bankruptcy case never came into court. The East India Company wrote off its losses. Equally important to Pedro, from the day his engagement to Judge Pereira's youngest daughter was announced, Martha renewed her confidence in him. Instead of founding her own company, she wisely followed the maxim of trade that water flows best where the channel is deep, and resumed her connexion with the house of Gonçalves Sequeira, this time overtly, as a full partner and with overwhelmingly the controlling interest. Pedro had emerged from the renewal of their partnership with increased stature, to which his judicious marriage and the much enlarged scope of his commerce contributed to place him second only to his father-in-law in power and influence throughout the city.

As he approached, Martha glanced helplessly down at her dress, a superb creation in deep crimson, with a long white and gold veil of transparently woven Benares silk. She had chosen crimson because the Portuguese would say it was extraordinary and the Chinese would say it was lucky, and the choice alone would enhance the *mystique* of wealth and good fortune which surrounded her. Should the priest refuse his blessing, it was a colour which would wear a very different meaning.

Pedro was at the door. The moment had come. She adjusted her long veil softly sweeping to the ground, put out her hand to him, and came forth into the glare of the sun.

There was a murmur of approval from the Chinese surrounding the palanquin. But she did not hear it. It seemed to her that silence had fallen over everything.

Dimly she saw the notables. Pedro had issued the invitations. Judge Pereira was there with his daughter, Pedro's wife. The Senators were there, leading Portuguese business men, Delfino Ribeiro the shipbuilder, Dominie and two of her cousins, the members of the Board of the Santa Casa with their wives. A remarkable number of women had come, each covered in a black mantle. For every woman, married or unmarried, it was in some inexplicable way an event of personal significance. The East India Company was represented, as she heard it would be, by its most junior supercargo, newly arrived. Talking to him was Mr. Humphrey the notary, apparently present in a private capacity. As he caught her eye he made a slight inclination of the head.

On the beach and clad in their best black silk were the bronzed Chinese labourers, men and women, who had done the heavy work in the building of the ship. For them too it was an important and happy day, and they were taking the precaution of giving the vessel their own special blessing. The women had brought a small Chinese table and stuck it in the sand. On it stood plates of persimmons and yellow star fruit and a censer filled with ash stuck with a spray of smoking joss sticks. On either side of this makeshift altar were high poles hung with red strings of firecrackers. As Martha turned to face in their direction the labourers cried out to her with cheery abandon.

Pedro beckoned her to join the guests, but she felt she was going to faint, and dared not move. She looked at the long black vessel with its proud masts.

"Where is it?" she asked Pedro quietly.

"Where is what?"

"The writing. The name."

"There, in white."

"So small!" she said with concern. She had expected it to be written in huge white letters down the ship's full length.

"That is the usual size."

"But can people read it?"

Pedro lowered his eyes to the stones.

"Too well," he whispered.

There was a movement among the Chinese on the quay. In their midst appeared a large red umbrella hung with silken tassels. Those nearest to Martha and Pedro drew back, creating a vacant lane into which walked first a boy swinging a silver censer from which the smoke of incense puffed out. Behind him came another boy bearing a lidded wooden cask of holy water. They wore red cassocks and white lace-bordered surplices, as did the two older boys who followed them, one with a tall crucifix, the other bearing aloft the red umbrella beneath which, in white cassock and surplice, wearing a cope magnificently embroidered in gold, lurched the weird figure of Father Montepardo, his white hair straying wildly across his forehead, leaning heavily on his knotted stick, twisting about from side to side as people shrank back from him in dread.

It seemed to Martha as if Pedro was no longer there. She was conscious of standing alone in emptiness and silence. A cloud of incense blew briefly past her. Before her the umbrella stopped. She kissed the priest's hand. With Father Montepardo beside her she walked slowly towards the gangway, a few feet from which she paused. The Father swung round characteristically, bent down, his eyes staring up at her. She was looking at the small white marks on the ship's bows.

She said:

"Ships, the Englishman once told me, can have women's names."

Father Montepardo followed her gaze. Without shifting

from his bent position he eyed her with satanic calculation. From the matshed the guests, led by Judge Pereira, were advancing to join them. She wanted to shout to them, 'Go back to your homes! I have changed my mind. The ship will never sail!' Instead she folded her hands to conceal their trembling, and watched the clouds in the blue sky.

The priest reared himself up, his face horrible with its eyes of different sizes.

"You are not afraid it will sink?" he demanded.

"No, Father," she exclaimed, astonished and coming at once to the defence of her ship. "Senhor Ribiero says it is very strong."

"I had in mind," Father Montepardo thundered, "the opinions of One Who is higher and more influential than Senhor Ribeiro, excellent man though he is. You do not fear you may be sending innocent men to their doom?"

"Of course not, Father! I pay them their wages."

But the old priest, who understood the ambiguities of Macao better than the Bishop ever would, had kept many a secret in his time, and one more made little difference. His face spread into an amazing leer. He chuckled.

"In that case, you are the *owner*," he stressed, indicating the way in which this particular ambiguity should be met. "Lead the way!"

He made a sweeping gesture. Martha stepped on to the gangway, Father Montepardo swaying and plunging forward after her. The bamboo and rice straw squealed beneath the weight of the procession.

The blessing took place in the captain's cabin, where there was an altar with silver candlesticks, and above it, fixed in a niche in the panelled wall, a statue of Our Lady. The cabin was filled with the scent of camphor and incense. While Father Montepardo, facing the altar, read the prescribed prayers, Captain Rodrigues and his officers, Martha, Pedro, the shipbuilder, and as many guests as could squeeze in stood about him in a semicircle, each holding a lighted candle. The rest of the company, also holding candles, crowded at the door.

Opposite Martha in the semicircle was the junior super-cargo whom the East India Company, judicious in protocol but unaware of irony, had sent as their representative. She watched with an unaccountable feeling of knowing him already as he stood, respectful like the rest, holding his lighted candle. He was young, simple, rather shy—no one to be afraid of—and with a profound inflowing of the past it was Thomas as he must have been, had she only known it, when she first saw him standing near the window, taking a step towards her. She wanted to tell someone. She wanted to cry out through the densening incense, above the droning prayers and muttered amens, 'This is what he was like! This is how it began!'

After the blessing Father Montepardo, conducted by the captain and officers and followed by the guests (only men had come aboard), visited each part of the ship, repeating his benedictions and sprinkling holy water. Martha went quietly up on deck and waited. As a woman she was not expected to go with them.

Before her lay the low, house-covered hills of Macao, one of them the house of her childhood on the Rua da Penha. Behind her rose the masts and rigging, and beyond this the pale green, grass-covered hills of China. Between the two stretches of land, the ship was a curiously separate world of perfumes contradictory and taut, the sharp, homely camphor of the furnishings, the cloying hardwood of the deck planks, the fragrant China fir of the masts and spars, and mingling with all of it the pervading smell of oakum and fresh pitch, scarcely dry paint, and the clean sweetness of new sail. Over the enormous crowd on the beach and quay-side, in all the surrounding junks and sampans, a hush of expectancy had descended. On deck the crew members, Portuguese and Chinese, stood quietly with bared heads as the procession mounted from the lower parts of the ship and went forward for the blessing of the bows. When this was done the guests drew apart, and in what was nearly an open-air silence Father Montepardo led the way back across the deck in brilliant sunshine, followed by the acolytes and the black-clad guests. They still held their candles. These sputtered in the breeze, and some of them blew out; but whenever the breeze relented, in a kind of gay vengeance they stood up with sudden bravery as if trying to rival the sun.

They were at the gangway again, and Captain Rodrigues was standing before her. Without saying anything, he looked upward and made a sign. She too looked up, to the top of the highest of the masts, from which alone no flag flew. And as she looked, a small bundle of material at the very top shuddered, loosened itself, and her long red and gold house pennant slung gently out on the wind.

At the same instant there was a deafening explosion as all around the ship the pendant strings of firecrackers were ignited, and burned and yelled their merry way. On the shore it was the signal the workers had been waiting for. The roar and sparkle of their own crackers on the beach answered those from the ship, while from the new shoreside office of Gonçalves Sequeira a prepared barrage hanging from the upper windows was unleashed. In a few moments crackers from the houses and the junks added to the din until the entire harbour was absorbed in a speechless fury of sound.

The captain was kissing Father Montepardo's hand. The guests, the acolytes, the priest, were on the precarious bamboo gangway making for the shore. Martha was with the captain, Pedro waiting to escort her. The weeks of excitement as the great vessel came to life were over. It was the high tide. They were going.

Men were moving to their positions in the rigging, waiting a word of command. The ship, which had been lying in placid repose, counting time in days or weeks, had become urgent. Without a word being said, its time was now being counted in minutes as, like an invisible spirit, that other life, the life of the sea, from which Martha was excluded, entered in and took possession of it, the real owner.

To Martha it was a moment entirely unforeseen. Preoccupied with so much else concerning the ship and its cargo, she had taken stock of everything except that the ship would go away. With an embarrassed frown Pedro observed that she was about to weep. She tried to say something, but could not, and above the thunderous roar no words would have been heard. She made a small gesture, and then as she looked at the men about her, every one with his attention concentrated on her, even the common sailors waiting to begin their work, her firm little chin rose slightly, her face composed itself. She had understood. The owner of a ship, even though she be a woman, does not weep before the men whose distant destinations she commands.

She extended her hand.

"Good luck, my captain," she said amid the inferno of noise. "May God go with you, every one!"

The captain did not hear, but he knew. They all knew. He bent and kissed her hand. The sailors grinned and waved. With a swift movement she turned to the bamboo gangway, bowing her head and raising it again in an effort of control, and made for the shore through white clouds of cracker smoke.

On the shore the noise was even more deafening than on the ship's deck. Threading her way through the people, she reached her palanquin and looked back. The breeze had shifted and loosened the smoke, and through a haze appeared the triumphant scene, the anchor coming up, the buoy ropes cast, and amid the stentorian blast of sound, bellowing smoke and spark along the shore and from the ship itself, the mass of people, the gaily coloured flags, the river so covered with craft that it looked like land.

But as the great sails unfurled one by one, and the Chinese people round her gasped with wonder, and the ship began to move, the sight was so beautiful and awful, the strange majesty of what she had created, without ever suspecting the true wonder of what a ship is, bore upon her in such terrible measure that she could look no more.

Grasping Ignatius by the arm she ordered her bearers, re-entered the palanquin, and a moment later was being borne away through the crowds.

Besides, she was in a hurry. Her day had hardly begun. Reaching Hospital Street, she swept into the house, throwing off her veil as she went, and hastening upstairs followed by Ignatius, resplendent in his new white uniform with gold braid, his compensation (received with supreme satisfaction) for foregoing his determination to enlist in the ship.

"Is everything ready?" she asked.

Shek hurried after her with business English reassurances.

She entered the dining room. Sixteen places at the long table. She surveyed it with an experienced eye. She had learned the way from Thomas. Judge Pereira would sit on her right, the President of the Senate on her left. Pedro would take the other end of the table. Dominie would sit somewhere down that end, between the two directors of the Santa Casa da Misericordia. And Pedro's wife?—next to the President of the Senate perhaps. On Pedro's right should be Father Montepardo, with a man, not a woman, on his right—he would be more at ease. She made the necessary memorization.

Unnecessary to inspect the kitchen. As the dishes were to be Portuguese she had asked Inez to come in specially to cook. Everything below was in sure hands.

With a word of approval to Shek she passed through to the living room.

Ignatius waited at the door. With nothing more to do now till the guests came she went to the Spanish armchair, which stood in its summer position, back to the fireplace. She laid her hands on the horns of it.

"How very angry he would have been," she said in sudden reflectiveness, "if what happened today had taken place when he was here!"

"Do you think so?" replied Ignatius. "I think in the end

309

he would have agreed."

She smiled in the negative. She knew better.

"You may be right," she answered. "It is something we shall never know." She paused thoughtfully and added, "Anyway, perhaps *not* being here he *does* agree with it."

As if signifying agreement with this, the little clock on the mantelpiece struck up in silvery tones 'For he's a jolly good fellow'—and struck two. Long inured to the clock, neither of them noticed it.

"Ignatius! If we climb on the roof, shall we not be able to see my ship from here?"

"It will mean fetching a ladder," he replied, politely but with reproof, "and what will the guests say? Besides, I'm not sure the roof is high enough."

She was dispirited.

"If you really want to see her," he said, "the best view would be from the Monte."

She glanced at the green hill filling the french windows.

"Can we go up?"

"I know the way."

"Give me my veil!"

They raced downstairs.

"The back way!" he cried excitedly.

They hurried out through the servants' area, past the kitchen, and out by the side door.

"Ah Shek! Give people wine when they come! We'll be back in ten minutes."

With Ignatius leading the way uphill at a fast pace they plunged into a twisting alley no more than five feet wide between decayed old houses. Some of them had actually met and joined above the alley, converting it into a tunnel. In no more than three minutes they turned a sudden corner and emerged on the lower slopes of the Monte, wild grass and rocks, the ancient battlements ahead of them, the blue sky filled with laughing summer clouds. Up and up they scrambled, the boy pausing occasionally to allow her to catch up with him. Leaping on a lone, flat-topped rock, he turned.

"There!" he cried proudly.

She came up beside him. Every house in Macao had sunk a little beneath them, and there beyond the roofs lay the two rivers and the sea, brown with silt but sparkling in the sun, and a view of innumerable islands.

It was the first time she had ever seen the sea. She had seen the rivers, and they were large enough, but faced with such an immensity of water—for from the hill a great deal of sea was visible—she was suddenly frightened, unable to understand it. She had expected to see her ship standing out large against landscape, as it had looked in the inner harbour. Instead there was only all this water, and her ship nowhere to be seen.

"Oh!" she exclaimed in utter disappointment. "It has gone!"

"No," Ignatius contradicted. "There she is."

To the left, before the Pearl River, lay the widest expanse of sea. She searched it anxiously.

"Where? I cannot see it."

"Not there," said Ignatius, pointing more to the right. "There, between Taipa and the other island."

Some way beyond the promontory of Macao a narrow channel glittered between two green, hilly islands.

"Where is it?"

"In the middle. The one with the big sails."

"That is not my ship," she exclaimed stubbornly. "That is only a small ship."

"She's far away, Senhora. All ships far away look small."

She still could not quite believe it; her ship was so large, after all.

"How do you know it's my ship?"

"I know, Senhora."

She compared the small channel with the wide expanse before the Pearl River. She was beginning to understand this new element of ocean, on which she had traded so long without ever knowing what it was like; and what she saw made her angry.

"So they have cheated me," she said darkly. "They said my ship would go out on the great sea, but look!—that one is only sailing on the little."

"Through there is the way to the great sea, Senhora. That was the way we went before."

She stared strangely at it. The wind made her white veil flutter. With a scurry of wings a bird rose from its nest in the grass and flew away.

"Then you believe it's true," she said, her voice calmer, "that my ship will sail on the great sea?"

"I'm sure of it. Look!" he said. There was a puff of smoke from the vessel's side—"Listen!"—and in the distance the hollow message of a cannon.

"What is it?"

"She's saluting the other ships at Taipa. That was what we did before we went out into the great sea."

"You understand it all, Ignatius," said she, comforted a little; and then tentatively, "Will my ship go very far?"

"Very far."

"As far as those places—from which people never come back?"

"Surely! But she will come back. She is very strong."

She was not entirely assured. The world was so much vaster than she had thought.

"Ignatius, about the writing on my ship . . ."

"Yes, Senhora?"

"In those places, will they change that writing?"

"Of course not! The writing is registered. No one can change it."

"Then, in those places"—she hesitated—"when they see my ship, they will say that writing?"

"Yes."

She sighed.

"It is my name, Ignatius."

"Yes, Senhora. I know."

She came to the edge of the rock, staring into the dis-

312